Hugh Carr was born in Dunkineely, County Donegal, and grew up in the Donegal Gaeltacht. After moving to Dublin he studied at the Royal Irish Academy of Music and later with Frederick May. In 1962 he entered the Irish civil service, where he worked in the district court until taking early retirement in 1988 to write full time. He has had plays presented at the Peacock, the Abbey, the Gate, in several Dublin Theatre Festivals, in London and in New York. His short stories have been broadcast by RTE and have appeared in the *Irish Press – New Irish Writing*. *Voices from a Far Country* is his first novel.

Voices *from a* Far Country

HUGH CARR

THE
BLACKSTAFF
PRESS

First published in 1995 by
The Blackstaff Press Limited
3 Galway Park, Dundonald, Belfast BT16 0AN, Northern Ireland
with the assistance of
The Arts Council of Northern Ireland

© Hugh Carr, 1995
All rights reserved

Typeset by Paragon Typesetters, Queensferry, Clwyd

Printed in Ireland by ColourBooks Limited

A CIP catalogue record for this book
is available from the British Library

ISBN 0-85640-545-0

for Hugh, Marina, Deirdre,
John, Neil, Frank and Lia

I REMEMBER years ago, it must be long ago, so long long ago I can't be sure whether dream or memory, and me drifting nameless in the gloom and gleam of that first dawning, before the world was made, before I or Why, long long before Dada, Mama, Baba.

In the night when I cry, Dada gropes for the matches and rises to boil a saucepan of milk over some rustling newspapers in the bedroom grate. Tall and grey-haired, the firelight flutters on his bald patch, flares of brightness and darkness leaping around the room as he stoops over the flames, white in his long johns.

The sudden roaring from Betty's cot brings Mama fleet-foot into the upstairs bedroom. 'Oh my God, what did you do now! Poor wee Betty. My God, the size of the bump on her forehead!' Mama picks up the can of Johnson's Baby Powder that I had flung at Betty. 'You're a bold boy to harm your poor wee sister – a bold bold boy.' Mama nests Betty in the crook of her arm, rocking her gently, and Betty's screams are stalling into quiet whinges. I stand looking up at them, roaring my head off.

At the fair a swarthy, craggy-faced man, stripped to the waist, bounces upright a huge cartwheel, with a high-ringing clang. The cartwheel has thick wooden spokes the colour of spilt chicken blood and an iron rim that sparks off the cobblestones in the square. It is so heavy that the man has to kneel to raise it, first on to his knees, then, groaning, he straightens up and his arm muscles slither and hump like giant snails as he lifts it high above his head. He is standing with his legs wide apart, his head thrown well back. Slowly he lowers the gleaming wheel on to his chin, then, ever so slowly, takes his hands away and stiffens his arms, holding them shoulder high, all the time never moving his eyes from the cartwheel. Watching from the front of the throng, I am terrified that the wheel will topple over; but even more, the wheel, the man and the wonder of what he is doing hold me in thrall.

In a jerky movement the man drops the wheel, which again bounces, higher this time, off the blue and grey cobblestones, before spinning itself to a clangouring flat-out stop.

Taking up a fat stick, he holds it in both hands at arm's length. With a shout, the stick uncoils, suddenly lengthening into a whip which cracks in the air, making me jump. The man cracks the whip several times, turning in a circle, the thong corkscrewing upwards over his head. Another wild shout and he begins to scourge himself, crying out every time the long lash of leather wraps itself around his flinching, sun-darkened body. His back and his chest are scored with thin red lines, slits of bleeding which open up after each cruel lash.

He stops and looks around, holding out the coiled-up whip. A thick-set man is shoved forward by the crowd and takes the whip, letting the thong dangle, wriggling like an eel along the ground. He raises the whip over his shoulder, then moves closer to the man and the thong curls downwards, opening up a new and deeper channel of bleeding. The man winces – and shouts, 'Harder!' Again the whip uncoils in the air, again and again it draws blood and groans. The man is bent over, his hands covering his face, shivering slightly; but he never begs for mercy. 'Harder!... Harder!... Harder!... Harder!...'

Sleet on my first day at school and Miss Rose has brought me up to the fire at lunch time. Sitting on the bench beside me is Aisling, the Master's daughter, her fuzzy red hair tied with a little green ribbon over each ear. She is the nicest girl in the world. It is also her first day at school and I am whistling for her with my arm around her shoulder.

'What tune is that?' Miss Rose asks.

' "White Are the Sails".'

'Can you sing it?'

Aisling turns her head towards me, her large tawny eyes opening wider as I begin.

> White are the sails on the emigrant tide,
> As white as the veil on the altar-stone wide –

but I can go no further until Aisling joins in:

> And broad is the ocean from windward to lee
> That rolls between Boston, my true love and me.

Now and then bicycles freewheeling down the Slope throw a flickering bluish light into our bedroom, flashing across the glass-framed picture of Saint Theresa and the damp-spotted wallpaper.

The big iron bed has a hollow in the centre and thick jaggy strands of horsehair prod us through the mattress when we are least expecting it.

'You're always squeezing me,' Betty complains.

'And *you're* always falling over on top of *me*.'

We each go to our own side of the bed, as near the high edge as we can get, but gradually we slide back again into the pit.

From the bar below, the voices of the men broadcast in odd words and phrases.

'Job is right, Jamie.'

'Up Dev!'

'Up Peadar Bawn!'

'Oh me galluses!'

'Sound man, Crusoe!'

'Raise it, Hudie, raise it!'

> 'It may be some day I'll go back again to Ireland
> If it's only at the closing of my day –'

'Keep it low, boys. After closing time.'

'Guess how many houses in the town?' Betty says.

'Twelve.'

'No.'

'Twenty.'

'No.'

'How many?'

'I dunno.'

'You're silly. If you don't know, you shouldn't make me guess.'

We begin to count: four pubs, six groceries, one drapery, one bicycle shop, one paper shop, and thirteen private houses – three with thatch, two with galvanised, the rest with slates – and the factory manager's house on the rise high over the pier – and Stonehead's garage, with the only private car in the town. On our way home from school we gape at it through a chink in the garage door, where it waits under canvas for the war to end.

'Why is Master O'Regan called Stonehead?' Betty asks.

'Do you not know that?'

'Why?'

'Because he's deaf as a stone.'

'And why is he as deaf as a stone?'

'You're always asking silly questions.'

'Why, Conor? Why?'

'Go asleep.'

'... Good man, Hudie. Give us, "The Girl from Donegal".'

'That'll do now, boys. Away after closing time.'

'Another round here.'

'Baby Powers, Jamie.'

'A wee wan, Jamie ...'

My first jigsaw puzzle has only twelve pieces but I have a lot of trouble fitting together the smiling yellow duck with a gold watch showing from his waistcoat pocket and a straw hat perched on his consaeity head.

Into the kitchen comes Francey Dubh, followed by the Duck Doogan. Nobody has much time for the Duck because he is always mocking people and taking a hand of them. The two men leave their glasses of stout on the table and watch me at the jigsaw. Before long they are both helping with the picture, fitting into place a waistcoat, a watch and chain, a high, starched collar, a stumpy tail. The Duck is ready to put down a beak, when he stops and glances across at Francey Dubh. Francey's face is stuck stiff like a lollipop. The Duck sticks his lips out further. He turns the beak around in his hand several times, then with a sweep, scatters the jigsaw all over the table. 'Kids' stuff,' he says. 'Come on. We'll go back to the bar.'

'Whoa! Steady there! Damn you ta hell for a stubborn bliddy baste!'

Dada looks out over the sash-curtain to where Uncle Neddy, a stunted, sour-faced man, is tethering his mule to the telegraph pole. The mule takes a few steps forward, then a few steps back, the empty cart swaying from side to side.

'Steady for Christ's sake! Steady ta hell ya bugger ya or I'll knock yer bliddy brains out!'

Mama has put her hands over her ears. 'God above, the language of that man! Somebody should surely call the guards. Go out and talk to him before he has us disgraced.'

'Do you want him to go crazy mad altogether!'

Uncle Neddy pokes his head around the kitchen door. 'Never buy a bliddy mule, Jamie, or he'll drive ye bliddy round the bliddy bend.'

'We weren't thinking of buying a mule,' Mama answers.

One look at Mama's face and Uncle Neddy turns and mule-backs out of the kitchen, Dada following him into the grocery.

'Your Aunt Molly was hard up for a husband when she married the likes of him' – Mama nods towards the grocery – 'do you hear him? Fit him better to say a few prayers; he hasn't been seen inside the chapel gate since the morning of his wedding.'

Mama has closed the kitchen door and Dada has closed the grocery door and the mule outside is roaring his head off – even so, Uncle Neddy can be heard clearly. 'Rotten bliddy day...Rotten bliddy country...Christ Jesus!...Dammit ta hell, man!...'

Jouncing down the lane after school, Boxty chants:

> Hicks, Hicks, full o' tricks,
> With his kind we'll never mix,
> Hell is for the likes o' Hicks,
> Heaven for the Catholics.

'Mama, where do the Protestants go to mass?'

'The Protestants don't go to mass; they don't believe in mass.'

'Where do they go on Sunday?'

'Sure there's no Protestants around here. The nearest Protestant church is in Killybegs.'

'Is Robbie Hicks a Protestant?'

'He's the only one in Glengreeny – the only one left – himself and old Dinny Frigg – though old Dinny spent so long in America that nobody knows what he is.'

'Where does Dinny Frigg go on Sunday?'

'He doesn't go anywhere. Dinny Frigg goes neither to church nor chapel. Forget about him.'

Sent for a bucket of water, I saunter to the top of the town in the hope of glimpsing Aisling.

'Is the lower pump dry?' Callaghan calls to me as I stop at the pump just beyond his door.

'No.'

'Then what are you doing up here when there's a pump outside Groarty's?'

I look at him dumb-faced, not knowing how to answer.

Callaghan has on him the faded green tunic of his old army uniform and underneath a grey flannel scarf for his stiff neck. If he wants to look up or down the street he has to turn his whole body; when he is reading the *Ireland's Own* at the table he can't glance sideways at the clock on the mantelpiece and has to ask Mrs Callaghan what time it is.

'This must be great water entirely,' he laughs, at what he thinks is my stupidity.

I am too embarrassed even to look towards Aisling's house, and slink off, water slopping into my boots.

The last day of the month and Tomkins and Riley have come in to drink some of their RIC pensions. Tomkins is a Hitler man and delighted with the way the war is going.

'The German Foorer will win the war, mark my words.'

'I wonder will he, now.'

'And who's going to stop him?'

'Churchill, maybe.'

'Churchill? Not at all, man. All Churchill is any good for is blather.' Tomkins takes out an old brown envelope bulging with war maps, which he has cut from the newspapers, and passes them one by one to Riley. 'You can see for yourself how things are going. Every day the German Reach is getting bigger.'

Riley barely glances at the maps. He is smaller than Tomkins, a thin man with a raw, perished-looking nose. Whatever Tomkins says, Riley will usually contradict him.

'That was the size of the Reach two months ago' – Tomkins points to a map – 'there it was last month, there it is this month, and the divil only knows where it'll reach to next month.'

'Maybe as far as Glengreeny. What would you say to that?'

'What I would say to that is the sooner the better.'

'And have us all under the German jackboot?'

'We'd be a hell of a lot better off than the way we are. Great bliddy man, Hitler. He put the German people on their feet. And he'll do the same for this country when he lands. Hitler is the man knows how to get things moving.'

'I'll tackle her when she comes in for her groceries' – Dada winks at Mama – 'you sing dumb, Cassy.'

'I won't open my mouth.'

Shortly afterwards Ellen Andy's long step and short step can be heard on the sidewalk. Ellen is our next-door neighbour and an old maid. Nobody makes any move towards the shop when the grocery door opens.

'Come down here a minute,' Mama calls to Ellen.

'What is it, Cassy?'

'You know well what it is' – Mama slams shut the kitchen door behind Ellen.

'Why did you sell the field to Ned Mary?' Dada asks from the head of the table.

'Sure he gave me the highest bid.'

'I would give you higher if you came back to me.'

'I left it to the auctioneer.'

'Peadar Bawn! Don't you know Peadar Bawn and Ned Mary are like that?' Dada holds up two fingers piggyback.

'Oh now, you're a right turncoat, Ellen,' Mama butts in.

'I'd have given you two hundred and twenty,' Dada continues. 'I'll still give it to you –'

'But you never told Peadar Bawn you would give two hundred and twenty.'

'Because I was doing business with yourself.'

'But Peadar Bawn was the auctioneer. You should have gone to *him*.'

'What would I go to *him* for – a Fine Gael man? I never voted for Peadar Bawn in my life.'

'You knew we wanted that field' – Mama's head is beginning
to shake nervously – 'Ned Mary had two fields already.'

'I don't know how many fields he had.'

'You know well how many fields he had; you would know
less. And you know well we would bid higher, only you wanted
Ned Mary to get the field – a man that never soiled his hands
in his life because he thinks he's too grand. How much did he
give you anyway?... Ellen! How much did he give you?'

'I'm not saying.'

'Is it sold at all?' Dada's eyes widen with hope.

'It's sold: signed, sealed and delivered.'

'All right. That's the end of it then' – Dada rises from the
table – 'we'll forget about it.'

Mama still holds her ground, standing between Ellen and the
door, her head shaking like an angry fist. 'You'll have no luck
and that's for sure. Any woman that'll go behind a person's back
– it's real devil's work.'

'Take it easy, Cassy.' Dada tries to calm Mama.

But Mama has worked herself up into a dizzy spin of temper
and is losing control fast. 'Look at the guilty face of her: a real
Judas face if ever I saw one. My God above, and all the credit
we gave you since we came to Glengreeny! You're a real Judas
– that's what you are.'

'That's enough now, Cassy.'

'Money is your God, and no wonder when you're too mean
to buy a bit of dried fish for yourself on a Friday or even a
packet of jelly for dessert –'

'That'll do now, Cassy.' Dada opens the door and Ellen Andy
springs hop-stepping like a frightened hen into the street. Ever
after, she buys her groceries next door in Ned Mary's.

Dada is a Yank: he spent six years in Chicago with his brother
Tom, and two and a half more years in New York with his

other brother Paddy, before he came home to settle down.

'Pity you ever went near the States,' Mama says. 'You never settled down ever since.'

Over two weeks since I left my winter boots in with Sammy Sly, but when I call for them, Mrs Sly, coming down the stairs with a full tea tray, says, 'He has the rummel-gumption, I'm afraid.'

I can see the boots with a hole the size of a shilling in each sole lying untouched on the counter along with a scatter of other boots and shoes, all waiting for Sammy to sober up.

'No trouble knowing when Sammy is on the booze: the bell tells on him.'

Every day the Angelus gets less and less punctual, with odd numbers of rings – until it stops altogether.

'Sammy's on the tear again.'

'Ah the poor cratur.'

'Wouldn't it be a godsend for his wife to ring the bell and not have him announcing to the whole parish the condition he's in?'

When Sammy's daughter Bredeen got a half-crown from her aunt on her birthday, Sammy cheated her out of it.

'I'll give you two brown pennies for the white penny,' says he.

'Sly by name and sly by nature.'

Spread out on the kitchen table are ration books, coupons, gum and brush – and Dada frowning down at them, trying to figure out where to stick how many of what.

'Drive you bliddy crazy, themselves and their coupons. As well as there's any call for the likes o' this: hundreds o' coupons all mixed up like a jigsaw puzzle. No wonder the public thinks it's all a game. Jamilla came in yesterday for a pair o' shoelaces

– the usual excuse. "How much tae will you give me if we leave you in our books?" "I'll give you what you're entitled to," says I. "Oh, is that all?" says she. "What do you expect," says I, "when there's rationing?" "I thought you'd be able to give us an extra share maybe," says she. "Well," says I, "you tell me whose share you'd like me to give you as well as your own and I'll ask them and we'll see what they have to say." "Then how is it Ned Mary can give the people as much as they want?" says she. "If Ned Mary can give the people as much as they want, then I don't know why you're wasting your time on me," says I. She went off with a *smut* on her.

'Ned Mary beat to have a pile o' tea in before the war and never touched it till now. He's selling away on the black market – but what good is it going to do him? The tea won't last for ever and neither will the war, and he'll always have the name of the black market. I'm glad I got rid of the extra chest I had. While it lasted, anyone that was deserving got their fair share at no extra charge, and now that it's all gone, I don't have to worry about who's deserving and who isn't.'

Across the street, in a bright splatter of sunlight between the gables, Sonny Moylan poses to have his photograph taken with Dada's American shutter Kodak. Sonny is wearing his Sunday-go-to-mass suit and his winter boots. The photograph is for Alice, who went to England soon after Sonny was born.

While Mama points the camera at Sonny, Old Con watches with a big photo smile of his own. Old Con is a weaver and on weekdays wears his shirt without a collar. 'That man has more worries than he has hair on his head,' Dada says of Old Con.

Alice is Old Con's youngest daughter and was only eighteen when she left home. 'She's doing well,' Old Con says. 'She has a steady job in St John and Elizabeth's Hospital in London.'

Sonny won't stop fidgeting and Mama gets Old Con to stand

beside him and hold his hand, but no amount of coaxing will get him to smile.

'Smile, Sonny; imagine it's Christmas,' Old Con says.

Two more down-in-the-mouth pictures and then Old Con brings Sonny into the bar; he orders a lemonade for Sonny and a bottle of stout for himself. Perched in all his finery on a high stool at the counter, Sonny looks into the glass of bubbling red lemonade, smiling at last.

'They're always telling me about Alice,' Sonny says to me afterwards, 'and I never even met her.'

Wee Groarty the tailor is fond of his half-un, but no harm in him. Whenever he has a spare shilling he sneaks out of his workshop at the back of the house and into our bar. Big Sarah, his wife, is a different kettle of fish. She's a tightener and Wee Groarty lives in dread of her. As soon as he sees her crossing the street he throws back his drink and ducks out the snug door.

When Con Moylan owned Canavan's Corner House, Wee Groarty was his best customer. That was before Old Con went burst.

'I'll never forget one day Wee Groarty was well on and didn't notice until Big Sarah was standing in front of him with the pram. Wee Groarty was after getting paid for a suit of clothes and had no notion of going home. Big Sarah listened to him without saying a word. When he had said his say she gave him a wee shove and he fell back into the pram. She had him wheeled out the door, up the street and into his own house before he knew what was happening to him.'

Captain Spearman has called again and Miss Rose, answering his knock, goes into the hallway, leaving the classroom door slightly open behind her. They both sit on the old wooden bench just across from the doorway, but most of the time only their legs can be seen – Miss Rose's freckled legs with pudgy calves, and the Captain's sturdy army marchers, stiff in his pressed green khaki uniform and tan, polished boots. The legs barely touch, then move away, and touch again. Only Captain Spearman's voice can be heard, but every now and then, Miss Rose shakes with the laughing.

Big Sarah shouts across the street to Mama: 'Imagine, Cassy, there's no such thing as the sky.'

'What, Sarah?'

'The sky. When you look up, you think you see the sky. Pure imagination.'

Mama looks up.

'There's not a thing in the world over our heads. I'm after reading it in the *Donegal Democrat*. Where we think the sky is, there's only emptiness. Nothing at all. And it goes on and on and on. I'll send you over the paper after a while.'

'That was the Silent Man. Looking for votes.' Dada returns from the bar after a duff errand.

'Why don't you give him his proper name – Peadar Bawn,' Mama grumbles.

'Sure, Peadar Bawn is only a nickname as well, but the Silent Man is a better one – because that's what he is – silent as a clod – except at election time – and even then he never makes a speech.'

'What did you say to him?'

'Sure, I said, I'll give you a vote.'

'He knows well you're Fianna Fáil.'

'Let him live in hope. No point insulting the man.'

'I think I'll give him my first preference this time.'

Dada frowns. 'So we're not even the one mind on that.'

'What did Fianna Fáil ever do for you? Tell me one thing they ever did for you.'

Dada looks as if he is going to explode – his lips forming the words, which he holds back – and heads in a huff to the bar.

The new sergeant, who is called Hobnails, has sworn to put manners on the publicans in Glengreeny. Last Sunday he appeared in Ned Mary's bar without even having to knock on the front door, which was wide open. Ned Mary had his head bent behind the counter, pulling a bottle of stout, and when he looked up, Hobnails was staring him in the eye.

'What do you think you're doing! You have only a six-day licence. You're not supposed to be open today at all.'

Ned Mary got such a shock that his false teeth jammed on him and he couldn't say a word.

The sergeant began to write the names down in his notebook. 'You've all been getting away with murder in this town for years – at least, that's what I'm told. Well, things are going to change. We may have no barracks here but the law applies in Glengreeny the same as everywhere else.'

Dada got the tip-off from Jellybob and had everybody out the back before Hobnails strode in.

'Still washing up!' Hobnails raised his bushy eyebrows at Dada.

'Just clearing up, sergeant, after the mass crowd. Will you have a wee drop yourself?'

'Me! Never touch the stuff. Anyway, you're supposed to be shut at this hour. It's an offence to have anyone whatsoever drinking on your premises during closing hours.'

'Righto, sergeant.'

'I don't know what sort of a town this is: everybody seems to be open all hours, Sunday and Monday. Well, this is going to change.' Hobnails looked in behind the counter and narrowed his eyes at the row of dirty glasses – some of them Dada had emptied just a few minutes before. 'Don't expect to get off so light the next time.'

★   ★   ★

'Small wonder we have no luck in this house: not a prayer, not a litany, not a rosary ever said in it – only what I say myself. From now on, the family rosary will have to be said every evening. You needn't be shrugging your shoulders, Dada.'

'I didn't say anything.'

For a week we persevere in a slow-quick-quick-quick-slow dance around the decades. Mama is a maudlin prayer, holding the rest of us back, especially Dada, who lets out the Hail Mary all in one gush of breath; rarely do we get to the Hail Holy Queen before he has to leave.

'It only takes fifteen minutes altogether. You can bolt the door for that length of time surely.'

'And what will I say to the customers? Put up a notice: CLOSED FOR EVENING DEVOTIONS.'

One evening Dada blesses himself hurriedly, rises, puts on his hat and heads for the bar, whistling as usual. Mama stops the rosary.

'I didn't hear anyone coming in.' She listens.

The sound of a cork being drawn. And Dada is talking to someone.

But Mama is still not satisfied. She tiptoes up to the bar – and finds Dada behind the counter, drinking a glass of stout, talking away to himself.

The busy hum of bees buzzing inside foxgloves, bluebells and the wide-eyed buttercups is drowned in the hubbub we raise dragging and hoisting our desks from the classroom into the afternoon sunshine. Only about half the desks have been taken out and arranged in a curved line on the grass and so we are three to a seat instead of the usual two.

I make a rush to sit beside Aisling; Footsie is already on her other side. We are all in our bare feet and my foot brushes against Aisling's leg as I crush into the desk.

'Conor O'Donnell, why don't you cut your toenails! You're after scraibing me.'

'Sorry.'

'You're crushing me as well.'

'Sorry.'

'You're always saying sorry, but you're not a bit sorry.'

'I am.'

'No, you're not.'

'Honest. I didn't mean to scraib you. I didn't mean to crush you.'

'Then why don't you go to another desk?'

I am so hurt that I feel like walking away and never speaking to Aisling, never looking at her ever again. But I sit tight, shivering with excitement, trying to think of something smart to say.

Crusoe has come down from the bar in a temper. 'Cripes, I'll kill him. I'll burst him! Ignorant gulpin! Who the hell does he think he is!' Crusoe paces up and down the kitchen, ramming his fist into the palm of his hand.

In the bar Big John McBride drinks by himself at the counter bothering no one. Crusoe can't stand Big John, although on this occasion all Big John said to him was 'What are you having, Crusoe?' Sometimes Crusoe gets annoyed if you call him Crusoe and sometimes he doesn't.

'Calm down, Patrick. Calm down,' Mama tells him.

'One o' these days I'm going to clock him one. I'm going to lose my temper and plaster him all over the floor.'

Crusoe tries to light a cigarette, but his hands shake so badly that the match goes out. He is blocky on his feet, sturdily built, but very short-sighted and wears glasses with thick lenses.

'Bring me down a wee brandy, Cassy. Cripes, I feel like clobbering him; I feel like giving him the old KO once and for all.'

In the First World War Crusoe was light heavyweight champion and knocked out Toronto Dick at the start of the third round. Whenever he has a few drinks taken he tells me to 'Put them up. Put them up and I'll show you how it's done.' When he is in this mood he sets my fists in a fighting pose and sticks out his chin. 'Come on. Hit me. Clock me one.' Every time I try to hit him he comes in under my guard and slaps me all over the face with his open hand. He is easily excited and begins jumping around the kitchen, swinging and jabbing and shouting 'Come on Irish. Come on Irish.'

Crusoe lives at the bottom of the town with his sister Margaret, but they don't get on. Sometimes when he comes home drunk he wakes Margaret up to cook a meal for him. Once, in a temper, he lobbed his plate of baked beans on toast across the kitchen and knocked the head off the statue of Saint Jude.

Sitting on the step outside his house, Sonny Moylan cocks the silvery new six-shooter that Alice sent him from London.

'Sammy Sly, up hands, clic, BANG!'

Nobody asked Jellybob to do odd jobs for us, it just happened. Jellybob got his name from the sweets he likes to suck in his small keyhole of a mouth, but since the war he has had to be content with lozenges or even dilisk. He has a happy face, with a narrow, off-beam nose, and eyes that don't always move in the same direction. On bottling days he used to look in hopefully over the half-door at Dada. After getting his free slug of stout from the jug, he would hang on talking, maybe give a hand with the corking, help to stack the cases, carry out empties – until gradually he found something to do every time he called. Payment was in free bottles of stout, and sweet cake, tea and sugar at Christmas and Easter.

'He's the right man to do lookout for you,' Crusoe said to Dada. 'I can never figure out when Jellybob is talking to me: he has one eye here and one eye there, and if he had a third eye, it would probably be looking over his shoulder.'

'God save us the day and the night, Jamie, what hurry is on you! Sure you're leaving clumps of it behind you.'

Dada pays no attention to Molly Dan, but continues to stride in hurried steps, the scythe levelling long uneven swathes to front and side of him.

'There's a big tuft' – Molly tries to pull up a tuft of grass, then moves on to another tuft.

Dada looks back at her and leans on the scythe handles. 'Listen, Molly: if you want to clear the field with your bare hands, go ahead, there's no one stopping you. But if you're let-ting the hay to me, then I'll do it my own way – which is with a scythe.'

Molly bites her lip. She is tall and bony and has broad feet like a man. 'That meada' always got the best o' care, Jamie. First it was mowed as clean as a platter, then I used to make grass-cocks –'

'Grass-cocks is a thing o' the past.'

'Oh glory be to God, and how are you going to save it!'

'Well, that's what I'm wondering, Molly – if *you're* going to be standing over me like a gaffer. You told me you were tired straikin' on your own; you'll be drawing the pension in time for Christmas, so why don't you go in and make a sup of tea for yourself like a sensible woman and leave the hay to me.'

Molly is not half-pleased and turns towards the house grumbling. Her legs are bare and her big boots with no laces in them have their tongues hanging out.

After the mowing we go across the ditch to visit Suzanne, who lives next door to Molly. Suzanne's house, like Molly's, has a thatch roof and a sweaty clay floor. Suzanne herself is bent down with age and has to turn her head sideways to look up at Dada. She is a great smoker and snuffer: on the hob is her clay pipe with the broken stem and beside it her small tin mustard box of snuff. As a sign of welcome she opens the lid and holds the box out to Dada. Even though he doesn't snuff, Dada takes a pinch so as not to insult her. Suzanne takes a good pinch for herself, dabbing each nostril and saying, *'Trócaire 's grásta'* – meaning 'Mercy and grace.'

'Trócaire 's grásta,' Dada answers.

'Do you like mints?' she asks me.

'I do.'

She hobbles to the dresser and comes back with a plateful of grass or some sort of shamrocks. I am still waiting for the mint sweets, when she takes up a few leaves of the green stuff and puts them in her mouth.

'Go ahead, *gasúr*, it's mints – *mismín*, some people calls it.'

The *mismín* tastes sharp and peppery and the stems still have some clay on them.

Dada smiles and helps himself. 'Every bit as good as mints,' he says, winking at me.

In the pulpit the bearded missioner reaches for the big timber crucifix, which he has slung in a belt around his waist, and raises it aloft. He can barely hold back the tears as he points to Jesus on the cross and shows us the five wounds. Suddenly he turns on us with an angry voice. We are the ones who put Jesus there. We spat on Him. We crowned Him with thorns. We drove the nails into His hands and feet and plunged the spear deep into His side.

Everyone is hushed going out of the chapel. Any one of us could die at any minute and maybe this is the last chance we will ever get to save our souls.

Coco looks up at the Captain, then back at Miss Rose.

The Captain takes a sixpence from his pocket and places it on Coco's palm. 'Now, Coco, make the sixpence disappear.'

Coco examines the sixpence, sniffs it and puts it in his mouth.

'I don't mean swallow it.' The Captain sticks his fingers down Coco's throat and rescues the sixpence. 'You're going to do magic. Now take the sixpence.'

Coco looks at the Captain. He looks at the sixpence in his paw.

'He doesn't understand,' Miss Rose says.

The Captain brings his lips close to Coco's ear. 'The magic word is abracadabra. I'll say it for you. Now close your paw ... Ready? ... Abracadabra.'

Coco opens his paw and the sixpence has disappeared.

'Where has it gone, children?' Miss Rose waits for us to answer. 'Does anybody know?'

Nobody has the faintest idea.

'Wait a minute' – the Captain is looking at Goldilocks in the front seat – 'what's your name?'

'Goldilocks,' we all shout.

'Let Bredeen answer for herself'– Miss Rose can't hold back a smile. 'Now, Bredeen, tell Captain Spearman your name.'

'Bredeen Sly, *a dhuine uasail*.'

'Is there something in your ear, Bredeen?' the Captain asks.

Bredeen smiles a frightened sort of smile.

'Check till you see.'

Bredeen smiles again. But when the Captain moves towards her she screams.

'She's frightened of Coco,' Miss Rose explains. 'Maybe you can check *my* ear instead.' Miss Rose lifts back her brown curly hair and stretches towards the Captain.

'There's something in there all right. Just hold your head sideways.' The Captain touches Miss Rose lightly on the head.

He holds her ear, which is the colour of chalk, and shakes it gently.

A sixpence rolls out on the floor.

In the middle of the night we are roused by loud knocking and a man's singsong voice outside: 'Kitty Mhici is dead! Kitty Mhici is dead!'

It is Kitty's nephew Paddy who has traipsed over three miles in the dark to buy provisions for the wake.

'What hurry is on him?' Dada grumbles. 'Does he think people are going to get up out of their beds to go to Kitty Mhici's wake?'

Jack Jumble and his long, scrawny wife and their nine scrawny, scraggly children have all crowded into the grocery with their ration books.

'What went wrong between yourselves and Ned Mary?' Dada asks.

'Divil a hait,' Jack grunts.

'Something must have gone wrong when you left so suddenly.'

'We had a wee differ,' Mrs Jumble says.

'Over what?'

'Och – we weren't gettin' our full share.'

'Did you pay for everything you *did* get?'

'Paid for everythin',' Jack answers, 'every dang happerthworth.' The midday Angelus is ringing but Jack hasn't yet come out from under last night's blanket of booze.

'If you take the books, you'll never be sorry, God bless yous' – Mrs Jumble turns to Mama, who has come to the grocery door – 'I'll pray for yous and I'll get all the childer to pray for yous. Look at the craturs, they're starvin': God bless yous and everyone belongin' to yous.'

'How are you going to pay?' Dada interrupts.

'Jack is drawin' the dole since we settled and we get the allowance. We'll pay every Tuesday, God bless yous.'

'What do *you* say?' Dada eyes Jack.

'Pay every Tuesday.' Jack is in the middle of the children, his cap screwed up in his hand, his shiny bald head barely an inch or so over the eldest. 'Every Tuesday, word of honour.'

'It would be a charity to take them on,' Mama pleads. 'Sure, Dada, they have to eat like everybody else.'

'A lot of extra work for nothing, that's what it'll be.'

'The weans won't be needin' half their tae or sugar' – Mrs Jumble puts a hand on the smallest head – 'the'll be rations left over.'

'You'll have to pay on the spot,' Dada warns. 'No credit any more for anyone.'

'We'll pay on the spot and God bless yous and every one of yous, that yous'll never be short of anything the longest day yous live. Maybe you'll give us some wee bite to be goin' on with. The childer hadn't a hait for two days; daisant man y'are and not like Ned Mary that wouldn't care if we all dropped out of our standin'; give us a loaf or if you can spare two and some tae and sugar –'

'Have you the money?'

'Oh God bless you, sure we'll pay you on Tuesday, that's a promise; isn't that so?'

'Word of honour.'

'Give us two loaves and a pound o' butter and some tae and sugar . . .'

Blackout, with the kitchen blind pulled down tight so that no glimmer can escape to help any German warplane. In the light of the tall-stemmed table lamp, with the pink glass bowl, Betty and myself concentrate on the game of Ludo we have just started. Without either of us noticing, Miss Dee has come in and stands looking over our shoulders.

Miss Dee teaches in Trá Gheal, where she has only a few scholars, but it is her home place. She has a notion of Arthur Moylan, Old Con's eldest son, and is always going into Arthur's bicycle shop to get a puncture fixed or a new bell or handlegrips.

When she pulls a chair in to the table and puts out a Ludo button for herself, we feel shy and uncomfortable. Betty shakes the dice in the eggcup and moves on a few squares.

'Pass the dice before you move,' Miss Dee commands.

I shake and move.

'Pass the dice before you move.'

It takes us a while to get used to this faster type of Ludo, and even when everything is going smoothly one of us will fall back into the old habit.

'Pass the dice before you move . . . Pass the dice before you move.'

'A hundred and ninety; a hundred and ninety I'm bid. Any advance on a hundred and ninety pounds?' Peadar Bawn stands on an upside-down fish box outside the post office, his pudgy hand raised, dabbing from side to side, scouring the crowd for offers. 'A hundred and ninety. Any advance on a hundred and ninety? . . . Going at a hundred and ninety pounds –'

'Two hundred,' Dada shouts.

'Two hundred pounds I'm bid. Two hundred pounds. Any advance on two hundred pounds? . . . Going at two hundred pounds . . . Going . . . Going . . . Sold to Jamie O'Donnell for two hundred pounds.'

Dada goes up to sign the papers and the Silent Man shakes his hand. 'May you have every luck in it, Jamie.'

A few other people come up to offer good wishes and Dada looks happy.

Old Katie, stooped over her blackthorn stick, is full of admiration. Old Katie was reared and suckled on Irish, and when she tries to get her tongue around the English it goes all stringy and sticky on her like butterscotch. She is shaking Dada's hand, looking up at him. 'It's not so much the field, Jamie, as what's on it. That's the school I was teached in myself. Your own mother was teached in it as well.'

'I know.' Dada is pleased.

'Waidean Veannai, times are changing. Did I ever think I would see the day when someone would bought the school?'

That evening Dada talks about bringing us over to view the property.

'What would I be going over there for?' Mama continues darning a hole in the elbow of my gansey.

'Surely you'd like to have a look at what I bought.'

'You didn't get the field you wanted.'

'Still harping on that. This is a much better buy altogether; much nearer and everything. You won't come?'

'Indeed then I won't.'

Betty and myself take the nearcut up the lane with Dada and across two stone ditches.

The old school itself is just a ruin: four bare, broken-down stone walls open to the sky. Two fields stretch back from the school yard: one narrow green strip slanting into the river; the other a big stony field with a huge slab of rock in the middle, and further back an old quarry, which is full of slaty grey water. Looking around from tumbledown school to river to quarry, Dada seems disappointed.

'I'll be back in a minute,' he says, 'I have to post a letter.'

What he means doesn't dawn on me until I see him crouched in the rushes with his trousers down.

★ ★ ★

> Where are you going to, my pretty maid?
> I'm going to the harvest fair, she said.
> Will you allow me to walk by your side?
> I might and I mightn't was how she replied.

We are high on the stage of the parochial hall, jauntily stepping in couples – the boys with their arms around the girls' waists, the girls in their straw hats, green ribbons floating out behind.

It is the first day of our practice for the Saint Patrick's Day concert and I can hardly believe my luck: I have been paired with Aisling. But I can't think of a single thing to say to her – or even if I should say anything.

She is wearing her straw hat slightly to one side, which makes her look like a grown-up, and smiling the sort of smile that is put on especially for the song. Miss Rose has told the other girls to copy Aisling but none of them can raise their eyes the way she does or tilt their heads or move in a way that fits the words of the song exactly.

I have never been so close to her before and for the first time I notice that her eyelashes are not red like her hair but sort of yellow. Every time we turn I can feel her breath on my cheek. In front of us, Footsie looks back and makes a funny face, twisting his mouth into a crooked snarl. Aisling smiles – a real smile.

Everyone laughs at Footsie's antics. On the football field he gets all the attention. People are always shouting 'Come on, Footsie' and 'Cut it out, Footsie.' He is called Footsie, not because he has big feet, but because of the peculiar habit he has of kicking the ball along the ground like a soccer player; also he is left-footed and left-handed. 'Raise it, Footsie! Get it in the air!', but Footsie keeps footing the ball in front of him with the side of his left foot so that no one can get near it. I wish he was behind us, where Aisling couldn't see him or better still if he had been left with the crows.

Around and around the stage we go, two-stepping, Miss Rose directing us.

'Boys smile at the girls... Stand in closer to each other... Girls look at the boys... Smile... Conor O'Donnell, you're not at a wake, you're on your way to the fair. You're happy. So smile.'

I am so nervous and excited that my false smile is cutting into my face like a cardboard mask.

Miss Rose moves ahead of us doing the steps, singing along with us:

> I have goats on the mountain and cattle and sheep
> And my mother she's doting and mostly asleep.

Aisling's body feels warm and sweaty under my hand and when we swing around, her long loose hair swipes me in the eye.

> I'll buy you a ribbon to tie up your hair,
> The best and the brightest for sale at the fair,
> And a ring for your finger that none will deride
> If you will allow me to walk by your side.

'Slowly... Slowly at the end... And turn... And kiss the girls... Come on. Don't be shy... A big kiss.'

Once a year, usually after the July fair, Dada and Mama have a day out in Sligo. This year when they arrive back the lumpy brown paper bundles of winter wear are passed over when we spy the oddly shaped parcel Dada holds behind his back – with a scrolled neck sticking out of the corrugated cardboard wrapping. A new fiddle. It is half-size and has a rounded, brightly varnished belly with two S-openings, and a back, glassy with the sheen of streaky wood grain.

The next evening Old Con tunes the fiddle and rosins the bow.

'It's going to be a tight squeeze for me to play this' – his knurled hand covers almost half the fingerboard as he fixes the fiddle against his chest. He sounds the strings raucously and does some more tuning. Some more bouncing with the bow, tearing across the strings, high and low and low and high and middle, until out of the muddle of sounds jumps 'The Rakes of Mallow'. Without stopping, he tears into another tune and then another still faster. He finishes, sounding the strings again several times as if he is about to launch into a further spate of playing as soon as he can think of a follow-up. Suddenly he shoves the fiddle under my chin. He pushes my head to one side and closes my fingers tightly over the strings. 'Away with you. Go on. Don't be afraid.'

I press hard on the bow and it grinds crookedly, rasping towards the bridge. My first lesson.

'Yous are only all a crowd o' tramps,' Scunsey shouts at Footsie, 'two generations off the side of the road.'

Scunsey is standing up for me because Footsie has been bullying me all week. Footsie is wary of Scunsey but he loses his temper when Scunsey calls him a tramp.

'Shut up your mouth you wee runt you! Why don't you go home and get your big sister to wipe your nose!'

'I have a better home than you, anyway,' Scunsey answers, wiping his nose on his sleeve. The sleeve of Scunsey's jacket has a waxy shine; he has a bony bump on each side of his forehead like the makings of two horns, which give him a dangerous look.

'Anything yous have yous got by robbing your poor oul' granny,' Footsie flares back, 'and then dumped her in the county home. Yous sent her off in the ambulance and her crying to be left where she was born and reared.'

'And what about your own oul' granny? Yous hadn't the

decency to give around a drop of poteen at her wake. Yous sent the people home without a bite or a sup.'

'And what about *your* uncle – oul' Magpie – with the ass out of his trousers and his elbows sticking out through his gansey, and his boots and his leggin's all cow shite, like a walking dunghill?'

'And what about your own oul' father with his hoppity leg and him swinging from side to side like a donkey coming home from the bog?'

Day after day the insults fly back and forth, but no blows are struck. In the end Footsie grows weary and leaves me alone.

'Sean Sly is in the long ones,' Betty announces coming in from the hall door – and, sure enough, he is, sitting on Moylan's windowsill with a new pair of homespun trousers on him that reach to his ankles. I watch through the sash-curtain until he stands up. What an almighty difference! He looks as if he is on stilts. July, he was in sixth class for the second year running and still in short pants. Now he's a man.

I wait until fair day, when everyone is busy, before sauntering down the far side of the street and suddenly ducking into Wee Groarty's front door.

'I want to be measured for long pants.'

Wee Groarty jumps with fright where he has been examining the calendar on the wall. 'You want to be measured for long ones! Are you sure?'

'Certain sure.'

Wee Groarty's cross face begins to slant into a smile. 'Does your father know about this?'

'He does,' I lie.

'Because he'll be the one who'll have to pay.' Wee Groarty has moved closer to me and I can smell the whiskey off his breath. 'Well, it's not going to take that much extra cloth altogether.' He looks down at my bare legs but seems in no hurry to bring me out to his workshop.

'Are you going to measure me?'

'I'm after taking your measure – with my eye. You saw Sean Sly, I'll bet?'

'I did.'

'I made a fine pair o' *báinín* trousers for Sean. Of course, Sean is fourteen. What age are you?'

'Seven and a bit.'

'Seven and a bit. Ummm. Sort o' young for the long ones, don't you think?'

'No.'

'Well, we'll see what your father has to say.'

'You'll have to wait another while, Conor,' Dada says. 'People would only be laughing at you.'

'How long will I have to wait?'

'A few more years. You won't feel it passing.'

'I would like to be in the long ones now.'

Dada smiles and pats me on the head. 'What hurry is on you? If myself could, I'd be in the short ones again; that's the truth. I'd give anything to be back in the short ones.'

'Where is he?' Maggie May calls to me as I pass the post office.

I know she means Corner Jim and I shake my head.

'Where can he be gone to? He was on his perch only a minute ago.' Maggie May glances up and down the street, blessing herself very quickly several times, before going back into the waxy dimness behind the smoky black counter, with its cargo of newspapers, *Ireland's Owns*, brandy balls, apples – and at the window end, the switchboard. Everyone laughs at Maggie May and the habit she has of blessing herself and fidgeting with her clothes.

The only person she will trust to deliver a telegram is Corner

Jim. He spends most of his time leaning against the gable of Canavan's Corner House or sitting on the windowsill of the post office, with his short legs crossed, smoking a butt.

'Little does Corner Jim know that he's working full time for the Government,' Dada says, 'on call twenty-four hours a day, in all kinds of weather. At a shilling a trip. If he only realised, wouldn't he be on strike long ago.'

'Why do you call him Big Jodie?' Dada asks me.

'Because that's what Scunsey calls him.'

Big Jodie is Scunsey's uncle and owns the carpentry shop, with the curved galvanised roof, just outside the town.

Dada laughs. 'I suppose compared to Scunsey he's big all right, but compared to anyone else – Big Jodie is one of the smallest men in the town.'

I had been telling Dada about the 'muwal' Big Jodie is making for the Christmas concert.

'What's a muwal?'

'It's what Big Jodie is painting on the wall.'

'You mean a mule.'

'Not a mule. A sheep. It's a huge field with a sheep in it.'

Most days after school we amble into the parochial hall to watch Big Jodie at work.

'The field hath to be g'een, boyth, becauth thath the colo' of grath.

> Thoses a' thead,
> Violets a' blue,
> Grath ith g'een
> And tho a' you.'

Big Jodie balances himself on a wobbly stepladder, brushing in tufts of grass, which stretch from one end of the back wall to the other and all the way up to the sky, which has a bulging white cloud in it to cover a bump in the plaster.

Jodie comes down off the ladder, his overalls speckled with fresh blots of green and blue and white paint.

'My oh my, I'm dead out f'om all the grath I'm afte' p'oducin'. The last time you boyth came in the' wathn't a thing sp'outing in that field and now look at it. Ithn't it ma'vellouth. Ith a theal metamophothith, thath what it ith – a theal metamophothith.'

Big Jodie loves using big words and then laughing at his own cleverness.

'Don't come too clothe, boyth, or you'll be in the muwal youthelves, and like the sheep you might neva get out of it.'

Jodie has changed brushes and is dabbing on thick blobs of white paint which, close up, don't look all that much like sheep.

'If you notith, boyth, the sheep a' lying down. Now why a' they lying down?'

'Because they're tired.'

'Not becauth they' ti'ed.'

'Because they're dead.'

Big Jodie almost jumps back from the wall. 'Do they look like dead sheep?'

'They do.'

'A bit.'

'Well, they' not dead sheep.' Big Jodie prods one of the sheep with the stick and moves back to take a cattle-jobber's look. 'The's nothing the matta with them. They' alive and well.' Jodie dabs on more white paint with the stick. 'The theathon they' lying down ith becauth if they we' standing up, people would expect them to move. You can't have th'ee sheep standing in the one spot all evening with people thinging and danthing all athound them and not ath much ath a nod out o' them.' Big Jodie gives the sheep a slap with the brush. 'My oh my, they' completely immobile. I think they' gone to noddy land. Well, all to the good – I won't have to put a fenth athound them.'

'Tell the Master we'll take an extra pound of coppers,' Dada calls to me from the bottling store.

I am delighted to have an excuse for going up to Aisling's house, but on the way I begin to feel discouraged, and the closer I get the lower my hopes sink.

Aisling is in the front garden, playing with a kitten on the wall.

'My father wants an extra pound of coppers on Sunday' – I talk to her through the railings.

'I'll tell Daddy.'

Every Sunday after second mass Stonehead counts the collection in the sacristy and divides the coppers into separate bags for the shops in the town.

I hang on, looking at the kitten and trying to think of something that will make Aisling laugh. The kitten turns away from me, raising her tail and sucking in her behind.

'Can she catch mice?'

'She's too young.'

'How old is she?'

'Three weeks.'

'Why don't you catch some for her?'

Aisling looks at me with a puzzled face. She doesn't laugh.

'You could catch them in a trap and give them to her.'

Aisling's long nose tilts upwards in a scornful way as she takes the kitten in her arms. 'You think you're smart, Conor O'Donnell, don't you? . . . Don't you?'

'No.'

'Yes, you do. But you're not half as smart as you think you are.'

I am standing at the railings like an eejit, my mind gone

completely blank from the shock of Aisling's words. Through the sash-curtain I glimpse Stonehead watching me. Time to skedaddle.

Old Cairbre's donkey swaying under the drag of the two heaped creels of turf slung across his back stumbles and topples on to his side. The creel on the underside gets squashed and the creel on top empties itself, scattering turf all over the street. Hee-hawing, the donkey kicks himself on to his back, his four bony legs searching for a foothold in the air and not a shoe on any of them.

'Come on! Hup! Hup!' Cairbre tries to coax the donkey to his feet but the donkey has rolled over on his side again and is breathing heavily, his teeth bared, his mouth twitching.

Once a week Cairbre goes to the bog for two creels of turf. The rest of the time the donkey spends grazing on the fair green or wandering the lanes and back gardens of the town. At night Cairbre brings him into the house. 'Move over there, Nedzer,' he shouts if anyone comes to visit after dark, but Nedzer mostly stands in the one spot with his bum cocked to the hearth. 'And who's more entitled to his share of the fire?' Dada says. 'Didn't he carry every sod of it down the mountain on his bare back?' Old Cairbre hasn't another soul belonging to him in the world. He is over seventy years of age and all he owns is his two-roomed galvanised cottage and a turf-bank in the hill. Even the different coloured patches on his clothes have patches on them and the peak of his cap is threadbare and grimy.

A crowd has gathered and between them they force Nedzer to his feet.

'What age is he anyway, Cairbre?'

'When had you him christened?'

'Is he ten years?'

'He's over twenty-one; hasn't he the key of the door.'

The creels are straightened out and we begin gathering up the loose clods. Nedzer has been standing in the one spot, his eyelids closing sleepily, like a sick hen.

'Put him to bed early the night and he'll be fine.'

'I think he needs a holiday.'

'He needs a good kick in the ass. That donkey is the greatest thief ever roamed the town.'

'True for you: he's in to everybody's back garden. If you didn't watch him, he'd jump over the kitchen table and take the bite out of your mouth.'

Old Cairbre gives Nedzer a sudden whack of the sally rod and the donkey goes around the gable swaying worse than ever.

From behind the counter Dada looks up as the voices of Tomkins and Riley are blown in the bar door ahead of them.

'I'm afraid he bit off more than he can chew this time.'

'Stalingrad was a quare mouthful all right. Give us two bottles o' stout there, Jamie. Still and all, Van Polis should have held out. He should have held out till he had the buttercups under his feet.'

'Didn't he hold out long enough – too long?'

'Hold out till the spring, that's what he should have done. On the other hand, things may not be as bad as they seem.'

'And on the other hand, they could be ten times worse.'

'I don't think so. A lot of what we hear is Allied propaganda. Propaganda and lies and the divil knows what. Though when it comes to propaganda you have to hand it to Go Balls.'

'Churchill, I would say.'

'Not at all, man. Go Balls is a good day's march ahead of him. I was listening to a speech he gave the other night in Ned Mary's –'

'Go Balls was in Ned Mary's?'

'How the hell would Go Balls be in Ned Mary's! A speech

he gave on the radio. Leebensroom, he was saying – leebensroom – that's German for "living room", which is what the
German people needs – more living room. He was shouting at
them at the top of his voice: Get up off your asses and fight for
leebensroom – every man, woman and child of yous. And the
cheers of the people – the Nassy cheers of them eggin' him on.
Damn yous for a crowd o' backsliders, says he – damn yous for
a crowd o' backsliders, this is all-out war. Every one of yous
should be involved in the war effort – making guns or bombs
or aeroplanes and the women making uniforms and darnin'
socks for the Weir March.'

'Sure I heard that myself on "Germany Calling". Haw–Haw
was at the same caper.'

'Aye, but did you hear it in the original? Leebensroom.
Leebensroom. Go Balls was in regular form that night. Do you
know the hair was standin' on me head listening to him. That's
the truth. I swear to me God I expected him to jump out of
the radio any minute and land on Ned Mary's floor and start
handing around guns and bombs to every one of us.'

On the narrow winding gravel road to the Hill, Betty and
myself, from where we sit on the bare floor of the cart, feel
every rise and dip of the iron-rimmed wheels. Going up
Coulter's Brae, Uncle Mick slides down off the back and leads
the donkey by the head.

'Hup! Come on! Gee up there!'

'Will we get off, Uncle Mick?'

'Stay where yous are. He's just lazy.' Uncle Mick gives
a swipe with the sally rod and the donkey bends his head
lower between the shafts, jerking us backward then forward.
Once over the crest of the brae, Uncle Mick again hoists
himself on to the back of the cart, flipping the reins over
our heads.

The Sunday before, Aunt Sally had invited us for a holiday: 'That is if yous wouldn't be lonely?'

'What would make them lonely?'

'You don't mind, Dada; you were born there; but the Hill is a lonely spot.'

'The holiday will do them good. Nothing like the mountain air.'

Uncle Mick sits sideways, his stocky legs dangling over the end of the cart. 'We'll soon be there now.' He points to a two-storey house in the trees at the end of a long lane. 'That's your Uncle Leo's place, the Lord rest him – where your father was born, and Sally – the first slate house in the Hill.'

'Where's your house, Uncle Mick?'

'You'll see it in a minute.'

The straggle of widely scattered houses runs in a wobbly line from the road, each house with a long, narrow lane leading straight up to it; most have a shelter of tall leafy trees as well. In some places the lanes are choked with briars and nettles and the stone cottage at the end has fallen in.

'She knows her way.' Uncle Mick slings a dark thong of tobacco spit into the ditch as the donkey turns into the last and longest lane.

In the yard the stones are sunken and rounded, marbled with hen droppings, and the withered thatch on the three-roomed, whitewashed cottage has a reddish glow in the evening sun. Rising close behind the house and slanting steeply upwards is the mountain with a few sheep and cattle grazing on the heathery slopes.

Aunt Sally comes to the door, smiling and red-faced. 'Welcome back sweet Caroline to Carolina town. Oh Waidean, yous are welcome, *céad míle fáilte*' – and she lifts Betty out of the cart and kisses her.

Standing on the bank behind the house after our tea, the four of us look down the Hill – slanting mountainside, rock and blue till – and not another house in sight.

'But you can see the smoke,' Aunt Sally says. 'Only nine smokes in the Hill now. Waidean, I remember when I was growing up counting seventeen smokes. And every house full of young people.'

'Are you lonely after Sean and Maura?' Betty asks.

'Wild lonely for ever.'

Uncle Mick takes the pipe from his mouth and points over his shoulder: 'Beyond the mountain is the sea; and beyond that – far, far beyond that – is New York – 315 East 206th Street, The Bronx – that's where they are.'

'Dawson might be raikin' the night' – Aunt Sally fills the kettle on the crook from a porringer – 'he often comes over to raik.'

'What's raikin', Aunt Sally?'

'Oh Waidean, do you not know what raikin' is? Raikin' is – well it's – stravaigin' – trailin'. He'll just come in and sit down at the fire. We'll have quare sport if Dawson comes over. We might get a recitation out of him; Dawson has lots of wonderful recitations. Or he might tell us a story. But he's a wee bit antic – a bit odd.'

Dawson, an elderly bachelor, lives in the nearest house with his mother, Old Joanne.

'Nobody in the Hill ever uses the lane when they're raikin'; they all cross over the ditch; it's a lot shorter. You never see anybody until they pass the kitchen window. They all come around the gable; we do the same ourselves. Oh Waidean, we're funny people in the Hill,' Aunt Sally laughs.

It is dusk when Dawson arrives but the red tin lamp hanging at the side of the window is left unlit. Dawson shakes hands with his left hand and looks at the floor when he talks to us.

We sit around the fire peering into the sputtering turf flames, telling what pictures we see in the coals. Uncle Mick puffs his clay pipe, the smoke curling up around the timber rafters. When you look above, you can see the scraws under the thatch, dark clay sods, tarred with the turf smoke of years.

Aunt Sally tilts over the sooty iron kettle steaming on the crook and rinses the teapot. Every hint to recite has been ignored by Dawson, but after the tea, without anybody asking him, he begins a story – The Story of Sullivan's Lost Child. Sullivan's grandmother was a witch and when she died she coveted the child. The story gets scarier and scarier and every time the grandmother is mentioned a shiver goes through Betty and myself. Dawson takes no notice but keeps his eyes steady on the turf flame. The dark has crept in on us from the open door and weird shadows without heads or legs jump about, waving at us from the flagstones and the whitewashed walls. Dawson has his hands crossed in an awkward way, but in the flickering glow from the hearth I can see what Aunt Sally has already told me – an extra stump of finger on his right hand. He is describing how Sullivan's child is playing on the strand. Out of the sea haze the granny's wizened face takes shape and her crooked knurled body begins stalking her granddaughter along the shore. We are waiting for her to pounce on the child; Dawson, acting the part, stretches both his hands towards the fire – when suddenly Betty lets out a screech that rocks Dawson in his chair. One screech follows another, sending Uncle Mick in a scurry to light the lamp. Still Betty lets out odd screeches, crying in between in a quivering voice: 'I want to go home. I want to go home.'

'You'll be all right, a stór, it's only a story. There's nothing to be scared of.'

Betty is looking straight ahead with wide terrified eyes, as if she can clearly see the granny witch. 'I want to go home. I want to go home, Aunt Sally.'

Everything is tried to calm her but her cries only grow more frantic. Uncle Mick has to hitch up the donkey; Betty is put sitting in the front corner of the cart with Aunt Sally's shawl wrapped like a bandage around her, and they head down the lane.

Dawson heads for home across the ditch.

Another deadner from Ferdia and the ball bounces off the pier wall, rolling into the tide before any of us can stop it. Ferdia is Aisling's older brother and has Aisling's long, straight nose and fuzzy red hair. Scunsey and myself stand watching the ball bobbing at the high-water mark, already beginning to wash around to the walled side of the pier.

'Too dangerous to chance it.' Scunsey turns his back on the challenge.

Ferdia moves nearer the edge, holding on to the pier wall to get a view of the far side, where the ball has now floated.

Scunsey is downfaced at the loss of his good sponge ball.

Suddenly Ferdia pulls off his shirt and throws it back to us. With a Red Indian whoop, he jumps feet first into the tide and begins to swim around the pier out of sight.

'Give us a leg up.'

I help Scunsey on to the high wall and he pulls me up after him. Ferdia has already captured the ball and raises it high in his right hand as soon as he sees us. He rolls over on his back, at the same time throwing the ball towards us – but it hits the pier wall, and lifted on a sudden gust of wind, is carried further out to sea. Ferdia follows, diving in and out of the waves, then turns and swims in closer to us. Again he throws the ball to us, again it hits the wall, and as it bounces off, he barely misses catching it. He is on his back, shouting and laughing, throwing the ball against the pier and jumping up out of the water to catch it on the rebound.

By the time he climbs up the slippery moss-green steps he is breathless and lies flat out at our feet. But no sign of the ball.

'Where is it?'

'You lost it?'

Ferdia stretches and the ball rolls out of his armpit.

More than once the sight of the Claddagh man passing the kitchen window has brought to a hurried halt a squabble between Mama and Dada. Claddagh works in the factory and most evenings comes in to have a few bottles of stout by the fire. He wears a wide-brimmed hat, a pair of horn-rimmed glasses, and when he sits, his waistcoat tightens and bulges over his stomach. A different pair of glasses, which he always gives a good polishing to, goes on as soon as he takes up the newspaper.

'I wish he would go up to the bar,' Mama complains; 'where he sits – always blocking the oven.'

The Claddagh man comes from Galway and has a room in Lambert's hotel.

'Claddagh is a true gentleman,' Dada says, 'and a good spender. Pity there's not a few more like him in the same factory.'

At second mass on Sunday Father Feegan's left eye has a black ring around it and his face looks puffy and bruised. 'There will be no devotions this evening,' he announces; 'instead benediction will be after mass.'

'He's back on the bottle again,' Dada says. 'He must have fallen somewhere.'

'And did you see the shake on his hands? He's a real pity.'

'Poor Father McGee was bad, but this man is beyond the beyonds. They must send all the boozers to Glengreeny.'

'That's an awful thing to say about the priest.'

'Well, it's the truth, isn't it? If he comes in, we can't give him anything. It'll be a charity to refuse him.'

'*You* can refuse him,' Mama answers.

Alone in the kitchen and wondering if Aisling or Ferdia will deliver the coppers, I jump when Father Feegan's hoarse command sounds behind me: 'Get me a naggin of Jameson from the bar.'

Dada frowns at me. 'Why didn't you run out the back when you saw him coming?'

'I hadn't time.'

'That'll be four and eightpence. Make sure he pays you.'

'That'll be four and eightpence, Father.'

'Tell your father I'll pay him again.'

'Are you doing the Ten Nights?'

'Oh sure I broke them. I had seven done when Francey took the flu. I had to start all over again.'

We make our way home from the chapel in the October dark, down the hilly and sideways-slanting street, with only the faint glow from each kitchen window we pass or a friendly flashlamp to keep us from tripping in the vannel or bumping into the pump. Voices ahead and behind take nearcuts through each other.

'– a tough cookie, that's for sure.'

'Is there any such thing as ghosts at all? I don't believe – that you Sammy?'

'Oh Con, how are you?'

'Cold the night. I can feel it in me shoulder.'

One night Dada heard a voice: 'Jamie is failed.'

'Did you hear that?' Dada sounded worried.

'What?'

'No – I thought I heard – somebody said, "Jamie is failed".'

'Who?'

'I dunno . . . Do I look all right?'

'Do you look all right! How does anyone look in the dark?'

But when we got home Dada examined himself in the mirror at the side of the kitchen window. 'Am I failed?'

'Then you are surely failed. We're all failed. We all need a good tonic.'

The following Tuesday, Dada went across to the dispensary for a bottle. He didn't look failed to me before he took the bottle, and he didn't look any better after he had it finished.

The last of the Sunday mass crowd cleared and Hackney Hill has pulled up outside, waiting to bring us to Mama's home place in Duhaigh for the day. All morning Betty and myself have been talking about last year's visit: the tall jaggy monkey puzzle in front of the house rising from an island of green, surrounded by sand and gravel; the crockery soldier on his fret-work shelf behind the bar; lemonade and biscuits and Aunt Laura, chubby and blond-haired, calling us 'dear'; and Uncle Harry and Dada telling each other stories of old times over glasses of Black & White whisky.

When we arrive, Uncle Harry, in his shirt sleeves, is busy clearing up in the bar and we all sit on high stools at the counter, where Dada insists on paying for the first round of drinks. Dada has his red silk handkerchief fluffed out in the breast pocket of his jacket, and in front of it, his American fountain pen and propelling pencil.

Aunt Laura journeys to and from the sitting room, rounding up empties until the counter teems with sour-scummed bottles and glasses. On the centre shelf behind the bar the redcoat soldier still stands to attention, a long-stemmed wine glass on each side of him.

'We had a big dance in the school last night,' Uncle Harry explains; 'we haven't the place cleared up yet.'

'Business is booming by the looks of it,' Dada remarks.

Uncle Harry produces a full bottle of whisky from under the counter and holds it up to the light. 'I haven't a drop o' stout left; they cleared me out completely. And I could sell as much more again.'

As soon as we finish our drinks we all move into the sitting room and Uncle Harry breaks the seal on the new bottle of Black & White, which he planks on the small table between Dada and himself. 'Help yourself, Jamie.'

'No rationing the day,' Dada laughs.

'Will you have a wee drop o' sherry, Cassy?' Aunt Laura smiles at Mama.

Mama makes a sour face and shakes her head.

Aunt Laura brings us in lemonade and biscuits on a silver tray. She sits for a while beside Mama and tries to make conversation. 'The children are getting big, the dears.'

Mama nods. Mama doesn't like Aunt Laura because she wears too much powder and lipstick – 'Always done up like a film star. That was how she got Uncle Harry – trapped him into marriage.'

'What ages are they now, Cassy?' Aunt Laura asks.

'Surely you know their ages.'

'Honestly, I forget.'

'You forget.'

Aunt Laura rises quickly and pours out another drink for Uncle Harry. 'You'll have another drop, too, Jamie.'

'A wee sup.'

'Dada, you're going to be drunk.'

'What if he is itself,' Uncle Harry snaps at Mama, 'one day in the year.'

Uncle Harry tells Aunt Laura to show us the new rockery and Mama and Betty follow her into the garden. Dada is sitting back in the brown leather armchair, his feet stretched in front of him, his hands loosely joined, thumbs circling each other. The nail on Dada's right thumb is black – a bad fright it got from a shovel in the steel mills. The nail didn't fall off but neither did it mend nor ever lengthen beyond where it reached on that day.

Dada is smiling a lot and talking about old times – about rationing in the States. 'Prohibition it was called – I'm sure you heard of it – a lot worse than rationing. Nobody was allowed to drink, so we all had to make our own. Me and my brother Tom had a bath of the stuff under the bed. You had to keep it hidden away on account of the Prohibition men. Every evening we used to give it a stir. We would be sampling it to see how it was coming along. Moonshine it was called. All over Chicago everyone was making moonshine. This evening me and Tom was after taking a good sample when a knock came to the door. Tom went to answer it and sure enough who was outside only the Prohibition man. "Any moonshine in the house?" "No. No moonshine," says Tom, and him reeking with the smell of the stuff. The Prohibition man strode past Tom, through the kitchen and into the bedroom, where myself was just after pushing the bath back under the bed. I was sitting on the edge of the bed trying to look innocent. "Nothing here," says I. But of course he saw the bath. "You Irish?" he says. "Sure, we're Irish," says I. He looked at the bath and he looked at me and Tom. "I always heard the Irish were great drinkers," says he, "but I never knew until now that you were such great pissers as well." '

Since early morning the raucous lowing of cattle in the street, cow coughs, hooves stomping, sticks skelping against dung-toughened hides and the harassed jobbers shouting and swearing.

'Put out your hand. Come on.'

'I'd be giving her away at that.'

'Houl' out your hand there.'

'I told you what I'll take. She's a fine wee heifer.'

'She's a bully wee heifer, I'm not denying it. I'll tell you what I'll do: if you give me luck's-penny – ten bob luck's penny –'

'Will you go way ourra that.'

'Come on. Spit on it. You'll get no better price...'

My job is to stand guard by the rusty iron gate leading to the cattle yard at the back of our outhouses. The charge is sixpence per beast, but most jobbers don't mind paying, as the cattle are safe for the day.

Everything goes well until Footsie danders into the fair green chewing an apple. I immediately stand in closer to the gatepost, hoping he won't see me, but he stops and lets out a jeer: 'Look at the *consaeit* of him taking money from the men. You better shout for Scunsey, you wee coward you' – and he rushes at me, his *ciotóg* raised.

My first thought is to take to my heels, but I am weighed down with two pocketfuls of sixpences, threepenny bits and pennies. Also the jobbers are looking on and I feel ashamed for being such a coward. In desperation I swing out wildly with both fists and by luck connect with his nose. Footsie gets such a shock that he fires the apple at my head, misses, and while he has his guard dropped I connect with a straight jab into the mouth. The jobbers are cheering me on and Footsie looks stunned. He is snorting blood up his nose and cursing me in Irish. He makes a comeback but I am not afraid of him any more and we slog it out fairly evenly matched, until one of the jobbers comes between us.

'That's enough now. That'll do. Make up, boys.'

The two of us shake hands and I give Footsie my handkerchief to wipe the scattered freckles of blood from his face.

'Where did you learn to box like that?'

'Nowhere.'

'You must have learned somewhere.'

'Crusoe.'

'Did Crusoe teach you?'

'Just a few lessons.'

'Cripes! Crusoe is mad. You're lucky he didn't bate the head off you.'

Out in the bottling store Dada has rolled the cill of stout up on to the stand and set the wooden tub underneath. To one side the corks are steeping in the enamel bucket. Next, the tapping of the barrel – two heavy blows of the mallet and the brass tap bursts its way through the bunghole. A sudden gush of froth. Dada turns on the tap and lets it flow until the tub is full. Dipping in the tin jug, he waits for the stout to shire down before taking the first drink. 'Haaah!' While there is still some stout in the bottom of the jug, he passes it to me.

'Go ahead, Conor. A wee sup never harmed anybody. *Sláinte!*'

The stout tastes ice cold and sour, but I drink it without making a sour face.

'You should say *sláinte mhór*, Conor; that's the answer whenever anybody says *sláinte*.'

'*Sláinte mhór!*' – and I finish off what is in the jug with a manly 'Haaah!'

'My father, the Lord rest him, could never afford to take a drink. Maybe one or two at Christmas time and that was the height of it. He died young from hard work – fifty-eight years of age. The only comfort the people had in them days was what they could take out of the land. I don't remember my grandfather. My great grandfather was supposed to have come all the way from Kerry, driving before him *dhá bhó dhéag agus tarbh dubh* – twelve cows and a black bull. I dunno how true that is. By the time it came to my father there was only one cow – and no sign of the bull.'

* * *

Against everyone's advice, Jellybob decided to ride his own donkey in the races on the strand. Then at the last minute he discovered that Francey Dubh was riding the young donkey that he had sold him earlier in the year. This is a son of the donkey Jellybob was riding.

'I decided to get in line beside Francey,' Jellybob told the men in the bar. 'I was hoping the donkeys would recognise each other and sure enough they did. But Francey didn't notice a thing. I kept the mother close to the son starting off. The other donkeys were all past their prime and no threat to either of us. Francey Dubh was certain he would have no problem passing me out, but as soon as I put on a wee spurt Francey's donkey fell into line behind me. Francey whipped and he kicked and he cursed till he was blue in the face but it didn't make a dang bit o' difference. His donkey was still the same distance behind when I passed the winning post. Francey Dubh was mad. "I know it's a cheat," says he, "but I don't know how you done it." "It's no cheat," says I. "Surely to God you'll agree it's a poor son that'll beat his own mother." '

Apart from the telegraph poles, where the long black and white posters are on display, and some other crumpled posters lying almost flat out in a few shop windows, there isn't a sign that Daniels' Travelling Show has arrived: no tent, no horses, no caravans. Old Mr Daniels, who is the boss, stays in Lambert's; the rest of the actors have lodgings in different houses around the town.

Every night in the parochial hall the show begins with a roll on the side drum, a long stretch of the accordion, and the big fat girl and the thin girl come dancing on sideways, singing:

> Honey, Honey, hold me,
> I'm so shy,
> But don't you kiss me
> Or I'll cry.

My ma she said
What I must do
Is stay away
From men like you.

The red silk costumes they wear stop well short of their knees, and when they kick their legs high in the air you can see their tight frilly knickers.

In the middle of the front row most nights Crusoe's broad shoulders block the view and at the end of the row Pete Post sits crouched against the stone wall.

'The Princess is a fine cut of a woman,' Crusoe says – meaning the fat girl.

The thin girl is called Ramsbottom and helps with the magic later in the show. After every trick Sulliman the Great says to her: 'Take it away, Ramsbottom; take it away.'

As the girls dance off at the beginning, two funny men are coming on from the far side of the stage. One man is smart; the other, not so smart, wears a yellow jacket chequered like a draughtboard.

'I heard you got married.'

'That's right. I married my mother-in-law.'

'You married your mother-in-law?'

'I married my mother-in-law.'

'Did your wife not try to stop you?'

'Sure, she did. She threatened to go home to her mammy.'

The main attraction is a play – every night something different: *Bold Robert Emmet, East Lynne, My Little Grey Home in the West.*

The show ends with another funny sketch, which always has old Mr Daniels in a starring role, getting tied up or beaten up or blown up. He wears a black bowler hat and a black jacket with tails and acts a bit like Charlie Chaplin, but he is too fat and too old for the part.

At Sunday mass Father McBrearty announces that on the following Saturday, the last night of the show, the play will be *The Story of Fatima* – proceeds for parochial purposes.

'We'll all have to go,' Mama says.

Dada objects. 'Saturday is my busiest night. I can't close down the bar.'

'It's for a good cause. Everyone will be there.'

'You can go yourself then. And bring the children.'

On Saturday Father McBrearty is led up the centre of the hall by old Mr Daniels to a special armchair with an embroidered cushion on it.

There is the usual roll on the side drum, the long stretch of the accordion – but no 'Honey, Honey, hold me'. Instead the two funny men come staggering on. Father McBrearty has a thick flabby neck, like a double chin put on backwards, and it lurches about when he laughs.

In the play the three children of Fatima go every day to pray before the statue of Our Lady. At the end they are on their knees in the grotto as usual, when slowly the blue and white statue comes to life. Our Lady glides off the rock, reaching her marble white hands towards the children. Everyone in the hall is holding their breath.

After the show old Mr Daniels, Sulliman the Great, and the two funny men talk and laugh in the back scullery and act at each other. Whiskey only, Dada decides – because they are not regular customers, the stout is too scarce, and anyway it is after hours.

All evening the men have been struggling to free Ellen Andy's black polly cow which lost her footing and slid down the bank into the rockiest part of the river. We watch from the fair green height, Footsie, Ferdia and myself, while Ellen, stooped in her tasselled black shawl, limps up and down the bank.

'Take her easy now. She's six months in calf. Go easy with her. Oh God help us, my poor cow; what am I going to do if anything happens to her!'

The cow stands without moving, trapped between two rocks in a swirling pool of water, her weary head turned to one side. Earlier the men had fixed hay bags under and around her belly to keep the ropes from cutting into her.

'One, two, three – heave!... One, two, three – heave!'

'Oh Waidean help us! Save my poor cow!'

Two men, bent low in the water, strain to free the cow's legs; two more are hauling on the ropes. The cow swings her head this way and that, frothing at the mouth. With each heave her body lunges forward then slumps back against the rocks with a splash.

The men take a rest, their hands on their knees, breathing hard.

'Do yous want more help?' Ellen calls out to them.

'We have as many as'll fit.'

'Don't lose heart whatever. God is good.'

The men settle the bags of hay back under the cow's twitching belly and take a hold of the ropes again. 'One last go. Come on, boys. We'll get her out this time.'

'Oh please God yous will. Waidean help us.'

'Lift. All lift together. One, two, three – heave!... One, two, three – heave!... This time. One, two, three – heave!'

The cow has sunk forward on her front legs, her long, sleek neck stretched awkwardly across the rock. The men look at each other and let the ropes fall from them.

'Oh what are we going to do, the poor beast?' Ellen claps her hands to her head.

'Come on home, Ellen.'

'What are we going to do?'

'We'll have to put her down.'

'Oh no, no. My lovely cow. You can't, Francey.'

'Her legs are broken, Ellen. It's no good.'

Francey Dubh takes Ellen firmly by the arm and leads her from the fair green. 'What are yous looking at?' – he shakes his fist at us – 'Go on home with yous!'

The other men splash up on to the bank and stand around dividing cigarette butts. In the muddy pool the cow stays slumped forward, barely moving, except for her belly, which heaves and glistens with sweat.

After a while Francey returns with Big John McBride. 'Are yous still here!' Francey makes a lunge at us and we run. 'Go on home, I'm telling yous.' But as soon as Francey and Big John have joined the men we straggle back on to the height.

Only Big John goes into the water this time. A few long steps and he is at the cow's head, fixing a hay bag underneath. Then he lines up, his big fisherman's waders searching for a grip in the river bed, his legs spaced wide apart. Very gently he touches the cow's neck with the blade of the axe. He takes a firmer hold of the axe handle and suddenly swings it back. The axe hovers in the air over his shoulder, and we look away. We hear the grinding blow and the terrible death roars. When I look again the cow has toppled forward, all bloodied and frantic, making wild plunges to get on to her feet. Big John raises the axe again and the blade crashes into the red bubbling gap in the cow's neck. Again and again the thick wedge of blade slices deeper into the wound. The roaring has stopped and the cow's head, now held to her body with a single raggle of skin, flops to one side of the rock. Blood oozes into the water, where the glistening black belly still heaves, and the rocks are splattered with dung.

'You're an eejit, Conor O'Donnell! Babies are not born in a cot.'

'They are so.'
'You don't even know how you came into the world.'
'I know well.'
'You said babies are born in a cot. Is that what your mammy told you? . . . And how did you get into the cot?'
'God.'
'Jakers Jack! You think God came down from heaven and put you into the cot?'
'Who else?'
'You're a skutterin' eejit. That's not how babies are born.'
'And how are they born?'
'They're born the same way as pups or sucks or bonhams.'
'They are not.'
'They are so.'
'How do *you* know?'
'Everybody knows that.'
'Everybody does not know it. Betty was born in a cot. I saw her.'
'You're a fierce eejit – and your mammy is a bare-faced liar.'
'*You're* a bare-faced liar.'
'All right, put them up!'

'Mama . . . Mama.'
'What is it, Conor?'
'Are babies born in a cot?'
'My goodness! What happened you? Had you another nosebleed?'
'I'm all right. Are babies born in a cot?'
'Why are you asking?'
'Footsie says they're not.'
'Footsie. And do you believe everything Footsie tells you?'
'He says they're born the same as – as animals.'
'Babies are a gift from God. They're born the way I told you.'

'In a cot?'

'How else?'

'Footsie says –'

'Don't mind what Footsie says. I don't like you playing with Footsie or any of that crowd. They're all too coarse. My goodness, you must have lost a pint of blood. What you need is a good tonic . . .'

'That was Wills's man and Con Moylan,' Dada says, shutting the bar door behind him. 'Imagine, Con is still paying off. It must be nearly twenty years since he went burst and the company men are still calling on him. He could have opted for bankruptcy – instead he's paying them all so much a month from whatever he earns at the weaving; hard earned money at Con's age. I saw him handing over four pounds to Wills's man and that was the last of what he owed *him*. "It took a long time," says Con laughing, "but I got there in the end." Wills's man shook hands with him and bought him a whiskey and a bottle o' stout. "I'm going to miss calling on you, Con," he says, "there's not many like you around." '

'Darlin' son. Darlin' son.' Jack Jumble lifts off his grimy, raggedy cap, scratches his head and grins at himself in the big mirror behind the bar. Jack's head is smooth and oily as a ballbearing, his face sweaty with booze, and his clothes have a sour, fusty smell, like stale bedding. 'Give us another one.'

I wait for him to put the money on the counter but instead his head disappears and I hear the tinkle of empty stout bottles at his feet.

Jack swings the clinking bag of bottles on to the high stool beside him and folds back the neck of the bag.

'We can't take any more bottles.'

'For why?'

'There was oil in the last ones.'

'Oil?'

'Snuggy got a taste of paraffin from his stout. He blurted it out in front of the whole bar.'

'Paraffin! Couldn't be.' Jack has lined up a row of dusty bottles on the counter. 'Your father promised me a penny a bottle for every one I collected out the country.'

'We're not taking any more. That's what he said.'

Jack snatches a random bottle from the line-up and sniffs. 'Smell that . . . Go on, smell it' – he waves the bottle under my nose.

'It doesn't matter. We're not taking any more.'

'No paraffin in that.' He picks up another bottle and dusts it on his frayed sleeve. His hands are small and rag-nailed, scuffed as an old pair of gloves, and the jacket he has on would hold his twin as well as himself. 'You can test every one of them' – he sniffs at another bottle – 'not a whiff o' paraffin anywhere.'

'It doesn't matter. My father said no more bottles from anyone.'

Jack takes off his cap again and rubs his head. 'Give us another one.'

'Have you the money?'

'I'll pay you again. Word of honour.'

'I can't give you any drink if you haven't the money.'

Jack's fingers keep vanishing up his sleeve as he lowers the bottles singly into the bag. 'You'll give us one more. Darlin' son.'

'No more.'

He stares at me from angry bloodshot eyes, his head just over the top of the counter. 'You're only a wee skut, that's all y'are.'

In a crowd Jack can be a menace and sometimes the indirect cause of a row. A favourite trick of his is to take a quick slurp from the glass of the man standing next to him, move off and do the same to somebody else. One fair day Jack took a big gulp from the Duck's glass, then moved down the line of drinkers.

The Duck now had nobody between himself and Crusoe, an old enemy and the most likely suspect. The Duck didn't say anything but waited his chance and took a big gulp from Crusoe's glass. Unfortunately Crusoe saw him in the mirror and was facing the Duck as he put the glass back on the counter.

'What do you think you're doing?' Crusoe demanded.

'Getting some of my own back,' the Duck said.

The old trouble between the Duck and Crusoe had been over a missing sheep and Crusoe now thought the Duck was casting this up.

'I'll give you some of your own back,' says Crusoe, landing the Duck a box in the nose that sent a gush of blood leaping over the counter.

Dada had seen who the real culprit was but decided to sing dumb: 'No point turning one row into two.'

'You promised you would let us,' Betty whinges to Mama.

'Now, you're both too young to be out this late.'

'You said you would.'

'Och, let the craturs go; they'll only be young once.'

'*You're* worse than *they* are.'

Dada takes Betty's green corduroy coat from the back of the door and holds it out for her. 'I'll bring them myself.'

'Don't be long then. It's no place for children.'

Great smuts, like black moths fluttering through the air, from the huge bonfire of branches and old bicycle tyres meet us going into the fair green, the heat rippling out in waves as we draw closer. Standing in a wide ring around where the sparks shoot upwards are boys and girls jostling and giggling. Big Jodie, who has emptied several bags of sawdust and chippings on the grass, sprinkles odd shovelfuls of the mixture over the flames.

We stay close to Dada, waiting for the sport to begin. After a lull Corner Jim flings a branch into the blaze and calls out two names.

Everyone cheers 'A hi!'

Somebody else calls 'Duck Doogan and Smilin' Sadie on the bonfire!'

'A hi!'

'James White and Máire Logan on the bonfire!'

'A hi!'

'Is Máire going with James White?' Betty asks. Máire is a niece of Dada's, and Mama has been talking about hiring her as a maid.

'I don't know,' Dada answers; 'maybe she is.'

'Captain Spearman and Miss Rose on the bonfire!'

'A hi!'

The names ring out and we raise a cheer after each.

Another lull – then John Sean sings:

> As I roved out on bonfire night
> No care was on my mind,
> My thoughts were all of divilment,
> Towards happiness inclined;
> I looked across the bonfire's flame
> A shimmering face to see,
> And when I looked I saw my love
> And she looked back at me.
>
> We danced around the bonfire's flame,
> A twelvemonth had gone by
> And in our hearts another flame
> Was dancing all as high;
> Though little pleasure did we feel
> When we remembered then
> That I would be in Tennessee
> Ere bonfire came again.

And bonfire came and came again
And still I stayed away,
Nor, till my fortune I had made,
Did I leave Amerikay;
Then I looked across the bonfire's flame
Her shimmering face to see,
And when I looked I saw my love
But she never looked at me.

Before anyone has time to clap, two more names are called: 'Dinny Frigg and Rosie Fry on the bonfire' – and wild cheering and whistling breaks out. Dinny and Rosie are two old Yanks who have been seen a lot together lately.

'Crusoe and Molly Dan on the bonfire!' – another big cheer.

'Pete Post and Maggie May on the bonfire!'

'A hi!'

'That's all there is to it' – Dada takes us by the hand – 'they'll be calling names till they run out o' couples.'

'Can we stay a wee while longer?'

'Mama'll be waiting for us. We better go home.'

Down with the flu, and Mama stokes and pokes into guttering flame the bedroom fire for Betty and myself. But the crows have built in the chimney and the downdraught weaves a puffy web of turf smoke around us, stinging our eyes and nostrils. Still the fire must be kept going or we'll both get pneumonia.

We talk about school and the Easter holidays, which are just around the corner. Aisling's name is mentioned. She has started taking music lessons from Miss Culleton, who travels from outside Killybegs on the bus every Saturday. Some evenings I hear the piano faintly, scales and snatches of melody carried on the wind from the top of the town. Other times I stand in the bar door listening, waiting for Aisling to touch the keys.

'She can play "Over the Waves" and a bit of "The Blue Danube Waltz",' Betty tells me.

My own ambition is to play the drums or the bagpipes in St Oran's pipe band. Me marching through the town with the men and a bulging bag of wind under my oxter or beating hell out of a side drum or maybe even the big drum. Aisling would take notice of that – a lot of other people as well. Unfortunately it's out of the question – for the moment anyway.

The turf smoke has got so dense that we no longer care whether we get pneumonia or not, and I scramble over the back of my small iron bed to get at the window. On the footpath opposite, Sonny Moylan stands looking up. 'Your chimney's on fire,' he calls. 'Your chimney's on fire.'

In the snug, Willoughby asks me if I ever heard of Sew Crates and Plateau: 'Two great men lived in Greece long ago. Sew Crates was the first man to discover that the earth is round. You know that the earth is round? Well, it is. Plateau said a lot of wise things. Know thyself, that was Plateau's saying. Know thyself.'

Willoughby was shell-shocked in the First World War and, as a result, has a British Army pension. His thick, rushy moustache, waxed at the ends, juts downwards like a thatch over his lower lip and he talks through it in a muffled sort of way. On pension day he orders several glasses of rum and sits at the counter or the kitchen table, a stack of envelopes and postal orders in front of him – so much for the black babies, so much for St Vincent de Paul, so much for the Maynooth Mission to China. His talk is mostly about ghosts and fairies, which he is not a bit afraid of – and Old Nick, the very mention of which causes him to suck in his breath and lower his voice as if he is saying the Holy Name.

'Old Nick is a boyo. He never gives up. And he never looks

the same any two times you meet him. He could be the man sitting beside you on the bus, or a young girl, or your next-door neighbour's cat – pretending to be, I mean, because, of course, underneath, Old Nick is always the same. Old Nick never changes, no, never changes. He never changes and yet he's always different.'

One evening when Willoughby arrived home from the town he found Old Nick in the house before him. 'The first thing I noticed was the holy water font on the floor, in smithereens. Then I saw him – Old Nick himself, struttin' around the kitchen, flappin' his wings, with a leer on his face. In the form of a crow he was. He was black with soot – straight off the hobs o' hell. And the sounds coming out o' him – like no crow on earth. "He never rose, He never rose," says he to me, before I even had time to get out of my topcoat. "He never rose", meaning Our Saviour, of course. "Go back to where you came from," says I, "back to your own kind, to the pit and the quicklime and all the damned souls o' hell." But divil a move out o' him. He was standing in front of the fire, like as if he was trying to sort something out in his mind. He was so close to the blaze it was unnatural. I expected him to go up in flames any minute. "What do you want?" says I to him, "or what brings you here?" I was afraid he came for my soul. "He never rose, He never rose," says he back to me again. I picked up a clod o' turf and let fly at him. Sure he only laughed at me. Up and down the kitchen with him, from the floor to the rafters, flapping his dirty black wings and mocking away and me follyin' him, firing clod after clod and anything else I could lay my hands on, and every clod I fired he was in a different spot when it landed: one minute, hovering in front of the picture of the Sacred Heart, daring me to fire – the next minute, perched up on the mantelpiece beside the clock. Then he disappeared altogether – flew up the chimney. If he did itself, I poked and

I jabbed at him with the sweeping brush till I got him down again and by that time I was as black as the divil myself. He fell straight into the fire but it didn't knock a flinch out o' him. Up he jumped, still blaspheming away in that croaky rauky voice of his, round and round the kitchen and me after him beltin' him with the brush. By the time I got rid of Old Nick the house was in a shambles.'

A tall thin priest with a pinched face has come off the four o'clock bus from Killybegs and now sits at the head of the table drinking a bottle of stout, an uneasy look in his eyes. Mama had a big shakehands for him and called him Father, but there is something odd about him – like a square medal or a hymn sung to the tune of 'Maggie Pickie'.

'Your mother will be glad to see you.'

The priest nods.

'I saw her last Sunday. She's in good form.'

'That's good.' He asks for another bottle of stout and lights another cigarette.

While Mama is getting the drink, Dada comes in and shakes hands with him but doesn't call him Father. 'Home for Christmas?'

'Just a short visit.'

Dada glances at him behind his back, dithers, then goes out again.

Two more bottles of stout, two more cigarettes, his round-collar thoughts kept to himself. He gazes at the empty glass as if he is expecting a second free drink and pushes it further down the table.

'You better go home to her, Father.'

'I suppose I better.'

'Poor Father Timony.' Mama shakes her head after seeing him to the door.

'Who is he?'

'That's Father Timony O'Boyle. You know Mrs O'Boyle – old Mrs O'Boyle? He's her son.'

'What's wrong with him?'

'Father Timony is silenced.'

'What is silenced?'

'Silenced means he can't say mass or hear confessions or anything. The bishop silenced him.'

'Why did he silence him?'

'Why? Oh, I don't know.'

'Did he do something wrong?'

'No, he didn't. I think he's a sad man, poor Father Timony. He's a real pity.'

Dada coming in with a bucket of Indian meal for the cow adds a twist and a knot to the story. 'What sort o' form is Ten-Minute Timony in?'

'A nice way to talk about the priest.'

'Well, that's what he's called, isn't it? Ten-Minute Timony.' Dada pours boiling water from the kettle over the meal and sifts it through his fingers. 'Ten minutes flat it used to take him to say mass. He would spend longer over a bottle o' stout. The poor man put himself out o' business.'

'Strange life, the publican's. Most of the time you spend waiting: waiting for people to come in, waiting for them to drink up and buy another round, waiting for them to leave before the guards arrive. You hear a lot o' wild talk, silly oul' *ráiméis* that they would be ashamed of next morning – if they could remember it.'

'I have four cills for you, Jamie.'

'Righto.'

Slowly and awkwardly, Morgan eases himself out of the

driver's seat and fixes a block of wood under the back wheel.

'Hold on, you.' Dada flings a bag of old corks behind the lorry, and Morgan lands the first cill on it. I help Dada to roll the cill of stout to the gable and stand it upright. Three more cills hop off the squashed bag, and our hands are red from the chalky paint on the rims: red paint for stout; white paint for porter.

Morgan's hands shake when he holds out the docket for Dada to sign. 'I'll have time for a quick one, Jamie.'

'Righto.'

Morgan always drinks the stout straight from the bottle. 'I'd never get my work done if I was to start drinking out o' glasses. I'd be half the night on the road.'

'Sure he *is* half the night on the road,' Dada says. 'By the time he reaches the end of his round he has to knock people out of their beds to take a delivery: him staggering around in the headlights with a bag of flour or salt or sugar on his back.'

'She's still there, is she?' He glances out at the lorry and the black collie dog that sits upright on guard in the passenger's seat.

The lorry is old and battered and half the step into the driver's cab has rusted off. Once, at the bottom of the town, Morgan didn't bother putting the block under the wheel and when he went out there was no lorry. Luckily it rolled only a few yards before coming to a halt in the sandpit.

'There's another four or five years in her. She'll do me for *my* day.'

'I don't know how he escapes,' Dada remarks; 'his eyesight is very bad and he's half-shot half the time. I think the dog knows his way around better than Morgan does.'

'The V-1 could finish it all yet. It's not too late yet. Did you see where it knocked down a church and a house in the south of England?'

'It's a powerful invention no doubt – a yoke that'll fly without a pilot.'

'Hitler's secret weapon.'

'Still and all, there's not much point knocking down a church – or a house for that matter.'

'That's only the beginning. They're only testing it at this stage, don't you know?'

'Well, they'll need to hurry up – if it's going to stop Eisenhower.'

'The V-1'll stop him – if Goering can get enough of them into the air.'

'Goering is only a windbag. Look what he done in Russia – left the whole German army stuck in the slush. They hadn't even a topcoat; they hadn't even a clean pair o' socks.'

'The Foorer didn't pull out all the stops yet. You'll find he still has a trick or two up his sleeve.'

'Well, things are looking pretty shady for him at the minute.'

'Things are not going according to plan, that's true; though I still think he'll come out on top. Do you know that when the Foorer put on his army uniform, he swore never to take it off till Germany was victorious?'

'Be God then, if he's going to be buttoned into the one uniform for that length o' time, I don't think he'll have many shaking hands with him – even if he *does* win the war.'

'Great wee man, the Foorer. He's not that tall at all, you know. Not near as tall as de Gaulle. It's his personality. When you think that in the First World War he was in the trenches. Hitler was shell-shocked, you know.'

'Like Willoughby.'

'What?'

'Willoughby was shell-shocked.'

'I'm talking about Adolf Hitler.'

'I know.'

'Surely to God you're not comparing Willoughby to the German Foorer!'

'All I'm saying is that he was shell-shocked.'

'Who was shell-shocked?'

'Willoughby. Come to think of it: the two of them was in the trenches. For all we know it could have been Willoughby that done it.'

'What are you blatherin' about!'

'All I'm saying is that Willoughby was in the trenches and Hitler was in the trenches – on opposite sides – firing at each other.'

'Who says they were firing at each other?'

'Well, they were hardly throwing each other Woodbines. So it could very well be Willoughby that done it to him.'

'You're telling me that Willoughby fired a shell at Adolf Hitler?'

'Why not?'

'Talk sense, man.'

'It's possible, isn't it? In fact they could have shell-shocked each other for all we know.'

'Shell-shocked each other! If you were having this conversation in Germany, you could be arrested – do you know that? – for disrespect to the Foorer. You could be taken out and shot as a traitor.'

'Well – I'm just thinking – about the shell shock.'

'What about it?'

'I'm just thinking – if it had the same effect on the Foorer as it had on Willoughby – I wouldn't hold out much hope for the German people.'

'Miss Rose looked gorgeous in her white veil and her big bouquet of white roses. He's coarse. Anything to do with the army – it's the last walkout. The chapel was packed. And the singing was lovely. But when they got outside they spoiled everything. He lifted her right off the chapel step to give her a kiss – lifted back her veil and kissed her. Imagine! Everyone was talking about it. I think she's going to have her hands full with that man.'

'Feel it, Cassy, it's pure silk. Yous can feel it, Betty and Conor. Go on, put your hands on it. Doesn't it feel nice and slippy? Yous never saw anything like this in your lives, I'll bet; none of us ever did. When James came home with it I didn't know from Adam what it was, the size of it – like a big white caul. The straps and the rest of it are all at home. I just brought the main part so as yous could see. Imagine the man that came floating down out of the sky in this. Whenever I look at it I think of him – and his mother back home in Germany, wondering what ever happened to her son. If I had her address I'd write to her and tell her that he's safe and well in the Curragh, that's the truth. Isn't it a lovely thing though and mustn't it be a strange feeling to fall down out of the heavens and land in a stripe of meadow all new to you – like being born a grown person – like it was your first step on earth?'

On Saint Patrick's Day the Ancient Order of Hibernians holds its annual parade. We straggle after the band – through the town, along the upper road and back again by Canavan's Corner House: the pipers with their cheeks puffed out, elbows going, faces stern as statues, drones and drums and drums and drones – 'A nation once again, a nation once again'. Carried proudly at the head of the procession is a huge canvas banner with Saint Patrick in green vestments on one side, his right foot stamping on a snake, and on the other side, a mournful-looking Saint Oran, patron saint of the village. It takes four men to control the heavy, flapping banner: two on the poles and two more on the steadying ropes. In the middle, between pipers and drum-mers, the Duck raises his legs in high goose steps, while he pounds out the beat on the big drum, every so often swinging the drumsticks in the air.

Anyone making Lent is allowed to break out on Saint Patrick's Day. Whatever has been saved in the line of goodies is dipped into. Sweets are scarce, so, apart from some brandy balls and butterscotch, we are mostly munching squares of jelly and dilisk as we strive to keep in step with the steady marching beat.

'Hurry up. What's keeping you?'

'My heel is skinned.'

'Take off your shoes.'

'I can't get me lace opened.'

At the parochial house the Duck gives two beats for a halt and the band spreads out in a curved line. A bleat on the pipes, the drones answering with a drawling grunt. 'Hail Glorious Saint Patrick' . . . 'Faith of Our Fathers' . . .

Nobody ever comes to the door and we move off without music, the Duck keeping us in step with single slow beats, his chin cocked up over the top of the drum.

After the parade the men crowd into the bar while Jellybob sits on the windowsill doing lookout.

'Are you drowning the shamrock?'

'Giving it a wee sprinkle.'

'When are we getting the kilts?'

'We should have them for next Saint Patrick's Day.'

'Oh, we heard that before.'

'Put us up another round there, Jamie.'

'What about a song?'

'Aye, give us a song there.'

'Give us one of the local man's.'

'Aye, give us one o' Rogan's.'

Saint Patrick's Day we gathered
To march behind the men,
'Twas the Old Hibernian Order,
I see them clear again,
I hear the pipers skirling
Their notes of ecstasy
And the drummers proudly whirling
In Glengreeny by the sea.

Uncle Neddy's mule and cart are tight up against the gable of
our house and for once Uncle Neddy hasn't a word out of him.
From the gable window, Máire, his daughter, throws down her
belongings: a bundle of clothes, shoes, a black patent handbag.
She stops when she sees me; Uncle Neddy turns and scowls. He
looks up again at Máire. 'Come on, Máire!'

'A'm not goin' down the stairs.'

'Then jump ta hell.'

Máire eases herself out on to the windowsill and drops with
a frightened cry into the cart. She has been with us barely a
month and hardly a day has passed without a row between
Mama and herself. Sunday last, Mama caught her writing a letter
in her bedroom.

'Who are you writing to there?'

'Nobody.'

'Nobody. And I suppose you're expecting an answer? Show
me the letter . . . "Dear James". This is to James White, isn't it?'

Máire doesn't say anything.

'You're the stubborn girl. How many times did I tell you that
you weren't to be running after the boys?'

'A'm not runnin' after thim.'

'What are you writing about, then, if you're not running after
them? . . . "Dear James. You wouldn't believe how lonely I am
since I left the Hill." What sort o' silly talk is that? Anyone

would think you were writing from Australia – and the Hill only three miles out the country. What other nonsense have you there?...''You would never believe how lonely I am without you.'' ' Mama raises her eyes and mocks Máire's broad country accent: ' ''Ya would nivir believe how lonely A yam without ya.'' Well, if that's not running after the boys I would like to know what is.' Mama tears up the letter and throws the pieces at Máire. 'Get down to the kitchen; there's plenty of work to be done if you'll only do it, instead of daydreaming about boys.'

'Goodbye, Conor,' Máire calls to me from the cart.

'Ya can tell your mother we're off,' Uncle Neddy grunts. He gives the reins a chuck: 'Gee up there! Go on A'm tellin' ya, out o' here ta blazes.'

Molly Dan and Suzanne come tottering into the kitchen, dead to the world.

'I think it'll be my last Lent doing Saint Oran,' Suzanne sighs; 'the oul' feet are giving up on me.'

Mama moves the kettle over the heat and gets delph from the scullery.

'Don't be setting any table for us, as the fella says; just a drop in our hands'll do fine.'

'None of yous taking milk or sugar, I suppose?'

'The milk or sugar doesn't bother meself, Cassy,' Suzanne answers, 'it's the tobacca.'

'Ah, that oul' tobacca has a *piachán* in you; it has you all choked up, as the fella says.'

'What are you talking about! Sure I hadn't a smoke or a snuff since Pancake Tuesday.'

'Then if you hadn't, you'll be making up for it once Lent is out.'

'Oh, I don't know how I'll manage to get through till Easter

Sunday. The first thing I think of when I open my eyes in the morning is the tobacca. Then I think if I could have a pinch o' snuff itself. Please God, I'll get the grace to carry on.'

Both women pour the scalding black tea from their cups on to their saucers, blowing into it. The currant bread is left staring back at them from the plate.

'Oh God save us the day and the night, Cassy, there wasn't one doing the station only ourselves. I remember when you wouldn't be able to get around the stones with the crowd was in it, as the fella says. What's coming over the people at all?'

'I don't think Father McBrearty is in favour of it,' Mama says.

'And why wouldn't he be in favour of it?'

'Well – haven't you the chapel above – with the Blessed Sacrament and all. What's the point in climbing halfway up the mountain to go round and round a heap o' stones?'

'Oh God save us the day and the night, do you hear this! And Saint Oran the patron saint of the parish.'

'Is he? Or was he a proper saint at all?'

Molly turns away from Mama and talks to Dada who is coming in.

'*You* know about Saint Oran, don't you Jamie?'

'Saint Oran? Sure.'

'The friend of Saint Patrick and born in our own parish,' Suzanne elaborates.

'Not born,' Molly corrects her, 'but lived here – and built his chapel.'

'You were doing the station?' Dada sits down beside the two women.

'We were, Jamie, and we think it might be our last time.'

'Not at all. You'll live for years yet the pair of yous.'

'We'll live with the help o' God, but I'm thinking our climb-ing days are over, as the fella says.'

'Must be a quare lot o' times since you started doing it first?'

'A quare lot o' times, surely. I started with my mother when I was twelve.'

'God save us the day and the night, I remember doing Saint Oran with my own mother, the Lord be good to her, and me only a gissa.'

'Then the both of you must be in fairly good standing with the Man Above.'

'Oh, you never know what sort o' standing you're in till you get there.'

'No, you never know whether you're up or down, as the fella says.'

The two women dally for a while chatting to Dada, then rise stiffly drawing their shawls around them and go out dragging their feet.

'I don't know what *they're* doing penance for,' Dada mutters. 'If *they* don't get to heaven, the rest of us may throw our hats at it.'

The sun dancing along the headboard of the creaky four-poster bed wakens Mama, Betty and myself on the first morning of our holiday in Duhaigh, Mama's home place – but Mama is not in a sunny mood.

'Imagine any woman that would put three people in the one bed; that's some welcome, surely. Did yous sleep at all?'

'We did.'

'We had a great sleep.'

'I don't believe yous had. I was tossing all night like a twig in a storm. There's a lump in the middle of the bed and it would give anyone a curve in their spine.'

A gentle knock on the door and Aunt Laura looks in smiling. 'Good morning, dears. Did yous all sleep all right, Cassy?'

'A lot you care how we slept: three of us crammed in here like pigs at the fair.'

'Were yous not comfortable? I'm sorry, Cassy.'

'Sorry, my foot. Some holiday this is going to be.'

'I thought yous all wanted to sleep in the big bed; that's what you said, Cassy.'

'What else could I say, when you put the words into my mouth?'

'I only asked if you would rather sleep with the children. How are yous, dears?'

'We're grand, Aunt Laura.'

'Oh then, they're anything but grand.'

'What would yous like for your breakfast? I'll bring yous breakfast in bed.'

'No thanks. We have enough of this ramshackle bed to do us for a long time.'

'I'm terrible sorry, Cassy. It was all a misunderstanding –'

'You're terrible sorry. You are I'm sure. My God above – I might have known from the welcome we got yesterday evening what to expect.'

'I was glad to see yous all, that's the truth.'

'When we arrived you were washing Joey's hair. You hardly looked at us.'

'Cassy, I welcomed you –'

'With a handful o' suds. Then you went back to latherin' away.'

'I couldn't leave the child's head in the basin.'

'After that, we were left hanging around while you washed the dinner dishes – at four o'clock in the evening!'

'Now, there's no need to get hurtful, Cassy.'

'Is there not? You came in here from the back o' beyond. You got a soft seat, me girl –'

'Cassy dear, can we not be friends?'

'Don't call me dear.'

'I'm only trying to be friends with you.'

'Friends, I'm sure. Who could be friends with the likes o' you? with your fancy airs and your false face –'

'Cassy, I don't want to fight with you on your holidays.'

'No, you don't want to fight with me on my holidays. You came in here without a penny to your name – and nobody belonging to you ever had a penny –'

Aunt Laura cuts Mama short with a crying voice: 'I'm going to tell Harry the awful things you're saying to me.'

'Tell away, crybaby,' Mama calls after her.

The commotion has brought the three of us upright into a sitting position. Mama now lies back haggard, staring at the ceiling, where a moth is walking upside down.

'Mama! Mama!' Betty tugs at Mama's arm.

'What?'

'I'm afraid.'

'There's nothing to be afraid of.'

'What are we going to do?' I ask, equally fearful.

'Nothing. We'll wait and see.'

While we are waiting, Betty goes to the potty. Then Mama goes. Then I go.

Uncle Harry doesn't knock. 'What's going on here!'

'What is it, Harry?' Mama bounces upright again. Betty rises on her elbows, and I slink back under the blankets.

Uncle Harry looks very cross. 'Laura tells me you're after insulting her, right, left and centre.'

'I am I'm sure. I never said boo to her.'

'Didn't you tell her she never brought a penny into the house?'

'Well, it's the truth isn't it, and she can't deny it. And neither can you.'

'Cassy, for God's sake, is that any business o' yours?'

'It is surely business o' mine. Da never wanted you to have anything to do with Laura Keane –'

'I won't listen to that sort o' talk.'

'You wouldn't listen to Da either, but now you see the mistake you made.'

'Mistake! What mistake?'

'You know well what mistake.'

'What are you talking about?'

'Oh, she has the wool nicely pulled over your eyes.'

'I don't want to hear any more of your ravings.'

'I'm not saying anything to *you*, Harry.'

'When you say it to Laura, you say it to me. She's down in the kitchen now, crying her eyes out –'

'Oh, she's well able to pretend. She should have been an actress. That's what she would have been best at.'

'In under God, what are you raving about, woman! You're not a day home yet and you have the whole house in an uproar. Keep a civil tongue in your head if you want to stay; that's my last word to you.' Uncle Harry glares at Mama and slams the door after him.

'Now, for you. That's what it is to have a stepbrother. Come on. Up! I'm not staying another minute in this house. We'll get our breakfast when we go home.'

'Who is it?' Betty holds up the hairlined photograph she found while rummaging through the chest of drawers in the top bedroom – a head and shoulders snapshot of a dark, wavy-haired man with a round honest face.

'No wonder for you to be asking who is it.' Mama glances at the photograph without taking it from Betty.

'Is it Dada?' I suggest.

'Dada before he went to the States. You wouldn't recognise him now, would you?'

★   ★   ★

Coming within sight of Stonehead's sun-scorched meadow, Aisling is uppermost in my thoughts when suddenly her flossy red head appears from behind an upturned handcock. I want to run towards her and I want to run a hundred miles in the opposite direction.

Further back in the field, her father and mother and Ferdia are busy shaking out the makings of a trampcock. Ferdia waves to me and I wave back. My feet drag as I wait for him to come as far as the ditch.

'Where are you going?'

'Tea for my father.'

Aisling, shaking out an armful of hay, turns towards us, her face browned from the long spell of August sunshine. I pretend not to notice and talk to Ferdia: 'It's very warm. I'm roasting.'

'There's a well in the corner' – Ferdia points – 'do you want a drink?'

'All right.' I sling the green shopping bag with the bottle of tea and sandwiches for Dada under a sward of ferns and hop over the ditch. Passing Aisling, I can't help looking straight into her big solemn eyes. 'We're going for a drink in the well.'

Aisling nods and follows at a distance.

Up the field, Stonehead strains under the weight of a handcock, which he is dragging along the stubbled ground with a long rope across his shoulder.

'Where's the can?' Ferdia scours around in the bushes. 'Where did you leave it?'

'Daddy must have it.'

'We can use our hands,' I suggest.

'Don't put your hand in the well. You'll only raise the dust' – Aisling touches my bare arm to stop me. 'Get the can, Ferdia,' she says.

Ferdia is going to argue, but changes his mind and runs to the top of the field.

Left alone with Aisling, a shiver of excitement runs through me. We are in our bare feet on the spongy scraw of clover and watercress, in the cool shadow of the overhanging hedge of summer leaves. I glance again at Aisling. She has turned to where Ferdia is taking the can from behind a handcock. I look up the field towards Ferdia. I look at the ground. I take a step nearer the well. As I do so, Aisling's face shines in the water, clear, yet unreal, as if I am seeing her across a great distance. Beyond her floating image the dense blueness of the sky hangs like a panel in the stained-glass window above the high altar, streaked with delicate lines of cloud. I stare into the well, fearful of being discovered, but unable to take my eyes away. Her hair, brushed back from her high freckled forehead and tied in a swishing ponytail, reaches almost to her shoulders. Every feature is imprinted clearly on the still film of water: her long, perfectly shaped nose, large questioning eyes, angel face – and in that instant I know for sure that I will never love any girl ever the way I love Aisling. I keep on staring in a sort of daydream, until tiny insects skidding around on top of the water cause a blur. Aisling turns her head and I look away. Has she sensed my stares? I look again and all I see is the blank face of the well.

After tucking us in for the night, Mama sits on the edge of my bed and takes up once more the story of 'The Children of Lir' – the four children of Eve who were turned into swans by their wicked stepmother.

'I had a stepmother myself. I never knew my own mother; she died when I was three weeks old. Then Da got married again – to Big Winnie Hannigan. That's what she was called: Big Winnie. She was all for her own children, Harry and Sadie. Most of the time she spent in bed, big lazy lump. She would rise in the morning to check the post and then back up the stairs with her. And not a thing wrong with her only downright laziness. The next thing was she took to the bottle. She was a secret drinker; wasn't it awful? As soon as Da would go out she would sneak into the bar and slip a naggin o' whiskey down her stocking. I used to have to clear the empty bottles out of her room and hide them in the dump. Imagine. And if I didn't do exactly what she told me, she would throw a tantrum. I used to be terrified of her. She wouldn't let me out to play, she would never let me down the town with Harry and Sadie. I had to wait hand and foot on her. One day she sent me over to McGlynn's for a knitting pattern: that's all she ever did was knit woollen cardigans for herself and for Harry and Sadie. McGlynns lived down the road from us. Nora McGlynn was the same age as myself and she brought me up the field to show me her pet lamb and I forgot all about the time. When I got home my stepmother was in a rage. She told Da a lot of lies about me, that I would do nothing she asked me, and that I was disobedient. Anything she said, Da always believed her. Then a lot of things were brought up. Da was complaining about all the sweets that were being taken. Harry and Sadie were taking most of them, but I got blamed for that as well. When I said it was Harry and Sadie, my stepmother called me a liar. "Get out of my sight," she said, "you wee liar you." Imagine! After all I did for her. She tried to turn my father against me. So I told about the whiskey. Of course she denied it. Da didn't know who to believe – but I think he knew she was lying. He left the room without taking anyone's side. I was terrified to be alone with my stepmother, she was in such a rage. But she never laid a hand on me – just gave me a look – I'll never forget it. From that day on we couldn't stand each other.'

Snuggy reaches down into the scaly sugar bag and pulls out a fresh salmon by the gills. He has a round baby face and the name of being a lazybones and a fly customer.

'How much?' Dada asks.

'Three shillings.'

'I'll give you half a crown.'

'Oh Jamie, I couldn't, honest to God, Jamie. I was out half the night to nab them few fish.'

'Half a crown.'

'Oh Jamie, you're very hard on me, and me risking jail and all.'

'Half a crown; take it or leave it.'

'We'll split the differ – two and ninepence, Jamie, and it's a deal.'

'Right you be.'

'And maybe you'll throw in a Woodbine for luck.'

On the sideboard in Con Moylan's sitting room I find a book by Shakespeare – *Antony and Cleopatra*. I have heard about Shakespeare from Willoughby: 'Bill Shakespeare, the greatest writer in the world; wrote *Hamlet*, the greatest play in the world. He lived a long time ago in England. To be or not to be, that is the question. Bill Shakespeare – remember the name – remember that Willoughby told you about him.'

Excited to have found a book by the greatest writer in the world, I ask Old Con for the loan of *Antony and Cleopatra*.

'Take it with you, son; it's no use to me or to anyone in this house.'

I can hardly wait to get across the street and start gorging myself on the tragedy of *Antony and Cleopatra*. I begin at the beginning:

> *Philo.* Nay, but this dotage of our general's
> O'erflows the measure. Those his goodly eyes,
> That o'er the files and musters of the war
> Have glow'd like plated Mars, now bend, now turn . . .

Puzzled, I glance a few pages ahead, then dip in at random:

> He needs as many Sir as Caesar has,
> Or needs not us. If Caesar please our master
> Will leap to be his friend, for us, you know
> Whose he is we are, and that is Caesar's . . .

A dense blur of befuddlement and doubt puts an end to my exploring. Can this really be the greatest writer in the world? I check the name on the cover: William Shakespeare. Is William Shakespeare the same as Bill Shakespeare? Or is there another Shakespeare? Or is Willoughby raving? Disappointed, I bring *Antony and Cleopatra* back to Old Con and thank him.

Of late Jellybob hasn't a good word to say for Miss Rose's new husband. 'The Captain is a right trick o' the loop. We were standing at Canavan's on Sunday, myself and Snuggy and Corner and a crowd of us, when the Captain says to us, "What about a game o' pitch and toss?" A penny a throw it was to be. Corner Jim said a ha'penny for a start but the Captain said no, a penny it would have to be. The Captain drew a circle – he had chalk and all with him – probably snigged it from the missus. Oh, it wasn't a very big circle. He told us to start pitchin': a dry run first. When Snuggy got a bull's eye straight off, the Captain moved the line away back. Then the pitchin' started in earnest. After every round the Captain scooped all the pennies into the circle and kept one penny for himself. "A penny for the house," he said. Whoever landed a penny in the circle after that would get the jackpot – but sure we were all so far back we were pitchin' away, round after round, and none of us could get the penny into the circle. And a penny for the house every time. It was five or six rounds before Corner landed in the circle. We had several more games after that and each round, a penny for the house. But the last game – the pitchin' went on and on, but Snuggy kept track of it – eight rounds exactly, which meant there should have been three and fourpence in the jackpot, allowing for the penny out each time – but all Snuggy got was three shillings even. The boyo must have hid the fourpence somehow in his hand or up his sleeve. I believe he's not in the army any more, either. He's hanging around the seven days of the week, so it's hard to know what he's up to.'

'. . . Sure, Dada. Conor should make his confirmation next May.'

'What age is he?'

'You don't even know his age. He'll be eight and a half when the bishop comes around.'

'Won't he be time enough the time after?'

'The time after he'll be eleven and a half.'

'Well, isn't eleven and a half time enough?'

'Eleven and a half is too old.'

'What's too old about eleven and a half?'

'Oh now, it's too old. This time is the time for him to be confirmed. Sure.'

'Well – what can we do when the teacher says no?'

'There's plenty we can do. We can go to Father Feegan; we can go to the parish priest.'

'There's no point getting up a racket over it.'

'Well, you're the easy-going man, surely. What I feel like doing is writing to the Department of Education – about Miss Rose.'

'Don't write to anyone. We don't want to get her into trouble.'

'She's only a Jam, that's all.'

'What do you mean – a Jam?'

'A J-A-M – Junior Assistant Mistress. She was never trained. By right she shouldn't be teaching at all.'

'Well – see what Father Feegan has to say; he should listen to you. He owes us enough.'

'I'll go down to Father Feegan tomorrow. He'll have to put Conor in the confirmation class.'

Mama and Dada have just come in from early mass still marvelling at the banns they heard announced from the altar.

'. . . A quare match surely. Any two that would think of getting married at *their* age. Are they not crazy?'

'Sure, they might as well. What harm can it do them?'

'Dinny Frigg is seventy if he's a day, and Rosie must be pushing sixty, if she's not dragging it. They're supposed to be loaded.'

'I have my doubts about that. Dinny worked as a pedlar out of New Jersey, selling pins and needles, shoelaces and combs and mouth organs; that was the biggest item he sold, the mouth organ. He told me himself. You don't make a whole pile at that. I'm not rightly sure what Rosie worked at; maybe she has money saved. She was a long time in the States.'

'Oh now, it's a shame for her – marrying an old Protestant.'

'Nothing wrong with Dinny.'

'They're well matched the pair of them: Rosie is fond of her drink as well.'

'She is surely. Well she won't be staggering very often if she's depending on Dinny to buy for her.'

Dada tells Betty and myself how he first came to Glengreeny: 'I was on my way to Donegal to book my return passage to the States, when I called in to the bar here for a drink. It was just to pass the time while I was waiting for the bus. Me and old Bernie McGee, who owned the place, got talking about one thing and another and he told me he was selling out. "How much are you asking?" says I. "Seven hundred and fifty," says he. I had more than that saved after my eight and a half years in the States. I struck the bargain with him there and then. Seven hundred pounds. Old Bernie put up the shutters and the two of us took the bus to Donegal and in to Solicitor Gallagher. I should have studied myself more. It was a wild mistake.'

A rain cloud drifting over Cnoc Oran turns the heather a rusty brown as its shadow creeps down the hillside. Coming up the street, Father McBrearty crosses over and stops in front of me.

'You're young O'Donnell, aren't you?'

'Yes, Father.'

'Why are you here?'

'I was just looking up at the hill, Father.'

'No. I mean why are you *here* – on earth? Why were you created?'

'To know, love and serve God, Father.'

'How many Divine Persons are there?'

'Three Divine Persons, Father.'

'Who was the first pope?'

The first pope has me flummoxed. I chance, 'Our Lord.'

'Our Lord! No, it wasn't Our Lord. Saint Peter was the first pope.'

'Hello, Father.' Mama has joined me at the door. 'Will you come in, Father?'

Father McBrearty ignores Mama's invitation. 'You want him confirmed this time around, I'm told.'

'Sure, Father, we do. He's old enough; he was one of the best in his first communion class.'

'Miss Rose thinks he's too young for confirmation.'

'He's not too young, Father. He'll be eleven and a half the next time the bishop comes around.'

'Well, well. I don't know. It's entirely a matter for his teacher.'

'If Miss Rose doesn't want to teach him, I'll teach him the catechism myself.'

'It's not just a question of knowing the catechism – it's a question of *understanding* it. What hurry is on you?'

'It's just that he's at an awkward age, Father. If he was a year older or a year younger –'

'Well, I'll talk to Miss Rose about it. She'll know better than anyone whether he's advanced enough or not.'

'He's well advanced, Father, whatever Miss Rose says.'

'We'll see. We'll see.'

Saturday morning and Dinny and Rosie sail in the bar door as soon as Dada draws the bolt.

'You're early afoot.'

'Early afoot,' Dinny wheezes.

'We're after getting married,' Rosie announces.

'Oh! Congratulations.'

Rosie is wearing a blue costume with a big yellow butterfly brooch on her chest; Dinny looks shrunken in the well-scuffed American suit of summer cloth as he squares up to the counter.

'What will it be, Rosie?'

'Brandy, of course.' Rosie lays her handbag on the high-backed seat by the window.

'Give us two wee brandies, Jamie.'

Rosie nods across to me: 'Tell your mother I want a word in her ear.'

'*I'll* tell her' – Dada sets the drinks on the counter – '*you* look after the bride and groom, Conor.'

'What is it you want her for?' Dinny asks, as Dada leaves.

'We have to have our breakfast, haven't we?'

'I had my breakfast before I left the house.'

'Our *wedding* breakfast.'

'Oh – aye – I was forgetting. Ah sure, we don't want

anything fancy. A few rashers and sausages'll do us fine.'

'Whist your mouth, man. We'll have a proper wedding breakfast.'

'Well, so long as it's not going to cost the earth.'

'Cost! Will you not be talking about cost on your wedding day.' Rosie looks across at me. 'He's only coddin'. The man doesn't know what to do with his money. You're loaded, Dinny boy, loaded.'

'Ah, now, you can't believe everything you hear either.'

'Will you listen to him – and you told me yourself you took every penny you possessed out of the Chase Manhattan Bank the very day before the Wall Street Crash. You didn't lose a penny piece. Not one cent. Amn't I right, Dinny boy?'

Dinny says nothing, but lets slip a sly sort of a half-smile across one side of his face.

'Out of one bank and into the other. Your money hasn't seen the light of day since. Well, I'm the one to give it an airing for you. Where are you taking me on my honeymoon?'

'Honeymoon! God almighty, woman, what sort o' crazy notions have you in your head!'

'What's crazy about a honeymoon?'

'What's crazy about it? Well – ahem – for one thing – ahem – the expense of it.'

'Bundoran would be a nice place to go.'

'Bundoran! That's miles away. We're not all rolling in money like you, Rosie.'

'We'll go to Bundoran after our breakfast.'

'Wait a minute. How are we going to get there?'

'Hill, of course.'

'Hackney Hill! All the way to Bundoran! My God, woman, are you clean off your rocker!'

'We're hardly going to foot it' – Rosie nods across at me – 'have a look in the kitchen to see if your mother is free yet.'

Because she doesn't want to have to get ready a wedding breakfast, Mama is anything but eager to make an appearance before Rosie.

'It's little'll please them,' Dada encourages. 'Sure, go up and congratulate them anyway.'

After more persuasion, Mama agrees. Going into the bar, she is ready to shake Rosie's hand, but stops in a quandary when she sees Dinny sitting sideways on the seat with his back to Rosie, and Rosie sniffling and dabbing at her eyes. 'I heard you got married,' Mama ventures.

Rosie is barely able to talk. 'Oh Cassy – we're ruined. Do you know – what that man – is after – telling me: he hasn't – a penny – not one – penny – to his name.'

'Tell her the rest of the story,' Dinny snarls. 'You haven't a penny yourself. *She* was the one was supposed to have all the money.'

'*You* were the one.'

'*You* were the one. Weren't you working as a housekeeper – living-in with the priests. What did you do with your money? Are you sure you're not coddin' me, Rosie?'

'Neither of us – has a penny' – Rosie blows her nose and turns again to Mama – 'what in the name o' God – are we going – to do!'

'Well, I'll get you some breakfast, anyway.' Mama is glad of any excuse to get back to the kitchen.

'Breakfast! Breakfast! I couldn't look at a breakfast. Why the hell didn't you tell me the truth?'

'Why didn't *you* tell *me* the truth – instead of your big talk – about the Wall Street – Crash?'

'And *your* big talk about all you could save on the priests' dinners. Leading me up the bliddy garden path. Ach!' Dinny again turns his back on his new wife.

Rosie looks straight ahead, occasionally snoking tears up her nostrils. She blows her nose again. Dinny crosses his legs. The silence stretches and stretches like a riddle that no one can answer. After a while Rosie takes out her vanity kit and examines herself in the small round compact mirror. Suddenly all business, as if she has just wakened up from a deep sleep and it is long past rising time, she dabs powder on her cheeks, puts on fresh lipstick, fixes her hair. Taking out her purse, she steps up to the counter and puts down a five pound note. 'Give us two more brandies – and make it doubles.'

Dinny continues to ignore Rosie, until she delivers the glass into his hand.

'Drink up, Dinny boy. What's done is done.'

Dinny takes a half-hearted sip from his glass. 'We're in a quare fix now.'

'You're an awful man for complaining, Dinny Frigg. Don't let me hear another word of contrariness out of you today. Now, how much have you on you?'

'I haven't a red penny.'

'Come on. Show me what's in your pockets.'

Dinny puts a hand in his money pocket and turns away from Rosie, but Rosie follows him around: 'It's too late for that, Dinny boy.'

Dinny throws a pound note on the seat between them.

'You have more than one pound, surely?'

Dinny flattens out another crumpled pound note.

'And what about the change you got?'

With a sigh, Dinny empties his pockets of silver and coppers: 'That's not going to get us very far, is it?'

'Whist your mouth.' Rosie takes the change of the fiver from her purse and lays it beside Dinny's scrapings. 'I was keeping this for Bundoran – but we can have our honeymoon here instead. We'll have enough for one good day's boozin', anyway.'

'And what about tomorrow?'

'Ara, will you not be talking about tomorrow when today is not rightly under way yet.'

'You should have told me the truth, Rosie.'

'Maybe I should and maybe I shouldn't' – Rosie holds up her glass and clinks it against Dinny's – 'you lied to me; I lied to you. We're evens, Dinny boy.'

Another visit by Mama to Miss Rose has done nothing to settle the confirmation question. Miss Rose won't budge; Father Feegan can't do anything, and Father McBrearty tells Mama, 'Have sense, woman.' At school everyone knows that I am trying to get confirmed before my time. I hope it will die down now.

Jellybob, sweeping out the bottling store, suddenly throws the brush aside and rushes across to the outdoor toilet.

'I think Jellybob has the V-2,' Dada says, 'unless I'm very much mistaken.'

The dose going around is called the V-2 after Hitler's latest rocket. Nearly everyone in the town has the V-2.

'I'll put him into the confirmation class,' Miss Dee had said to Mama. 'I'll make sure that he passes.'

Miss Dee has only twelve pupils in her school; it is very cosy, she says, and she will be able to give me extra lessons in catechism. 'You should send Betty as well. It's a pity to separate them, Cassy.' But Betty remembers the game of Ludo and 'Pass the dice before you move', and she doesn't want to have anything to do with Miss Dee or her cosy school. In the end it is decided that Betty will stay on in Glengreeny; I will have to board out in Trá Gheal, as the school is over three miles away.

'This is turning into a right laughing-sport,' Dada says. 'Who is he going to board out with?'

'He can board with Nanno McGinley, a second cousin of your own. She'll be only glad of the money. Her son Barney will be company for Conor, as well.'

'Sure, Barney is nearly a grown man.'

'Well – they can be friends.'

'And what about Man-Hat-On?' ('Not Man-Hat-On, Conor. Manhattan. Because that's where he worked, and he used to sicken the people talking about it.' But I still think of him as Man-Hat-On.)

'Forget about Man-Hat-On. Man-Hat-On won't even know he's there.'

'How much are you giving for the eggs this week, Jamie?'

'Same as I was giving last week, Molly, same as I'll be giving next week.'

'Oh God save us the day and the night, and how is a poor person to live at all?'

'And how is the shopkeeper to live at all when we're back to the barter system: so many eggs for this and so many eggs for that – and half of them cracked or rotten by the time Benny Egg calls to collect them?'

A dull, drizzly Sunday evening with dense waves of mist completely blotting out Cnoc Oran, as Barney leads the donkey and cart through the big gate into the yard.

Dada has already stacked my small iron bed in sections outside the back door, ready for loading. 'You'll be all right, Conor. I'll cycle out to see you one o' these days.'

Mama helps to bundle the bedclothes into the cart: pillows, a hot-water bottle, shirts and socks. Last, she stuffs a brown paper parcel under the blankets: a currant cake, sweets and butterscotch.

'Sit in,' Barney tells me. 'I'll lead her till we get down the town, in case she slips on the tar.'

I climb up on the spokes of the cartwheel and sit with my back to the donkey. The yard, the fair green, the sloping street, all begin to roll away from me like a scene in the pictures where you don't want the story to end: Aisling's house on the hill, Con Moylan's tall chimneys, Ned Mary's 'Guinness Is Good For You' sign, Crusoe's tin roof. Betty has crossed to the far side of the street and I wave back to her until we turn at Canavan's corner.

The site for Trá Gheal school has been quarried out of the hill, with room for just one person to pass at the back: in front is a narrow track of winding, stony road, high-walled on the sea side, and beyond – a dead drop down the jagged cliff face into the deep green swell of Cromleach Bay. Far to the left, wrapped around the level sweep of sand and jutting out into the Atlantic, is the massive glinting black headland, Land's End, where the tide gusts up in the air great throws of water like white flames. Ships passing to America take a long time to travel the broad length of the horizon.

From the hallway, where I sit alone with my catechism, I watch through the open door the big ships, warships, maybe, headed for battle with Hitler's U-boats. I watch the trawlers seesawing their way around the headland, and the odd rowboat out for a day's fishing in the bay. I watch the tide lazily stretching itself out on the strand, and the low fluffy clouds darkening, sweeping like a paintbrush across the ocean. I watch everything that is strange to me in this strange place, until Miss Dee moves my desk back again into the classroom, where she can keep a closer eye on me.

All day long I do nothing but catechism. Even so, when catechism class comes around I am not any better than anyone else and a lot worse than the best.

'You should know more by now' – Miss Dee impatiently taps

the ruler on the table – 'your mind is not on your work. You'll have to do better – a lot better.'

Of the twelve pupils in the school, five of them – the Meehans – come from the one family. The Meehans talk a lot about their uncle who lives with them: M'uncle says this and M'uncle says that. Andy Meehan, who is called Big Andy, is the eldest of the family and also the biggest in the school. He should have been confirmed the last time the bishop was around but he failed. I am put sitting beside him, but we don't hit it off. Whoever sits beside Big Andy has to take on the very risky job of prompting him, which is almost a full-time job, because Big Andy knows next to nothing about anything. In catechism I can feed him very little and I get even less thanks.

'Why didn't you stay in the school you were in instead of sitting beside me? I don't want any dumbbell sitting beside me.'

Once when I tried to give Big Andy a prompt, Miss Dee told me to stand up. I wasn't sure that my prompt was right, but I thought it best to venture something. Miss Dee asked me for the answer and everyone in the class laughed when they heard it. Big Andy laughed as loud as any of them, with his big mouthful of crooked, rotten teeth. Out in the yard at lunch time he laughed again: 'You were number thirteen when you came into the school – the unlucky number. M'uncle says you'll never pass.'

The deck of cards has been fanned out on the backless chair in front of the fire, and starting with two cards placed like a roof, we begin to build a house over the spread. With every card added, the house gets bigger and the foundations get scantier until the slightest shake of the hand in placing a card is enough to bring everything tumbling down. Barney claims to be the best builder, but his mother doesn't lag far behind.

Nanno is about sixty, with scraggly white hair sticking out

from different parts of her head like icicles. She is good-humoured and loves to see the neighbours coming in to raik, but there aren't many neighbours around, so most evenings we are left to ourselves with the cards. When we get tired of House we play Strip Jack Naked. The crickets are chirping away under the hearthstone and from the strand we hear the slow, heavy sighing of the sea. Odd times from the lower room other muffled sounds are heard: a cough, a garble of words, a bed creaking – this is Man-Hat-On. When he first came to Trá Gheal, Man-Hat-On built the two-storey stone house we are now in, but he ran out of funds before he could plaster it or put ceilings or partitions upstairs. After that, he got married to Nanno; he cleared the garden and planted a crop of early potatoes; a year or two later he took to the bed. None of the neighbours has set eyes on him since.

I watch to see if Nanno or Barney will bring him down his tea or his supper, but they never go near the lower room while I am about. Neither is there any sign of him around the kitchen – his socks or his boots – and his name is never mentioned. Once when we were playing House something crashed in the bedroom. I was expecting Nanno or Barney to check what had happened; they looked at each other and listened – then Nanno added a card and Barney added another.

'How are you getting on at the catechism?' Nanno asks.

'Fine.'

'If you don't pass, it'll be a terror; your mother'll be a laughing stock. Oh, you're after knocking all! Well, it's time for bed. Barney, light the candle.'

Our nearest neighbour, Rogan, lives behind a towering stone wall that hides all glimpse of what lies beyond.

'His father built it for protection against the sea gale,' Barney tells me; 'there's not a stone in it out of place. Rogan doesn't do a whole lot on the land. He has only himself to look after, so it's little does him. When he's scarce o' money he works at the weaving. But he doesn't do a whole pile at that either. He could have the one web in the loom for months. Then he'll take a figarie and finish it off in a few days. He's a sort of a poet as well – a bit light in the head.'

Rogan takes the cards from the mantelpiece shortly after we arrive and tells us to pull our chairs in to the table. He shuffles and cuts the cards very fast, throwing the deck from him after dealing. 'Turn up a card there, Barney. Cards is one of the oldest games in the world and still one of the best. Other games you have to concentrate – even draughts – you have to think about what you're doing. Cards frees the mind. You can be playing away and your mind the far side of the gap into fairy-land. And still you're part of the company.'

We play several games and Rogan wins most of them.

'What about a game o' House?' Barney suggests.

Rogan shakes his head, smiling: 'House takes too much out of you. It makes you concentrate. House imprisons the mind.'

'It's simple,' Barney says; 'there's nothing to it.'

'It's simple, surely; that's where the trap is. You know, if you were building a real house you wouldn't have to concentrate half as much.' Rogan shuffles the cards and deals out another game of Twenty-Five. He is a small stocky man with lively dart-ing eyes, but there is also a hint of sadness in the way he looks at you sometimes.

'I hear you play the fiddle,' he says to me.

'I'm learning to play.'

'Did you bring it with you to Trá Gheal?'

'It's under his bed,' Barney says.

'You must bring the fiddle the next time you call.'

'I'm not much good at it.'

'You'll get good if you practise. A fiddle under the bed is no use to anyone. Take it down to the kitchen tomorrow and hang it on the wall. If it's within arm's reach, you'll play it.'

'He has no time,' Barney says.

'Of course he has time.'

'He has to do his catechism.'

'He'll do better at the catechism if he plays a tune now and again. What about poetry? Do you like poetry?'

'I do.'

'Would you like to hear some?'

'Of your own?'

Rogan laughs. 'Who else's?'

'I would.'

'I'll say you a bit of a poem I'm making up. It's a long poem – about the town. Everyone'll be in it. Maybe you'll be in it yourself before it's finished.'

'I don't want to be in it.' Barney sounds annoyed. 'Have you *me* in it?'

'It's about Glengreeny. I'm not touching on Trá Gheal.'

'Just as well. They'll have your life if you do.'

'These few lines are about myself' – Rogan looks me in the eye and pauses before he begins –

> I earn my living at the loom,
> Shuttlecock and bobbin boom,
> Weaving threads of triple tone:
> Plain and twill and herringbone.
> By night I weave from other skeins
> The ravelled yarn of living veins,
> Unwinding promise and despair,
> The warp of joy, the weft of care,
> Crossthreads of amity and strife –
> The history of village life –

'Oh, that'll do you,' Barney interrupts. 'It's time we were going home anyway.'

November now and I lie in bed listening to winter scurrying like a rat across the slates. My bed has been set up about the centre of the big upstairs bedroom that sprawls the full length of the house. In the corner Barney sleeps on a shakedown, with nothing between him and the floorboards only a home-made tick filled with straw.

Almost directly over my head is a skylight. I pay little attention to it until the first clear night, when I glimpse faintly a single shimmering star – and immediately I am smitten with homesickness. Other stars flicker into view, and others ever fainter – an immensely distant ocean, silent, still. And below me, across the headland, that other ocean, so close that I can hear every throw and turn of the tide. The more I think about them both, the more lonesome I feel. I think also about Man-Hat-On: is he still awake, does he talk to Nanno when she closes the bedroom door behind her for the night, do they sleep in the same bed, how does he spend the day or what does his mind turn on? Any man that would build a house – half-build a house – in such a wild and desolate place must surely be out of his senses. Always my own thoughts are drawn back into the vast still world beyond the skylight. I lie without moving, looking up at the myriad hypnotising eyes, gradually drifting in and out of sleep, until I doze off or Barney breaks the spell.

'How do you like Miss Dee?'

'She's all right.'

'A bit cross, isn't she?'

'Yea.'

'I'm glad to be finished with her. I left a year before my time because I had to help at home, and she kicked up a terrible racket. But sure, what good is knowing where Africa is or

Australia or the Sahara desert, when I'll never be next or near any of them?'

'Would you not like to travel?'

'What good will it do you? Anyone that ever travelled, they're never half-right again in the head afterwards. I'm content where I am.'

Armada Pat looks in over the half-door. 'You didn't see two stray sheep in your travels at all?'

'No then I didn't, Pat,' Barney answers. 'Are you missing two?'

'A coupla' wethers I bought at the fair; they're after wandering off on me.'

'Give him a hand to search, Barney' – Nanno rises from her chair at the fire.

'Oh it's all right. There's not much two can do that one can't. I'll have a look around the headland. Maybe they're gone over the bank.'

'Please God they're not.'

'You have a new add to the family I see.'

'That's Conor O'Donnell from the town.'

Armada Pat squeezes my fingers together in his big grainy hand. 'I hear you have your work cut out for you.'

'He's busy with the catechism, all right,' Nanno agrees.

'If you come across the sheep, take them in.'

'I will sure, Pat.'

'Well, I'll be off.'

Armada Pat is tall and lithe and his dark, leathery skin gives him a foreign appearance.

'Why is he called Armada?'

Barney looks to his mother to answer.

'Do you know about the Armada?' Nanno asks me.

'No.'

'The Armada came from Spain. They were headed for England – it was when England and Spain was at war – but they ran into a storm and most of the ships was lost at sea. One of them was washed up on the rocks around the coast, and this Spanish sailor made his way overland as far as Trá Gheal. So the story goes. He stayed with an ancestor of Pat's. She was a widow woman. It's all a long time ago – but the blood follows the line. There's a house beyond in Carraig Mór – the Moloneys' – where they have Spanish blood as well. Sure what does it matter? Aren't we all the one human race?'

'Please Miss, the inspector is outside, Miss!'

Miss Dee gapes through the window then turns to us, talking very fast: 'Sit up straight, everyone. Pay attention. Remember – *Fáilte romhat, a dhuine uasail* . . . Conor O'Donnell, put away your catechism. And take out your Irish reader. Quickly.'

A smart knock on the door, and without waiting for an answer, a small dapper man with shiny grey hair, a grey serge suit and carrying a dark brown satchel breezes in.

Miss Dee motions us to our feet and tries to smile.

'*Fáilte romhat, a dhuine uasail.*'

'*Go raibh maith agaibh, a pháistí.*' The inspector shakes hands with Miss Dee, leaves his satchel on the table, and they turn towards the fire, talking.

We all have our heads down, pretending to be studying. When I look up again the inspector is sitting in Miss Dee's chair with the brown-covered roll book open in front of him. He casts his eye over the class, counting us. More secrets pass between Miss Dee and himself. Miss Dee points to me; the inspector looks from where I am sitting to where he has his finger on the page, and back again.

'Conor O'Donnell, come up here . . . You're for confirmation?'

'Yes, *a dhuine uasail.*'

'What age are you?'

'Eight and a bit, *a dhuine uasail.*'

'Eight years and a bit. Young for confirmation, aren't you?'

I don't know what to say, so I try to force a smile.

'Why do you want to be confirmed so young?'

I can't answer anything to this either.

'Can you tell me why?...I don't bite, you know.' The inspector turns to Miss Dee. 'A bit backward, is he?'

'No. Just a bit shy.'

'Don't be shy. Whose idea was it that you should be confirmed this year?'

'My mother's.'

'Your mother's idea. And why does she want you confirmed so young?'

I had never thought about the why and have to sing dumb again.

The inspector shakes his head and turns to Miss Dee. 'You have a problem on your hands, I'm afraid...Well, I don't know. I'm not happy about the reason for changing schools. You shouldn't have encouraged him.'

'It was his parents' decision,' Miss Dee explains respectfully.

'Even so. Parents aren't always the best judges in these cases. What sort of student is he?'

'He's about average.'

'About average. And now he has to learn all this catechism. How is he going to do it?'

'I'm giving him all the help I can, inspector.'

'Well, so long as it's not at the expense of his other subjects.'

Miss Dee looks worried. 'He's fallen a bit behind at the moment, I'm afraid, what with the change from one school to another.'

The inspector turns to me again, points to the map of Ireland behind him and hands me a ruler. 'Can you show me where Limerick is?'

I search high up and low down for Limerick, the ruler hovering like a one-eyed hawk over several places but not daring to land anywhere.

'Do you know anything about Limerick?...What's manufactured there?...Any industries?...Anything that happened there – in history?...To do with a stone?'

I can't think of a single thing to say about Limerick or its manufactures or its mysterious stone.

'All catechism and nothing but makes Jack a dull boy.'

'He hasn't really settled down yet, inspector.'

'I think you'll have to concentrate more on his other subjects. Treat him the same as every other pupil. If he passes, he passes; if he fails, he fails.'

'It's going to be hard on his parents if he fails.'

'That's *their* business. They began this. I don't think you should go along with it. What do you say?'

'All right, inspector.'

'I'll be back another day to see what progress he's making.'

On my way to the well for a can of water who do I see wobbling down the rutted stony track on his bicycle only Dada.

'Boys o' boys, Conor, the sea air is agreeing with you. I think you're after growing.'

From the house, Nanno has heard Dada's voice and comes to the door to shout a welcome: 'Come in, Jamie. You're a big stranger in this part of the world.'

After leaning his bicycle against the gable, Dada hands me the brown paper parcel from the carrier: 'Mama sent you this. It's a cake.'

We sit at the table while Nanno gets ready the tea and cuts

two thick slices from the sweet cake. Behind her back, Dada winks at me and nods towards the lower room.

'How is himself?' Dada asks Nanno.

'Oh he's the one way.'

'In good enough health?'

'In good enough health.'

'Well, that's good. The health is everything.'

'Health is everything.'

'Never moves out at all, does he?'

'No.'

'It would do him good to get out for a while – meet the people. Don't you think?'

'Ah sure he's rambling a lot.'

'Rambling?'

'In his mind. The rememory is gone.'

'Completely?'

'Very near.'

'Would he know me, I wonder?'

'He wouldn't know you from a crow, Jamie. The man hardly knows himself.'

'Ah, is that the way?'

'That's the way.'

Nanno doesn't say any more about Man-Hat-On and Dada asks no more questions.

After tea Dada is eager to explore. 'I'll bet you weren't up at Land's End yet, Conor?'

'Not yet.'

'We'll have a look at Land's End – see if it's still there.'

At Land's End we are closer to the sky than we have ever been in our lives – or so it seems. A cool wind, contrary and gusting, curls upwards from the sea, blowing the gulls sideways off their course and bringing with it the sigh and sprinkle of the waves. On the level sward of scutch grass at our feet, written in giant letters with big stones, is the word EIRE.

'A message for Hitler so that he won't bomb us all to kingdom come. I hope he can read Irish.'

We walk around the stones, the sea rumbling below us on three sides.

'Did you see Man-Hat-On at all?' Dada asks.

'I never laid eyes on him.'

'Not once?'

'Not even once.'

'Isn't that a fright; never shows his nose outside the bedroom door. The last time I was here – it must be four or five years ago – there wasn't sight or sound of him then, either. You would think Nanno would find some way of coaxing him into the daylight. Hard to know who's to blame. Well, it's none of our business, I suppose.'

Dada moves away from the stones and stands with his hand over his forehead, looking out across the bay. 'Do you see the white dot on the far side, Conor? That's Kerrigan's house. That's where I was hired as a boy.'

'Was it hard – being hired?'

'Ah no. It was all right. The work was hard enough; money was scarce in them days.'

'How much did you get?'

'How much did I get!' Dada laughs. 'I didn't get a penny. My father got – I don't remember how much – a few pounds, I suppose, for the year.'

'And what had you to do?'

'Everything. Everything that had to be done on the farm, I done it. Kerrigan ruptured himself and had to go to the hospital. When he came out, he was afraid to lift the latch of the door in case he'd rupture himself again. But I wasn't so badly off. I was well fed. The woman of the house – old Sally Kerrigan – she liked me. Plenty o' spuds and butter and salty mackerel.

Some of the craturs that were hired out had a terrible time of it. You know Crusoe? Well, Crusoe was hired with a man in Glenties. He usen't to have enough to eat half the time. And sleep in the barn. In the end he ran away – which was a terrible thing to do, because it would come back on the father. But nobody blamed him. Crusoe's father was a wild man for the booze. How Crusoe came to be hired out was like this: the two of them, father and son, came into the town for the fair and towards evening the father had all his money spent. What does he do to get a few pounds only hire out the son. For the price of a couple o' drinks he sold his son into slavery. Crusoe told me the story himself one night he was well on. Crusoe never came near home after that till the father died. That's how he was in the war and in France and everywhere else. Ah well, them days are gone now and all to the good. Many's the time I looked across that bay. Wild lonesome, the sea.'

Any day the inspector may walk in to examine me again, so there is no more extra catechism during class. After school I sit in the front desk with my catechism open but turned face down. Across the aisle from me, Big Andy sits with another blind catechism. Between us, Miss Dee walks up and down, across the front, around the back, up and down and up and over and back. 'What is transubstantiation? . . . What is viaticum? . . . What is simony? . . . Name the seven deadly sins. . . . Who goes to hell? . . . What is limbo?'

Even though Big Andy has stumbled across this stony station-ground before, he is more often on his hands and knees than I am. Small consolation to me: if I can't keep ahead of Big Andy, then I might as well pack up my bed and go home.

The funny thing is that Big Andy is better at the hard questions than he is at the easier ones. Among the things he never gets right is the difference between limbo, purgatory and hell. People who deserve to be in purgatory, Big Andy lets them off with limbo, and the ones who should only be in limbo he chucks them into purgatory or even hell. No matter how many times Miss Dee explains the rules to him he still has everybody in the wrong place. Another thing that mixes him up is the Three Divine Persons in one God. 'Don't think,' Miss Dee tells him, 'just answer – the way you answer *calumny* – the way you answer *gluttony* and *blasphemy*.' But as soon as any of these questions is asked, Big Andy puts on his thinking cap and in no time he is shuttling souls between limbo and purgatory and hell and calling out numbers of Gods and Divine Persons like the multiplication table.

When I tell Rogan about some of Big Andy's answers, he has a good laugh. 'If he's as bad as all that,' Rogan says, 'the bishop shouldn't just fail him, he should get the pope to excommunicate him.'

Almost halfway across the strand, with the schoolbag under my oxter, I remember that I have left my catechism propped up against the jug on the kitchen table. Passing Man-Hat-On's room, I am surprised to see the window open at the top and to hear a sort of singing – Barney's tuneless voice – then another voice, more musical but frail and shaky, joining in. Chanting. The bedroom door has been left partly open and the chant is clearer when I go into the kitchen – a song I never heard before – a sort of droning – a jolly song, sung with a mournful lilt. I take up my catechism and go out without making a sound.

Rogan glances towards the chimney corner when he arrives, but passes no comment on what he sees there. If only Nanno and Barney would carry the mattress upstairs before Old Hannah comes in to raik. Old Hannah's nickname is Bean Rua – the red woman – and she has a tongue like a scythe. We all sit at one side of the fire, with the big watery eye of the mattress staring across the hearth at us.

'Give us a tune on the fiddle.' Rogan breaks the silence.

'I never took it down since.'

'Take it down now.'

But my journey upstairs is for nothing because the strings have gone slack and I don't know how to tune them.

'You're a terrible man. How many tunes do you know?'

'Five or six.'

'Before you learn another tune you must learn how to tune the fiddle – otherwise you could be the sweetest fiddler that ever drew a bow on strings, and damn the bit of good will it do you if after all that your instrument is going to sing dumb.'

'Will we have a game o' House?' Barney suggests.

'Leave the cards for the time being, Barney.' Nanno gets up and starts to turn the mattress around like a big slice of toast. Barney and Nanno have the mattress swinging between them when the latch rises and Old Hannah's rusty white head nods in at us.

'Come in, Hannah.'

Hannah walks slowly to the centre of the floor and stands viewing the mattress. She turns her eye on me and lets out a shrill cackle:

The man will sweat and the boy turn red
And the nervous child will wet the bed.

'Sit down, Hannah.' Nanno draws up a chair for her.

'Many's the time I wet the bed myself,' Rogan says, 'and damn the bit o' harm did it do me – or the bed, either.'

'It's a true saying all the same.' Hannah's words seem to be said more to me than to Rogan.

'Maybe and maybe not,' Rogan answers her.

Hannah shakes her head and begins her rime again:

The man will sweat and the boy turn red
And the nervous child will wet the bed.

'But don't stop there, Hannah,' Rogan says, 'for

After years and years go by
Who'll know the man or child or boy
Or care if maid was dark or red
When all alike will wet the bed.'

Everyone laughs at this except Hannah.
'I never wet the bed,' Hannah snaps.
'Sure I'm not saying that you do.'
'You're talking about the woman with the red hair, aren't you?'
'I'm talking about us all, dark or red, man or woman. It's only a matter o' time until we're all back at the nappy stage – if we live long enough.'
'Well, there's a truth in that surely,' Nanno agrees.
Barney reaches for the cards on the mantelpiece and begins to shuffle them, in his eagerness letting several fall on the floor.
'What about a song? Will you sing for us?' Nanno turns to Rogan.
'I will surely – but maybe Hannah will give us a wee breeze first?'
'Ah sure I know only the one song, and all I can remember of *it* is one or two verses.'
'One or two verses is better than a fiddle under the bed. Sing us what you know of it.'
Old Hannah clears her throat and never moves from the note she begins on – more saying than singing:

'Who is it ruffles the gravel?
Who is it knocks on the door?
Nobody there, it's only the wind.
Don't be frightened, *a stór*.

Last night I heard a stranger
Whispering my name,
Tapping at my window –
Was it only the rain?

That's all I know of it.'

'Good on you,' Rogan says.

Nanno rakes the coals closer together with the tongs. 'But what happened the rest of it?'

'The rest of it is gone where my voice is gone and my red hair. Now, Rogan, it's your turn.'

'Give us one of your own – about Trá Gheal' – Nanno balances two fresh sods of turf around the reddening coals.

Rogan doesn't need any more encouraging. He throws back his head and closes his eyes and the notes come out with a clear deep ring to them:

There are mussels in the shallows, there are salmon in
the deep,
And mackerel and herring running free,
And the *bairneach*s and the dilisk cling to rocks along
the beach,
There is kindness in the bounty of the sea.

With rod and line, the fisher boy will pass the summer days
And longingly he'll linger on the quay,
Till his father feeling lonesome takes him riding on
the waves,
There is nature and contentment on the sea.

We have salt fish when we fancy, we have ling and we
have soles,
We have mackerel as fresh as they can be,
And on Sundays we have haddock or a lobster on the coals,
Oh, you'll never die of hunger by the sea.

No humans sow where mussels grow, where hake and
   salmon run,
And the harvest of the ocean it is free,
But every generation gives a daughter or a son
And they are called the children of the sea.
   O the sea
   O the sea
And we are all the children of the sea.

'Put out your hand' – Miss Dee brings the rod diving on to my
palm, where it crashes like a kamikaze pilot. Big Andy has just
been dive-bombed twice and is nursing his hand under his
oxter. 'Barely a week left and the two of you are dithering over
the simplest questions.' Miss Dee holds on to the rod, banging
the table and lashing out at our desks whenever we falter. Like
two tired donkeys nearing the end of a hard race, there is
nothing for us now but the stick, and plenty of it.

Out in the yard Big Andy talks about 'avenge'.

'If I don't pass this time, there's nothing surer than I'll put a
match to it. I would have passed three years ago only M'uncle
says she kept me back so as the numbers wouldn't go down.
When I leave she'll just have the twelve. *You're* her last hope.
And you needn't think, when you get as far as sixth class and
you know everything, that she'll let you go. She'll find some
reason to hold on to you. She'll slow you down as much as she
can. M'uncle says she would have us all trottin' around with our
schoolbags on our backs till we were grown men, if she could
get away with it.'

'Are you free some day next week?' Armada Pat calls to Barney
without getting off his bicycle, one leg balancing on the
doorstep.

Barney turns around from his tea – 'What is it, Pat?'

'We'll have a go at the lobsters.'

'The few creels I have are all holes.'

'I have plenty o' creels.'

'OK.'

'A nice lobster would go down well after all the salty mackerel –'

'And the rabbits,' Nanno adds; 'there's not a pick on them.'

'Maybe we'll have a feed o' lobsters next week then' – Pat looks back to check the parcel on the carrier of his bicycle – 'I'm after coming from the town. Hitler is doing bad. The Russians are swarmin' all over him.'

'The worse he's doing, the better.'

'Will you come in for a drop o' tea, Pat?'

'I'm in a hurry, thanks. We'll fix a day next week.' And Pat pushes himself off, wobbling out on to the road.

'He's always in a hurry,' Nanno says, 'for what, I don't know.'

Her black hat and her coat hanging from the side of the dresser and we are finishing the rosary close to the smoke-darkened, wooden bed in the kitchen where Old Hannah is laid out.

White pearl rosary beads around pearl fingers, pearl face, pearl lips. I am not really sorry over Old Hannah's death; I am even a wee bit glad.

'Glory be to the Father and the Son and the Holy Ghost, as it was in the beginning, is now and ever shall be, world without end, amen.'

The chairs are drawn back tight to the wall and the after-prayer calm fills out the space of a few breaths.

'She went fast in the end.'

'She did. She was at mass on Sunday. Sunday evening she didn't feel well, Nanno was telling me. Barney went in for the priest; Father Feegan gave her the last rites and all. On Monday morning when Nanno went up to see her she was dead in the bed.'

'Hannah was a popular woman in her day.'

'She had plenty of admirers, anyway.'

'Bean Rua. You used to be after her yourself, Peter.'

'I used, surely. No point denying it. What is it – fifty, nearly sixty years ago?'

'We were all after her. You remember the dances in the old schoolhouse?'

'Why wouldn't I remember them?

> On winter nights with happier cheer
> The youth around all gathered here
> And freed from daytime's chant and rule
> We danced till dawn in Claren school.'

'The house'll be closed down now, I suppose.'

'Another empty hearth in Trá Gheal. The grass and the nettles'll take over soon enough.'

I had been looking forward to the setting of the lobster pots, but when Armada, standing on the slipway, lifts me over the gunnel and Barney pulls me by the arms into the swaying boat, all I can think of is the drowned man who was washed up on Malin strand.

'Sit in the front,' Armada tells me – and the boat rocks with every step I take towards the narrow seat at the high end. Armada passes the lobster pots one by one to Barney, who has no trouble keeping his balance standing between the two long seats in the middle. 'I think that's everything' – Armada reaches in the last pot – 'get rid of some of the bilge.'

The boat lurches sideways as Armada slides the oars down along the seats and climbs in. 'How are you doing there?'

'Job is right.'

Barney has thrown out only a few canfuls of dark scaly water when Armada lodges an oar against the slipway and leans on it with all his might. Slowly the boat swings away from the shore, the two men quickly lifting and dipping the oars, not yet in time.

The boat sinks lower in the swell, swaying from side to side, then spurts forward between the plash and skreak of the oars. Once out from under the black shadow of the cliffs, the bay opens wide and flat around us. In front of me the men's hunched shoulders close in then straighten up together. I turn my head to look at the water lapping past us in slanting rocking whelms, and immediately I feel dizzy.

The creels stacked in the middle of the boat have a strong fishy smell, each with a stone securely tied, and a bait of gurnet in the bottom. Armada and Barney row without talking. The slightest movement causes the boat to tilt in that direction and when Armada hands me back his jacket I can feel myself sinking into the waves before the boat rises again and steadies. Even though I have a firm grip on the prow with both hands, I am terrified that I will either fall overboard or that the water will gush in over the side, levelling us all.

'Are you all right there?' Armada looks back at me. 'God, you're very pale.'

'I'm all right.'

Armada takes in his oars and stands to drop one of the creels over the side. It sweeps backwards before being sucked under, the hollow ball of green glass bobbing in the water to mark the spot. Five more creels to go and the boat begins to swing around in a wide circle. Another drop, another buoy floating behind us; another swing around and my head is reeling. I close my eyes against the heaving water and the swaying cliffs and sky. In the bottom of the boat the stale bilge squelches around between the floorboards. Suddenly my bare feet feel icy cold.

'I'm going to get sick.'

'Put your head over the side.'

When I hesitate, Armada steps across the seat and grips my shoulders firmly with both his hands. My chin is forced down on to the gunnel and I am drooling at the mouth, my face just a few inches above the dark swirling water. I had been sick on the bus and I had been sick from tobacco, but never before had I felt in my stomach the vast and hopeless emptiness of the sea; I really don't give tuppence whether I fall overboard or whether the Atlantic swallows me in one greedy gulp.

'You'll be all right in a wee while. Just take it easy' – Barney looks back and laughs – 'the first time is always the worst.'

'That's true. Once you get it over with, you'll never be seasick again.'

'Dada, wait till I tell you: who do you think is after calling?'

'Who?'

'Armada Pat.'

'The man that never left me a penny in his life. Did he give you a fright? You're as pale as a ghost.'

'No wonder for me to be pale. Do you know what day today is?'

'Wednesday.'

'Wednesday! It's the day of the catechism exam.'

'Oh, so it is.'

'So it is. That's all it means to you – and I have the knees prayed off myself all week.'

'Did he pass?'

'Wait till I tell you. Remember I told Miss Dee to send us word. Well, who does she send word with only Armada Pat. Imagine!'

'Did he pass?'

'I'm coming to that. "I have news for you," says Pat. I knew immediately what he was on about. "What is it, Pat?" I said, and I was quaking. "Bad news," he said –'

'He failed!' Dada blurts.

'Will you not always be in such a rush.'

'Either he passed or he failed.'

'That's what I'm coming to. "Is it about Conor?" I said to him. "It is," he said. I had to drag every syllable out of him. "And what's the news?" I said. "He failed," he said –'

'Well, there you are, he failed. After all the fuss.'

'Will you let me tell the story?'

'What more is there to tell? He failed: he failed.'

'Listen a minute. "Are you sure he failed, Pat?" I said to him. He was looking at me with a sort of a sarcastic smirk on his face. I never liked Armada Pat. "Who told you he failed anyway?" says I. "Miss Dee told me," says he, "when I was passing on the bicycle." Well, I nearly fell down with the fright I got. He was looking at me, still smirkin' away, as if he was delighted to be bringing us bad news. Then he burst out laughing. "Ah no," says he, "he passed." '

'He passed?'

'Isn't it great news?'

'Are you sure he passed?'

'Am I sure? Of course I'm sure. That's the message Miss Dee sent with him. Conor passed.'

'He passed. Well, that's a good one.'

'What did I tell you? I was right all along.'

'That's great news. Let them all chew on that.'

'We'll see what Miss Rose will have to say now – and Father McBrearty. With all their smartness, I knew more myself than any of them. I'm mad with Armada Pat – the purgatory he put me through; he's a bad article.'

'Well, what do we care, so long as he passed?'

'That's not the best of it. Wait till you hear. "The other fella

passed as well," says he. "What other fella?" says I. "That big
son of Andrew Meehan's that failed the last time," says he.
Imagine! Putting Conor in the same class as that big stupo. I was
rippin' with him. It's a true saying: There's bad blood in Armada
Pat.'

Consternation when I arrive back from school: Nanno sits
hunched over the fire, the bedroom door wide open. 'He's
gone,' she blurts out.

This is the first time she has ever mentioned her husband to
me and I don't know how to answer.

'I went over to Claren to visit my sister; Barney went to the
hill to check on his sheep. When I got back the kitchen door
was off the latch, the bedroom door was open and himself
nowhere to be found. Where in the name o' God can he be?'

A glance from the table to the fire tells me to forget about
dinner – at least for the moment.

'Barney is out searching for him now with Rogan.'

'I'll give a hand.'

'He's not in the hill; he's not on the strand,' Nanno calls after
me.

Only a few yards down the road and I meet Barney and
Rogan coming against me. Wedged between them like a trapped wether and wearing only his frayed woolly long johns is a
stunted wisp-haired spook of a man. Man-Hat-On is in his bare
feet, limping and hopping along the road, scowling with
discomfort every time he steps on a pebble or anything sharp.
Around his neck he has an old blackened scapular. Barney nods
to me and I follow them in silence back to the house.

Nanno, still crouched over the hearth, blesses herself with
relief. 'Where was he at all?'

'Land's End,' Barney answers, guiding his father towards
the fire.

'Land's End! God bless us and save us all!'

'He went as far as he could go.' Rogan tries to make light of the whole affair.

'Sitting on a stone,' Barney adds.

'He was sitting on EIRE,' Rogan says, 'guarding the Free State. Well, I'll be off.'

Barney backs his father closer to the fire to heaten him up.

Nanno turns away from him. 'You're a terrible man, putting the heart crosswise in us all.' She goes down to the bedroom and comes back with fresh clothes, which she lays out on a newspaper on the hob.

Man-Hat-On hasn't moved and seems content toasting his bum and the backs of his skinny legs. Barney must shave him every few days because he has a prickly growth of grey hair on his sunken wizened face, but not too much. The rest of his face is as white as his feet – and almost as blank. I wonder if he is aware of me being in the house, or if he thinks I am one of the family. He doesn't seem to take any notice of us at all, and after a while puts his hand into the fly of his long johns and starts to play with his winkie.

'Sit down.' Barney talks crossly. 'Go on. Sit down.' Barney forces his father on to the chair. He reaches for his hand and takes it out of his long johns, holding on to it for a while, as if he is after shaking hands with him. But as soon as he lets the hand go it wanders back again into his fly.

I know that Barney feels ashamed; I want to leave but I am too embarrassed to move; also I am curious.

Barney takes his father's hand again: 'Are you going to sing? . . . Come on. Give us a song.'

Without changing his expression, Man-Hat-On begins in a shaky ghostly voice:

> Driving through the Bowery in my motorcar,
> Waving, smiling, nodding, smoking my cigar,
> Money in my pockets, young and fancy free,
> Driving through the Bowery, I was happy as can be.

He comes to a dead halt, his eyes glassy, and Barney has to prompt him before he can go on:

> Swinging into Broadway, I give a hoot or two,
> All the ladies turn around, smiling as they do,
> Who's that happy millionaire, with his big cigar,
> Driving round the city in his motorcar?

> In Central Park before it's dark I let the throttle out,
> The cyclists wave their fists at me, the strollers scream
>   and shout,
> The horses shy as I go by and cops and robbers roar,
> For some of them had never seen a motorcar before.

'That'll do you now.' Nanno hands the aired clothes to Barney.

Man-Hat-On looks happier after his song and doesn't want to leave his chair.

'Come on inside till I change your clothes.' Barney has to force his father on to his feet and across the floor. Man-Hat-On fights every step of the way, trying to shrug Barney off, but he has no more strength than a child. I feel sorry for him; he looks so helpless and undernourished, with his bony arms and chest and his pale, skinny chicken-neck.

Barney bundles his father into the room ahead of him and pulls the door shut on them both.

Sports day in Killybegs and Dada has been gone since early morning to help in Fitzgerald's bar.

'What on earth is keeping that man? He was supposed to be back at seven. He's always home by seven – a quarter past seven at the latest – and now it's nearly eight.' Mama gets more and more impatient with each tick of the clock and sends Betty to the door several times to see if there is any sign of Dada. 'Where can he be at all?'

It is after nine when we hear Dada's whistle in the yard, as he lifts his bicycle down the cement steps.

'What in the name o' God kept you to this hour?'

'Is there something wrong?'

'Look at the time it is!'

'Never mind what the clock says, it's still clear: a fine summer's evening.'

'You were drinking.'

'I had a few drinks.'

'Oh then, you had more than a few.'

'I met Crusoe and Jellybob. We went for a few drinks in Rogers' after I finished.'

'Crusoe and Jellybob – nice companions. My God above, look at you – and the eyes swimming in your head!'

'There's no need to be getting up in the moon: one day in the year.'

'I'm waiting for you here since seven o'clock and not a sign of you.'

'Well, you knew where I was.'

'I didn't know from Adam where you were. You're gone since dawn – out all day – supposed to be earning money – instead of which I'm sure you spent every penny you made.'

'Well, I didn't spend any of yours anyway.'

'A nice way to talk to his wife.'

'It's the truth, isn't it? You still have your two hundred pounds dowry in the bank. Anything I ever spent was my own.'

'Nice talk, I must say. I'm the pity, surely: left in the house from morning till night – never brings his wife anywhere.'

'Because you won't go anywhere.'

'I would go plenty of places if I was asked.'

'You'll go nowhere. I'm blue in the face asking you to come to Donegal for a day – or Bundoran – or the Hill.'

'The Hill! Some day we would have in the Hill.'

'Nothing wrong with the Hill. Not a thing. But you won't go with me to see my relatives; you won't even go to see your own brother.'

'Harry is not my brother; he's my stepbrother.'

'Brother, stepbrother – what does it matter? You're the one flesh and blood.'

'We're not the one flesh and blood – anything but the one flesh and blood.'

'Then what are you?'

'What am I? You're the ignorant man.'

'Just looking for something to fight over, aren't you?'

'Keep your voice down.'

'Just looking for a fight – because you would fight with your toenails.'

'There was never any fighting in our house. My father was a gentleman, a member of Donegal County Council –'

'And a far out relation of Cardinal O'Donnell on your mother's side; we heard all that a hundred times.'

'I'm the pity, surely. Fit you better to look after your wife and family instead of streelin' around Killybegs all day.'

'I was working. Nothing wrong with me. Not a thing.'

'Oh then, there's plenty wrong with you. Any man that'll come in like that to his wife and family. Some example you are to your children.'

'You're going to turn the children against me now. Is that what you want?'

'You're a disgrace to your children' – Mama puts her arm

around Betty and myself drawing us towards her – 'no wonder they're ashamed of you.'

'Ashamed of me?' Dada looks at us and his eyes begin to fill up. 'I never done anything to make anyone ashamed of me.'

'No, you never *done* anything. You're an ignorant man – a thick ignorant man.'

Dada has been trying to put on a brave face in front of us, but now he loses all control and breaks into wild fits of crying. The outburst is so sudden that we are all frightened.

'Well, you're the big baby. Look at him – crying like a baby' – Mama tries to laugh it off.

Dada turns away from us, his voice rising in a throbbing roar of pain: 'Leave me alone, woman! Leave me alone!'

Since changing schools I haven't come face to face with Aisling and I often wonder, when we do meet, if she will ignore me.

As we come down on to the strand Ferdia is nowhere in sight, but Stonehead, wearing a straw hat, leans back on his elbows, and Mrs O'Regan has just taken up a towel, which she is spreading out on the sand. Aisling stands with her back to us, pulling down the edges of her blue swimsuit over her bottom. We are going to pass right in front of them, with Dada and Mama a little ahead of Betty and myself.

'Do you know the joke about Paddy the Irishman, Paddy the Englishman and Paddy the Scotchman, when they went out for a dip one day?'

'I'm sick of that joke. You're always telling it,' Betty says.

Betty's putoff doesn't discourage me. I want to be talking and laughing as I come up to Aisling, so I begin: 'Paddy the Irishman, Paddy the Englishman and Paddy the Scotchman went out for a dip one day after work. "Wait a minute," Paddy the Englishman said. "I'll go first because I'm the cleanest." So Paddy the Englishman dived in and he had a good swim and the sea wasn't all that dirty after him – just a bit of a scum on it. "I'll go next," said Paddy the Scotchman, "because I'm not as dirty as Paddy the Irishman, *he's* filthy." So Paddy the Scotchman dived in next and he splashed around for a while and he came out as clean as a fish. "It's your turn now," says he to Paddy the Irishman. Irish Paddy was looking into the sea and he had a face on him as if someone was after asking him for the loan of his head. He didn't take off his clothes or even his cap –'

'Hello. Lovely day,' Dada greets the O'Regans.

'Hello, Jamie,' Stonehead answers, 'hello, Mrs O'Donnell.'

'Hello.'

'Hello.'

Aisling, pouring her long fleece of shiny red hair into her bathing cap, raises her head in an inquisitive glance. For a moment we are looking into each other's eyes.

I wait for Aisling to speak; she tucks some stray skeins of hair in under the edges of the rubber cap, almost frowning with the effort. I try my best to smile – but my face won't budge. In a fluster I turn back to Betty: 'Paddy the Irishman jumped into the sea with all his clothes on and disappeared under the waves. He was down for a long time before he came back up again. "What kept you?" says Paddy the Englishman. Irish Paddy was dirtier than when he went in – all silt and seaweed. "You don't think I'm going to bathe in the filth you two left behind you," says he, "I was searching for the plug to let the water out."'

Dada picks a place on the far side of the rocks, so that we are cut off from view of the O'Regans. I don't see Aisling again until she appears near the water's edge tiptoeing unsteadily out into the tide, both her arms raised. She stops when the water reaches above her knees and looks back. Mrs O'Regan, who is wading towards her, splashes Aisling's shoulders. 'Don't splash me, Mammy! Don't splash me, please!' Aisling stands shivering for a while until a wave swells upwards, covering the bottom of her costume, then she ducks up and down in the water, her hands held out from her sides, her bathing costume clinging to her like an extra skin.

Dada frowns at me. 'You shouldn't be staring at them, Conor.'

'He has a notion of Aisling,' Betty says.

'No, I haven't.'

'Well, what harm if he has itself?'

'Conor hasn't a notion of anyone' – Mama's prophecy rings in my ears even before she pronounces it – 'Conor is going to be a priest.'

Dada has unwound the bandage from his sore leg and the skin is pale and streaked with purple where he has had his varicose veins taken out in the States. 'Come on, Conor, we'll brave it.'

I run past Dada, shouting, kicking sand with my heels, and dive into an oncoming wave. Aisling looks across at me, unsmiling, as the water gushes up my nose and down my windpipe.

Even though they always walk together to mass, Molly Dan and Suzanne sit in separate seats. Suzanne's perch is on the outside of the third seat from the top, where she is kept busy stretching and ducking and twisting until everyone squeezes in past her. Molly sits far down the chapel, well beyond the halfway mark, at Christ Falls for the Third Time.

When they come into the kitchen after mass for their usual glass of port wine, Molly is in a terrible state of befuddlement: Father McBrearty has had two seats removed to make a passageway and so there is no longer a seat at Christ Falls for the Third Time.

'God save us the day and the night, I got the land of my life when I went to go into my usual place. Just a big empty space where my seat used to be. I wondered was it in the Protestant church I was by mistake.'

Suzanne stops with a pinch of snuff halfway to her nose: 'Why don't you come up to the front where you can see what's going on?'

'My seat is Christ Falls for the Third Time. That's where I always sat and that's where I'll sit now.'

'How will you sit, unless you're going to sit on the floor?'

'The kneeler is still there – on the seat in front – but when I want to sit I have to go way back, and I have nothing to support myself on when I'm on my knees. God save us the day and the night – all the seats in the chapel and he had to pick on Christ Falls for the Third Time.'

'Offer it up' – Suzanne nods at Molly – 'maybe it's what you need to do penance.'

'I wonder would you be so glib about the need for penance if he took out the third seat from the altar. You'd have a different tune then.'

Idling at the river's estuary, our bare feet dipping in and out of the crosscurrents, the three of us wonder how best to enjoy the bright sunny day.

'Will we go to the Island?' Scunsey suggests.

Ferdia is doubtful. 'We don't know where it is.'

'It's somewhere up the river – a good bit.'

'Is it beyond Brugh?'

'I dunno.'

'It must be.'

'No. Big Jodie said it's not beyond Brugh and it's not this side of it either' – Scunsey sounds mysterious.

'How could that be?'

'He said there's a fork in the river; half of it goes off on its own. Guess what?'

'What?'

'There's an apple tree on the Island. And plenty of blackberries.'

'How do you know?'

'Big Jodie told me.'

'Was he on the Island?'

'Plenty o' times.'

We are already splashing upstream, wading near the bank where the sandy river bed slopes downwards, holding on to clumps of grass for a hand grip, or the branches of overhanging sally trees. At the factory a current of warm green outflow swirls around our feet.

'They're dyeing green today,' Ferdia says.

The river straggles its way behind the houses, discoloured and sluggish from the dumping of many slops. Beyond Mulligan's house, the first house in the town, the water clears and the drowsy smell of hay and heather from the opposite bank tingles in our nostrils.

At the Rock Pool we stop to look for trout. Through the still water we watch until our eyes get used to the hazy dreamlike world, where dappled shapes mysteriously appear, flashing for an instant, nosing in the gravel on the river bed or hanging in midwater, like ancient ferns imprisoned in glass. Occasionally they dart upwards, zigzagging just below the surface, then dive, swimming level with the bottom, their shadows floating beneath them, bending, folding over stones, trailing behind or suddenly stretching ahead until all disappear in a nervous flutter of tails and fins.

'Come on,' Scunsey says, 'we can look in there any time.'

We don't rest again until we reach Lahan bridge, where we lean against the cool, shady arch of lime-drenched stone. All three of us are already showing the rigours of the journey. Scunsey got a ducking when a branch he was swinging from broke; I got stung with nettles; and Ferdia got stung, and scratched with briars as well.

'I wonder is it much further?'

'It shouldn't be too far now.'

'We didn't come to the fork yet.'

'We should reach it any minute.'

On we go, hopping from stone to stone where we can, expecting to glimpse the Island or the fork around every bend.

'Shhhh!' Ferdia holds up his hand.

Ahead of us, in the middle of a shallow pool, balanced on one long, spindly leg, is the biggest bird any of us ever saw in our lives. It stands very still; its other leg hinged back under its body – until we try to creep up on it, when it spreads its huge grey wings, flapping, and slowly lifts off.

'It's a heron,' Scunsey announces.

'How do you know?'

'Because I know.'

In the heat and heavy silence of the countryside we feel less inclined to talk. Now and then small birds whizz and dart about when they hear us approaching, flying like furry arrows out of the bushes. On either side of us the stubbled fields are raked clean, the hay in handcocks and trampcocks.

'There it is! The Island!' Ferdia points to where a hawthorn rises crookedly from a grassy mound out in the river.

'It could be the Island.'

'If there's an apple tree on it.'

'There's honeysuckles!'

We hurry forward, splashing on to the rise of short, wiry grass and rushes. Scunsey begins plucking the honeysuckles and we join him, greedily sucking in the cool driblets of nectar.

'This must be the Island.'

'Look!'

'What?'

'It's not an island at all.'

'It *is* an island. It's out in the middle of the river.'

'But it's joined to the far bank. You can't go around it.'

'And what about the fork?' I ask.

'Maybe there's no fork.'

'Maybe there's no island.'

'There is so.'

'How do you know?'

'Because I know.'

'We only have Big Jodie's word for it.'

'It has the reddest apples ever you saw. And that's not all.'

'What else?'

'There's something else, Big Jodie said.'

'What?'

'He wouldn't say.'

'Just something else?'

'That will astonish you.'

'Something that will astonish us?'

'That's what he said.'

'When was Big Jodie on the Island?'

'When he was wee.'

'Come on. We're only wasting time.'

Into the water again, jumping, drenching each other all over again, shouting and splashing forward from bend to bend, the sun pressing on the backs of our necks like a hot poultice. Before long we are breathless and moving in single file, slow as homecoming cattle. We are far beyond the farthest distance we have ever walked, wading through country which is as unfamiliar to us as the prairies of Wyoming or the wild jungles of Borneo.

A big red bull stops muzzling in the grass and raises his head, staring blankly at us. Whose bull is it? None of us knows.

In another field: slabs of stone half-standing, leaning this way and that, moss creeping over them – an old graveyard maybe.

Further on, at the bottom of a ripening field of corn, a woman sits on the ditch herding a cow. When she turns we get a fright: at the side of her eyes purple clusters of flesh bulge out like grapes; more purple growths hang from one of her eyelids. We had decided to ask the first person we saw what townland we are in, but none of us speaks until we are well past the woman.

'It's Mary Kyle.'

'She has the curse on her.'

'No, she hasn't,' Ferdia says; 'that's the way God made her.'

'Where does she live?'

'I dunno.'

'A long way away. She hardly ever comes into the town.'

'See my toes! They're white from the water.'

'Mine are all shrunken.'

'I'm hungry.'

'We should have brought sandwiches.'

'Jakers! See!'

Suddenly, across the further bank which is clear of bushes, we get a glimpse of a bald, stony valley, where the river swirls and twists in loop after loop until its sparkle dims on the horizon.

'Is there an island?'

'Look!'

'I don't see any island.'

'Away in the distance.'

'It's the Island!'

'Could be.'

'Hard to say.'

'We'll know when we get there.'

Around the next bend we lose sight of the Island. The flow of the river has slowed, falling into step with us, but the bottom is griddled with small pebbles, so that we feel as if we are walking on pine cones. On we go into the next stony loop – and the next. The backs of our legs ache and our toes feel numb and rubbery. Ferdia rests against a rock that is shaped like an anvil. Scunsey and myself each sit on rocks nearby.

'What if Big Jodie is coddin' us?'

'He's not. You saw the Island yourself.'

'It could be just part of the bank – like before.'

'It's the Island. I know it is,' Scunsey insists.

'We'll go up on the bruagh and take another look.'

From the height above we have a clear view across the immense floor of the valley to where the sun and the river seem to merge in a fiery pool of light.

'It's like the end of the rainbow.'

'And the nearer you get to it the further away it goes.'

'I can see the Island! Clear as can be.'

'Where?'

'I'm nearly blinded. I can't see anything.'

'Don't you see?'

'I can see something – but it mightn't be an island at all.'

'It's definitely an island. See the way the water is shining all around it.'

'But we can't see the far side.'

'It could be a mirage.'

'A what?'

'A mirage.'

'You have to be in the desert to see a mirage.'

'It could be a *sort* of a mirage.'

'I say it's real.'

'Even if it *is* real, it'll be dark night by the time we get to it.'

'I'm awful hungry.'

'So am I.'

'At least we saw the Island even if we didn't reach it. We can always come back another day.'

'Then we'll get stung and cut and drenched all over again.'

'It'll be worth it for the apples.'

'And the blackberries.'

'And something that will astonish you.'

'If Big Jodie would come with us.'

'He wouldn't have time.'

We are slow to turn away from the bluey-green speck on the horizon, hazy in the shimmering brightness, in the far shining arrows of the sun.

'We'll definitely be back.'

'Definitely.'

'Me and Mama was talking: you won't have to stay in Trá Gheal any more, Conor. You're big enough now to make the journey on foot. Next year, maybe, I'll buy you a bicycle.'

'Will you buy me a bicycle this year?'

'You're too young yet.'

'I'm well able to cycle.'

'Going round the Rock is dangerous; you need to get used to it first. There's some terrible squalls there in the wintertime. The hat was blown off myself one evening. I had to race after it down the road; it was going mad, twisting and turning like a rabbit. I thought it would get away on me over the bank.'

Just before the consecration, Ellen Andy is short-taken and has to flee her place in front of the altar rails, hurrying the full length of the chapel to escape. Will she come back or will she go home? Everyone in the chapel seems to have stopped praying and to be waiting for the answer.

A short while later, Ellen's ringing hop-step is heard coming up the centre aisle – and then Ellen herself with her shawl folded reverently over her head and her long, black skirt caught in the waistband of her knickers. Ellen's knickers are home made, from an old flour bag. Sideways over her bum in capital letters is printed SPILLERS FLOUR.

★ ★ ★

'We'll have to pay Morgan a call,' Dada had said after mass. 'Delivering stout to me since I came here – he's out of hospital nearly a fortnight and we never went near him.'

Morgan says he is in good form, but his left leg, in plaster of Paris, rests on the chair in front of him and every time he moves on the sofa (which is the bench seat from a lorry) his face twists with pain. As he tells us about the accident his hand dangles down, playing with the dog's floppy ears. 'He's the only one escaped without a scratch,' Morgan says, 'himself and Snuggy.'

'Snuggy was lucky.'

'Lucky, surely. He was asleep in the back of the lorry when it happened. The crash woke him up. It damn near knocked out everybody else – arms and legs broken.'

'You were lucky you weren't all killed.'

'We were, surely. We all had a wee drop too much taken after the AOH demonstration in Donegal. Coming down the Slope, I put my foot on the brakes – nothing happened; she kept gathering speed. I could see McGinley's cement wall at the bottom of the hill. We're done for, I thought. And that's the last thing I remember. Isn't it funny, I don't remember trying to take the turn, or the crash or a damn thing? We were all brought into McGinley's and laid out on blankets and sheets in the kitchen. When I came to, I didn't know where I was. It was frightening. Patrick Joe was next to me. A splinter from the back window went into his eye. Jodie was on my other side with a broken leg. One of us worse than the other and nobody able to do anything for us. Father Feegan was moving between us, trying to keep our hearts up till the ambulance came from Donegal. I didn't know a thing about Francey Dubh. We were all in such pain: every man was thinking of himself. I must have passed out again; I don't remember much else – except the bell – the chapel bell ringing – not very loud – you could just barely hear it. When I mentioned it afterwards, some of the others heard it as well. Why the chapel bell would ring at that hour – only it was a very windy night.'

Dada and Morgan go on talking, but my own thoughts are on the way I heard Paddy McGinley telling the story a few days after the crash. 'We heard this terrible bang that wakened us. I said to Mary, somebody is after crashing into the wall. I had that feeling the minute I woke up. I thought it was Morgan. Well, he's the first you would think of. By the time I got the lamp lit in the kitchen, the wild knocking was at the door. Snuggy it was. He hadn't to say anything. I could see the lorry across from us and the cab all crushed in. I called Seamus and between the three of us we got the men out of the wreck and into the kitchen. Mary took the clothes off the beds; the children were all up and frightened at the sight of so many people hurted. From the start we knew that Francey Dubh was in a bad way. Some of the others looked worse off: they were losing a lot of blood. Francey wasn't bleeding at all, but he was hardly able to breathe, and the sweat breaking out on his forehead with the pain. When the priest came in he went around to everybody. Francey waited his turn, but when Father Feegan asked him how he was feeling he said, "I think I'm dying, Father." "Not at all," Father Feegan said, "you'll be all right." "I don't think so, Father," Francey said. "Will you hear my confession?" Father Feegan heard his confession and anointed him. After that, Francey asked to have a word with Mary. Mary and Noreen – that's Francey's wife – they're first cousins. He put out his hand to Mary – he didn't say anything – just held her hand. Then he said, "Tell Noreen I was thinking of her." When the ambulance arrived he was dead.'

Even though the wind is howling outside, Meehans' kitchen door is open and the screen of netwire to keep out the hens hinged on for the day.

'Will you have some porridge to warm you while you're waiting?' Mrs Meehan asks me.

I hate porridge and have already had a bowlful with country butter added, which makes it taste even worse, but which Mama insists Betty and I take every morning.

Mrs Meehan reads the answer from my face. 'A cup o' tea then?'

'Thanks.'

The Meehans have all slept it out and the children are crowded around the table gulping down their breakfast and pulling on cardigans and ganseys and jackets at the same time.

M'uncle comes up from the bedroom, a small, round-bellied man with loose red eyelids and watery eyes; he stretches his braces over his shirt. From the blackened teapot on the hob he pours a cup of strong tea for himself and stands with his back to the fire.

Mrs Meehan hurries from the dresser to the table to the fire, pouring tea and porridge and spooning sugar from a brown paper bag.

At the head of the table sits Big Andy smiling all around him, laying into the home-made bread and butter. Standing beside him Wee Peadar and Wee Nora, the two youngest of the family, barely reach up to Andy's shoulder. On his other side, gulping down porridge, are the twins, Johnny and Tommy, also standing and just level with Big Andy's chin. 'They gave all the height to Andy,' Rogan said; 'they kept nothing over for the rest of them.'

'Gimme more tea, Ma.'

'Get it yourself, Andy. Can't you see I'm busy?'

Big Andy brings his porringer to the hob and tops it up before standing beside M'uncle, his backside to the fire. He watches contentedly the hubbub going on at the table and takes a slow satisfied slurp of tea.

'Are you finished your breakfast?' M'uncle says to him.

'No.'

'You would need to get a spurt on then.'

'For what?'

'Aren't you going to bring them around the Rock?'

'Me?'

'Who else?'

'But I'm finished with school.'

'Get on your coat, Andy, and take the wee ones by the hand' – Mrs Meehan elbows Andy.

Andy's face has curdled into a sour glob. 'I thought I was finished with school, Ma?'

'You *are* finished with school. This is just to bring them around the Rock. You won't have to go near the school.'

Big Andy is in such a temper that he gets himself all tangled up in the sleeves of his overcoat. 'Come on with yous if yous are coming. I'm ready. I'll have the rest of my breakfast when I get back. Keep the kettle on the boil, Ma.'

Big Andy strides ahead of us with grown-up steps, looking back over his shoulder and telling us to 'Hurry up with yous.' The nearer we get to the Rock the fiercer the storm rages and the harder we have to push against it to make any headway. Wee Nora and Wee Peadar cling to Andy until he takes them by the hand. I have a grip of Johnny's hand, who has a tight grip of Tommy's hand, who has a strangle hold on the tail of Big Andy's coat. We are all squashed in tight against the overhanging bulge of rock, so that the freak squalls blundering down from the hill pass howling over our heads. Seldom anybody talks because the wind grabs the words out of your mouth and blows them up in the air, scattering them East and West.

'Andy!'

'What is it?'

'What did you say?'

'What's that?'

'What?'

Every so often a sly squall squeezes in between us, tugging, trying to blow us out of line. On the far side of the road a stone wall blocks our view of the sudden dizzy drop into the tumbling sea. 'Whatever yous do, stay well in against the Rock,' Mrs Meehan had warned us.

Once past the Rock, the wind slackens and we can walk out on the road again. Looking back, we see the dust swirling and the ferns waving frantically on the hill. A little further on and the grey slate roof of the school comes into view, with thick sworls of turf smoke belching upwards, telling us that the fire is well lit and that we are late.

Big Andy stops and waves us past him. 'Yous better run for it or she'll have your lives. Go on! Run! Run! Yous are as late as late can be.' Big Andy opens his big mouth and sends a mocking laugh chasing down the hill after us. 'Run, let yous! Run! Ha-ha-ha-ha! She'll be in a wild temper the day. Ha-ha-ha-ha! Run! Run! She'll malafuster yous! She'll kill yous all! Ha-ha-ha-ha!'

'Himself has the flu but Sally will take your measure. Go up the garden to the workshop.' Big Sarah brings me through the scullery smelling of stale dishcloths and cabbage stalks, and opens the back door for me.

In the workshop Sally sits cross-legged on a sort of low stage at the end of the room. Spread out on her lap is some canvas material which she is hand-sewing – the lining for a coat or a jacket.

'Conor O'Donnell – and is it the long ones you want?'

'No. I just want an overcoat for the winter.'

'Don't mind me. I'm only taking a hand of you.' Sally leaves her sewing aside and steps down from the platform. She is a big girl, twenty-one on her last birthday, with short curly hair and a round, rosy face.

Big Sarah is very hard on Sally and never lets her go anywhere. Shortly after her birthday, when there was a long dance in the hall, Sally asked Mama for the money to go. Mama gave her a half-crown – never thinking that Big Sarah would find out. Sally had sneaked out the bedroom window to the dance, but she wasn't long gone when her mother missed her. Big Sarah went up to the hall and marched Sally home in front of her. Next day Big Sarah came into the kitchen to Mama and threw down a half-crown on the table: '*You* look after *your* knitting and *I'll* look after *mine.*'

Sally has taken up a small notebook with a shiny red cover and writes my name in it with a pencil stump. She opens out the length of tweed I have brought, testing it between her fingers. 'Herringbone. This is going to make a lovely coat. Where did you get it?'

'Con Moylan.'

'You're going to be a great swank in this, Conor. You'll have a sweetheart in no time. Maybe you have one already?'

'No, I haven't.'

'Are you sure?' Sally is looking straight into my eyes. I wonder if she knows about Aisling.

'You're blushing, Conor – a sure sign you have a sweetheart.'

'I haven't. Honest.'

'Well, you're time enough.' Sally circles my waist with the measuring tape, her fingers touching me for an instant on the arms and legs and shoulders. She is humming a tune I remember from Daniels' Travelling Show:

> Yesterday I saw you passing
> Heedlessly upon your way,
> Never knowing how I love you,
> Melanie, O Melanie.

If I met you in the garden,
Would I know what words to say?
Would you sense my awful yearning?
Melanie, O Melanie.

'You're never sure; no, you're never sure. You can never relax, never trust him. I was very nearly home. I was thinking – do you know what I was thinking about? A good smoke. I ran out of matches and the pipe was dead. Fire was all that was a bother to me. I would give anything for a light. Or would I? I began to think about it. *Would* I give anything? Would I give my soul? Hardly was the thought full grown in my head when I heard the croaking behind me: Cro-cro-cro-croak! Cro-cro-cro-croak! I listened for a while, trying to figure it out, trying to remember where I heard the words before. It wasn't long till the meaning of it dawned on me. Of course, I knew immediately I was in trouble. Big trouble. What was I going to do now? I hadn't a stick or a cross or a drop of holy water or a thing to protect me. Well, I'll have to face you anyway, me boyo – so I turned around real quick, raising my arms in front of me in the form of a cross. There was a shriek – a long, drawn-out shriek – and then silence. The cross did the trick. There's no divil in hell can stand the pain of the cross. On I went. I had no more annoyance from him. Not a sight of him. Not a sound. Not a smell. There's a fierce bad smell off Old Nick, you know. Rotten. I don't know how I could describe it to you – like an oul' maggoty hedgehog that would be dead a long time in the ditch. Anyway, there was no smell. I'm finished with you, me boyo, I thought; I have the upper hand of you at last, and me ready to spring the sign of the cross at him again as soon as he let the slightest croak out of him – when, God above! – I felt myself being tripped from behind, and before I had time even to hit the ground, I got this ferocious kick in the backside that lifted me clean up in the air and landed me a good five or six feet away on my mouth and nose in the drain. At the same time the croakin' started again, worse than ever. Luckily the drain was dry, otherwise I was a gonner, because I went in head first and I was stuck there like a cork in a bottle. What was I to do now and me barely able to keep my head out of the muck and the *clábar*? There was no way I could make the sign of the cross, except maybe with my legs, and I didn't want to chance that in case I might be doing myself more harm than good; for there's nothing worse than a crooked cross, so we're told. See how it put the cockanony on Hitler. Anyway, I was trying to figure out what was best to do when I felt something slimy crawling along my neck and down under my collar. Back with a vengeance they were. That was just the first of them. Before I had time to say Christ have mercy, the buggers were all over me and every one of them croaking and cursing and blaspheming – every one of them a filthy stinking divil out o' hell. That wasn't the worst. The croaking got louder and louder with more and more divils answering to the call, slithering down the ditch, leapfroggin' into the drain beside me, up my sleeves and down my gansey and into my trousers, he-divils and she-divils stuck in each other, squarting their filth all over me and them croaking at the tops of their voices and blowing and belching from all ends. I thought every minute I was going to choke on the foul stench I had to breathe in. When I tried again to lift myself up, I got the greatest shock of all: I must have weighed about a ton. Christ, am I after turning into a bullfrog myself or an elephant or what, or has the soul gone out of me, for they say when the soul leaves you that you're as heavy as the down side of a quarry? And all this time the head boyo himself was perched up on my backbone, where I couldn't shake him off, and him cro-cro-cro-croaking away to beat the band. Oh, Old Nick, he's a boyo; there's no getting the better of him; there's no putting him down.' Willoughby breaks off to curl the ends of his moustache, shaking his head, blinking his eyes and muttering to himself about Old Nick, so that he loses all track of the story he is telling. 'The next time your dog comes home late take a good look at him. Look to your hearth and the crickets chirping at your feet. Listen to the hens in the yard and what they're saying, and the crows and the magpies. Listen well. Especially at night when you're in bed. Even the flies on the wall have a voice and they're either praising God or cursing Him.'

After devotions on Sunday evening, Claddagh brought a stranger in with him. 'This is Michael Jordan; he's a county man of my own.'

Dada shook hands with the good-looking young man and got me to bring the drinks to the kitchen table.

'Michael is in charge of the dyeing section,' Claddagh said; 'he'll be here on a permanent basis from now on.'

When Michael's turn came to buy, he took out his wallet, which had his photograph in a little celluloid window; ten shilling notes were in one compartment, pound notes in the other. His hair was oily and smelt of Brylcreem; a small black comb stuck up over the top of his breast pocket.

As usual, Claddagh listened to the Sunday play on Radio Éireann; because he didn't like any interruptions, we had got into the habit of listening with him.

'Who plays the fiddle?' Michael asked at the end.

'Conor does – a bit,' Dada said.

'Will you play us a tune?'

I played 'Saint Patrick's Day' and 'The Irish Washerwoman' which everyone present, except Michael, must have heard me play a dozen times at least. As I was putting the fiddle back in its case, Michael reached out and I let him take it from me.

'I'll bet you play yourself?' Mama said.

Michael nodded. He tuned the fiddle to his satisfaction, took out his handkerchief, folded it and placed it on his shoulder under the fiddle. Drawing the full length of the bow across the strings, he began a tune that I had never heard before – a tune that climbed higher and higher, like the warbling call of a bird. His fingers were far up on the strings and trembling, which gave the notes a sweeter, fuller sound. In the second part of the tune he played two strings together, note sounding against note. I felt a tingling at the back of my neck. I didn't think it possible that such music could come from a fiddle – especially my own little half-size fiddle.

Claddagh has no liking for music. Any time Con Moylan took out my fiddle, Claddagh looked bored and then annoyed, but even Claddagh sat still, occasionally glancing around at the effect Michael's playing was having, every bit as enthralled as the rest of us. At the end we all clapped.

'What's the name of that tune?' I asked.

'It's called "Souvenir".'

'Will you play it again?'

Michael hesitated. 'I'll play you a fast tune for a change: "The Mason's Apron".'

I longed to ask Michael if he would teach me. I would give anything to be able to play like him.

'Did you find a place to stay?' Mama asked as they were leaving.

'I'm staying across the street – in Groarty's.'

When they had gone, Mama fretted. 'Imagine Big Sarah keeping a lodger.'

'Well, what's wrong with that?'

'Haven't they a tailoring business? Isn't that enough for them? We could have given him the spare room.'

'Well, he didn't ask us.'

'It's a wonder Claddagh didn't tell him.'

'How could Claddagh know you would keep a lodger? I didn't know myself till this minute.'

The Sunday of Johnny O'Brien's funeral and the bar is crowded. Mama has got so used to Molly Dan and Suzanne having their wee sniffle after mass that she brings down the two half-uns of port wine as soon as the women step into the kitchen.

Suzanne does a lot of carfufflin' over payment, scrummaging around in her bag – in the end she takes out her mustard tin and dabs snuff in each of her nostrils: '*Trócaire 's grásta.*'

'*Trócaire 's grásta,*' Molly answers, adding, 'it's *your* turn to pay this week.'

'Are you sure?'

'Sure I'm sure. Certain sure. I bought last week, you bought the week before that, now it's your turn again.'

'Oh Waidean!' Suzanne goes back to her bag and takes out her purse, but she changes her mind. 'I don't think I'll have anything to drink the day, Cassy.'

Mama has been standing with the cinnamon and the kettle of hot water waiting to mix the drinks.

'Don't mind her, Cassy' – Molly moves her glass nearer the kettle – 'pour away there.'

'No. Hold on you, Cassy.'

'What is it, Suzanne?' Mama hesitates, the spout of the kettle tipping Molly's glass.

'Oh, I don't know. I'm not feeling well.'

'Are you not feeling well, Suzanne?'

'No, I'm not, Cassy.'

'If you're not feeling well, all the more reason you should drink up,' Molly advises. 'It'll cure you.'

'No, it won't. Take them back, Cassy.'

Molly looks longingly at the two glasses on the table. 'Well, whatever you're going to do, I'm going to have my drink as usual.'

'Wait a minute!' Suzanne grabs Molly's hand as she takes up the glass.

'Wait a minute for what?'

Suzanne says nothing but she tightens her grip on Molly's wrist, forcing her to surrender the glass back on to the table.

'God save us the day and the night, what's coming over you at all!'

'That's what's coming over me' – Suzanne snaps open her grey canvas purse, holding it upside down.

Molly gapes at the empty, tattered purse. 'You *must* have money.'

'Not a farthing.'

Mama waits to see if Molly will offer to pay, but Molly sits tight.

'You can pay for them next week, Suzanne,' Mama says.

'Oh no, Cassy, I can't. Every penny out of my pension is a marked penny.'

'Did you lose money?' Molly asks.

'No, I didn't.'

'You must have lost a two shilling piece.'

'I didn't, I'm telling you.'

'Then what did you do with the rest of your pension? We agreed to leave over the price of a wee sniffle, didn't we?'

'I left it over.'

'Then where is it? You got your usual messages, as the fella says: tea, sugar, bread, butter, your half-ounce o' snuff and your ounce o' tobaccy.'

'I had an unexpected outlay.'

'An unexpected outlay? What sort of unexpected outlay?'

Suzanne turns to Mama, who has left the kettle back on the range: 'I may as well tell you, Cassy, what happened. I was in the chapel listening to the offerings being called for Johnny O'Brien.'

'You didn't pay offerings, surely?' Molly interrupts.

Suzanne gives Molly a sharp sideways look. 'Don't you know that Johnny O'Brien is a second cousin of my own?'

'Well, what if he is itself?'

'What if he is itself!' – Suzanne turns back to Mama – 'I was in the seat behind the mourners, Cassy, listening to the names being called – Peter O'Brien, two and six; Annie O'Brien, two and six; Patrick Groarty, two shillings – and there was I holding on to my own two shillings for the wee sniffle afterwards, and I thought to myself, Is it worth it? – because everyone was waiting for my name – and if I didn't pay over my second cousin, who's going to pay over me when my own time comes? – so I went up to the table and I put down my two shilling piece –'

'You were foolish enough,' Molly butts in.

'I done the right thing,' Suzanne says, 'and I'm surprised you didn't hear my name called out, which was loud and clear – Suzanne O'Flaherty, two shillings – but I expect you weren't listening as usual because you never pay at anyone's funeral yourself. Anyway, I'm glad I had the two shillings in my purse; whatever about the drink, I can rest content that I paid over my second cousin Johnny O'Brien, a decent man.'

From the street, a fiddle sounds, high-voiced, over the clink and chatter of the tea table. I rush to the door, my mouth full. Wee Groarty's window is down, the music streaming out as if the house is a big radio . . . Two strings sounding together . . . the main tune returning – rising – soaring – lifting our hearts.

Ellen Andy comes to the door in her black cotton apron . . . Callaghan and Mrs Callaghan . . . Nora Mary . . . Con Moylan . . . Dada.

'He can play, Con.'

'No mistake about it.'

'Oh Waidean, when did I hear music like that!'

Big Jodie comes strolling up the street, limping slightly, Snuggy tagging along beside him; they stop outside Groarty's. 'Bthavo! Bthavo!' Big Jodie calls in the door. Snuggy gives a Hi!

The music has stopped. Michael Jordan comes to the door as if he is going to take a bow, his fiddle under his oxter.

'Good man yourself!'

'Give us another one. Don't go back inside.'

Michael nods to us.

'Play away,' Con Moylan calls.

'What would you like to hear?'

'Give us "The Coolin".'

'Give us "The Pigeon on the Gate",' Snuggy suggests.

Sally squeezes past Michael and sits on the windowsill; in her hand is a small piece of yellow cloth, which has the rosin for the bow in it. She raises her eyes to Michael's face as he fixes the fiddle under his chin and the first notes of 'The Coolin', like starlings risen, flutter over the town.

'Oh Waidean, isn't that lovely! I could listen to that music for ever.'

'How do we – how do we know but it's all propaganda?'

'What's propaganda?'

'All propaganda.'

'It's no propaganda – no, no, not this time. The man is dead. Dead as – as Humpty Dumpty.'

'Then I'd like to see the body – I'd like to see a photograph.'

'You'll see no photograph.'

'My own guess – my own guess is that he got out – out at the last tick o' the clock.'

'Out? Out where?'

'Out. Somewhere. Somehow. Japan, maybe.'

'A lot o' future he'd have in Japan. He'd be lost. Sure he – he doesn't speak Japanese, does he?'

'Doesn't speak Japanese! What does it matter whether he speaks Japanese or Chinese or – or Portuguese? He's the Foorer. God dammit man – the leader of the German people! Will you have another one?'

'No. I'm full.'

'The Foorer, you'll find, is safe and sound in some neutral country – some neutral country. He'll rise again.'

'And what's he going to do?'

'What do you mean, what's he going to do?'

'In some neutral country?'

'What are you talking about, man?'

'In the meantime – I mean – what's he going to do?'

'What's he going to do!'

'That's what I'm asking you: what's he going to do?'

'He'll lie low.'

'How is he going to live? Hah? Answer me that. Would you – would you give him a job?'

'Would I give Hitler a job? I would. I would surely give him a job. Certainly.'

'He started off as a – as a dishwasher, you know.'

'No, no. Hitler was never a dishwasher – never a dishwasher.'

'Then he'll be damn lucky if he doesn't end up as one – if he's alive – damn lucky.'

'He was a painter – that's what he was – Hitler was an artist; hadn't a penny. He came up the hard way.'

'Went down the hard way as well – left nothing behind him only a heap o' rubble.'

'Heap o' rubble is right.'

'A heap o' rubble, that's all.'

'You know, I – I cried the night I heard he was dead.'

'I thought you said he was alive?'

'They said on the radio he was dead. I cried my eyes out.'

'Foolish man.'

'I was following his career – from the very beginning. I was for him all the way – all the way – when no one else was for him – not even the German people themselves.'

'Heap o' rubble.'

'He could have done a lot o' good – could have done great things the same Hitler.'

Out for the Sunday stroll we meet the factory manager who always wears plus fours and has never been known to darken the door of a pub.

'This could be the last walk any of us will ever take,' the manager says.

'It could indeed,' Dada agrees with him. 'It looks as if they're going to blow the world to smithereens.'

'That is, if they go ahead with the test.'

'They'll go ahead all right. They're not going to pull back now.'

'I read in the paper,' the manager says, 'that it might set off a chain reaction, which nobody could control. One atom will hit another atom which will hit another and another, until every atom in the world is destroyed. Imagine taking a chance testing something like that.'

'The scientists are mad, surely.'

'They won't stop until they blow up everything.'

'It's prophesied by Saint Colmcille that the world will be consumed by fire.' Mama's words toll over our heads like a warning knell.

'We'll all know tomorrow when the bomb goes off.'

'Is it the end of the world?' Betty asks in a frightened voice.

'No. Not at all,' Mama answers quickly. 'It's only all talk.'

In bed that night Betty lies awake worrying: 'I think it's the end of the world. Do you, Conor?'

'I don't know.'

'I think they don't want to tell us in case we'll be frightened. Are you frightened?'

'No.'

'I am. Why else would the factory manager say it? And Dada agreed with him. And Saint Colmcille said it too. I hate the atom bomb.'

'Stop talking about it.'

'. . . Conor.'

'What?'

'I'm afraid.'

'Go asleep.'

'I think it's the end of the world.'

Mama has gone to a wake in Duhaigh and Dada and Old Con talk over a neighbourly drink in the kitchen. They both agree that what the town badly needs is a proper dancehall. After a few more drinks Old Con has a brainwave: the outhouses behind his house could easily be turned into a dancehall, only it would take money.

'I'm your partner then,' says Dada.

'All we have to do is knock down the inside walls,' Old Con says. 'After that it only needs a stage and some plastering. It wouldn't take that much altogether to slap it into shape.'

'We'll have to do a right job on it though – a mineral bar and all. We'd make a fortune on teas and minerals alone.'

Next day when Mama hears of the idea she puts the damper on. 'What do you want to go into partnership with Old Con for; why can't you build a hall yourself?'

'Where?'

'In the old school yard.'

'You're right.'

'It's walled in and everything.'

'It is.'

'You have only to knock down what's left of the old school.'

'Maybe that's what I'll do. Me and Con was only talking.'

'Anyone that would think of going into partnership with Old Con must be dreaming the dream of the man in the moon.'

'Nothing wrong with Old Con.'

'He went bankrupt once already, didn't he?'

'Out of pure goodness. Old Con had the biggest business in the town, only he gave out too much credit.'

'Well, he's too old now.'

'He is.'

'You'll have to be fly. Don't say a word about this to anyone.'

'Not a word.'

'They'll all get the shock of their lives when the hall is up.'

Sunday evenings I go down to Scunsey's house, where a swing dangles lopsided from the big oak tree at the bottom of the garden. We take turns shoving each other higher and higher, until our heads are skimming the branches, lopping in and out over the river.

One Sunday the sky suddenly starts popping hailstones at us and the two of us run for shelter to the kitchen. On top of the dresser the red bellows of a melodion fades to dark purple as the light filtering through the livid clouds begins to narrow.

'Can you play it?'

'A bit,' Scunsey answers.

'Play a tune.'

Scunsey rests the melodion on one raised knee and plays with short hurried spurts of air 'The Rakes of Mallow', followed without a stop by 'The Drake in the Corn'. He is an absolute wizard at the traditional – and never let on to anyone that he could play.

'If he practised, he'd be great,' his father says. 'He's a natural musician, like his mother, the Lord rest her.'

'Where is everybody headed?' Betty runs out the door to stare after the rush of children and grown-ups. 'Conor – oranges – Mama – oranges – the oranges are in! . . . Dada, will you give us some money? – the oranges are in.'

'Here, get a half-dozen.'

'Get a dozen.'

'All right. Here. Get a dozen.'

'Come on, Betty – quick – before they're all gone.'

We hurry up to Maggie May's, where a crowd blocks the footpath, busy scattering orange skins, spitting out seeds, sucking, gobbling, slobbering.

Inside, a noisy crush at the counter – arms waving, sixpences and shillings and half-crowns held up – and Maggie May blessing herself and twitching at her cardigan and doing her best to please everyone.

'Maggie, four. Maggie, four.'

'Six. Six here, Maggie.'

'One, Maggie dear.'

'Give me the money, Betty. I'll get them.'

'No. I'll get them.'

'Twelve, Maggie.'

'Twelve, Maggie, please.'

'Maggie, four. Maggie, four.'

'Seven, Maggie, seven.'

'I'm hoarse calling you, Maggie Maggie Maggie.'

'Here you are, Maggie, the money for five.'

'There's just four left.'

'Four here, Maggie, four, Maggie, four.'

'Here, Maggie!'
'One, Maggie.'
'Three, Maggie, two, Maggie, Maggie, Maggie.'
'One Maggie, Maggie one.'
'Maggie dear, gimme the last one.'
'Oh Maggie.'
'Oh shite!'

Joe Scully's wrinkled blue Ford van, backed up on the footpath outside the parochial hall, tells us that the pictures will be on tonight. Joe is devil-may-care and 'too good-looking for his own good'. The posters he has on display around the town say EVERY WEDNESDAY AT 8 P.M. SHARP, but more than once the only entertainment on offer at 8 p.m. sharp was Corner Jim reading from a telegram to the people waiting on the footpath: 'Can't make it Stop Mechanical fault Stop Sorry Stop Joe Scully Stop'.

'The drink is his downfall,' Jellybob says. 'Thon man could make a fortune if he only steadied himself.'

One night Joe got the reels mixed up. He put on the third reel after the first one, but didn't discover his mistake until all the bad guys had been shot and the hero was riding into the sunset, with his girlfriend side-saddle in front of him on the horse.

When the next reel came on, all the bad guys were alive again and rustling away like mad and they beat up the hero and tied him and gagged him and threw him down a well.

Everyone was very confused, and the longer it went on, the more confused we got. But the worst of all was much later when the hero's cattle were grazing on the prairie and it was getting dark and the moon came out and the cattle began to lie down for the night. And that was the end.

Tonight the picture is *Gentleman Jim* and is all about boxing.

Ferdia saw the trailer last week and says it will be 'great stuff'.

On our way up the hall Betty and myself look across to the platform, where Joe usually works on the projector, getting everything ready for the show. Beside him tonight a chubby blonde woman moves jauntily from one foot to the other in perfect time with the record which is playing:

> Can you tell me where she's gone, where she's gone?
> She had lipstick and a garish costume on,
> She was wearing dancing shoes
> And her hair was flying loose,
> Can you tell me, can you tell me where she's gone?

Her earrings, flashing with the movement, scatter around broken rainbow beams of light; thrown loosely about her shoulders is a bright red headsquare. Aunt Laura! Or is it Aunt Laura? When we turn to go over to her, she quickly looks away. We don't know what to do and Betty bumps into me when I suddenly change direction. Red with embarrassment, we traipse up the hall to our seats.

'It's definitely Aunt Laura,' Betty confirms, looking back to check.

'But why did she pretend not to see us?'

'Maybe she didn't know us.'

'She must have known us . . . Don't be staring.'

'It's definitely Aunt Laura.'

Going out, we catch a glimpse of Aunt Laura's blonde head and sparkling silver earrings, but she has moved in behind the projector and has her back to us.

'Mama. Guess who was at the pictures? Aunt Laura.'

'Aunt Laura?'

'She was helping Joe Scully when we went in.'

'Are you sure it was Aunt Laura?'

'It was.'

'Were you talking to her?'

'She never spoke to us.'

'She didn't see us.'

'She did so.'

Dada, who has been listening and casting worried glances from Mama to Betty and myself, can no longer hold back. 'Now, what did I tell you?'

'Shhh. Not at all. It couldn't be Aunt Laura.'

'It was definitely Aunt Laura.'

'Maybe she'll come in.'

'She won't come in,' Dada says.

Demolishing the old school was an easy job and for the past few days Barney from Trá Gheal and Jellybob have been busy in the school yard making blocks. Barney shovels the gravelly mixture of rough sand and cement into the mould, which is open at the top and bottom; Jellybob packs in the concrete, smoothing it by drawing a float of timber across the top and finally lifting off the mould. The blocks are left where they sit for a few days until they have hardened, then stacked at the end of the yard. People passing ramble in to see what's going on, sometimes trying to slag Jellybob.

'Are yous building a house or what?'

'A hall.'

'A dancehall?'

'That's what we're at.'

'Oh, this is Jamie's new hall. I heard the rumour but I didn't think he would go ahead with it. Going to cost a quare penny, I'd say.'

'It'll cost a quare penny, true enough.'

'Just shows you: there's money in the booze.'

'Money in the booze.'

'When'll it be up?'

'Hard to say. A year or so, I suppose.'

'At the rate you fellas are going it could take for ever.'

'You're in a hurry to see it finished.'

'No hurry in the world. I don't know where's the need for a second hall. The parochial hall done us all this time.'

'Will you dance in it?'

'The new hall?'

'Maybe you'll get a woman for yourself.'

'Go way ourra that!'

'If you got a woman out of it, you mightn't have so many complaints.'

'Go on with you, Jellybob.'

While Jellybob's back is turned, Barney whistles at any girls that pass and calls after them.

'Quit, I'm telling you,' Jellybob warns him, 'before you get us a bad name.'

'It's only for the gas.'

'Even so. You know the way people talk. They'll be saying there's two boyos making blocks in the old school yard and they're mad after the women. The next thing is Jane'll hear it.'

Barney holds back for a while, but when he sees Mary McBrien in a flowery, short-sleeved summer dress, wheeling her bicycle up the hill, he can't bear to keep quiet.

'Mary! Mary! Come here.'

'What is it?'

'Come here.'

'What do you want?'

'Take your time.'

'I'm taking my time ... What have you to say?'

'There's something wrong with your bicycle.'

'What's wrong with it?'

'The wheels are going round.'

'You're very smart.'

'Hold on a minute.'

'Let go of my bike!'

'We're making blocks.'

'I can see that.'

'Barney! Come back here and top up this mould. You left it only half-filled.'

'Take your time, Mary. We're busy making blocks.'

'You're not all that busy.'

'Do you know how many we have made?'

'One and all the rest.'

'McGinley, come here I'm telling you!'

'I'm coming. Hold on you, Mary.'

'For what?'

'Do you go to the pictures?'

'An odd time.'

'There's a good one on next Wednesday: *Down Mexico Way* – Gene Autry and Smiley Burnett.'

'Will you get back here on the job before I give you a good kick in the behind?'

'Goodbye.'

'Hold on you, Mary.'

'Goodbye.'

A crowd of children in their Sunday best, smirking and giggling, follows Mrs Ned Mary down the street after second mass. She wears a black hat with a black veil over her face and a long, black dress which reaches to her ankles. This is the New Look. From behind the curtains we watch the comical procession: Mrs Ned Mary saintly solemn, as if she is coming from communion, which indeed she is, while the children mimic her stately walk from a safe distance.

'Easy for her to be in the height of fashion: hasn't to lift a finger from morning till night.'

At last the bar has been locked up and we sit back in Hackney Hill's car ready to take off for Uncle Mick's, when Dada suddenly reaches for the door handle and steps out again on to the footpath.

'What are you rushing for now? Take your time.'

Dada unlocks the bar door and we can hear him foostering around in the dark.

'Always in a mad rush. What is that man thinking about at all?'

'Can you fit this in the back?' Dada reappears with a three dozen case of stout. 'They'll have a bigger welcome for us now.'

As soon as the engine is switched off in Uncle Mick's yard we hear the hi-diddle-di of the fiddles and the heavy stamping and sliding of feet on the flagstone floor. A gust of hot smoky air, which mists over my glasses, swirls out the kitchen door at us from where the dancing is in full swing.

'Welcome back sweet Caroline to Carolina town,' Aunt Sally greets us, shaking hands. Uncle Mick clears a path for Dada through the swinging couples and the case of stout is carried in procession to the lower bedroom, Uncle Neddy, Aunt Sally and Dawson taking up the rear.

'Stay where yous are until I bring yous down a cup o' tea.' Aunt Sally's broad smile of welcome still capers around her eyes.

'Mick, have you such a thing as a corkscrew? I'm after forgetting to bring one,' Dada admits.

Uncle Mick turns to Dawson: 'Have you a corkscrew, Dawson?'

'Where would *I* get a corkscrew?'

'Damn it to hell, break the neck, use a bliddy knife or something!' Uncle Neddy splutters.

'Wait a minute. You'll be drinking broken glass and corks and everything.'

'Christ almighty, has nobody a corkscrew!' Uncle Neddy is staring down at the case of stout as if he is ready to swallow bottles and all.

'Well, you're a smart man, surely. I told you to take your time.'

'No harm done. We'll sort it out – won't we, men?'

'I think young Hayes has a penknife,' Dawson says.

'Maybe there's a corkscrew on the end of it.'

'Where is he? Get him down here to hell!' Uncle Neddy slams open the bedroom door. 'Hayes! Paddy! Come here! PADDY!'

Young Hayes sidles into the bedroom, the sweat pouring off him, looking as if he has been caught doing something he should be ashamed of.

'Have you a penknife?'

'A penknife?'

'You have a penknife, Paddy.'

'I have.'

'Is there a corkscrew on it?'

'A corkscrew?'

'A bliddy corkscrew – for pulling bliddy corks! Dammit to hell, man! Show us . . . We're saved!'

'Give the man a drink.'

Mama, Betty and myself have eased ourselves on to the bed I used to sleep in when I was on holidays a few years back; Dada and Uncle Mick sit on the big double bed where Sean and Maura were born. Uncle Neddy stands by the window with Dawson and young Hayes, three heads nodding back and forward, slurping greedily from the bottlenecks and burping.

'Here yous are. Can yous manage there at all?' Aunt Sally squeezes into the room, with tea and currant cake on a

'Guinness Is Good For You' tray, which Dada gave her at Christmas. Through the open doorway we can hear someone being asked to sing in the kitchen.

'Come on, Hudie.'

'Good man, Hudie. Rise it!'

'Quiet! Quiet!'

'Come on, Hudie. "The Girl from Donegal".'

Silence falls gradually, until the sods on the hearth can be heard sizzling – a silence that stretches, and stretches.

'Hudie . . . Come on!'

'Come on, Hudie.'

'Come on, McGee!'

'Give the man space.'

'Give him a chance.'

'Shhh . . .'

'Shhhhh . . .'

At last Hudie clears his throat. 'I'll sing later on,' he announces.

There is a murmur of disappointment – and the fiddles are away stringing out another tune.

'Will yous come up for a dance? "The Siege of Ennis". Come on' – Aunt Sally leads us on to the floor.

'Will you have a dance, Cassy?' Dada puts an arm on Mama's shoulder.

'Are *you* crazy!'

'Will you not join in?'

'Do you want us to be trampled to death! We'll watch.'

Dada stands beside Mama and the four of us move back against the wall. Uncle Mick and Aunt Sally are sucked into the swirling, sweltering whirlpool of dancers, side-stepping, swinging and bumping; Aunt Sally covers a lot of ground, moving with broad hopping steps, drawing Uncle Mick after her. In and out the dancers weave, stooping and straightening up, the bobbing lines opening and closing and opening again, advancing in sweaty waves from wall to wall. The two fiddlers sweep the tune along with short flicks of the bow, sing-low, sing-high, sing-high, sing-low, over and over again until everyone on the floor is dizzy and breathless.

Dada winks at the musicians and places two bottles of stout at their feet. Uncle Mick has given the tip-off to some of his pals and they follow him to the lower bedroom. The girls huddle together talking and laughing shyly; the men, some of them Brylcreemed, pass cigarettes; more tea, more talk, more dancing. The bedroom door squeaks open and shut; a few times the dog tries to make his way to the hearth, each time he gets stood on and slinks from the kitchen squealing.

'Time for a song.'

'Hudie.'

'Come on, Hudie.'

'Good man, Hudie.'

'Quiet! Shhh! Shhhhh!'

'Dawson. Come on! A recitation.'

Hudie closes his eyes and begins in a high-pitched voice 'The Girl from Donegal', but Dawson has also started and forges ahead with his recitation regardless:

> When the British Empire's crumbling and there's
>   havoc everywhere,
> And the houses are all tumbling and the streets in disrepair,
> Who will bolster up the nation, cover in each
>   widening chink?
> Who will fill the gaping craters? Who do you think?
>
> When the power lines are sparking and the gas about
>   to blow,
> And the water mains is leaking, who's the sucker
>   down below?

When the sewer is overflowing and we're swooning with
   the stink,
Who's the sod that's got to clear it? Who do you think?

As the building rises higher, many lose their
   climbing nerve,
Only certain men will venture where the planks
   unsteady swerve,
Where the scaffolding's so shaky that it's suicide to blink,
Who's the spider on the catwalk? Who do you think?

We work holydays and Sundays, a thing we oughtn't do,
We get overtime a plenty and danger money too,
We smoke our fags, we back the nags, on Saturday
   we drink,
We're all so blinkin' busy that we haven't time to think.

For the past while Ferdia has been complaining of a pain in his
right leg. The Jubilee nurse wrapped a tight bandage around his
knee but it stayed on only a day and now Ferdia is limping
slightly. 'I think it's growing pains,' his granny said to him;
'you'll be better before you get married.'

So many people talking to Dada about the new hall and wishing
him the best has put him in great humour.
   'The sooner it's up the better, Jamie. Prices are only going
to soar.'
   'It's badly needed; sure, the old hall is a disgust to the town.'
   'Somewhere for the young people to go besides heading off
for Dunkineely every Sunday night.'
   'It took yourself to think of it, Jamie. You're after stealing a
march on the rest of them.'
   The blocks have all been made and stacked at the end of the
school yard, waiting for Dada to decide on a builder – whether

to get Bertie Hicks or someone from outside.

'We'll give the first dance for parochial purposes – that way the clergy won't be annoyed. You have to keep in with the clergy. And I'll open on Saint Patrick's night – the best night in the year. They'll come from all over to see the new hall. There's a big population on all sides of us; it won't be able to hold half of them. I should make enough the first night to nearly clear the roof – which is going to be the single most expensive item.'

'I thought you were giving the first night to the priest?'

'Oh. So I am. Then we'll open some other night. Doesn't matter what night you open, you'll get a full house anyway. We'll keep Saint Patrick for again.'

'And what are you going to call it?'

'I dunno. Just The Hall, I suppose.'

'It has to have a name, hasn't it?'

'Oh – well – we'll call it – The Roseland Ballroom.'

'What sort of a name is that?'

'It's a dancehall me and Paddy used to go to in New York – The Roseland Ballroom.'

'That's no sort of a name. If you want to have any luck you should call it after some saint: Saint Colmcille or Saint Brigid or Saint Patrick.'

'Saint Patrick, then.'

'Saint Colmcille is the Donegal saint.'

'Saint Patrick's Ballroom – that's what it'll be called.'

'God save us the day and the night, Jamie, you couldn't put up with thon woman. As you know, I took her in out of pity. Her house is falling down around her and anyway I thought it would be cheaper for the two of us living together. Well, I didn't get a day's peace or a night's rest since she arrived. First thing she does is plonk herself in my cosy chair at the fire and no matter how many times I remind her, that's where she heads as soon as her feet hit the kitchen floor in the morning. Another thing: she won't sleep only on the outside of the bed, next the hearth. And she's in and out all night to the po. When I wake up in the dark there's not a stitch of clothes on me, as the fella says; she has everything wrapped tight around her, sheets and blankets, as snug as a baby in the cradle. And in the morning the bed is full of ashes and sparks. I open my eyes in a cloud of smoke. The same when I'm going asleep at night. She's propped up against the bolster, with that oul' broken bit of a clay pipe stuck in her gob and her puffing away like a steamroller. I'm scared out of my wits that the both of us will be burned to a cinder some night and not one to bury us itself. "It'll have to stop," I said to her; "this can't go on." We had a wee fallin' out over the jam as well. She'd eat a half-pot o' blackberry jam in the day if she thought she could get away with it. The other thing is my belongings. Anything she takes a fancy to, she'll swipe for herself. She won't show her nose outside the door unless she has my good blackthorn stick helping her along – or my pixie or my shawl. "You'll have to keep your hands off my things," I said to her. "You have your own things and that should be enough for you." Well, you ought to hear the givin' out of her. She has a temper like a wildcat – what she didn't say to me, glory be to God! She was puce in the face with vexation. Then the packin' started: every stitch o' clothes belonging to her went into the bundle and away with her. She wasn't gone a half-hour till she was knocking on the back door. Her house was damp, her bed was damp, her chair was damp, and she would get her death of cold if I didn't take pity on her. I'm stuck with her now, Jamie, and I don't know from Adam what to do. I can't get a heat of the fire with her huddled over it all day; I can't get a wink o' sleep, and at the rate she's going she'll have me eaten out the door before the winter is half over. God save us the day and the night, I didn't realise how well off I was when I was single, as the fella says.'

'Tom Tim is after going into Maggie May's again. There's nothing surer than the'll be a wedding there yet.'

'Oh then, she's hard up if she marries Tom Tim.'

'What are you talking about! Nothing wrong with Tom Tim.'

'Big lazy lump, that's all he is. Never did a hand's turn in his life.'

'Tom is fond of his comfort all right.'

'He's surely looking for a soft seat – glad to get out of the Hill, I suppose.'

'What are you talking about! The happiest days I ever spent were spent in the Hill. They could be as happy as Larry the two of them.'

'Provided Maggie does all the work.'

'Tom won't exert himself too much, that's true. I remember one day my father, the Lord rest him, sent me over to Tom's for the loan of a spade. Tom had no idea where the spade was. I didn't want to hurt his feelings so I let him search for a while – and all the time I could see the spade winking down at us from the rafters. That's where his father used to keep it. Since the day old Johnny died, the spade was never touched. It's the only fault Tom has – a wee bit lazy. He's an innocent sort of a man.'

'He's a big fat lazybones, good for nothing. Máire told us all about him.'

'What did she tell you?'

'She told me that it's all hours before he gets out of bed. When his mother was alive – poor old thing would be milking the cow and feeding the pig, and Tom would still be snoring away.'

'Tom was spoiled from he was a young fella. That's the way with the only child.'

★   ★   ★

Mama lays her prayerbook and her brown suede gloves on the windowsill after coming in from benediction before turning to us: 'Ferdia has polio.'

'Ah, the poor cratur.'

'What's polio?'

'It's not good.'

'I always liked Ferdia,' Dada says from the top of the table, 'he's a manly wee fella.'

'Will he be all right?'

'Sure, Conor, he'll be all right.'

But I know from the way Mama speaks that she doesn't mean it.

Budget Day and another ha'penny on the stout.

'What are we going to do? Sevenpence ha'penny. We'll be all day searching for change. Eight pence would be a sensible price. But we'll have to wait and see how the rest of them are going to handle the situation. When I started trading, the farthings were still on the go. Now even the ha'pennies are on the way out.'

The first customer to appear the day we put the price up is the Duck, who calls for a bottle of stout. He lays out seven pennies on the counter as if he hasn't heard.

'Another ha'penny, I'm afraid.'

'Another ha'penny! Sevenpence ha'penny for a bottle o' stout! That's going beyond the beyonds. Nobody'll be wetting their whistle after this.'

'Ah what are you complaining about! Aren't you getting value for money?'

'Value!'

'Sure, you're getting value. It never reached its price. Never will.'

★ ★ ★

'Michael Jordan just asked me if we'd give him lodgings?'

'Close the door.'

'He's waiting in the bar for my answer.'

'Michael Jordan is fly. There's something after happening between himself and Groarty's.'

'What do you think is after happening?'

'I wonder.'

'What?'

'I didn't see Sally Groarty in a long time.'

'Did you hear some rumour?'

'I'm just putting two and two together.'

'I thought you would be delighted to keep him. We have a room lying idle above –'

'If he asked us in the beginning, it would be a different matter. But now?'

'Putting two and two together: what do you mean?'

'Well, you're the innocent man . . . Conor, go out and play.'

'Go on. Do what your mother tells you.'

'I don't think we should have anything to do with Michael Jordan . . .'

'Jamie, I'm after being up in Maggie May's. Who do you think is sitting in front of the fire, his legs stretched out, drawing his pipe?'

'Tom Tim?'

'The very man. Maggie was out the back when I went in. "Shop, Maggie! Shop!" Tom calls out to her.'

'He'll make a fine shopkeeper, Tom. A fine post master.'

'Last week I brought Maggie in a cart load of turf and afterwards she was blessing herself and making tea for me. Sitting at the head of the table was Tom, with an empty plate in front of him – after polishing off a big feed. "Have you more pie there, Maggie?" says he. "More pie!" '

'Oh that would be Tom all right.'

'I hadn't time to get a bite into my mouth before Tom was clamouring, "More pie there, Maggie! More pie!"'

Passing the forge on my way home from school, Scunsey follows me and speaks in a low voice: 'Sally Groarty is dead.'

'Sally Groarty! She couldn't be!'

'She is. She died this morning. Everybody is crying about her.'

'What happened to her?'

'I'm not sure, but . . .'

'What?'

'I think she had a baby.'

A few nights later in the bar the men are talking.

'It shouldn't have happened.'

'No, it shouldn't have happened. Imagine, the mother never let her outside the door. How could she hope to cover up a thing like that?'

'Hard as nails, that's Big Sarah.'

'Wee Groarty is heartbroken over it. I didn't know what to say when I met him. After a while he started talking about it himself. They didn't realise a thing till the last minute. She hid it from them completely, he said. But I have my doubts about that.'

'They say she asked them to send for the doctor – but the mother wouldn't hear tell of it. She died without the doctor or the priest.'

> I have seen you in the chapel,
> Solemnly you knelt to pray;
> But my prayers were all confusion,
> Melanie, O Melanie!

Then I heard of your elopement,
Can I credit what they say?
Silently you left one morning,
Melanie, O Melanie!
Left without a word of warning
In the stillness of the morning,
Melanie, O Melanie!

'Dada, have a look at this!'
'What is it?'
'Look!'
Dada has just divided a Sweet Afton in two; he puts one half of the cigarette back in the packet and lights the other half before joining Mama at the kitchen window, towering over her.
'Keep your head down or he'll see you' – Mama tugs at his jacket.
'Tom Tim. What about him?'
Tom is driving his cow up the street as he does every evening. The cow looks bloated after a day's grazing and Tom ambles behind her in easy step with the cow's slow wobble.
'Isn't he a real laughing stock? You would think it was a funeral he was following.'
'Tom likes to take life easy.'
'He's after putting on a stone weight since he got married – at least a stone.'
Tom's loud lazy drawl calls across to Con Moylan standing in the doorway: 'Heavy kind of a day, Con.'
'It is then. It looks like thunder.'
'Aye. It's close enough for that.'
The black polly cow casts a sideways glance at Tom and turns around by our gable of her own accord, Tom following at a distance, puffing his pipe.

'Isn't it a wonder Maggie wouldn't try to shake him up? He looks as if he's asleep on his feet – and the cow roaring her head off every morning, begging to be milked.'

'What you're looking at there is the happiest man in Ireland.'

'The laziest man, you mean.'

'Tom Tim hasn't a contrary thought in his head. He milks his cow, he drives her to and from the field – and his day's work is done. Maggie does all the rest.'

Jenny Scotchie's sunny spurts of laughter fill the kitchen and ring around the house. She is spending her first holiday since the war with her cousins, the Monaghans, and calls on us whenever she comes into the town. Jenny is tall, with long dark hair shaped in a fringe across her forehead. Her mouth is broad and full of spittle and when she laughs her fleshy upper gums show over her large even teeth. She wears stylish clothes and shoes, and a pair of ebony earrings. The earrings are from Spain – two tiny castanets clacking from each ear.

'My father gave them to me; he used to never come home without something, he was in the merchant navy; his ship was one of the first to be sunk by the Germans. We were expecting him home on leave and we got word that he'd been torpedoed. It was terrible. I tried to not let it get the better of us, but my mother never got over it . . . I work at home. Dressmaking. I'll never be rich, I'm afraid, but so long as we have enough to get by I'm happy . . . No, indeed, I have no sweetheart. And no sign of one either. . . Why *wouldn't* I marry an Irishman when my father and mother were Irish? I'd be more than a match for any Irishman.'

'Jenny would make a great wife for Claddagh,' Dada says later. 'She has a notion of him, too, I think.'

Mama agrees: 'Did you see the way she changed her mind about going to the dance. She came in all bangles and earrings, jangling like a pony – but when she saw Claddagh wasn't going she sat in the kitchen all night.'

'Claddagh'll never get married.'

'If he's not married already. I always think he has the look of a married man about him.'

'Not at all. Claddagh is as free as the four winds.'

The sideways sweep of the bus around the last downward turn into Killybegs brings the ocean into sudden view, the ravenous seagulls diving and squealing, and, across the bay, the old industrial school, red in the clear morning light. I feel conspicuous carrying my fiddle case through the town but it is too early yet to go in to Mr Hart for my music lesson.

In the shallow inlet, where the pier begins, a scuttled rowboat lies on its side, its fishing days far behind it. A stout copper-skinned man looks down at the boat, his pudgy hands joined on top of the cement wall. Across the street Peadar Bawn is buttoning his overcoat outside Rogers' hotel. It is Saturday and the only fisherman in sight sits cross-legged on the old wooden pier stitching up a net. The net stretches across the full width of the pier, so that to get by I have to walk across it.

'Watch where you're walking, sonny.'

'Sorry.'

'I don't mean the net – but the pier. It's in pretty poor shape.'

I go past him, picking my steps over the loose shrunken planks; between them I can see down into the dark slick of water, which is the colour of squashed caterpillars. On each side the rust-stained trawlers nudge against the bulwarks and the air has a sour, fishy smell. At least there is no one here to stare at me. To pass the time I sit on an upturned fish box, my fiddle case across my knees, idly scanning from shore to horizon, from headland to headland, and like so many times at Trá Gheal, soon lost in the mystery of the ever-changing, never-changing sea...

Heading back up the town, I pass three empty barrels waiting for collection outside the hotel. More empties in the square and several rows of stout barrels and salt barrels on the platform of the railway station. The day of my first music lesson Mr Hart had looked out the window at this sight:

'Killybegs, barrels and kegs,
Kilcar for making *báinín*,
Carrick town is broken down
And Glen's not worth a *tráinin*.

Did you ever hear that rime?'

'I did.'

A torch-beam of sunlight points into the open hall door of Mr Hart's house; I go up the linoleum-covered stairs to the music room, with its empty marble fireplace and Collingwood piano. Mr Hart's son works in the bar below, which is out of bounds for Mr Hart.

The sound of me practising the scale brings Mr Hart from the bedroom. He is in his shirt sleeves, trying to button on his collar:

'Early to bed and early to rise
Makes a man healthy, wealthy and wise.

Did you ever hear that?'

'Yea.'

'Say the space notes for me.'

'F – A – C – E.'

'And what are the line notes? . . . You've forgotten. Do you remember the rime I gave you?'

'Every Good Boy Deserves Fags.'

'So?'

'E – G – B – D – F.'

'Now the scale of C. Go ahead. Play away there.'

During the scale, Mr Hart disappears into the kitchen, from where I can hear him clattering with the delph and coughing. He returns, a cigarette dangling from the corner of his mouth.

'Play it again, Sam.'

Mr Hart's cheeks are yellow and sunken and his hands shake as he struggles to fasten his cuff links.

'Stop! Stop! You're resting the fiddle on your wrist again. Forget everything you were taught by the traditional crowd. Put it out of your mind. You're starting again from scratch – literally from scratch. So hold the fiddle with your chin, the way I showed you. *That* way your hand is free to move up and down the fingerboard. Any other way and you're stuck in the one diddly-i position all your life. I think the kettle is boiling. Play away there – the scale of C – and watch your intonation.'

I bow my way from the fourth to the second string, steel to gut and gut to steel until my neck feels more and more of the weight, and the neck of the fiddle gets closer and closer to collapsing on my wrist.

'You need a new fiddle.' Mr Hart comes in with a mug of steaming tea held shakily in front of him. 'You've outgrown your instrument.' He is fully dressed now but his bushy white hair still has the toss of the bed on it. 'Tell your father a new fiddle will cost around eight pounds. I'll get one for you in Sligo. Now, start again. Fiddle under your chin. Take away your hand. You should be able to support the fiddle between your chin and your shoulder. Don't be afraid, it won't fall. Even if it does it'll be no great loss.'

I am wondering if Mr Hart is a bit tipsy, but it is too early in the day for that. His wife, who comes from Glengreeny, lives downstairs in her own quarters and they never speak or meet. Mrs Hart is a narrow-shouldered, skinny woman who always dresses in black. She has sworn that the day Mr Hart dies she will wear a red feather in her hat.

★　★　★

In the grocery with Mama, Aunt Sally wipes her eyes, which are red and puffy from crying over Uncle Mick: 'He's in bed nearly a week and he's not improving any.'

'Did you get the doctor for him?'

'He won't hear tell of a doctor. He'd never speak to me again if I brought a doctor into the house.'

'What's wrong, Sally?' Dada stops at the grocery door.

'It's Mick; he has congestion of the lungs.'

'Well, sure, many a person had congestion.'

'If you heard the coughs of him. He can't draw his breath and every day it's weaker he's getting. I just don't know where to turn.'

Mama looks to Dada. 'We'll go up to see him this evening, Dada.'

'Yea. OK.'

'I'll make a poultice and we'll put it on his chest. He'll be all right.'

'Dry your tears, Sally' – Dada puts an arm around Aunt Sally – 'there's years left in thon man.'

'Oh, I hope you're right.'

'What age is he, anyway?'

'I don't know what age he is and that's the truth. He would never tell me his age.'

'Fly man,' Dada laughs.

'I'm wondering if I shouldn't write to Sean and Maura. They'd be wild upset if anything happened to their father and them so far away.'

'Write to them anyway. They'll want to know how he is.'

'Oh Waidean! What am I going to do? If anything happens to Mick I'll be lost.'

'Are you going to join us?' Con Moylan turns towards Jenny Scotchie, who has stopped to look in the kitchen door.

'Will I be disturbing you?'

'Not in the slightest' – Old Con sits closer to Claddagh on the long seat.

Jenny steps down into the kitchen, almost missing the step, and laughs nervously; she sits at the head of the table, opening her green swagger coat, which is buttoned to the neck.

'Will you have a drink, Jenny?' Claddagh asks.

'Och I dunno.'

'Go on. Have something.'

'I'll have a wee sherry then.'

Claddagh has had two or three drinks already, otherwise it would be ages before he would make so free with Jenny.

A few evenings before this, Jenny had come in early. As the evening wore on and there was no sign of Claddagh she delayed – talking to Mama, flicking through the *St Anthony's Annals*, listening to Victor Sylvester on the radio, until about a half-hour before the ten o'clock bus was due she left so as not to miss it. 'She's hoping to find Claddagh in Ned Mary's,' Mama said, 'but I could have told her he never goes near Ned Mary's.'

After another drink Old Con starts teasing Claddagh: 'You're looking for a wife, aren't you, Dan?'

Claddagh forces a smile and pours what is left of the bottle into his glass.

'I heard you were looking for a wife – and that you would prefer a Scotchwoman to any other nationality under the sun.'

Claddagh avoids Jenny's eyes. She smiles across at the two men, little specks of spittle bubbling in the corner of her mouth.

'Too late now to get married,' Claddagh says.

'Too late? Not at all, man; you're never too late. What do you think, Jenny?'

'I'm sure Dan would make a fine husband – but I'm afraid he's spoiled having his own way all this length of time.'

'Now, Dan, do you hear that? You're spoiled from being on your own.'

'You get tired being on your own,' Claddagh answers.

Jenny hasn't taken her eyes off Claddagh; she looks as if she would like to have a heart-to-heart talk with him.

'If you're tired on your own, then you know the remedy,' Con says.

Claddagh laughs it off and washes it down with a long drink of stout.

We hear the ten o'clock bus throbbing outside Ned Mary's, every so often missing a beat – but Jenny never moves. Later, when they are all leaving, she says she will have to get Hill to drive her home.

'I'll be down the town with you,' Claddagh offers. He holds back to let Jenny through the hall door before him; Jenny hesitates and they both end up stuck in the doorway. Claddagh has put his arm around Jenny and suddenly he pulls her closer and hugs her. Jenny hugs him back. For a moment they are pressing together, arms around each other, faces almost touching. Old Con doesn't see any of this because he is already halfway across the street to his own house. They are all a little tipsy.

'You haven't half enough clothes on you, Conor. I got a new vest for you and a nice warm pair of knickers.'

'Knickers are for girls.'

'It doesn't matter; they'll keep you warm.'

'I don't want any girls' things.'

'Put them on you now and do what Mama tells you, that's the good boy. You need all the clothes you can get, going round the Rock, otherwise you'll catch your death of cold.'

'I don't want any knickers.'

'Do what you're told now, Conor. Mama knows best.'

★ ★ ★

Something has gone wrong with Dada's plans for the new hall. The subject is never mentioned any more and when someone brings it up Dada's face freezes over before he says, 'We'll have to see. There's not all that much money floating around.' I wonder if the banker might have put his frown on it. 'He's only a wee snatch-penny,' Dada says. 'You'd think he owns the town; probably does too. Four pubs all scrambling for the same few pounds and each of us marvelling how the other three manage to survive.'

Yesterday evening Dada was up on the ladder, clearing the eave shoots, when Tom Tim crossed the street with his cow.

'Did you give over the idea of the hall, Jamie?' Tom shouted, broadcasting his question to the whole town.

Dada scowled down at him. 'We'll have to see. There's not all that much money in circulation.'

'There's not, Jamie. Maggie was saying the very same thing. Even the weans haven't their pennies and their ha'pennies for the butterscotch. We thought when Hitler was done for we'd all be rolling in pound notes. Do you know, there was more business during the war?'

'It wasn't any slacker, anyway.' Dada came down two steps of the ladder.

'It wasn't. Maggie was telling me she couldn't keep sweets with them. She wouldn't have the jar o' brandy balls opened till it would be empty. Now there's several jars standing idle on the shelf, puffed up to the neck with brandy balls and toffees and what not and divil a one bothering about them. Ah well, I'm sure there'd be a lot o' trouble too with a dancehall.'

'A lot o' headaches.'

'And a lot of expense to get it launched. Where's my cow gone?'

'She went around the gable; she knows her way home at this stage' – Dada begins to climb back up the ladder.

'Only the last leg of it. No matter how many times I bring her up and down the street, she'd never chance it on her own. Funny. They're lazy animals cows; you have to do everything for them. The dog, now, will look after itself – and the cat – they'll always find their way home.' Tom is puffing his pipe and has his usual contented grin spread across his face like shaving cream. 'Well, I better go. Maggie'll have the sausages frying for me. Good luck, Jamie.'

'Good luck, Tom.'

Dada, Betty and myself have stopped to rest on the big level flagstone above the old school yard; Dada talks about his mother: 'She reared seven of us; did her best for us all on very little – and she was expecting her eighth. I was hired out with Kerrigan at the time. I was after coming in from milking the cows when I got word to go home immediately. I slung my boots over my shoulder and took the nearcut across the mountain. On the way I met Tommy coming to tell me that our mother died that morning, and the baby died with her. The two of us sat down on a stone and we cried our fill.'

At the side of the stove Claddagh sits with a vacant look in his eyes, his glass of stout gone flat from neglect. Is he thinking of Jenny Scotchie and all the laughing they had together and how she won't be calling tonight or any other night?

'You'll be back next year, Jenny?' Mama had said to her on her last night.

'Och God knows. A year is a long time.'

Claddagh was sitting in Dada's place at the head of the table with the *Independent* opened out in front of him, taking everything in, but he never raised his eyes or said a word.

He is probably wondering where Jenny is now and what she

is doing. I often wonder about Aisling, where she is in her house and if she ever thinks of me.

Harris's van has arrived with the Christmas stuff and Harris's man is checking over the items on the counter with Dada. It is the one time in the year when Dada buys in sweets, which he puts in the Christmas parcels for the families that have children. Betty and myself always get a fistful to divide between us.

'Are you forgetting something, Jamie?' Harris's man asks.

'Forgetting?' Dada casts his eye over the jar of sweets, Christmas cakes, spices, raisins and lemon peel. 'No. I don't think so.'

'What about Mick for Mick?'

'Oh.'

'The one tin o' Mick McQuaid tobacca for your brother-in-law.'

'Well – no – I won't be needing it this year.'

'Is he – not the best?'

'He's sick this last while. Congestion of the lungs. His smoking days are over.'

'Ah the poor cratur.'

'Yea. I don't think poor Mick is going to mend.'

Big trouble over the ring competition, which began in early October: a penny a throw, and the sealed wooden box of pennies has several customers' names scrawled across the sticky-paper seal over the lid. Dada has put prize night back as late as possible – the twenty-second of December – and whoever has the highest score then, gets the jackpot. Nearly all the players are regular customers – but a problem has arisen. In every other pub the Captain has won outright – and with just one throw. During the year he never shows his face except in Lambert's, then on prize night he strolls in, buys one bottle of stout, puts a penny in the box and clocks up the highest score.

'It's not right,' Mama says; 'he shouldn't be allowed in the competition.'

'How can I keep him out?'

'Tell him it's for regular customers only.'

'I can't do that.'

'Well, it's not fair to everyone else; poor craturs paying their pennies night after night and then this fly boy comes in and scoops the lot. It's a disgrace – and his wife a teacher and all. He shouldn't get away with it.'

On prize night the bar is crowded, everyone in a happy Christmas mood, yet when the Captain appears with his slick clean-shaven smile, all he gets back is a lot of empty stares like a stranger at a wake. He stands at the end of the counter on his own, rubbing his hands, orders a bottle of stout and flicks through the score book.

'I was just going to close it off,' Dada tells him.

The Captain picks a penny out of his change and drops it in the box as if it was a five pound note.

'You're going to have a go?'

'I'll have one go' – the Captain looks around at the blank gable of faces in front of him – 'let me stand or fall on that. Is that fair?'

'It's a free country,' Dada says.

'What have I to beat?' – the Captain looks again in the score book.

'You have me to beat,' Corner Jim pipes up, 'forty-three.'

'Forty-three, is it, Jim? I'll see what I can do.' The Captain has to reach across Crusoe's shoulder to get the rings from the counter. He turns one of them over in his hand, weighing it to get the feel of it. Nobody moves back to make room for him at the chalk line and he has barely space to raise his arms.

'Give the man a chance now' – Dada leans on the counter to watch – 'equal rights for everyone.'

Most people throw the rings from the waist upwards; the Captain shoots straight out from eye level as if he is firing from a gun – and his first ring lands on thirteen. The second lands on twelve, the third on eleven, the fourth on ten, the fifth on nine. Before he can throw the sixth ring somebody jostles him. He waits and points to the board.

'There's fifty-five there already. I'll try to hook another thirteen for the sport of it.' The Captain closes one eye and gets jostled again.

'Come on now. Give the man a chance,' Dada calls.

The ring shoots out, hits the thirteen, but bounces back off the board.

'Fifty-five' – Dada writes in the score book – 'keep the record official. Do you want another throw?... Does anyone want another throw?...'

Nobody wants another throw, least of all the Captain, who looks around, barely able to hold back the smirk of victory edging up from his tightly closed lips.

'All right' – Dada draws a line with a sweep across the page – 'that's it. Now the outright winner... I have all the highest scores here at the back. There's Captain Spearman with fifty-five' – Dada pauses but nobody cheers – 'there's Michael James with a hundred and ten –'

'Wait a minute!' the Captain interrupts.

Dada ignores him. 'And there's Jim with a hundred and seventeen – which is the highest.'

A big cheer goes up, though everyone seems mystified as to how these miraculous scores came about.

'Hold on you now,' the Captain protests. 'There has to be a mistake. The highest you can get in any throw is seventy-two

– and that's landing two rings on thirteen, twelve and eleven, which is next to impossible.'

'Highest of three throws,' Dada tells him.

'Three throws!'

'That's why I asked you if you wanted another throw.'

The Captain puts a hand in his pocket: 'I'll take another two throws then.'

'Too late now, Captain. The line is drawn. And the winner is Jim. A big hand for Jim.'

Uncle Harry and Aunt Laura have invited us to the last night of the play they are doing in Duhaigh school. Mama is in two minds about going: none of us has been in Duhaigh since Mama's row with Aunt Laura, though Uncle Harry continues to call on us whenever he visits Glengreeny.

'Why wouldn't you go?' Dada shrugs. 'Let bygones be bygones.'

In the play Uncle Harry and Aunt Laura are two old beggars who have lost their way in the hills. One is blind, the other is deaf, and every faltering step they take lands them on a slithery slope of arguments.

The school is packed and the laughing hardly stops from beginning to end.

Afterwards in the sitting room Uncle Harry has the bottle of Black & White on the coffee table between Dada and himself. Mama and Aunt Laura are being overpolite to each other, but from the look on Mama's face and the way her head is shaking nervously I know that an explosion could come any minute.

'Did you see how the stage was made, Jamie?' Uncle Harry asks Dada.

'I didn't pass any remarks.'

'Just some planks thrown across a few empty Guinness barrels. I was scared of my life all week that Guinness's man might call. We would have no stage – and worse, I might get no more stout either.'

'He's always on to me about the labels,' Dada says. 'All I ever label is the front row of bottles. "What have you in there behind?" says he to me. I took out two bottles – and the row behind was labelled as well – or it looked as if it was – but it was just two bottles. I label the front row and two bottles out of the row behind as well. I'm at it for years and he never tumbled to it yet.'

'He caught me so often that I have to label the lot now. You can't afford to fall out with him.'

'Wait till I tell you. One day he came in and Con Moylan was at the counter, dallying over a bottle of stout as usual. It takes Old Con nearly a half-hour to empty his glass. Of course, there was no label on the bottle. I could see your man glancing at it now and again but he didn't say anything. He didn't want to commit himself because the label could be on the side that was away from him. So I poured out what was left of the bottle to put it under the counter. While I had the bottle raised in the air he grabbed my hand. He still couldn't see the far side, but he was holding my wrist, looking me in the eye. I was sure the game was up. "Ah, you'll have to give me the benefit of the doubt an odd time," says I. He was still staring me – the big red Guinness face of him; the same boyo can fairly let it back himself. "Fair enough," says he, and he laughed.'

Aunt Laura still has on the make-up from the play: her eyebrows and her eyelashes are darkened with mascara and her cheeks are all rouged up. When she comes around with the teapot to fill Mama's cup, Mama looks her straight in the face.

Aunt Laura keeps her eyes on the spout.

Before we left home, Dada had warned Mama to say nothing to Aunt Laura. 'I won't say a word to her,' Mama promised, and so far – apart from 'Hello' – she hasn't. Dada also called Betty and myself up to the bar and told us to keep quiet about seeing Aunt Laura at the pictures.

'If she says she saw us, what?'

'If she says it herself, that's all right. But she won't. You're both to sing dumb about the pictures.'

'Why?'

'That's the why.'

'Does Uncle Harry not like Aunt Laura going to the pictures?'

'He sure doesn't.'

Around the table nobody says anything except Uncle Harry and Dada, who are enjoying themselves. Betty and myself work our way through the apple tart and biscuits, and Mama has her head held high, looking shakily in front of her at nothing in particular.

'Are yous all right there, dears? Are *you* all right, Cassy?'

Mama keeps looking ahead. She doesn't say anything, but nods a few times. The way Mama nods, it could mean anything.

Uncle Harry is telling about a dream he had: 'I had this awful fight with Laura – in the dream; I was never as mad in my life. I don't know what the fight was about, but I remember grabbing her by the throat and I was squeezing as hard as ever I could. She let out a scream – I thought my heart stopped beating – it was such a wild scream – and then I woke up and I had my hands closed tight around Laura's throat and she was screaming for me to let go of her.'

'I was screaming for my life, that's the truth,' Aunt Laura says.

Mama looks at Aunt Laura as much as to say, You'd be no great loss.

'I started to say an act of contrition. I really thought he was going to choke me.'

When Aunt Laura tops up Uncle Harry's glass he puts his arm around her waist. Uncle Harry is a little bit tipsy and draws Aunt

Laura closer to him. 'When I think what I nearly did – and she's the love of my life.' Uncle Harry glances at Mama. 'You're welcome to stay the night, Cassy. You can all stay. You're always welcome.'

'Sure we know that, Harry,' Dada says.

'You'll all stay the night; what do you say, Cassy?'

'We'll go home,' Dada says. 'Hill'll be here for us any minute.'

Corner Jim's legs dangle from the high stool at the bar as he tells Dada a story we have all heard several times already.

'I was standing outside the post office – to tell you the truth, Jamie, I was hoping that Maggie May would come out with a telegram so that I could earn a shilling for a smoke. The dole wasn't due till the morrow. I had exactly tuppence in my pocket when Pete Post handed me an envelope with my name written on it in type. It was a letter from an attorney in the States asking me if I was Jim Clear, the nephew of my Uncle Jim in Philadelphia, and, if I was, that he had fifteen thousand dollars for me. The old boy was after snuffing it and leaving a pile behind him. I brought the letter in to Maggie May to make sure I wasn't dreaming and I can tell you she blessed herself a good few times before she got to the end of it. "It looks as if I'll have to find a new telegram boy," says she. "That seems to be more or less the gist of it," says I. Last week I got the cheque. It's lodged in the Ulster Bank in Killybegs. Jamie, I'm set up for life.'

'You are if you watch yourself. I'll bet you weren't sober all that many days since?'

'No. Not all that many. But cripes, Jamie – a shilling now and a shilling again for telegrams! I'm due a wee celebration.'

'The time to spare the turf is when the creel is full.'

'I'll never see it spent.'

'You'll see it spent soon enough if you don't steady yourself.'

'Will you have something on me, Jamie? And give Conor a wee soda.'

'Well, seeing it's the occasion that's in it. But take my advice: spare the turf.'

Corner Jim throws out a crisp new ten shilling note on the counter. 'There's more where that came from.'

'Good luck to you, Jim.'

Corner Jim smiles and gives a fly wink. 'I'll never see it spent, Jamie – not if I live to the age of Mathusala.'

The sudden stark sunlight of early spring has turned to lighter blue both the sky and the sea glimpsed beyond the classroom window, and all morning I long to be in the open air.

At lunch time, stretched full length on the hillock above the school, the furious waves hurrying landward seem to lift me on their fleecy backs, surging all around, and I imagine myself floating on a raft, adrift and free at last from the rusty anchor of catechism.

Below me, resting on one elbow, Johnny Meehan half-turns to say something. He stops and stares, then takes a closer look up the leg of my trousers. 'Conor O'Donnell is wearing knickers!'

'No, I'm not.'

Johnny grabs me by the leg before I have time to bound away: 'He's wearing knickers! No coddin'. He's wearing knickers!'

The silence that follows seems to stretch as far as the horizon, filling the whole vault of heaven with its throbbing; the girls have stopped playing tig, everyone looks to where I feel myself sinking into a bottomless pit of shame. Suddenly the boys surge forward, crowding around me. I am held down kicking, while Johnny pulls up the leg of my trousers, bringing the hated pink knickers into full view.

'Conor O'Donnell is wearing knickers! Shame! Shame! Shame! Conor O'Donnell is wearing girls' knickers!'

The following morning I feel numb, sick with dread, and drag my feet all the way to Trá Gheal, so that the Meehans are gone on well ahead. At the turn which brings the schoolhouse into view I stop and lean on the wall, looking down to where the tide is drumming against the grey rocks far below. I look from the chilly grey depths to the schoolhouse and back again, not able to move a step further. Slowly the water bulges, rising towards me in a great blob, until the surface skin tears apart and the horrible dripping head of a horse bursts through, its eye sockets empty, bared teeth gnashing savagely. I turn and run like hell for home.

Is Willoughby in league with the devil?

Yesterday, the radio was on in the kitchen and in between addressing envelopes to The Black Babies, The Maynooth Mission to China, and St Vincent de Paul, Willoughby managed to carry on a muttered conversation through his moustache with the announcer. *Hospitals' Requests* was the next programme and he cocked his ear. He turned towards the radio and brought his mouth close to the loudspeaker. 'Give us "The Oul' Plaid Shawl",' he mumbled. The announcer paused for a moment: 'And now we'll have "The Oul' Plaid Shawl",' he announced. The only one who showed no surprise was Willoughby.

'We were known as the Winter Birds,' Dada tells Betty and myself. 'We only went to school from October to March. The rest of the time we were helping on the land. Oul' Master Brannigan used to be raging. "The Winter Birds are back again," he would say. "Where were yous all year?" Every one of us would be quaking. "On the land," we would say. "What land?" he would say. "Sure there's no land around here – only the moor and the hill and the black bog. Is that where you Winter Birds are going to build your nests?" he would say. "A hungry life you'll have of it." He was mad against the Irish as well. "Much good your Irish'll be to you when you're tramping the high roads of Scotland or America looking for work!" He was right.'

Going home from school the Meehan twins have again run on ahead leaving me on my own. The reason I know only too well and I have been thinking over what has to be done. Dragging my feet, I let the distance between us lengthen still further.

Beyond the graveyard a strangled thorn tree gropes its way out of an old tumbledown house. Once behind the crumbling stone walls I pull the hated pink horrors down over my shoes and kick them into the tangle of briars at the butt of the tree. To make sure they don't surface, waving from a prickly thorn branch, I roll a stone over on top of them. The job done, I feel like having a piddle. No need to say where.

A lot of talk about Corner Jim and how he is going around with a 'fancy woman' from Killybegs. She is much taller than Jim, very good-looking, but 'no chicken'. Regularly Jim hires Hackney Hill to drive him to Killybegs, where he spends the day drinking with the lassie in Rogers' hotel. Sometimes they go for a drive to Donegal or even further afield. Hill has a good laugh over it with Dada: ' "Where will it be today, Suzie?" Jim says to her. We were after picking her up outside Rogers' – handbag, gloves and all. "Were you ever in Belfast?" she says to Jim. "No, I wasn't," says he. "Were you?" "Never in my life," she says. "Why don't we give Belfast a turn then?" Jim says. Off we head for Belfast – but we didn't even get through Dunkineely before the two of them wanted to stop for a wee warmer-upper. Two brandies. And I drank a bottle of stout myself to keep them company; it would be a dull day for me if I didn't. After the first brandy Jim switched to stout, but your one stuck to the Hennessy – and Craven A cigarettes – and there was no question of putting the brakes on, either. "Will you have another one, Suzie?" "Ah sure, we might as well." That's all you'll hear out of Suzie all day long: "Ah sure, we might as well." And the handbag snapping for cigarettes and lighter and lipstick every couple of minutes. She drank glass for glass and smoked fag for fag and at the end of it all she was steadier on her feet than Jim was. On to Donegal town with us, where there was another stop – for lunch – but first – a wee drink – just one drink to give us all a bit of an appetite. Well, I needn't tell you that one drink called for two and two called for its twin – until lunch time was long past and we had to make do with ham sandwiches and more drink at the counter. Back into the car. Will we hit Derry before tea time? We will if we don't make any more stops, but there's little hope of that. The last town we stopped at was Strabane. Both of them had long forgotten that we were supposed to be heading for Belfast; all the talk now was about Derry. I let them off at Strabane and I stretched out on the back seat of the car to try and sleep off the load of booze that was weighing me down like a tombstone. It was well after closing time when the knock came to the window. The two of them were nicely at this stage and talking about Belfast again. That's where they started out for and that's where they were going. I knew better than to begin an argument. "Righto," I said, "you're the boss." They fell into the back seat with their arms all over each other, talking about staying the night in Belfast. "How long will it take us to get from here to there?" Jim asked me. "Oh two – three hours," I said, knowing well that they'd be fast asleep in a matter of minutes. "Put the boot down then," says Jim. "Whatever you say," says I – and I drove around the corner and pointed the car for home.

'One morning early we had set out for Dublin, and after a long day's journey going nowhere, it was dark night and time to wake Jim up in the back seat. "Are we in Dublin already?" says Jim, staggering out of the car and into a puddle in his own back yard.'

Lately Betty is cracked in the head about Anthony McGill. Anthony works with Big Jodie, serving his time at the carpentry.

'He's far too old for you,' I tell Betty.

'No, he's not.'

'He's at least sixteen years.' But Betty doesn't care if he was sixty.

Whenever we come within sight of Jodie's workshop, Betty wants to pay a visit. She stands at the workbench watching Anthony planing timber, or hammering, or collecting sawdust into bags for burning. When he looks at her she smiles back at him, but there is very little talk between them. Outside, Anthony's motorbike, chipped and dented, with a scuffed black pillion, leans against the gable: an old machine, it grumbles every inch it has to travel. Getting ready for school in the morning, we often hear Anthony backfiring his way through the town.

'Will we go up to Jodie's this evening?'

'What for?'

'Just to see.'

'Big Jodie is sick looking at the pair of us.'

'We weren't up for ages.'

'Only last week we were up.'

'Big Jodie doesn't mind.'

'Why don't you go up on your own?'

'I'm too shy.'

When we go into the workshop, with its crisp woodland

smell of pine shavings, sawdust and resin, Anthony is usually whistling at the bench. He whistles the same tune over and over – which is not a tune at all but a weird invention of his own, all off key. I know that Betty notices this, but we never mention it. Anthony is good-humoured and keeps on working all the time we are there. He has a square sort of a face, with flat brown hair that keeps falling down over his forehead in a cow's lick.

Sometimes, if Jodie is not around, Anthony will imitate him. Once Betty asked him what he was making. 'I'm making a thoof for a houth,' Anthony lisped. Unknown to him, Jodie was standing in the doorway; he came over to Anthony. 'If you open you' eythes, McGill,' says Jodie, 'you'll thsee that what you' making ith a thegula donkeyth poo.'

Suzanne, stooped over the grocery counter, her tasselled black shawl pulled down from her skimpy grey hair, holds open her shopping bag. 'These are the last groceries I'll be buying from you for a while, Jamie. Oh – I need a candle – and – can you sell me a half-box o' matches?'

'A half-box?'

'I'm going into the county home for the winter. If I buy a full box, the half o' them'll be gone mouldy by the time I get out.'

'You have the situation well studied.'

'Oh God help me, sure I have to.'

'Well, I can't sell you a half-box. But I'll tell you what I'll do: seeing that it's the last roundup until the spring – you'll be out in the spring, I suppose?'

'Oh I will surely – if God spares me.'

'Then I'll give you a full box – as a present.'

'Oh God bless you, Jamie. I suppose you're thinking there's a poor way on me?'

'I'll tell you what I'm thinking: I'm trying to figure out which

of us is the worst off – you for asking to buy a half-box o'
matches, or me for – I'll put it this way: if ever you want to say
a good word about me, don't say that I gave you a box o'
matches as a present... So you're going inside for the winter?'

'I am, Jamie, giving it a try. I'm going in next week – whenever the ambulance calls for me. Isn't it a terrible way to end,
too?'

'What you ought to be saying is that it's a great thing there's
such a place as the county home. Won't you be well looked
after for the blackest months: you'll have your fill to eat, a warm
bed, sleep as much as you like – then when the first glimmer
o' sunshine hits the windowpane you'll be out again like the
daffodils.'

'Oh, I don't know. Many's the person went into the county
home and never was seen more.'

'Of course you'll be seen and well seen. Pity though yourself
and Molly couldn't agree.'

'The saints in heaven couldn't agree with *her*. Everything had
to be *her* way. I couldn't make a drop o' tea but it was either
too weak or too strong, or I was using the wrong cups, or the
teapot was on the wrong side o' the hob. I couldn't wash the
delph, I couldn't sweep the floor; she wouldn't even let me put
a clod of turf on the fire – she had her own special way of stack-
ing the turf and no other way would do. If I wanted to take a
snooze in the middle of the day, she would start spring-cleaning,
clatterin' and bangin' around the kitchen until I'd have to give
up trying to sleep and get out o' bed again as cross-tired as when
I got into it. All her life living on her own, that's the problem.
I had my man for thirty-two years, so I know there has to be
give and take. But there's no give in *her*. "Is it all right," says
I, "if I bring over my own clock?" The oul' pandy clock she
has – it was always gaining time – so much every day – which
she was used to. Every so often I would have to ask her what

time it was. The clock might say a quarter past nine – she'd look at it, and she'd say twenty to three or half past seven or whatever. I could never figure out how she knew the time and she could never explain it to me, no matter how she tried. But would she let me take over my own good alarm clock that never misses a tick? Oh no. That would upset everything. I put up with it for as long as I could and then I hit on a plan. What I did was – the next time I was raikin' in Meehans' I took a look at the clock when I was leaving. I knew it would take me about a half-hour to get from Meehan's to Molly's house – plus whatever little extra for stopping on the way to have a chat with Mickey Mhór. Then I had to wait my chance till I was on my own; so when she went out for a creel o' turf I took down the clock and I set it to the right time. Everything was grand until the Angelus rang. She took a look at the clock. And she took another look at it. She took it down and she shook it. She put it to her ear. She looked at it again. Then she looked at *me*. We got over the delph and the bed and the jam and everything else. The clock was what finished us. She never trusted me after that. We could never live together again.'

A flat timber body, two wheels, two legs, two shaftlike handles. Betty and myself study the strange contraption in Big Jodie's workshop.

'What is it, Anthony?'

'What does it look like?'

'A boxbarrow – only it's too high.'

Anthony McGill is busy sandpapering the handles, not bothering to look up at us. He has changed his hairstyle, with a parting in the middle, but his cow's lick still hangs down over his eyes. 'It's not a boxbarrow,' he says.

'A cart. For a jennet?'

Anthony doesn't laugh. 'Guess again.'

'I dunno.'

'It looks like – for selling fish,' Betty suggests.

'A fishcart? No.'

'Tell us,' Betty says.

Anthony eyes the two of us. 'It's a bed.'

'A bed?'

'What are the wheels for?'

'Going round.'

'And the legs are for standing. You're very smart.'

'I'm not coddin' yous at all: a bed is what it is. Stonehead ordered it last week. It's for Ferdia.'

Every Thursday the bundle of comics, securely tied with string, arrives on the four o'clock bus: *Radio Fun*, *Film Fun*, the *Beano*, the *Dandy*. I like *Radio Fun* best, because as well as the funnies, it has a story – usually a detective story in which something *priceless* gets stolen. I wonder why the jewels and the paintings and the vases are always *priceless* – a word I haven't come across anywhere else.

Today the bus was late and after we have finally handed over our clammy pennies to Maggie May, we stand around on the footpath browsing – Scunsey, Aisling, Nora Mary and myself. Aisling is dipping into the *Dandy*, skipping through the funnies until she comes to Marzipan the Magician. Standing beside her, I call out the caption with a fine riming ring: 'Marzipan the Magi Kan.'

'The what?' Aisling's big chestnut eyes open wider.

'Marzipan the Magi Kan,' I repeat.

Aisling and Nora Mary laugh.

'Not the Magi Kan,' Nora Mary sniggers. 'The Magician, you eejit!'

I had never heard the word pronounced before and my awful blunder stuns me. Magi Kan. Magician. Magician sounds posher, but it doesn't rime with Marzipan, the way my wrong pronunciation did. The two words keep sparking off each other in my head. What must Aisling think?

My own comic hangs open at the crime story. 'You know in the crime stories –' I begin. Scunsey and Nora Mary look at me. I turn the question on Nora Mary: 'I'll bet you don't know why the things that are stolen are always *priceless?*'

'That's obvious,' Nora Mary says.

'Why?'

'Because it makes the story better.'

'I know it makes the story better. But do you know why?'

'Why what?'

'Why they're *priceless?*'

'I'm after telling you.'

'You're not after telling me why all the things are *priceless.*'

Nora Mary looks puzzled. 'You don't know what you're talking about.'

'*You* don't know why the things are *priceless.*'

'All right, smartie. *You* tell us.'

Aisling's eyes are on me as I begin my explanation. 'The reason is because crime doesn't pay. Sometimes the thieves get away with the loot – so then the things stolen have to be *priceless.*'

Nora Mary looks even more puzzled. So do Aisling and Scunsey.

'You don't know what *priceless* means,' Nora Mary says.

'I do so know what *priceless* means.'

'What does it mean?'

'It means – *priceless* – it's not worth anything.'

Nora Mary glances at Aisling and they both snigger.

'It means the opposite.' Aisling's words hit me like an elbow in the face.

'*Priceless* means it's so valuable you can't put a price on it,' Nora Mary says.

'Girls think they know everything,' Scunsey mocks, but I hardly hear him. *Priceless*. So valuable you can't put a price on it. The stories would make a lot more sense that way. One thing I could never understand was why, if the things had no value, the crooks would bother to steal them in the first place. My comic still hangs open at the *priceless* crime story, like a mouth in shock; Nora Mary and Aisling wait for me to say something.

'I was only coddin'.'

'You were not,' Nora Mary snaps.

Aisling closes her comic and goes home – no doubt convinced that I'm a complete fool.

The writing pad, the blotting paper, the brown business envelopes and Mama sitting at the head of the kitchen table filling the fountain pen from the bottle of Quink ink. To one side Dada stands, looking over her shoulder, his long back slightly bent, his face changing from satisfaction to doubt to impatience, as always when something important is afoot.

' "Dear Miss Glenn",' Mama writes. 'What next?'

'Tell her we would like to know what price she's asking.'

'I'll have to say we heard she was selling her premises.'

'Righto.'

' "Dear Miss Glenn, we have heard your premises is for sale and we would like to know what price you are expecting." '

'Good. That's it.'

'Are we doing the right thing, I wonder?'

'Sure, we're doing the right thing. If we get Anastasia's place we'll be landed; it's a great stand. I'll do twice the business I'm doing here. Glengreeny is a lousy wee town. Nothing in it only jealousy.'

'I hope the news that she's selling is true and not just a rumour.'

'It's no rumour. Sure, the woman is nearly eighty years of age. She's long past being able to run a pub.'

'What am I to say next?'

'Say we're interested in buying it – if the price is right.'

' "We – would – be interested – in – purchasing – your – premises – as – we – are – thinking – of – moving – from – here." '

'If the price is right.'

'I said that already.'

'Oh. OK.'

'What else?'

'That's all.'

' "Please – let – us – know – as – soon – as – possible – if – you – are – interested – in – selling – Yours – sincerely – James – O' – Donnell." '

'That should do the trick.'

'Please God we're doing the right thing.'

'Take your time! Let me spit on it.'

'You and your spitting!'

'There you are. It'll bring us luck. Now, the next problem is to sell the pub I'm in.'

'Why don't you do it properly and get an auctioneer?'

'No auctioneer. If it's not sold at the auction I'm sunk altogether. Word of mouth is the only way: a word here, a word there. That's what Anastasia is doing. Fly woman.'

'Then Jellybob is the one to tell; he'll spread it all over the countryside, and so will Jane.'

'We'll let it slip to Jellybob – but nothing definite. Just a hint: If I got the right price, I mightn't say no. Something like that. With a bit o' luck we'll be up and away by Christmas and settled in Anastasia's place. God help the poor fool that's going to be taking over from me here!'

★　★　★

Another angry sermon from Father McBrearty about all the selfish bachelors strolling around with not a thought for anyone only themselves. They have a holy duty to get married and no excuse for letting old age catch up with them.

Father McBrearty is planning a house-to-house tour of the parish and a lot of the old people are terrified. An epidemic of thatching and whitewashing has broken out with everyone trying to put the best shine they can on their belongings for the parish priest.

'I wish to God he'd stay at home!' Crusoe complains. 'Margaret has everything in the house topsy-turvy with dusting and polishing. This morning I couldn't even find my good boots. As if he's going to have time to examine under the beds!'

Shining from the front seat of the chapel is the bald oily head of Jack Jumble, his hoarse 'Holy Mary mother o' God' rising above and trailing behind everyone else.

'What's he doing at the rosary when he never goes to mass?'

'It's his way of getting into people's good books.'

'He's barred from every pub in town, I hear.'

'After this, he won't be. If they don't let him back now, he'll be at the rosary again next Sunday. Maybe mass as well.'

'There must be great power in his prayers.'

'Jack Jumble always gets whatever he prays for. You'll find he'll be back on the tear in no time.'

Dada has left a customer drinking at the counter and comes into the kitchen flurried and downfaced: 'Anastasia's is sold.'

'Now. What did I tell you?'

'To Barney Flanagan. Wasn't she the right rascal that never answered our letter?'

'We're as well off without it.'

'We are.'

'We'll have to be fly. Don't say another word to anyone.'

'I won't mention it to a soul. Jellybob'll have the news well broadcast by now, though. I can tell him I changed my mind. Ah what the hack!'

'Can I take them out?'

'There you are.'

'Will I put them on?'

'Sure. Go ahead.'

Dada had unlocked and opened back his tall upright American trunk to check his papers; in the bottom compartment lay a pair of well-scuffed sparring gloves. My hands easily slip into the padded brown gloves, which Dada laces up.

'Me and Tommy bought a pair each in downtown Chicago. We used to box each other around the apartment after work. One Sunday Tommy was out and a friend of ours, Jeremiah Muldowney, came over. Jeremiah had trouble with his mouth – pyorrhoea of the gums – and he had to get all his teeth out. He was a sight, the poor fella, and none of the girls would have anything to do with him. When Jeremiah saw the gloves he wanted to have a go, so I laced him up. It was a scorcher of a day and we were after drinking the last two bottles o' beer in the icebox. "I better get a few beers to keep us cool," says I. "I'll nip round to the saloon on the corner for a half-dozen." Off I went, leaving Jeremiah boxing the air, warming up for the bout. In the saloon who should I meet only the Man from Mullinavat. I don't believe I ever found out what his real name was; all me and Tommy ever called him was the Man from Mullinavat. He was working on construction and every cent he earned went down his throat. Nothing would do him only stand me a drink. Of course, I had to stand him one back. The Man from Mullinavat had got married to an Irish-American girl since the last time I met him and things were going far from well. He was telling me all about it: how much she was costing him and how he couldn't please her no matter what he done. He said he was thinking of skipping it to New York or somewhere and leaving the wife high and dry – when, the next thing, the door of the saloon nearly burst off its hinges and Jeremiah Muldowney stood facing us with the gloves up and him in a mad rage. He made one lunge at myself with the gums bared, so that I had to run in behind the counter to save myself. You see, he couldn't get out of the gloves on account of having no teeth and he was prancing around the apartment like a tiger in a cage, until the heat and the frustration went to his head. When he couldn't reach myself, he took a swipe at the Man from Mullinavat and floored him – which was no great achievement, because the drink had the work half-done for him already.'

Dada puts up his fists and punches the gloves. 'Come on. Box me back...That's it...And move around. You have to be nimble on your feet as well. Many's the evening me and Tommy punched each other around the kitchen, the sweat pouring off us. Happy times then.'

We haven't been in Tessy Ann's since the day we heard the laughing record, and now in the bar, after her funeral, the mourners are remembering.

'She had a hard life, the cratur.'

'She had indeed – a heavy cross to bear.'

'They say she was blind before the first child was born.'

'She was then.'

'Tessy Ann never saw one of her children and she reared eight – four boys and four girls. You heard how the tragedy struck?'

'Well, I heard several versions.'

'I'll tell you now – and you can believe this version, because I had it from my brother, Father Michael, the Lord rest him.

He was the curate here at the time and a great friend of Tessy's. About a year after Tessy and Patrick John got married they were whitewashing the kitchen, getting ready for the birth of their first child. Tessy Ann was chatting to Patrick John, looking up at him as he worked. When a skite of lime struck her in the eyes, they washed it out and thought no more of it. But that night the pain was so bad that Patrick John had to cycle in to Killybegs for old Doctor McBride. When the doctor examined her, he was horrified. Tessy Ann was expecting her baby in a matter of days, but even so, the doctor insisted on her being driven through the night to the hospital in Derry. With that and all, it was too late. They kept her in the hospital until after her delivery and then she came home with the child. Her eyes were still bandaged and they hadn't told her that the lime had burned away the pupils. Patrick John was to break the terrible news to her after she settled in at home, but he couldn't bring himself to do it. The day the Jubilee nurse came to remove the bandages, she brought Father Michael with her. "There's no good way of breaking bad news," Father Michael said to Patrick John. "I'll have to tell her straight out." And so, before the bandages were removed, Father Michael told Tessy Ann the truth. She listened to him until he had finished. When she spoke, her words sent a shiver through the priest and the nurse and Patrick John, who was standing at the bedside. "What good will I be to my husband or my baby or anyone? I'll only be a burden all my life. Wouldn't it be a blessing for myself and for everyone belonging to me if I was dead?" Patrick John did his best to console her, but all to no avail – and so did Father Michael. "If I was in your situation, I would probably feel the same," he told her. "I wouldn't see any point in living either. You'll have a lot of time on your own – a lot of time to think. Maybe the thought will enter your head to take your own life." He said it straight out to her. "If ever it does," he said, "I want you first

to think of this: what happened to you is a terrible thing –
and yet you don't know how your life is going to open
out before you from now on. It may be that the Lord has
some special reason for putting this heavy sorrow on you.
He may have some special work for you to do – something
that you couldn't or wouldn't do if you had sight. It mightn't
be anything grand as the world judges. Maybe all He's asking
you to do is to accept – which at twenty-six years of age
is no small thing. You must have trust in Him. Just by living
you'll be a strength and a hope to other people." But Tessy
Ann paid no heed to his words. All the time she was crying
away to herself and when the nurse took off the bandages
and she felt what was left of her ruined eyes she started to
scream and flail about like a mad woman. "I don't want
to be blind. Oh why did I look up at you Patrick John when
I did? And why didn't you bring me to the doctor in time?
Oh Christ have pity on me!" Her baby, which was asleep at
the head of the bed, woke up in terror, crying nearly as loud
as its mother. Neither her husband nor the priest could console
Tessy Ann. Her wild screams were heard all over the town, in
every house, cutting in on every conversation, stilling all that
was going on. When every effort to soothe her had failed, the
nurse, who was holding the baby, gave it into her arms. As is
nature's way, Tessy Ann brought the screeching child to her
nipples. She sank back on the pillow, and mother and child
found comfort in each other. She never complained from that
day on.'

Dada has one hand gripping the seat of Jack Jumble's trousers,
the other closed tightly on the collar of his jacket, steering him
towards the bar door.

'Don't tear me good clothes!' Jack struggles to hold his
ground, grabbing at the counter and the doorjamb.

'Come on! Out! You're only a dang nuisance! Out with you! And don't come back.'

The old, frayed homespun jacket that Jack has on him – where did I see it before? And the trousers? And the gansey?

'Dada, he's wearing all Uncle Mick's things!'

'What?'

'Aunt Sally must have given him Uncle Mick's clothes.'

'You know, I thought there was something odd about him.' Dada turns back to the door to have another look at Jack, who is zigzagging down the footpath towards Ned Mary's. 'Well, that's a good one. If you came on him from behind, wouldn't you swear it was Mick, the Lord rest him – except that Mick could never afford a stagger in his life. Well, I'm sure Mick doesn't begrudge them to him now – though he'd find it hard to believe that he was working all them years to put clothes on Jack Jumble. It's a funny world.'

The ringmaster has called for volunteers, while the low squat piebald ponies continue to canter around, heads bobbing, harnesses jingling. In the centre of the ring, waiting nervously for the word to mount, are Scunsey, Footsie, Sonny Moylan, Boxty, Big Andy and myself. We are also waiting for the ponies to halt, but the ringmaster keeps them jogging at a steady clockwork pace with regular cracks of his whip and we have to manage as best we can. Sonny Moylan crawls on to the pony's back and survives two rounds of the ring flat on his belly, like a dead outlaw, until he slides, head first, down the other side. The rest of us are sitting upright, clutching the animals' manes, jogging mechanically in a big circle with the crowd cheering us on. Will we be trotting next? Then galloping? With all the experience gained riding stray donkeys after school, I think I should cut a fine figure – especially in front of Aisling, who is on the end of a ringside seat, with Ferdia in his wheel-bed beside her.

'Stick 'em up, cowboy!' the ringmaster barks. 'Hands in the air! Everybody.'

This is far from what I was expecting, but shouldn't be beyond me.

'Come on! Hands up!'

Hesitantly we raise our hands – higher and higher – until Scunsey topples over, followed by Boxty and Footsie. The riderless ponies keep jogging around as if each has a phantom jockey on its back.

A loud crack and the ringmaster curls his whip over our heads. The crowd gives a louder cheer. Two full rounds of the ring with hands in the air. We are barely finding our balance when another command jolts us: 'On your knees! Get on to your knees!... Come on, boys!'

I have just got my second knee under me when my glasses fall off and I am plunged into a soapy sea of unclearness. My fingers again desperately clutch at the pony's mane, but I continue to slip backwards. To anchor myself, I wrap both arms tight around the animal's neck, but now I am leaning so far forward that any instant I may be thrown out over his head. Another agonising round of the ring. Big Andy is still upright, followed by four riderless ponies – and the ringmaster moving in closer to us, cracking away, louder and faster, and calling out our praises: 'The bareback riders of the big top – yes, ladies and gentlemen, we still have two fearless daredevils, who are going to attempt the dangerous feat of standing up – yes, ladies and gentlemen, standing straight up on their bucking broncos. Come on, boys! Up! On your feet!' Crack! Crack!

The crowd blurred and open-mouthed goes rinsing past. A loud cheer tells me that Big Andy is on his feet.

'Good man, Meehan!'

'Ride him, Andy!'

The ringmaster viciously cracks his whip at me. 'On your

feet! Come on! Up you get!' And the crowd joins him.

'Get up, O'Donnell!'

'Up, you boy you!'

'Come on, O'Donnell! On your feet!'

But I remain knotted around the pony's neck in a death hug, knowing that, unless the tent collapses or the world ends, nothing can now distract from the awful calamity facing me.

'Straighten up, man!'

'Sit up!'

'Stand up!'

'What are you afraid of!'

'You'll fall no further than the ground!'

Without loosening my hug, I begin to straighten my legs. I am now arched upwards at a steep angle, my backside in the air, my head between the pony's ears.

Another raucous ignorant laugh from the crowd. Has Big Andy fallen off? Maybe I'm not doing so badly after all.

'Get up, O'Donnell, you dying-lookin' eejit!'

'Stand up on him!'

Whatever I do, the pony will keep going, so if I fall out over his head, I could very well be trampled to death.

'Get up your head, O'Donnell!'

'Get down your ass, you eejit you!'

Somewhere in the dizzy blur of faces I know that Aisling is a witness to all this, but I don't care any more, so long as I escape with my life. My only hope now is to get back into a sitting position. This is what I am attempting, when, without warning, the pony stretches his neck in a shivering shake that pitches me headlong into the sawdust. Helping me to my feet, the ringmaster fixes the glasses back on my face – just in time for me to glimpse Big Andy cantering past, his body bent between a stand and a crouch, his arms seesawing, his black teeth bared in a wide frantic grin.

★   ★   ★

'Are you going to the strand?' Ferdia calls to Scunsey and myself, as we freewheel down the street, our swimming togs held across the handlebars.

'Just as far as the pier.'

'I'll go with you.'

Ferdia never says, Will you bring me? but always, I'll go with you.

The glassy dark apron of sea wrack clinging to the pier wall hasn't yet been covered, each heave of the tide straining to lift higher its teeming burden of ocean. We settle Ferdia's wheel-bed near the steps, where he will be able to see us over the side, then sit low on the pier to change into our bathing togs.

Scunsey and myself are tumbling about in the water, looking up at Ferdia, when something in his eyes stops both of us dead. We come back up the steps shaking the brine from our bleached skins, like two guilty dogs.

'It's too cold,' Scunsey says.

The two of us have moved close to Ferdia. I know we are all thinking of the day he swam out for the ball.

Nothing but the low murmur of Irish coming from the scullery, where Seán Ó Heascaigh and Seán Ó Faoistin are partitioned off, sharing a hideaway drink after mass.

'*Gaeilge ar fad anseo. Gaeilge ar fad,*' Seán Ó Heascaigh says.

The odd time they come in, the two of them head for the privacy of the scullery, where Seán Ó Faoistin sits just inside the door with his wooden leg stretched out in front of him. One night Crusoe got short-taken in the kitchen and bounded for the back door, tripping over Seán Ó Faoistin's leg and bumping his head off the table. 'Why the hell can't he sit back from the door,' Crusoe said, 'instead of having his leg stretched across it like a bush in a gap!'

Seán Ó Faoistin has an office job in the factory and walks his bicycle to and from work every day, but never gets up on it. He hails from the Gweebarra Gaeltacht.

'*Gweebarra na sléibhte, Gweebarra na dtonn,*' Seán Ó Heascaigh says to him, which means 'Gweebarra of the hills, Gweebarra of the waves'; by repeating this line now and again he manages to coax a smile out of the gloomy Seán Ó Faoistin.

Seán Ó Heascaigh also hails from the Gweebarra direction. He always asks for his drink in Irish – which we know is a bottle of stout anyway – but he wouldn't satisfy us to ask for it in English. Mama has no Irish, so the best she can do is nod and smile at him.

Seán Ó Heascaigh is a school inspector somewhere up the country; he comes home about once a month, never wears less than his Sunday best and cocks his fist at any child he hears talking English.

'If I was paid at the same rate as Ó Heascaigh,' Dada says, 'I'd go as far as box people's ears for talking English.'

When the two Seáns meet, most of their talk in Irish is *about* Irish – how few people are talking it nowadays and how it is gradually dying out. Through two or three mournful rounds of drink they grumble and groan, their voices sometimes sinking into a black litany of whispering, then rising as they answer each other's complaints with more bad news. The one familiar word we hear over and over is 'Seán'. 'Seán' comes at the beginning of sentences and at the end and in the middle and sometimes twice in a row, as one of the Seáns finishes speaking and the other Seán begins – and they go on like this nodding and agreeing with each other so that it would make very little difference if they were both talking to themselves.

'*An Béarla salach,*' Seán Ó Heascaigh says, meaning, 'the dirty English language' – and Seán Ó Faoistin echoes back, '*An Béarla salach. An Béarla salach.*'

★ ★ ★

At a spot directly above the old school yard we halt, Dada carrying a sledgehammer and a sign nailed to a timber post.

'There's room for four houses here and a bit of a garden behind each of them. What more does anybody want? People in the factory are always complaining that there's nowhere to stay. And young couples getting married. Hold it steady there, now, Conor.'

Dada gives the post a few good whacks and stands at arm's length to examine the lettering: block capitals in black, against the painted white of the signboard: SITES FOR SALE.

'I forgot to tell Jodie to make the writing big enough to be seen from the road. Still and all, when people see a sign in the field they're hardly going to think it says AMERICA THREE THOUSAND MILES. Now we'll have to wait and see if we get a bite.' Dada gives the post a final whack and spits at the sign: 'Come on, you boy you, do your work!'

'Break! Break! You have to break when I say *break!*' Ferdia leans forward in his wheel-bed trying his best to enforce the rules in the boxing match between Scunsey and Footsie.

A few weeks back Scunsey and myself had started sparring with the gloves. Soon there was a queue waiting to have a go and so an elimination contest was held to be followed by a title fight. Having only one pair of gloves is a bit of a drawback. The toss of a coin decides who will wear the right glove and who will have to box southpaw. You hit with the gloved hand, but you can block with either, and after five rounds you swap gloves. Battling all week for a crack at the title were Joe Scunsey Louis, Jack Paddy Anne Johnson, Gene Sonny Tunney, Billy Boxty Con, myself (Gentleman Conor Jim) – and Footsie, who insisted on fighting under his own proper name, Charlie, which he is sorry for, because we christened him One Glove Charlie.

There have been so many disputes that Ferdia now referees

with a long stick, so that he can get at the contestants to enforce his decisions; he also has a shorter stick, which he bangs on an empty sweet can: this is the bell. The present fight between Joe Scunsey Louis and One Glove Charlie is the final and is for the heavyweight championship of the world. Gene Sonny Tunney Michael O'Hehir Moylan is the commentator.

'Box on,' Ferdia says.

'And now One Glove Charlie is moving around Joe Scunsey Louis looking for an opening. Louis has his naked fist up and looks dangerous, even though he lost the advantage since the change of gloves. But One Glove Charlie also lost the advantage because he is a *ciotóg*, or southpaw, and now has to box north-paw. And Louis is back-pedalling and One Glove Charlie is circling him and the two fighters have their guard up and now it is One Glove Charlie's turn to give ground and Louis is circ-ling One Glove Charlie and One Glove Charlie has his one glove up and Joe Scunsey Louis has his one glove up and they are circling each other and the crowd is beginning to boo and the referee is telling them to box and everyone is booing them and Louis rams in a straight left into One Glove Charlie's stomach and One Glove Charlie is bent over in agony –'

'Stop! Stop!'

'And the referee is stopping the contest and is lashing Joe Scunsey Louis with his stick.'

'Foul! Below the belt! Foul!'

'The referee is taking points from Joe Scunsey Louis for a foul punch and Louis is angry because he got a whack of the stick on the backside and the referee is warning him –'

'You can't hit below the belt.'

'You're after hitting me below the belt with that big brute of a stick!'

'The referee is giving out to Louis for dirty tricks and Louis is giving out to the referee –'

'Box on.'

'And now the fight is on again – but the bell is ringing for the end of the round, which was another action-packed round and the crowd is going wild here in Madison Square Garden. And at the ringside I see a lot of famous boxers who got themselves knocked out on the way to this great fight: Jack Paddy Anne Johnson and Billy Boxty Con, and Gentleman Conor Jim, who owns the boxing gloves, and now the bell is ringing for round eight and the boxers are back on their feet and One Glove Charlie lands on Louis's nose with a real stinger and Louis staggers backwards and he is feeling his nose with his free hand and he is shook and One Glove Charlie is coming at him with a whole lot of punches and Louis shoots out his left and hits One Glove Charlie bang on the nose and now the nose of One Glove Charlie is dripping blood and Joe Scunsey Louis's nose is dripping blood and the crowd is going wild here and shouting for blood and One Glove Charlie lands another right and another and another and Louis runs around behind the referee and One Glove Charlie is following him and the referee is lashing out with his stick and he just got One Glove Charlie on the legs with a vicious whack and One Glove Charlie turns on the referee but he changes his mind and lashes out at Louis instead and Louis is after tripping over the referee's stick and Louis is down and One Glove Charlie is on top of Louis and One Glove Charlie is punching Louis with his two fists which is a foul and the referee is calling for them to break and the bell is ringing for the end of the round and did you hear that mad shout from the ringside which was Billy Boxty Con who just jumped in over the ropes and landed on top of the boxers and Boxty Con is punching all around him and now Gentleman Conor Jim is in the ring with his fists up and Paddy Anne Johnson is in the ring and the referee is lashing right, left and centre at everyone with his stick and ringing the bell with his

other stick and now here comes the greatest of them all, Gene
Sonny Tunney, with my fists flying and look out lads for the
greatest heavyweight champion of all time . . .'

Overnight, colour has vanished from the face of the earth and
the chill January sun glints from white roads, white roofs, white
fields and hills and a glassy white sky.

'If it freezes over this, nobody'll be able to move a step.'

'When I went to fother the cow the mouth of the haystack
was solid white. I never seen that before.'

'No buth, no newthpaperth – and wust of all no thkool. My
oh my! What a' we going to do at all!'

'The hens took one peep out the byre door and turned on
their tails.'

'I saw Wee Groarty pouring a kettle o' boiling water down
the pump and Big Sarah standing over him directing operations.
She's a tightner.'

'Take the geranium out of the window, Dada.'

'My toes are freezing!'

'You'll get chilblains that near the fire, Betty.'

'Hooray! It's snowing again!'

'It'll be colossical when it's finished, true as God – it'll take
six people easy. There's a rudder for steering at the front
and a high seat at the back for the driver, and ropes and
everything coming from the rudder, so that Big Jodie can
go around corners or anywhere he wants. He's going to
bring it to the top of the Slope and it'll freewheel all the
way to the bottom. It'll be ready tomorrow or the day
after. There's a carbide lamp as well and a ship's bell. The
name of it is the Silver Bullet. He'll bring us all. It'll be
great sport!'

★   ★   ★

Claddagh, Con Moylan and Crusoe enjoying a cosy after-hour drink in the kitchen complain about Hobnails.

'The only thing in his favour,' Crusoe says, 'is you always hear him coming.'

'Not the night,' Con Moylan remarks. 'You wouldn't hear him with the cushion o' snow he'd have under him.'

'Unless he's completely out of his mind, he won't be out tonight,' Claddagh says.

'I'm afraid Hobnails *is* completely out of his mind' – Dada heartily wishes they would all go home.

'I was over in Kilmore a few weeks ago when he raided Anastasia's,' Crusoe begins. 'Barney Flanagan has it now and Barney doesn't seem to have got the hang of things yet.'

Dada laughs. 'I'm not surprised. Sure thon man has no experience of a pub – straikin' on a farm all his life.'

'He had no experience this night, anyway. The rat-tat-tat came to the door and Barney opened up expecting it was some-one looking for a late drink. When he saw Hobnails standing before him he slammed the door shut in his face. We were all expecting another rat-tat-tat, but it never came. Instead the boots started – up and down and up and down. And they would stop for a while. And we would be getting ready to make a dash for it. And they would start up again, left-right, left-right, ring-ing off the sidewalk like a half-shod donkey. The hoor kept us there until two o'clock in the morning. Barney wouldn't give us any more drink and the four of us were biting our nails with the tension. Myself was sleepy and hungover and nervous as a cat in a bag o' stones. At two o'clock the stepping stopped for good. Dead silence. Was he gone home to bed? Or just foxin'? Barney stuck his head out the door. Not a sinner in sight. But the Boots could be hiding at the gable. At either gable. Barney walked at his ease to the near gable and just as he got there he heard the Boots coming at him from the far gable. When he turned around, Hobnails was standing on the doorstep with his notebook out.'

'He's a sly boyo,' Dada agrees, 'all out for revenge.'

'I was in the hotel the last time he raided,' Con Moylan says. 'Every one of us got down the river bank.'

Dada begins collecting up the empty bottles. 'I had a crowd in myself, but I got them all out the back. He raided every pub in the town and he didn't catch one.'

'He'll be back,' Old Con says.

'I'm expecting him any night' – Dada eyes Old Con's glass, which is still half-full.

'He's a dangerous bucko.' Crusoe finishes off his drink.

Claddagh, returning from the WC, scatters a bright flutter of snowflakes from his shoulders: 'It's coming down heavy outside.'

'Give us another round, Jamie' – Crusoe holds out a ten shilling note – 'I think we can relax the night.'

Dada frowns at Crusoe. 'This'll have to be the last round.'

RAT-RAT-TAT!

'Christ almighty!'

'It's him surely!'

'Quick men! Under the stairs!'

RAT-RAT-TAT!

'Who's there?'

'It's me.'

'Who?'

'Tom.'

'Tom who?'

'Tim.'

'Oh – Tom Tim. Take your time, Tom. It's all right, men. Yous can come out . . . Tom. Is something the matter?'

'I think I have a wee touch o' bellyfounder. Maggie told me to get a brandy.'

'Come into the kitchen. It's a terrible night.'

'I woke up with this pain in me belly. I think it must be the weather.'

'Wait till I turn up the lamp . . . You know everyone here.'

'You have people in! Well, that's a good one.'

'Hello, Tom.'

'How are you, Tom?'

'I'm not all that well.'

'Sit down there till I get you a drop o' brandy.'

'You're not feeling the best, Tom?'

'I'm not, Con. I had to take a fother o' hay across the river to the few sheep I have. I think I got a touch o' bellyfounder.'

'The brandy'll leave you all right.'

'That's what Maggie said. "Go down to Jamie for a drop o' brandy," she said.'

'The brandy'll do the trick.'

'I didn't think there would be anyone out at this hour only myself.'

'We were just having a quiet drink.'

Dada returns with the brandy for Tom and bottles of stout for the others. 'There yous are men, the last round the night. Now, Tom, swallow that down nice and easy.'

'Do you know, Jamie, I'm after coming out without a penny.'

'That's all right. You can pay me again. And *sláinte!*'

'*Sláinte mhór*, Jamie! . . . Boys o' boys, it's strong!'

'It'll do you good.'

'Would you believe this is the first drink I ever had in a public house; in fact it's the first drink I ever had anywhere and I'm the age I am.'

Tom sipped his brandy to the last drop and the others finished their glasses of stout.

'That's it. Time we were all in bed.' Dada got up and led the way out of the kitchen. He opened the front door and a whirl of snowflakes blew in, striking Tom in the face, who was at the head of the line. For a moment Tom stood shivering, then headed into the flurry. He stopped and turned back. Outside on the footpath, blocking the way, was a big snowman. Hobnails.

Snug in bed with our crockery stout-bottle hot-water bottles we listen to the shouting and laughing and the girls' high-pitched pleadings as the Silver Bullet screams past. At the bottom of the town it streels to a halt and a new crowd begins pulling it to the top of the Slope. We count the trips and try to guess the passengers from the excited mingle of voices, snatches of song and a tuneless mouth organ. 'I wish we were older,' Betty says, 'the big people have all the fun.'

'Keep the kettle on the boil, Cassy. A lot o' people asking for punch.'
    'I always have the kettle on the boil.'
    'Snuggy came in last night, home from England, and the accent of him. Asked for a hot toddy, if you don't smile. "A what?" says I. "An 'ot toddy," says he. "What kind of a drink is that?" says I. Of course, I knew well what he meant but I wouldn't give him the satisfaction. "Do you not know wot an 'ot toddy is?" says he. "It's not an Irishman's drink anyway," says I. "It's a glass o' punch," says he. "Then why don't you ask for a glass o' punch?" says I. "If Oi assed for a glass o' punch beyond," says he, "thai wouldn' know wot Oi was talking about." "Well, we don't know what you're talking about here, either," says I.'

'Yous are all crazy. Yous'll all be killed,' Wee Groarty calls to us from Canavan's side door as we take up the steering ropes,

Scunsey, Boxty and Footsie pulling on one side of the sleigh, Sonny Moylan and myself on the other. At the rear, Big Jodie, wearing gloves and a red peaked cap with earmuffs, prepares us for the dangers ahead: 'We' going the full dithtanth, boyth, to the top of the Thlope – or ath the explo'eth thay, the thoof of the wo'ld. Ou' dethination ith the teleg'aph pole at Maggie Michaelth – which ath eve'y thkool boy knowth ith the No'th Pole.'

We no longer believe anything Big Jodie tells us, but we play along, sometimes adding original touches of our own.

Some of us have managed to scrounge a few pennies for sweets: I have a Peggy's leg, which I divide, and Sonny bites off small rubbery pieces from a liquorice pipe, handing them around; happily we munch our way towards the Pole.

'Evyone pull thei' weight,' Big Jodie orders, 'and keep tight togethe'. Many famouth explo'eth came to g'ief th'ough pa'ting company with thei' thleigth – wandething athound in the thackleth wildth, oh my oh my.'

The Silver Bullet, which slid along smoothly at the bottom of the town, as easy as push penny, gets heavier with each steeper, slippier step we take up the Slope.

'What do you think of thith, boyth?' Big Jodie stops and points in the snow.

'What is it?'

'Animal thrackth.'

'Looks like a cat's paws.'

'Or a dog's.'

'At thith latitude! A' you dheaming! Ith a pola' bea'. Maybe even a Yeti. Imagine if we found the legenda'y Yeti, my oh my! What do you think it ith?'

'Probably a gorilla.'

'I think ith a Yeti mythelf – and a big one at that. Oh look!'

'What?'

'Do you not thsee? On the hothizon!'

At the far end of Dunne's field two children with a bucket of water are straggling across a snowdrift.

'It's the Dunnes.'

'A' you out of you' mind! We' on ou' way to the No'th Pole – no whe' nea' Dunneth.' Jodie joins one hand to the peak of his cap and stares into the distance. 'Take anothe' look, boyth. I think ith two Eskimoth.'

'You're right, Jodie. It's Eskimos all right.'

'That meanth we' somewhe' in the A'tic Thircle. My oh my! We' that fa' advanced al'eady. Time fo' a thong, boyth.

Keep thight on to the end of the thoad,
Keep thight on to the end...'

On we trudge, with Jodie's low lisping chant leading the chorus. When we reach the school yard everybody wants to stop for a breather. Jodie says we must be nearing the polar region and tells us that he is going on ahead to do some reconnaissance. Left on our own, the complaints begin.

'We should have stuck to the main road,' Boxty says. 'Jodie is leading us all on a wild goose chase.'

'What are we doing in the school yard anyway?' Sonny Moylan grumbles. 'I don't want to be anywhere next or near the school.'

'I'm thick of thith whole expedithion,' Footsie mocks. Hardly has Footsie's mouth let out the words when a phantom snowball hits him smack in the teeth. 'Who shaggin' fired that shaggin' snowball!'

We are each swearing we had nothing to do with it when Boxty gets hit. Then I get hit myself – a real stunner on the cheek.

We begin to arm ourselves, each of us looking suspiciously at the other, each with a growing pile of hard-packed snowballs ready to let fly. Suddenly Footsie sweeps the icy crust from the school wall into Boxty's face and the battle is on. Snowballs are now coming at us from all directions. We fire what we have gathered, then race up and down the length of the wall, clapping together ammunition as fast as our freezing fingers will allow. In a mad frenzy we scoop from chinks in the wall, delving into crannies and corners, raiding the school doorstep and windowsills, where the snow is set and frosted and can be fired in splintering sheets.

'*Damnú ort! A diabhal! Droch bhreith ort!*'

Curses in Irish add their barb to the stinging blitzkrieg, as we fire and sweep and kick all around us, yelling and jostling, until we collapse breathless on the Silver Bullet, limp and fluffy as burst pillowcases.

From behind the WC, Big Jodie's red muffler-cap appears bobbing along the top of the wall. 'Oh my oh my! Thith ith what I wath af'aid of – thnow madneth. The itholation and the cold – in the thackleth wildth – it dhriveth people inthane. Come on, boyth – headth down and fathe into the wind – befo' the A'tic night dethendth on uth.'

At Maggie Michael's, Jodie stands to attention and salutes; we screw up our eyes at the telegraph pole, frost-capped and glittering: the North Pole. Solemnly Jodie tells us that this is what countless heroes gave their lives for. All the great explorers that perished, trying for years to do what we're after doing in a while of an afternoon. Now we're ready for the return journey and, as everybody knows, from the North Pole to the equator is downhill all the way.

The five of us crush on to the long, narrow sleigh, our legs arched up, our arms wrapped tight around the rider in front. Big Jodie, enthroned on the high seat at the rear, flicks the steering ropes like reins, which pass outside each of us. But before we take off, he tells us, there is the question of scientific experiments. One of the things we have to find out is if we can travel faster than sound. A sure proof that you're travelling faster than sound is if you hear yourself saying something that you haven't even thought of yet.

The Silver Bullet depended on leg power to get started, but once under way, along the tracks it had already delved out for itself, it quickly picked up speed. Not one of us but is cheering and shouting, as much out of terror as excitement, the sleigh dipping and wobbling in and out of the uneven furrows of ice, tilting sideways at every turn, the white swirling ditches leaning over us like icebergs – and always the danger that a cow might decide to cross at her ease in front of us or a startled sheep suddenly jump out of a gap.

From the rear we hear groaning. Big Jodie tells us that he is suffering from frostbite to his toes and he can feel snow blindness coming on – but we can't stop because the danger of falling asleep and freezing to death is too great.

When the first snow-dumb roofs and the birdless chimneys at the head of the town come into view, Big Jodie clangs on the bell. 'Thivilithation! We' thaved, boyth, we' thaved!'

Big Jodie crunching down the street in his brown army boots calls across to Scunsey and myself. With a serious face he tells us that he is on his way back from the far North, where he was chasing the Yeti and the great grizzly bear. The bad news is that the glaciers are retreating, the icebergs are beginning to melt. Next morning I waken to a bright splash of sunshine in the bedroom and the plink of random dripping from the eave shoots.

'Conor! Time to get up! School today! Betty! School!'

When will they come again, the enchanted snows of '47?

Con Moylan's second son Conall has got married to Monica, who comes from Duhaigh. Monica suffers from homesickness and is over to Mama every other day, wondering if she will ever be able to settle in Glengreeny: 'I was never used to living in a town, Cassy. I miss the green fields and the sound of the river and the view of Sliabh Liag from the back door. I never thought anything of them when I was among them but, ah, I miss them terrible. And when I think of Mammy and Kathleen and Sean I can't stop crying. How did you ever settle here, Cassy? It's fierce lonesome forbise Duhaigh.'

Mama has a good laugh over Monica's homesickness. There are only five houses in the whole of Duhaigh and you could walk the roads all day long and meet nothing only crows and magpies.

'Cassy, do you know what's going on in Ned Mary's? Come out to the back door till you hear.'

'What is it?'

'Listen ... Do you hear?'

'Fiddle music?'

'A full *céilí*, that's what it is.'

'In Ned Mary's?'

'The two Mickeys are playing. They'll have everyone at the fair in to them.'

'Who's going to bother listening to the two Mickeys?'

'What are you talking about! Mickey Beag and Mickey Mhór – the two finest fiddlers in the county. Jellybob is after telling me: the two of them are sitting in the bar window, playing away to beat the band. There's people dancing and swinging. Mickey Mhór is storytelling as well. Why didn't I think of getting them?'

'You're better off without them. If you have to stoop that low to bring the people in – forget it!'

'Aye. You're right.'

'Ned Mary is only going to make a laughing stock of himself. Who has time to listen to music on a fair day?'

'You're right. Let them play away; what the hack about them! Close the door. Sicken you, the same Ned Mary!'

'My God, you have a wild mouth there!'

'You never saw anything like that, I'll bet.' Crusoe opens his mouth wider, facing the kitchen window so that Dada can get a closer look.

'There's a big hole where your palate should be.'

'It's like that for ages – well, maybe not as bad. I noticed it first a while after I came home from France. Just a sort of a welt. I think I got it in the trenches. There were all sorts of things going. I saw a man and the feet nearly rotted off him from standing in the slush and the mud.'

'Why don't you go to the doctor?'

'I often meant to, but I kept putting it off.'

'Show me . . . My God! The whole roof of your mouth is gone. You should go over to Doctor Bergin, he'll see you right.'

'I must go in one of these days.'

'Sure, man – go in the next dispensary day. It's a lot better than worrying about it.'

The row has been going on while Dada stands shaving at the small round ivory-framed looking glass hanging from the side of the kitchen window. Mama continues to pity herself: 'Poor thing that never had a day's pleasure in her life: stuck in the house here from morning till night. I would be better off dead and that's the truth – a lot better off dead than married to someone like you.'

'You were glad to get me – damn glad to get me.'

'Oh you fairly pulled the wool over my eyes. Pity I didn't listen to my father. And Harry. And Sadie. They were all against you from the first day they met you. None of them had a good word to say about you.'

'Had they not.'

'Not one of them.'

'I never fell out with any of your family. *You're* the only one of your family I ever had a cross word with.'

'Oh you're very smart. They advised me often enough to have nothing to do with you.'

'Then I wish to God you had taken their advice!'

'They saw through you the very first day. They just couldn't believe that I would think of marrying you.'

Dada's hand trembles as he draws the cutthroat razor down along the length of his cheek. He turns from the mirror to face Mama, a thin line of blood oozing across his cheekbone. 'Why do you hate me so much, Cassy?'

'I don't hate anyone.'

'You hate *me*. Why? Just tell me why... I never done anything on you.'

'No, you never *done* anything on me.'

'What is it you have against me? Come on! Out with it!'

'Keep your voice down.'

'If you have some grudge in for me, tell me, and then maybe I can do something about it.'

'You can do nothing about it.'

'Nothing?'

'Not a thing.'

'You're going on like this for years. I can't take any more. I'm at the end of my tether.'

'We should never have got married.'

'Well, I'm damn sure if I knew the sort of life you were going to give me, I'd never have got married. Not in a hundred years.'

'Don't start shouting.'

'That's all you care about – the neighbours.' Dada swivels back to the mirror, blood streaking down his cheek. I watch anxiously as he dabs with the towel then brushes more shaving cream along his jawbone and under his chin.

Mama rants on: 'There's not another woman in the world would put up with you. My God above, when Father Feegan came in yesterday I was ashamed of my life – me down on my two knees scrubbing the floor. What must he think of you – any man that has his wife down scrubbing the floor –?'

'Did *I* ask you to scrub the floor?'

'Somebody has to scrub it.'

'I couldn't give a hang if you never scrubbed the floor.'

'No, you couldn't give a hang.'

'When you *had* a girl to scrub the floor, you never gave her a minute's peace.'

'Some girl – Katherine Breen!'

'And Brede. And Máire –'

'Máire – your own niece – a stupid slob.'

'Leave me alone, will you? Just give me five minutes' peace.'

'Leave you alone. Too long you were left alone, too long. And I'm the one that has to suffer for it. I'm certainly doing my purgatory on this earth.'

'Then if you are, you're making damn sure that everyone else is doing it as well.'

'Nice talk to his wife! That's a nice way to address your wife. You're a stubborn man – a real headstrong man.'

'Oh shut up!'

'Shut up, no less! Now for you! I'm the pity surely that has to put up with this sort of treatment. I should have left you years ago – that's what I should have done.'

'Why don't you then?'

'Oh Sacred Heart of Jesus!'

'Why don't you leave? Get to hell out of here and we'll all have some peace!'

'Maybe I will – and for good.'

'Nobody stopping you.'

Mama's head shakes and her lips quiver before the words come tumbling out. 'I'll do away with myself, that's what I'll do. I'll throw myself in the river.'

Dada freezes. 'In the name o' God, what sort o' talk is that!'

'I'll do away with myself, I'm warning you.'

'You'll do away with yourself?' Dada turns again towards Mama, the razor, blood-streaked, held at his throat, his voice rising. '*You'll* do away with yourself, is it? *You'll* do away with yourself!'

'Leave him alone, Mama!' I shout.

Dada slams the razor down on the table, his hand held on top of it. He stands trembling with his back to us, his two arms tensed stiff on the table, his head bent.

Fair day and an excited heifer jumps in over the pole that Ellen Andy has placed across her gateway. Ellen's daffodils are the pride of her life and the red heifer is leaping in and out through them, kicking her hind legs in high spirits. Ellen rushes into the garden shouting and cocking her fist, but she forgets to remove the pole. Around and around goes Ellen hop-stepping after the heifer, the two of them tramping all before them. When her mistake dawns on her, Ellen stops to clear the gateway; the heifer stands watching her. Ellen stares back and shakes her fist. She picks up a stick and the chase is on again – but each time the heifer passes the gateway. Ellen stops; the heifer stops – one as confused as the other.

'Leave her alone, Ellen! I'll get her out for you,' Father McBrearty, coming down the street, calls to Ellen.

'Oh Father, she's after destroying all! Look at my lovely daffodils and them only coming into their own.'

'Leave her to me now, Ellen. Shoo! Shoo!' Father McBrearty puts his hand on the heifer's rump. The heifer looks around at the priest and begins to amble at her ease towards the gateway and out on to the street. Father McBrearty turns to Ellen, laughing: 'Easy knowing you were born in the town, Ellen. I was reared on the land. As soon as I touched her she knew the game was up.'

A slight, sallow-skinned man with close-cropped white hair and wearing a baggy American suit bounces in, followed by an equally slight, blonde woman. 'Does James O'Donnell live hereabouts?' the man sings out in a jaunty voice, loud enough for everyone in the kitchen to hear.

Dada starts up from the table. 'Tom! Good God, man! You're the big stranger!' Dada throws his arms around his brother.

'This is the Wee Doll,' Tom introduces his wife to us with a laugh in his voice.

Mama knows the Wee Doll well: they used to meet at the dances in Duhaigh school when the Wee Doll's hair was 'as brown as the heather' – and she went to the States the day Mama's father was elected to the Donegal County Council for the first time.

'Sit down the two of you. You're looking well, Tom.'

'So are you.'

'How are times beyond?'

'The best. Never better. Dollar is strong at the moment.'

'The mighty dollar.'

'You and your mighty dollar.'

'When was it you came back home, Jamie?'

'Thirty-Four, yea.'

'Fourteen years ago.'

'Big changes since then. How is Paddy?'

'Paddy is the same as ever.'

'The wife died on him.'

'Two years ago. He was a bit down for a while, a bit lonely – but he's after finding a wee doll for himself. I think she's trying to talk him into marriage.'

'Foolish man if he listens to her. Paddy is well off – his own saloon and all.'

'He's doing all right.'

'You're in the saloon business now yourself, Tom?'

'Yea – for the past nine years.'

'He bought a second saloon,' the Wee Doll chimes in, 'out in Rockaway.'

'Rockaway. That's a long way from where you're living, isn't it?'

'Too far. I had to hire a manager. I just call out once or twice a week – keep an eye on things.'

'Plenty o' money in the saloon business?'

'No scarcity o' money. How are things here?'

'Good. Yea. Good.'

'Tell him the truth, Dada. Things couldn't be worse.'

'No – well – a bit slack at the minute. We were expecting an upsurge after the war.'

'Country hasn't come on any, so?'

'Not a whole lot. No. You did the right thing to stay beyond.'

'I guess so.'

'We haven't the population in this country.'

'You haven't the population and you haven't the natural resources and the country is too small. It'll never amount to anything.'

'Oh, now, that's a terrible thing to say about your own country.'

'Well, it's the truth, isn't it?'

'Tom is right. Nothing here for anyone.'

'Poor wee Ireland.'

'You'll have a drink – the two of you. Come up here, Tom, till I show you the place. See what you think of this for a saloon.'

       ★   ★   ★

Jellybob has the inside story on the appearance of the ambulance outside Ned Mary's. 'Ned wasn't himself for the last while, you know. When you went in, he would be sitting on the sofa in the kitchen and not a mum out o' him. It was the very same as if he was asleep, except that he had his eyes open. The first day I noticed anything wrong – I was after bringing him a cart o' turf. I threw it into the shed and all for him, and then I came in to get paid. Ned was on the sofa with his hat on as usual and I stood in front of him expecting he would know what was on my mind. Not a bit of it. I was looking at him but *he* wasn't looking at *me* – more, looking through me. "I'm after throwing in the turf," I said. Well, I might as well have blew my nose for all the effect it had on him. "I'm finished the job, Ned," says I, looking him in the eye. He was still looking through me. He said nothing, he did nothing, just sat there like a big cat blinking his eyes. Says I to myself, Ned Mary, you're gone through the Gap and no mistake and God only knows if you'll ever find your way back again. Margaret came in and she got the money out of the till. Enough said. I wasn't a bit surprised when I heard the ambulance called – to bring him you know where.'

'Where?'

'Oh, now, I'll say no more.'

'The hospital, is it?'

'I'll say no more.'

How do we know it's spring?

The hedgehogs are out, the daffodils are out and Suzanne is out. Her first Sunday of freedom and Suzanne has come in for her wee sniffle as usual, with her old friend and sparring partner.

'I'll tell you the truth, the county home is a place I wouldn't wish on anyone. There's about twenty of us sitting in a long draughty room – sitting looking at each other from morning till night like geraniums in a windowbox, and half of them asleep.

Very little talk, either. Some of them you couldn't talk to – they're gone with the fairies. Some of them that'll never see the road rising in front of them again. There's one oul' one – Katie they call her – and she had my heart broken from the day I went in. She was certain sure I was her sister and nothing could get it out of her head. Everywhere I went she was after me like a shadow. Biddy she was calling me. Biddy this and Biddy that – and if I didn't answer her, she was over nudging me. In the end she had me nearly as mixed up as herself. I got so used to answering to Biddy that I nearly forgot my own name. I'll tell you one thing: the county home is no place for sensible people. You might go in knowing the days of the week, but before a month is out you'll be lucky if you're able to tell day from night or whether it's awake or dreaming you are half the time.'

Suzanne has paid for the two glasses of port wine, and when Molly Dan orders two more to celebrate, Suzanne says she'll pay for them as well.

'No, you won't' – Molly reaches for her black knitted shopping bag, where she keeps her money knotted up in a handkerchief – 'you have the whole week ahead of you yet.'

'If I have itself, I have plenty to see me through.'

'What have you only your pension, or what's left of it, the same as the rest of us, as the fella says.'

Suzanne gives a croaky cackle and jingles her purse. 'Put away your money, Molly. I'm standing this, and the reason I'm standing it is because what I have in my purse is not one pension but two.'

'Two pensions! Glory be to God! How could you have two pensions?'

'I'll tell you how I could have two pensions. Before I left they gave me my pension and I put it in my purse. Well, I was passing down the hallway to go into the ambulance when the nun at the glass kaboosh called after me, "Suzanne did you get your pension?" I don't know what divil got into me – I didn't say I didn't get it, but I didn't say I did, either. I sang dumb. The nun reached into her money box and she counted me out another pension. So I thanked her and she shook hands with me and she said, "We'll be seeing you again, Suzanne, next winter." And I said to myself, You'll never see me here again, me lassie, and off I went. I suppose it was a sin, but I was so long in that oul' county home that I swore I'd have a good fling for myself when I got out – and I don't care if I have to do a bit of purgatory for it itself.'

'You have two pensions! God save us the day and the night – two pensions – and another one coming next week!'

Suzanne counts out sixpences and pennies for the drinks and gives Molly a quick squint at what she has left in her purse. 'Isn't it wonderful, Molly? As long as I'm going, I'm in the money at last.'

Monica has been telling Mama about Old Con and Sonny. 'Con was in the kitchen and he called Sonny in and told him to sit on the seat beside him and he put his arm around him. "I have something to tell you," Con said, "and I hope you won't take it bad. You're going to be confirmed the morrow – you're growing into a wee man and it's time for you to know. What I have to tell you is about myself and Nora, the Lord be good to her. You always called us Mammy and Daddy. But Nora wasn't your mother. And I'm not your father. I have to tell you this now because you're going to hear it sooner or later and it's better you hear it from me. You always thought Alice was your sister – but Alice is your mother. You might have felt she had a special love for you – I know she's in England since after you were born, but she always sent you things and she came home to see you as soon as she could. Your father was from Derry – he's in Scotland for years – if you ever want to find out about him, Alice'll tell you." Sonny was crying and Old Con was hard put not to break down himself. "I don't want you to think, Sonny," he said, "that this is going to make any difference between you and me, because it's not. As far as I'm concerned, you're no different from any of the rest of them that I reared. Anyway, you're so long calling me Daddy that I came to look on you as my son – and so you are – my grandson – and the first. So you have to take it like a man, Sonny. From now on you'll be calling me Granda." '

'Is your father in?'
  'He's in the kitchen.'
  'Tell him I want to see him. You know me, don't you? Brogan – Brogan from the Hill, tell him – Oh, how are you, Jamie?'
  'How are you, Weeshie?'
  'I'm running for election, Jamie – you probably heard – for the new party – Clann na Poblachta – the party of the future. Can I rely on you for your number one?'
  'Well, now, we'll see.'
  'Ah now, Jamie. I'm depending on you. The other crowd is in long enough; the Silent Man is in long enough, for all he has to show for it. Isn't it high time for a change, Jamie? Time to give the new man a chance, and that's myself. I'll see you right. I guarantee you things'll be a great deal different under Clann na Poblachta. And we're going to win. We're going to sweep the country. So now is the time to throw in your lot with us.'
  'A new party – I dunno – still – I'll give you a vote.'
  'Good man, Jamie. You'll give me your number one. Sure, aren't you a Hill man like myself? You won't forget me on election day? Good man, Jamie.'
  When Weeshie went into Lambert's there was a crowd there from the factory, among them Crusoe. Weeshie and Crusoe

never got on, but Weeshie went up to Crusoe as if they were the best of friends: 'Good man, Crusoe, you'll give me your number one.'

'Of course I will, Weeshie,' says Crusoe, 'and now if you'll excuse me, I have to go out the back to do my number two.'

'What are you doing?' Mama stops at the kitchen table to look over Dada's shoulder.

'Just dropping a few lines to Tom.'

'I'll do it for you.'

'It's all right – I'll manage myself.'

'He won't be able to read a word of that.'

'Tom'll make it out all right.'

'What are you writing about, anyway?'

'Well – you might as well know now as later: the thought struck me – if I went out for a while –'

'To the States!'

'I have to do something before we're all in the poorhouse. We'd have a decent life in the States. We'll all go out. What do you say?'

'What do I say! Springing it on me like this!'

'Sure, maybe it won't come to anything. I'm only broaching the subject at this stage. Everything depends on Tom – if he puts up the affidavits.'

'I knew you were discontented since the day he walked in the door.'

'He set me thinking, that's all.'

'Then you need to *think* – and *think* very carefully about what you're doing.'

'I know what I'm doing. America is the only country. We'd all be well off. Nothing in this wee hole of a town for anyone. Tom would give me a job and all in one of his saloons; he's looking for someone he can trust. No harm in writing to him anyway. See what he has to say.'

'Show me and I'll write it for you.'

'OK. I'll tear this up. Start again.'

'You're one discontented man and that's for sure.'

'Tell him all I want is the affidavits. I'll look after everything else myself, he needn't worry. If he wants to give me a job, well and good, but I'm not going to ask him.'

' "Dear Tom" . . . What next?'

'I was thinking things over after you went back –'

'You better ask him how he is first.'

'Oh. Right. Dear Tom, I hope you are in the best of form –'

'In the name of the Father and the Son and the Holy Ghost, amen. Saint Anthony guide us. Our Lady guide us. Now, start again.'

'Weeshie Brogan is a poor choice for any party.'

'A poor choice. Sure he never went beyond National School – and he made no great impression there.'

'What about Peadar Bawn? I never heard of *him* going to no university.'

'The Silent Man is sound.'

'You *think* he's sound – because he never *makes* a sound.'

'More cute than sound, I'd say.'

'He's a fly member, the same Silent Man.'

'Oh, a fly member.'

'Brogan is a bit of a clown. Most of the time he starts off, he says the opposite of what he means.'

'He'll make a good politician, so.'

'Brogan'll never get in; he'll lose his deposit.'

'Weeshie might surprise us all. He's a brave wee man.'

'He gets too excited; loses the head too easy. That's no good in politics.'

'Brogan has one weakness I don't like. You all know what I mean.'

'What's that?'

'Oh, now, you have ears like the rest of us.'

'Supposed to be fond o' the bloomers.'

'Fond o' the bloomers is right. There's not a woman in Trá Beag'll put out her washing the day he's collecting the rates.'

'Isn't that a fright!'

'I think it's all made up.'

'No made up about it. It's not long since he whipped a pair on Noreen Waters – and another pair on Smilin' Sadie.'

'Weeshie'll be all right once he gets married.'

'Imagine if he started that caper around Dáil Éireann.'

'Sure there's no clothesline in Dáil Éireann.'

'Brogan'll never get next nor near Dáil Éireann.'

'I think you're right. The Silent Man has it sewn up.'

'Of course he has. Brogan can rant and rave till the crows come home to roost; the Silent Man'll lie low, he'll never open his mouth, but when the votes are all counted, *he'll* be the one that's nice and snug in Leinster House.'

A terrible row between Mama and Dada, with Mama again threatening to throw herself in the river. After this, Dada is silent, but Mama rants on: 'Seven of yous reared on the side of the mountain with not a bite to put into your mouths half the time . . . a crowd o' tramps, that's what yous were . . . you fairly pulled the wool over my eyes . . .'

We listen in a daze, fearful of what may come next. When she has used up all the insults she can think of, both old and spur-of-the-moment, Mama heads up the stairs, her head shaking, stopping halfway to hurl back one final threat: 'I'll cut my throat, that's what I'll do. I'm warning you.'

'Go after her, Dada!'

Dada rushes to the banisters – and stops. 'It's no use. She won't listen to *me*. Maybe if one of yous went up . . .'

I tiptoe up the creaking steps and gently turn the knob of the bedroom door. But the door is locked.

'Mama . . . Mama . . .'

Beside me, Betty leans her face close to the keyhole, her voice rising then trailing off in a drawn-out, terrified wail: 'Mamaaa! . . . Mamaaa! . . . Mamaaa! . . .'

News that Cairbre's donkey was sick brought us to the half-door after school.

'What do yous want?'

'Just to see how Nedzer is.'

'He's no better.'

'Can we see him?'

Cairbre looks back over his shoulder into the peaty dimness of the kitchen. 'Well yous better be quiet, he's asleep now.'

We gathered around the heaving shaggy body stretched across the hearth.

'Is he for death?' Scunsey asked.

'For death! Well damn your bliddy eyes! The fever is on him but he'll get over it. Won't you, Nedzer?' Cairbre patted the donkey's bony rump.

Footsie had brought a cure and when Cairbre's back was turned he took the matchbox from his pocket, lifted Nedzer's tail and fired the ginger up his hole. We waited for the explosion – but nothing happened. Footsie left disappointed.

'Cairbre's donkey is jiggered,' he said, 'his shaggin' bum is dead already.'

A few days later Cairbre was in the bar after coming back from Father Feegan, where he had gone for a cure. 'He had the salt out and all and was ready to bless it when I let slip that it was for Nedzer. "Nedzer who?" says he. "Me donkey," says I. "An office! For a donkey!" says he. "Go home and have sense, man. There's nothing I can do for your donkey." I felt like telling him that if there's nothing you can do for a donkey then there's damn all you can do for a person either.'

'What age is he anyway?' Dada asked.

'That's what I don't rightly know myself. Between the two of us, he was a stray. He wandered in to me the morning after a fair – stuck his head in over the half-door. He was just a foal at the time. The poor divil was hungry and I took pity on him. That was nineteen years ago the twenty-fourth of July coming – and he's with me ever since.'

'Nineteen years in a donkey must be about the same as seventy in a person.'

'He's a spry seventy then . . . There wouldn't be a hait on him only the awful duckin' he got a few weeks back. The night of the big rain he was out till morning; that was the beginning of it.'

Next day we heard that Nedzer was dead.

'When is the wake?' Corner Jim asked Cairbre.

'Wake? Damn your bliddy eyes! You're very smart, aren't you? There might be a hell of a bigger crowd at that animal's wake than the'll be at your own.'

In the evening Big Jodie and Jellybob helped Cairbre to dig a grave at the bottom of the garden.

'We'll give him a good thend off,' Big Jodie said.

A crowd began to gather, some in the garden, some in the kitchen where the donkey was stretched out on his side, a bolster of hay under his head, a sugar bag covering his hind quarters, his front legs together, touching. 'The only thing missing was a rosary beads,' Crusoe said.

The sugar bag was taken off and forced under Nedzer's upper body; another sugar bag was drawn up under his rump. On each side three men strained and lifted, short trippity steps as far as the door – and they could go no further.

'We'll have to cut off his legs,' Jellybob said.

'Put him down a minute' – Big Jodie dropped his end – 'thole him ove' on hith back. Hold up hith legth.'

They try again, bare hooves in the air, head upside down, dragging over the threshold and down the garden.

Everyone seemed to be expecting some sort of ceremony, so after the body had been tipped over into the hole, Big Jodie moved to the head of the grave and threw in the first shovelful of clay.

'Dusth tho a't and unto dusth tho sha't thetu'n... We all knew thith donkey well,' Big Jodie began in a reverent tone. He then made a long speech about the great donkey Nedzer was: how he worked hard all his life, earning his bread by the sweat of his brow. But of course he wasn't perfect: there were times when he was inclined to wander from the straight and narrow and jump the ditches. Sometimes he would bring with him a crowd of ravenous young donkeys and they would lay waste all around them. 'But let him who ith without thin among you cast the fust sthone...'

Outside Canavan's Corner House the fair day crowd has gathered to hear Weeshie Brogan making his first speech in Glengreeny. Behind the table on which he stands a banner flaps, gusting between two upstairs' windows:

CLANN NA POBLACHTA
VOTE NO. 1
WEESHIE BROGAN

'... and anyone that trusts a politician is a fool, which is one of the reasons I'm asking you to vote for me, because I'm not a politician – I'm one of yourselves.'

'Hear! Hear!'

'The other crowd'll tell you what all they're going to do for you, once they get in power – they'll promise you sun, moon and stars. Well, I'm telling you the truth, I don't know what I'm going to do until I get elected because I don't know what it's like in Dáil Éireann – though I have a fair good idea – lying and cheating and robbing the people that elected you. But under Clann na Poblachta, all that is going to change. That's one promise I'm making you. Elect Weeshie Brogan and you'll have a new brush – a clean sweep of Dáil Éireann. The present government has the country destroyed. In the beginning they were all right – fair dues to every man – they were all right for a while in the beginning; they were green then, like a bunch o' bananas, then they got yella, and now they're rotten.'

'Good man, Weeshie!'

'Some of yous might be thinking to yourselves, Why should we elect Weeshie Brogan when we already have a TD in Dáil Éireann? Why not stick with the divil you know? Well, the question I'm asking yous is, *Have* yous a TD? This TD of yours – who shall be nameless – has been in Dáil Éireann now for twenty-two years. And what did he ever do for Glengreeny in all that time? Does anyone in Dáil Éireann, except himself, know that such a place as Glengreeny exists? Did this TD of yours ever say anything in Dáil Éireann about the hardships of the people of Glengreeny or Trá Gheal or the Hill?'

'True for you!'

'Hear, hear, Brogan!'

'Did he ever say anything in Dáil Éireann about anything? Your TD is a quiet man, you'll say, and he gets things done in a quiet way. But what did he ever get done? The only public work he ever done to *my* knowledge was to get a set of signposts put up after the war, with Malin, Killybegs and Kilcar written on them in Irish – and they're all pointing in the wrong direction!'

'Good man, Brogan!'

'Up Clann na Poblachta!'

'Up Dev!'

'Up Peadar Bawn!'

'Up the Silent Man!'

'Oh, he'll apply for the pension for you – in Irish, and he'll write out a reference for you – in Irish –'

'Like the one he wrote for yourself, Weeshie Brogan.'

'And got you a good job at the rate collecting.'

'Your TD is a silent man all right. Not once in twenty-two years did he ever come before you to give you any reason why you should vote for him. And as for his election campaigns! What sort of campaign does the Silent Man run? I'll tell you: he runs the sort of campaign that's the nearest thing there is to a silent campaign – which is a whispering campaign. A wink and a nudge and vote the Silent Man. Everyone will tell you to (Wink. Nudge.) vote the Silent Man. But the Silent Man himself will say nothing. He has a chance to put his cards on the table here today –'

'You're a quare-lookin' card yourself, Weeshie!'

'He has a chance to put his cards on the table today. Do you think he'll make an appearance? Oh no. As usual, the only appearance he'll make will be outside the school gate on election day – smiling and winking and shaking hands – and his motor-cars will be ferrying oul' ones from the county home and the chimney corner and their dying beds to vote for him. And not one of those people will know from Adam what they're voting for. Nobody that votes for the Silent Man has any idea what they're voting for. And the Silent Man himself, when he comes to cast his vote, has no idea what he's voting for.'

'Well said, Brogan!'

'Up Fine Gael!'

'Peadar Bawn for ever!'

'And if any of his supporters are wondering where he can be contacted the day, then I can tell them. You'll find him at home in slumberland – trying to snore off last night's load of after-hour booze –'

'Ah, now, come on.'

'Shut up your mouth, Brogan!'

'I'm not telling you a word of a lie – because I saw the Silent Man slinking out of Ned Mary's between two of his AOH buddies at one o'clock this morning –'

'And what were *you* doing abroad at one o'clock in the morning?'

'Taking in the washing?'

'This Silent Man of yours – my advice to him is to say out straight, once and for all, what his policy is –'

'And what's your own policy, Brogan?'

'Let him say what his policy is and stop all this goddam smiling and nodding and winking –'

'Who robbed Noreen Waters' big red ones?'

'When are you starting up the drapery, Weeshie?'

'All this goddammed handshaking and smiling and winking is not going to bring down the price of butter, and if you're taken in by it, then you're a crowd o' bliddy eejits and you deserve as good as you get!'

This morning the affidavits arrived in the post from Uncle Tom, and Dada is whistling around the kitchen and smoking full length cigarettes. Mama's humour is anything but cheerful.

'Oh, now, you're going to be a right laughing stock going off to the States at fifty years of age.'

'What are you talking about fifty? I'm forty-seven.'

'Forty-seven or fifty, it's all the one.'

'Three years in the difference. A lot can happen in three years.'

'Nothing will happen – except you'll be three years older.'

'Three years older! What sort o' talk is that?'

'Anyone over twenty-five has no business going to the States.'

'And what should I do then?'

'Do the same as everybody else. You don't see any of the other publicans leaving their wife and family and going off, do you?'

'Ned Mary is gone off – to the nuthouse. Maybe that's where you want me to go.'

'Oh you have an answer for everything.'

'I'm a lucky man I can go to the States. Every day I spend here is a day nearer the Mother Hubbard cupboard.'

'How did we ever get into such a situation? There's surely a dark cloud over this family.'

'No dark cloud. Everything'll turn out for the best yet. Anyway, Tom'll probably give me a job in the saloon. All I'm afraid of now is the medical. I hope the leg doesn't come against me.'

'How many times did I tell you to see about that leg and you wouldn't listen?'

'Nothing wrong with my leg, only it's a wee bit itchy now and again . . . Have you a pen there? We'll have to send these on to the American consul.'

'God save us the day and the night, Jamie, it's a terrible thing to have to go behind anybody's back, but what could I do? If I left her where she was, she would be famished. She hadn't even a drop o' paraffin to put in the lamp except what I brought over to her myself – for all the thanks I got. She was after getting wild forgetful entirely. The good saucepan she had – she burned the bottom out of it and couldn't remember ever doing it. She could remember nothing. "Had you your dinner?" I asked her. She couldn't remember whether she had her dinner or not. Sitting in the dark, stooped over the hearth, with the fire going down and that oul' dudeen of a pipe stuck in her gob. That's what was keeping her alive, as the fella says – snuff and tobaccy.

"Would you not go to bed itself?" I said to her. But she had enough of the bed. As soon as she lay down the pains would start – in her legs and her neck and all over. I was scared of my life she would doze off in that oul' wobbly chair of hers and topple headlong into the hearth. Eventually I got her as far as the bed and under the clothes, and it was no easy job, because she changed her mind a half-dozen times on the way. Once she was in, I knew she would stay there, because it would be too much of an effort for her to get out again. That evening I went in to the Jubilee nurse and told her the story. The day after, the ambulance came for her. Glory be to God, I was ashamed to show my face outside the door. I never looked out once till I heard the ambulance going down the road. I'm sure she knows it was no one but myself informed on her – but it was either that or have her famished or burned alive or God knows what. Do you know, Jamie, I'm dreading the spring. She'll destroy all when she gets out; she'll have my life, as the fella says.'

'Is Weeshie Brogan bonified?'

'No, he's not. Sure he's well inside the three mile limit.'

'You'll have to leave, Weeshie, I'm afraid. It's after closing time.'

'Wait a minute, Jamie, I'm sleeping with my aunt tonight – I mean – not sleeping – I mean . . .'

Just beyond Ferdia's house the ambulance has stopped. The driver steps down from the cab, and from the passenger's side a nun appears in a long black habit, her white cowl flapping in the wind. The driver swings open the doors at the rear; he draws out a canvas stretcher; the nun takes out sheets and a pillow, and they both go into the house, leaving the ambulance doors gaping behind them.

'Ferdia is going to Derry to see a specialist,' Scunsey says.

'Will the specialist make him better?' Paddy Anne asks.

'Maybe he will.'

We have broken off the game of handball we had been playing against the gable of the old hall and have moved out on to
the sidewalk.

'Should we go up to wish him the best?'

'They mightn't like us to.'

The driver and Stonehead carry Ferdia out on the stretcher,
the nun walking beside them, one hand holding down her
cowl, the other on the sheet over Ferdia's chest. They are
followed by Mrs O'Regan and Aisling, who has Ferdia's rug
across her arm. As the men turn with the stretcher and the
driver steps up into the ambulance Ferdia sees us. He smiles and
waves. We raise our hands and Scunsey gives the victory sign.
The nun stands aside until Stonehead steps down, then, taking
the rug from Aisling, she goes into the back of the ambulance.
The driver closes the shiny white doors with a clang and Aisling
and her father and mother stand stiffly together waiting for the
ambulance to move away.

'. . . The last night I was up in Maggie May's, Tom came in, after
being at the pictures. He has another two stone put on him, at
least. Collapses into the chair at the fire, takes out the tobacca
and starts to rub a smoke for himself. "*Lady be Good* was no
damn good," says Tom. "Maggie, take off me wellies." '

'She had her tea in the hotel; driven all the way from the county
home in a motorcar and back again: herself and Kitty Doogue
and two oul' fellas from Malinbeg. I had it all from Smilin'
Sadie. The two oul' fellas ordered two bottles o' stout, Kitty had
a lemonade and Suzanne ordered a wee sniffle. Nobody in the
hotel knew what a wee sniffle was and Suzanne couldn't
enlighten them, as the fella says. She couldn't remember. Is it

whiskey? No. Is it brandy? No. Is it sherry? No. In the end somebody mentioned port wine. That's it. They were all laughing at
her. God save us the day and the night, she disgraced herself.
She drank two full glasses o' port wine, without a drop o' water
or cinnamon or a thing in them – and paid for none of them
because she forgot her purse. Going out the door, she discovered
it was on a string around her neck all the time. She was staggering getting into the car, as the fella says. And after all that, Peadar
Bawn lost his seat. He might as well have left her where she was.'

'I was terrible worried going in to the doctor on account of the
leg. He knew as soon as he looked at it. "You got your veins
out," he says. He gave me a prescription for the chemist. I have
to put ointment on twice a day. Not a bother on me otherwise.
"You're as healthy as a man of thirty," says he. Away with me
on the bus to O'Connell Street to get something to take the
hunger off me. I was crossing at Nelson's Pillar when who
should I meet coming against me only the Silent Man – Peadar
Bawn himself. Big shakehands for me. How are you, Jamie?
and all that. Brought me into the Gresham Hotel and stood me
a half-un o' whiskey. He was after being made a senator himself.
He's a decent man, Peadar Bawn – no malice in him. You
know, drinking his whiskey, I felt ashamed of myself that I
never gave him a vote in all the years – except last preference.
Too late now. The next election I'll be voting in will be for
president of the United States.'

A cold, drizzly March morning seeping down the windowpane
and Dada's heavy step creaking around in the upper bedroom.
    'Betty! It's time to get up . . . Betty! Come on! Dada is up.'
    Dada's new gaberdine coat, his hat and his paisley scarf are
laid out on the banisters from the night before; on the long seat
the battered brown suitcase has its lid open.

Mama is at the range, sulk-faced, frying eggs. Dada wipes the lather from his cutthroat razor, folds it back and pushes it down in the corner of the case.

'What's this!' He turns around to Betty and myself, holding up an envelope addressed 'Dada'.

'Don't open it,' Betty says. 'It's for when you're in New York.'

We had both written the letter yesterday and Betty put in the five dollars that Uncle Tom gave her – not thinking that the case would be opened again until Dada arrived in the States.

Dada lays the envelope back in the case on top of everything else. 'Don't be sad. We'll all be together again soon.'

None of us feels like talking during the breakfast and when Hill pulls up outside, Dada rises suddenly and in a flurry flings on his hat and his scarf and reaches into his inside pocket to check his passport and sailing ticket.

'My God, take your time! He'll wait for you.'

Dada grabs his gaberdine from the banister. Turning, he folds his arms around Mama, lifting her off her feet and kissing her. He draws Betty and myself towards him and holds the three of us tight.

As he goes out the door with his well-labelled case Mama shakes holy water after him.

Betty and myself stand in the doorway and watch the car straining up the Slope, Dada waving to us through the back window.

For the first time ever, Mickey Beag is playing my new fiddle in the kitchen, when, down from the bar, comes the Yankee McGee. The Yankee is very fond of music and has been up in Mickey Mhór's house already to hear him playing and storytelling. Mickey Beag and Mickey Mhór are first cousins but two more unalike it would be hard to come across. Mickey Mhór takes the fiddle and all to do with fiddling very seriously and is inclined to be short-tempered with other musicians. Mickey Beag's attitude is light-hearted. He is a much better fiddler than Mickey Mhór, but because Mickey Mhór talks so much he gets most of the attention. Some fiddlers like to give themselves a build-up before each tune. Mickey Beag never goes in for this sort of thing, but Mickey Mhór won't draw the bow across the strings without first telling the story of what he is going to play. The stories are all about fairies and ghost fiddlers, who had been overheard playing the tune, and so it was handed down the generations.

Mickey Beag plays the flute as well as the fiddle. He also made up two tunes of his own, one fast, one slow – 'Two oul' fideraries', Mickey Mhór calls them.

MICKEY BEAG'S REEL

FAREWELL TO KILCAR

When Mickey Beag had finished playing a three-part reel, the Yankee asked him what the name of it was.

'Call it anything you like,' Mickey Beag answers.

'Come on, now, it's gotta have a name.'

' "Butter and Crame",' Mickey says, off-hand.

' "Butter and Crame"? That's funny. It reminds me when we were growing up – if someone asked your name – What's your name? Butter and Crame.'

'That's what it's called – "Butter and Crame" – though the proper name of it is "The Donkey on the Gate".'

' "The Donkey at the Gate", I guess,' the Yankee corrects Mickey.

'No. "The Donkey on the Gate".'

'I heard of "The Pigeon on the Gate",' the Yankee says, 'but "The Donkey on the Gate"! That's a noo one on me.'

'That's what it's called,' Mickey says, ' "The Donkey on the Gate".'

'I guess there's a story behind it?' The Yankee looks hopeful.

'A story?'

'Your cousin Mickey Mhór has lots of stories to go with the toons he plays.'

'Oh there's a story behind it all right,' Mickey agrees.

'Are you gonna tell it?'

'I'll tell you now' – Mickey sounds the strings with his thumb and rests the fiddle on his knee, the bow dangling from his other hand. 'There was this fiddler from Kilmore – it all happened a long time ago – McCall was his name and he was after burying his father and mother – the both of them got killed by a bull when they were taking a nearcut across the river; anyway, McCall was on his way home from the funeral, d'ye see? and he had the fiddle under his oxter. It was late at night because he drank a fair sup after the burial and when he came to the estate wall he noticed that the big iron gate was off its hinges – it was lying flat on the road and a white donkey sitting on top of it. Just as McCall was going to pass, the donkey hopped down off the gate and on to the road blocking his way. "Sorry for your trouble," says the donkey, "and will you play 'Butter and Crame'?" McCall was too frightened to argue, d'ye see, so he put the fiddle under his chin and he started to play "Butter and Crame". Well, he was gone no distance into the tune when the donkey let a hee-haw of a snort out of him. "Stop! Stop! You're playing that all wrong," says the donkey. Now McCall was a pretty nifty fiddler and he didn't like anyone telling him that he wasn't playing a tune right – especially a donkey – so he quit playing altogether. "Play it yourself, so," says he, "seeing that you're so smart." Well, the donkey took the fiddle in his shank and he took the bow in the cleave of his foot and he sat on the gate, and boy could he play! McCall was standing with his mouth wide open – as wide as any donkey's – listening to this powerful tune being hoofed out of his fiddle. He could have been an hour listening, he could have been two hours, when it dawned on him that there was something terrible wrong about all this. "Hold on you now," says he to the donkey, "that's not 'Butter and Crame' you're playing at all. The first few notes was 'Butter and Crame' all right but after that you're gone to the four corners of the world." Sure the donkey didn't take a dang bit notice of him but kept on fiddling away. McCall was following the tune the best way he could, because, whatever else, he didn't want to lose it. The donkey kept playing the tune over and over, and every time it got more complicated than the time before, with more and more high parts and low parts and slurs and all kinds of birrells and twists. McCall was dizzy in the head trying to keep up with it and learn it at the same time, when all of a sudden the music stopped. It was morning, d'ye see, and the donkey took to his heels across the field and was never seen more. McCall grabbed the fiddle from the gate and he started playing like mad the donkey's version of "Butter and Crame" and be damned but hadn't he it off note for note. He played it all the way home, over the ditches and across the river for a nearcut, so that it was well sunk in by the time he got to his house – and then he played it sitting in front of the fire until he fell fast asleep. Sometime in the middle of the night he woke up with the fiddle still under his chin – straight away he lashed into "The Donkey on the Gate" – that's the name he was calling the tune now – but be damned if he could remember a single note. It was gone completely, d'ye see. There wasn't a scrape of it left in his head or in any of his fingers. And that's how the tune came about – "The Donkey on the Gate" – and that's how it was handed down the generations to this very day.'

'Sure, Conor. Miss Dee is only feathering her own nest. You'll be much better off in Rathar school. Everyone is talking about the wonderful teacher Master Brick is – two and three scholarships every year. Ned Mary wouldn't be sending Nora to Rathar if it wasn't the best school.'

'How am I going to get there?'

'We'll sort all that out.'

'It's five miles to Rathar.'

'Hill drives Nora Mary over every morning. Maybe we can share the expenses. Betty can go as well. The two of you will be together again. Yous should never have been separated the first day; I said that all along.'

'I don't want to change school again.'

'Mama knows what's best. You'll be much happier in Rathar, yourself and Betty. You'll have a comfortable drive over every morning with Hill.'

'And how will I get home?'

'How does Nora Mary get home?'

'She has to take the nearcut across the bog.'

'Well, aren't you as well able as Nora Mary to cross the bog?'

'I don't want to have to cross any bog. Betty won't be able to walk across the bog.'

'That's enough about it now. We'll go over to see Master Brick early next week.'

'Listen to this boys: "Ex-Army Officer in Neelons Haul. Before a special sitting of Dundalk district court on Tuesday was Dermot Spearman, Glengreeny, Co. Donegal, former army captain, who was remanded on a charge of smuggling forty pounds worth of neelons" –'

'What!'

'Neelons. Forty pounds worth of neelons.'

'What the hell is neelons?'

'Neelons – would it be? – it must be some sort of – neelons – I dunno.'

'Forty pounds worth of neelons – that's what it says.'

'What the hell is he up to at all!'

'Some sort of cigarettes, maybe.'

'I don't think it's cigarettes, because it says forty pounds worth of neelons and seventy pounds worth of cigarettes.'

'Would it be whiskey?'

'I never heard of Neelon's whiskey, did you?'

'Never.'

'What about you, Crusoe? Neelons?'

'Never heard of it.'

'Probably some sort of new stuff. There's all sorts o' new inventions on the go since the war.'

'It must be something people wants and is willing to pay for. I mean – if he's smuggling it – forty pounds worth of it – that's a hell of a lot of – of neelons.'

'Here's a man will know. We have a wee problem here, Dan. The Captain is after being nabbed with forty pounds worth of neelons on him.'

'Neelons?' Claddagh looks puzzled.

'See. It's in the *Donegal Democrat*. "Ex-Army Officer in Neelons Haul".'

'Oh. Nylons.'

'What did you call it?'

'Nylons. It's stockings.'

'Forty pounds worth of stockings! Come on.'

'They're made out of a new material. Not wool. Nylon. They're called nylons.'

'Who the hell is going to pay for smuggled stockings?'

'The ladies go crazy for them, so I hear.'

'Ladies' stockings! Oh, that's a different matter.'

'Nylons are – ladies' stockings?'

'That's what they are.'

'He was smuggling ladies' stockings!'

'Christ almighty!'

'It's not a man's game.'

'Far from it.'

' "Ex-Army Officer in Nylons Haul"! Did you ever hear worse than that?'

'Isn't he the right trick-o'-the-loop the same Spearman.'

'Miss Rose has her hands full with thon boyo.'

'If it was cattle he was smuggling itself, or butter, or tea. But neelons!'

'You're not pronouncing it right. What is it again, Dan?'

'Nylons.'

'Nylons. That's it.'

'Nylons. Well, that's a good one. The man is disgraced for life. Nylons no less.'

Rathar school, like Trá Gheal, consists of just one open room, though much bigger, and there are two teachers. Betty has been placed with Mrs Crean, who holds sway at the chimney end; Master Brick has the bigger space – two windows to Mrs Crean's one. In between is no-man's-land, where Mrs Crean talks to Master Brick in a whining voice and at other times walks back and forth with him until he gets over one of his 'wee turns'.

Mrs Crean is a gentle, sad-faced worrier who has a terrible time with her husband The Bottle Crean. The Bottle is also a teacher and is on his last chance. At Easter Mrs Crean went around all the pubs in Rathar telling them to give no more drink to The Bottle.

'You were in Trá Gheal?' Master Brick wheezes at me, a little clump of grey hairs bristling on each of his pudgy, purple-veined cheeks.

'Yes, *a Mháistir*.'

'And before that you were in Glengreeny?'

'Yes, *a Mháistir*.'

'Will you settle down here, do you think?'

'Yes, *a Mháistir*.'

'Well, I hope so. A rolling stone gathers no moss, you know.'

Master Brick is a small barrel of a man, with piggy eyes and puffy cheeks that gradually turn from purple to flaming red as his temper rises. Whatever class he teaches stands in a half-circle in front of him. 'Close the line!' he wheezes, when anyone is pulled into the centre for punishment. Everyone is called by their surname and you must answer up immediately, loud and clear, otherwise you get an elbow in the ribs or a jostle, or, if you're McGinley, very likely a box in the face. Nobody feels safe in any of Master Brick's classes and I have been only a few days in the school when he gets one of his wee turns. He is laying into McGinley, who has missed several questions, punching him and swinging him around the floor by his gansey. Master Brick's cheeks are turkey-cock red and puffing with temper: 'I'll take no more nonsense from you, McGinley.' (Punch) 'Stupid ignorant –' (Swipe) 'clod.'

McGinley has his hands over his head trying to ward off the blows that are following him like a Big Wind around the room.

No more questions are coming from the Master – just louder and angrier insults. 'Why do you bother your head coming to school?' (Swipe. Swipe.) '*Amadán!* Meenaroan bog-eejit!'

McGinley is darting this way and that, with the cruel pudgy fists flailing at him.

Suddenly the Master's leg shoots out and McGinley sprawls on his face. Master Brick is breathless and shaking with rage. He lashes out with one boot and then the other, while McGinley hops and jumps around, trying to avoid the vicious kicks aimed at him. The Master's insults have turned into mocking roars, his fists and his feet ready to lash out at anyone who gets in his path.

McGinley's eyes plead for a way of escape through the closed line, but none of us has the courage to let him through. In the end it is from the other side that the line is breached. Mrs Crean stands beside the Master, her hand on his shoulder. She is taller than Master Brick and guides and partly forces him to no-man's-land.

Master Brick, still shaking and puffing, walks up and down and up and down, while Mrs Crean's mournful voice whines in his ear. McGinley is also shaking as he shuffles back to his place, all our sad eyes following him.

'. . . the silly talk about Old Nick; we used to be laughing at him, but there was something in it, all the same. There was something about him – even the daftest things he came out with – like the day I met him on the way to the fair. I was driving the two wee heifers before me, hoping to make a sale. "Put it off till another day," he said. "Put it off till another day." How could I put off selling the two heifers? I had no hay for them. And the next fair was a month away and prices would be further down. But that was the fair day I had the accident. Squeezed in against the wall and the cart on top of me, I remembered his words: "Put it off till another day." Old Nick was never far from his mind the last week. He talked of nothing else only how Old Nick was out to get him. "*He's* getting stronger all the time and *I'm* getting weaker", that's what he said. "*He's* getting stronger and *I'm* getting weaker." I met him coming down the lane on Saturday. "I'll take him with me," he said, in that peculiar way he had of talking into his moustache. "Who do you mean?" I said. "Who do you think?" says he. "Is it Old Nick?" says I. "Who else?" says he. "I may not be able to save myself but the'll be nothing left for *him* to hang on to, either." He got a terrible death. He made it out of the bed – as far as the kitchen – but the fumes and the smoke must have suffocated him. He was lying outside the bedroom door. You wouldn't recognise the body. Everything in the house was burned to a cinder. Only the four blackened walls were left standing.'

★   ★   ★

'Do you know what I am, Conor?'

'What do you mean, what you are?'

'In the stars, I mean.'

'What are you talking about?'

'Gemini is the star I was born under.'

'You weren't born under a star.'

'I was so.'

'Only God was born under a star – the star of Bethlehem.'

'Everyone was born under a star.'

'They were not.'

'They were so.'

'Who told you that?'

'Nora Mary.'

'How does *she* know?'

'It's in the *Woman's Own*. She showed it to us. Nora Mary is Scorpio. I'm Gemini. Do you know what Gemini is?'

'I don't believe you were born under a star; I don't believe Nora Mary was born under a star.'

'Well, we were. Gemini is the twins. That's what I am.'

'We're not twins.'

'Do you know what Aisling is?'

'What?'

'Aquarius.'

'Aq – ua – ri – us?'

'It means, the water carrier.'

'What does water carrier mean?'

'I dunno. Carrying water, I suppose.'

'From the pump?'

'Or the well. Do you know what you are?'

'How would I know?'

'I forget the name of it – but it means a goat.'

★　★　★

Dear Cassy,

I hope you are well as I am very well here myself. I hope
Conor and Betty are well too. Tell them I was asking for
them and that Im thinking of them always. I am in the best
of form myself and begining to get the hang of the job.
Everything here is on draft all beer. The stout is in bottles
and so thick you couldent drink it. Even the Irish doesent
touch it. Me and Tom went out to see Sean and Maura
Sally's children on Sunday. The two of them have there
own apartment in the Bronx. Sean works full time on the
buildings and Maura has a job minding an old Yankee
woman. They coked us a lovely dinner sweet potatoes and
all and told myself to come out any Sunday I want. The
two of them are doing well so you can tell Sally. There is
not much news around here. I am bussy during the day but
in the evening it is lonely. I miss you all. There is a lot of
Donegal people around here from inside they come into the
saloon after work at all hours of the day because they are on
different shifts. They are lovely people and great spenders.
No scarsity of work at the moment. When the turf comes
tell Jellybob to put it in the old byre it will be less trouble
than building a turf stack. Tell him first to take out the sith
and the spade and the shovel and anything else hel be
needing later on. Tell Claddagh and old Con I was asking
for them. I met Cons son Arthur out in Paddys place and he
told me all about Ned Mary he was definitly in the asilum
and very bad too. Funny you have to travel 3000 miles to
find out about your next door naybour. Tell Con I met
Arthur and he is doing well. I miss you all terrible. You can
lodge the dollars I am sending in the Ulster Bank in
Killybegs. I want to keep it seperate in case the income tax
might get on to me. The few extra dollars are for Conor
and Betty. I wont be able to send anything next week or

the week after because I have to get somewhere to stay and I will have to put down a deposit. I cant expect Tom to put me up any longer. There is three bags of corks in the bottling store so you needent order any untill the first bag is run out. We are lucky to have Jellybob to do odd jobs as he is a great worker. Just let him do things his own way and you wont have a bit of bother. I forgot to mention Paddy is getting married on Saturday out in Long Island so we will have a big day there. The girl he is marrying is from Alabama her grandfather was Irish and ten years younger than him. Well I have to finish now and I will be thinking of yous all. Tell Conor and Betty to write to me.

Your loving husband
Jamie.

Between each sweep of the windscreen wipers I watch the curved, tapering bonnet rising and dipping through the downpour, like the prow of a fishing boat. In the back sit Betty and Nora Mary cold and glum, their schoolbags between them. We pass the old limekiln, the crossroads where Peadar Bawn's signpost in Irish points into the bog – and further on, the blackened hulk of Willoughby's house with the roof fallen in. Every so often Hill wipes the damp from the windscreen with an old knitted glove and tips the Woodbine he is smoking against the edge of the ashtray. The only sound is the swish of the wheels through the wet and the louder gurrell of the engine as the road rises steeper in front of us. At the top of the hill the blurred outline of the big gable rock out in the bay comes into sudden view – the same that I saw every morning on my way to Trá Gheal. Little did I realise then how well off I was.

Leaning on the counter, Mama wets the pencil in her mouth and writes in Aunt Sally's passbook: '¼ tea, ½ sugar, cocoa, ½ butter –'

'Any word from Jamie?'

'Any word from Jamie' – Mama glances up sharply at Aunt Sally's round innocent face – 'that's all I hear from morning to night – any word from Jamie.'

'Don't bite the nose off me. I only asked.'

'He should be at home minding his business, that's where he should be – not three thousand miles away in the States.'

'Oh Waidean! Hadn't he to go beyond to make some money?'

'Who told you that? Plenty money to be made here, if he only put his mind to it. No wonder people are talking about him.'

'Who's talking about him?'

'Oh, you're the innocent. Any man that'll go off, leaving his wife and family to fend for themselves –'

'Isn't he sending you money? You told me he sent you money regular.'

'An excuse for staying away, that's all it is. If he was any good, he wouldn't have to go to the States.'

'Oh Waidean, the way she talks about her husband!'

'America is all any of yous ever think of. That's all yous were reared for – the emigration boat.'

'I'm not going to stand here listening to you insulting Jamie and the whole family. You can keep your groceries. There you are – tea, sugar, butter – you can do what you like with them. This is the last time you'll see me in here.'

'Then you better pay what you owe. You have a hefty bill in your passbook.'

'I'll pay what I owe to Jamie, when he comes back. Though if he has any sense, he'll stay where he is.'

'Get out with you this minute!'

'I'm going, never fear.'

'And take your eggs with you too.'

'Waidean, but you're the spitfire!'

'You're no asset to anybody – everything on tick.'

'Plenty glad to have me. I'll go where my custom will be appreciated. Next door – that's where I'll go – straight into Ned Mary's.'

On the long grey-blue summer evenings, after going to bed, I lie on my back listening to the music crackling from the fair green. Doherty's Amusements haven't many records and the few they have they play over and over again. One of my favourites is:

> Soldier from the wars returning,
> Patriotic fervour burning,
> Safe from musket and from shell,
> Brave the stories that you tell . . .

After school we stroll around the deserted fairground – the red and green and orange swingboats leaden above their shiny braking-boards, the rifle range with last night's punctured cards still on the shelf, the sour-sweet smell of trampled grass and drenched canvas, and the battered, tented lorry, where the slot machines wait in line for a feed of pennies and a hopeful shakehands. If no one from Doherty's is in sight, we pull each handle in turn. Sometimes one of us might have a few coppers, the rest crowd around offering advice until a machine is chosen, fed and pumped, before being cursed for a dirty rotten greedy gut. None of us so far has made any money from the slots. Once, Footsie managed to stack up nine pennies before his luck turned, and Sonny Moylan, starting with only two pence, had rung up rows of bells and cherries and bananas and had lost track of his wealth, but then Lobbylugs turned nasty and swallowed everything back again.

By now we have got to know the peculiar habits of each

machine; the grown-ups have already given them names. The most generous is nicknamed The Toff; the meanest – a squat, hunched, crooked-handled trickster – is called Go Balls. Whenever Go Balls is fed he rattles and rumbles as if he is going to cough up the jackpot, but very seldom anything comes out. At night people call the boss over to complain about how tight-fisted Go Balls is. The boss, a burly man with a grouchy, pock-marked face, takes out a handful of pennies to coax Go Balls. In no time he is putting money back in his pockets. 'Nothing wrong there,' he says, but as soon as he turns on his heel Go Balls starts gulping down everything again and sits tight like a stingy drinker who never stands his round.

'Try The Toff, Boxty,' Sonny Moylan suggests.

Boxty is jingling seven pennies in his pocket, the remains of a shilling that Corner Jim gave him for finding his good over-coat in the ditch. Sonny Moylan, Footsie, Paddy Anne and myself follow Boxty up and down the line of machines, our fingers feeling around each for any left-over pennies; Footsie searches in the grass where he found a threepenny bit one Sunday morning – but now he finds only a bent shoe nail.

'Try Blue Pete,' Paddy Anne advises. 'I won four pence and three pence last Sunday. Blue Pete is the best.'

'Blue Pete is a cheat. Try Lobbylugs.'

'Come on, Boxty. Chance something.'

Boxty has stopped at The Toff. He puts a penny in the slot, holding it there with his thumb. When the penny drops we cheer and Boxty pulls the handle sharply, sending fruit and bells whirring around . . . One for The Toff.

None of us says anything while Boxty bites his lip before chancing another penny . . . Two for The Toff.

Hurriedly Boxty offers up another penny. And another. All for The Toff. He dithers, fingering the three pennies still itching in his palm.

'Don't give up now, Boxty.'

'Try Blue Pete.'

'Try Lobbylugs.'

Boxty feeds another penny to The Toff. Then another. 'Damn you, Toff!' He looks at his last penny and rubs it on his bare arm.

'Chance it, Boxty.'

'Maybe the jackpot is coming up.'

Without moving from where he stands, Boxty lets his eyes wander warily over the pawky machines. To the left of him, Footsie is trying to hoodwink Go Balls with a Ludo button. Go Balls swallows the button but gives no handshake.

'I'll chance Go Balls' – Boxty quickly drops his last penny in the slot.

Go Balls clears his throat. His three crafty eyes roll in his head, whirr around in a blur and come to a jolting, unfocused halt. A rumbling in his guts, a sort of smothered fart – the usual Go Balls trick – and then nothing.

'Why didn't you try Lobbylugs?'

'Or Blue Pete.'

'Or even Skinner.'

Suddenly Boxty's fist shoots out and lands Go Balls a vicious punch in the belly. Go Balls groans and shivers. He looks as if he is going to start up again. Then a pile of pennies comes vomiting out.

'Good old Go Balls!'

'How much did you get, Boxty?'

Boxty scoops up his winnings and shoves another penny in Go Balls's ear. He jerks Go Balls roughly by the arm and more pennies come spluttering out. Another punch in the belly, another groan, and still more pennies spitting on to the ground. We all dive, elbowing and jostling, except Footsie, who gives the twisted arm of Go Balls another vicious jerk.

Boxty springs up just in time to catch the few pennies that are dribbling from the jutting iron mouth. He shoulders Footsie out of the way and gives Go Balls a dig in the ribs, followed by a fist into the face. A golden shower of pennies rains down on our heads.

'Hand them over. They're mine.' Boxty collects from each of us.

I look up at Go Balls. His eyes are still spinning dizzily, his guts rumbling as he throws up all around him. Boxty has one trouser pocket stuffed and is filling up the other. The pennies keep coming out in belches and burps. When it looks as if Go Balls's stomach is beginning to settle, Boxty sticks his fingers far back in his mouth and gives him another haymaker under the belt.

'What do you think you're doing!' The pock-marked face of the boss glowers down at us.

We scramble to our feet, fearful of the big hairy fist the boss has raised. Boxty scoops up a rake of pennies and, with his hands in his pockets, takes to his heels.

'Come back here! Come back with my money!' – the boss lumbers after Boxty, shaking his fist.

In his panic Boxty has made the mistake of running towards the river and is now trapped in a corner between the fair green wall and the river bank, which is waist high with nettles.

'Ah ha! You're nicely caught. By Jesus, I'll put manners on you!'

Where the wall ends, a tall chestnut tree slants towards the bank, its higher branches dangling out over the water. Using one leg as leverage against the stone wall, Boxty hoists himself up the tree trunk and for a moment is lost in the branches.

Thwarted, the boss tramps around the base of the tree, scowling upwards. When Boxty appears again he is well out of reach and still climbing.

The boss grabs at a branch and holds it, hesitating. 'Come down out o' there, you blackguard you! Come down before I shake you down!'

'Shag off!' Boxty shouts over his shoulder, making his way out to a thick, sturdy branch, which overhangs the Deep Hole.

The boss lets go of the branch he is holding and it springs upwards out of reach. 'By Jesus, you'll pay for this – if I have to wait here till cockcrow!'

We watch from a safe distance, wondering what we can do to help.

Boxty looks down at the boss and makes donkey's ears at him: 'Hee-haw, hee-haw, hee-haw!'

'Good man, Boxty!'

'You have him bate, Boxty.'

The boss turns on us: 'Clear off to hell, you crowd o' blackguards! Off with you!'

'Up here!' Boxty taunts the boss again. 'Why don't you come up after me – if you're able? Big Boss!' Boxty is enjoying himself, riding the swinging branch like a bucking bronco and making faces. 'Come on and get me, you big gulpin you. You're just full of piss and shite and Christmas Day farts!'

Suddenly Boxty topples sideways with a frightened scream.

The boss starts back from the tree: 'Hold on you, for Christ's sake! Don't let go!'

Boxty, dangling by his legs over the Deep Hole, tries to raise his upside-down head, his arms flailing around wildly like stripling branches blown about in a storm.

'Christ's sake, don't move! Pull yourself up with your legs . . . Take it easy . . . Hold on there!'

Slowly Boxty draws himself upwards until one hand grasps the branch supporting him. There is a splash in the water like a trout jumping, then another splash – and another – and another – as down through the trembling leaves rains a magical shower of pennies, spinning, sparkling, plop-plop-plop! We look from the river to Boxty, who is now holding on to the branch with both hands, too frightened to staunch the burnished treasure downpouring from his pockets.

'Well dammit, if that doesn't beat anything I ever saw! That takes the biscuit and no doubt about it.' The boss turns his face upwards, almost smiling. 'Come down now and I won't touch you. Nobody will lay a finger on you. Only let this be a lesson to you. You're after getting a fair warning from the Man Above.'

'Why was she called Big Winnie?'

'Because she was big, I suppose.'

'Was she as big as Big Sarah?'

'Bigger.'

'As big as Big John McBride?'

'Oh, Betty, don't be annoying me.'

'Have you a photograph of her?'

'No, I haven't. I saw enough of her – far too much for my own good, big lazy lump! She had so many cardigans on her she was like a bale of wool; she was barely able to put one leg in front of the other. And a black skirt and a red flannel petticoat on the hottest day in summer. She had the petticoat on her when she got up and she had it on her in the bed. No man should ever get married a second time. A stepmother is the last walkout. Da, the Lord rest him, didn't realise what he was doing. She was one of the Seán a' Táilliúir's; they were all very good-looking – she was good-looking, I'll grant her that, but she had the spoiling of it. The worst thing about her was her silence. She could sit for hours and not say a word – not one word. If you spoke to her – especially if you asked her for something – she would pretend not to hear. She used to sit all day long at the fire, knitting or sprigging. When her meals were ready she would pull up to the table and eat her fill. After dinner

she always went to bed for a snooze. You wouldn't see her again
till tea time. From tea time on, she got crankier and crankier.
After hours of saying nothing she would let a yell out of her,
"Don't bang the cutlery!" If I made the slightest noise washing
the knives and forks, she would put her hands over her ears and
yell, "Don't bang the cutlery!" Oh, she was a real tyrant. When
I finished school Da was all for sending me to college, but she
wouldn't hear tell of it. "We need Cassy for the housework"
– as if I was just a skivvy. And that's the way she treated me.
"Bring in the turf. Sweep the floor. Feed the hens." All I ever
heard from her was grumbling – grumbling whenever she
opened her mouth.'
    'Tell us the other thing.'
    'What other thing?'
    'The other thing she did on you.'
    'When you're older I'll tell you.'
    'Tell us now.'
    'You wouldn't understand, Betty.'
    'Was it bad?'
    'It was bad.'
    'Did you cry?'
    'I cried for many a day – for many and many a day.'

'Here he comes now' – Mama turns to Jenny Scotchie as
Claddagh passes the window.
    Jenny ducks behind the kitchen door, so that Claddagh has
put his hat on the table and is settling himself in Dada's place
before he sees her.
    'Goodness gracious! Where did *you* come out of!'
    Jenny laughs open-mouthed. She moves towards Claddagh,
who rises to greet her. Claddagh has his hand out but Jenny is
expecting a hug and a kiss and has moved too close for a handshake. The hands don't know what to do but the two heads

touch and one of Jenny's earrings gets caught in Claddagh's glasses. Jenny laughs as she manoeuvres to free her ear. Claddagh takes off his glasses and untangles the earring, which has several strands of little coloured beads hanging down. They stand looking at each other not daring to talk . . .

'Are you glad to see me?'

'Sure he's glad to see you,' Mama butts in, before Claddagh has time to answer or even clean his glasses properly.

'You're as welcome as the flowers of May,' Claddagh says.

Jenny laughs again and little beads of spittle form at the corner of her mouth. She is wearing a two-piece costume of blue shiny cloth; her fringe has disappeared, her hair, which has been shortened and brushed back, looks darker than before, as if it has been dyed.

'We were expecting you last year,' Claddagh adds.

'Oh . . . Did you miss me?'

'I did.'

'We all missed you,' Mama says.

'Well, I'm here now.' Jenny looks at Claddagh as if she expects wonders from him.

'How long are you staying?' Claddagh talks in a strained way, shy in front of us.

'I'll be going back on Saturday week.'

Claddagh treats Jenny to a sherry and they sit together on the long seat talking, mostly remembering Jenny's previous visit. The sports in Killybegs is mentioned and Jenny says she would like to go.

'Why don't the pair of you go?' Mama butts in again. 'You would have a lovely day out together.'

'Maybe we'll do that,' Claddagh says.

Jenny smiles. 'That would be nice . . . I mean to see a bit of the country this time. Eileen is giving me the loan of her bicycle.'

'You won't go too far afield on the bicycle.'

'And why not? If there's somewhere I fancy, I can always stay overnight. You can have a great holiday on a bicycle. Last year I went to the Highlands with a friend of mine. We cycled everywhere.'

'I suppose if you get the weather it's all right.'

'Did you take your own holidays yet?'

'Not yet.'

'How long do you get?'

'Just two weeks. I usually go back to Galway.'

'I was never in Galway. I believe it's lovely.'

'It can be.'

Jenny nudges Claddagh, her eyes twinkling. 'Are you going to bring me?'

Claddagh looks frightened. He doesn't know what to say.

'Bring me,' Jenny pleads, 'for a day. Ah go on.'

'Of course he'll bring you,' Mama says.

Claddagh says nothing; he tries to laugh it down with a long drink of stout.

'Into the back seat, the pair of you,' Hill orders through the half-open window of the car.

I get a glimpse of Nora Mary on the floor in the front, her head well down, but I pretend not to notice. Since Mama has had a row with Ned Mary we are not allowed to have anything to do with Nora.

'That's the end of that arrangement,' Mama had said to Hill. 'In future you'll have to drive Conor and Betty on their own.'

'Supposing I put Nora in the front seat on her own,' Hill suggested. 'Conor and Betty can have the back of the car all to themselves. They won't even see Nora Mary.'

'Oh then, they'll see her all right.'

'Even if they do, it'll be the same as if they were on the bus.'

'And what about the fare? We'll still be sharing the fare with Ned Mary, won't we?'

'Half and half. Sure.'

'I don't want to have anything to do with that man ever again, I told you.'

'You won't have anything to do with him. You'll pay the fare to me.'

'And Ned Mary will pay you the other half and it's still sharing.'

'All right. I'll tell you what I'll do. I'll make it the same as two journeys. I'll charge both of you the full fare. Is that fair?'

'Are you crazy!'

'It'll be the very same as two runs.'

'And Nora Mary still in the front seat?'

'They won't even know she's there.'

'Don't say that again. Nora Mary is the noisiest child in the town. She never closes her mouth. The only way is to drive Conor and Betty on their own.'

'And then come back and drive Nora Mary on her own?'

'I don't care what you do with Nora Mary. I'm employing you to drive Conor and Betty.'

'All right. Whatever you say. It's *your* money.'

Every morning since, Hill drops us in Rathar before the school opens, turns the car and rushes back to collect Nora Mary. This morning there has been a hitch.

'I haven't time for the two runs the day,' Hill tells us. 'I have to drive Peadar Bawn to the train.'

As soon as we turn at Canavan's corner Nora Mary uncrumples herself and slides up on to the front seat.

'Not a word about this to your mother,' Hill talks back to us.

'Mum is the word.'

★ ★ ★

Claddagh's face falls when he comes into the kitchen and finds Corner Jim sitting beside Jenny Scotchie on the long seat.

Corner Jim is well-oiled and has made several attempts to get his arm around Jenny; each time she sidled away from him, Jim following, so that they are both near the end of the seat.

Claddagh sits at the other end, his face trying to pull itself out of a contrary slump.

Jenny has been cool towards Jim, barely answering anything he says; now she smiles at him as if they are the closest of friends.

'I'm trying to get her to take a wee trip,' Jim says to Claddagh.

'Is that so?' Claddagh remarks sourly.

'Where are you thinking of bringing me?' Jenny asks, although she has already told Corner Jim that anywhere she wants to go she'll go on her bicycle and on her own.

'Were you ever in Belfast?' Corner Jim's flushed boozy face beams at Jenny.

'No, I wasn't.'

'Belfast is ahead of Dublin. We'll hire Hill to drive us to Belfast. What do you say?'

'I wouldn't mind seeing Belfast,' Jenny agrees.

'You're on then. We'll have to leave early. Belfast is a full day's work.'

Claddagh shakes his head and passes a frown to Jenny across Corner Jim's shoulder. Jenny smiles back at Claddagh; Corner Jim turns in time to catch the tail-end of the smile for himself.

'It's a deal, so?'

'You're on for anything, Jim.'

'I am surely. Nothing venture, nothing win.'

'What are you having?' Claddagh talks across to Jenny, ignoring Corner Jim.

'I'm all right, thanks' - Jenny holds up her glass, which still has a tawny sparkle in the bottom - 'Jim bought me a drink.'

Corner Jim rises, staggering slightly, steadying himself with one hand against the back of the seat. 'This round is on me. You'll have another one, Jenny?... Ah go on.'

'OK,' Jenny says.

Corner Jim buys a round for the three of them, which doesn't improve Claddagh's humour one bit. When the time comes to leave, Corner Jim says he'll get Hill to drive Jenny and himself home.

'I have my bicycle outside, thanks all the same,' Jenny smiles sweetly at Jim.

The three of them rise together. In the hallway Corner Jim tries again to get a squeeze out of Jenny; Claddagh has his arm around her from the other side.

After trudging across the bog we throw our schoolbags on the long seat, Crusoe watching us.

'The happiest days of your life,' Crusoe says. 'You don't realise it at the time, but when you're at school that's the happiest you'll ever be.'

The way Betty looks at me I know she is thinking the same: Crusoe is definitely cuckoo.

'You know, you'd miss the war.'

'You would surely.'

'Great excitement there for a while.'

'Great commotion. I often wonder what would have happened if they made peace the time Hess came over – and let the Foorer loose on the Russians.'

'You'd have no Communist threat the day.'

'You would not. No, you would not.'

'Big letdown now when you open the newspaper. On the front page, what MacBride said and what Aiken said. I stopped buying them.'

'Churchill was the man gave them something to write about.'

'The greatest go-boy of them all was the Foorer himself. Never a dull moment while *he* was around.'

'He caused a bit of a stir all right.'

'And when you think that he told them all beforehand exactly what he was going to do!'

'Told who what?'

'The Foorer, man. The Foorer.'

'Told everything he was going to do?'

'Down to the last detail. Attack Poland. Attack England. Attack France. Attack Russia. Years beforehand he told them.'

'Sure if they knew what he was going to do, they'd have stopped him in the beginning.'

'Did you never hear of the book he wrote?'

'What book?'

'I'm talking about the Nassy handbook – written by Adolf Hitler himself.'

'Never heard of it.'

'You never heard of Mine Camp?'

'No then, I didn't. Is it a war story?'

'War story! It's a blueprint, man – Hitler's master stragedy – strategy – the Nassy bible.'

'Nasty bible is right.'

'Not nasty bible. Nassy bible – or to be exact – the Gnatsy bible. All the Foorer's plans for the Third Reach were set out in Mine Camp ...'

In the kitchen Jenny Scotchie dabs at her eyes with an embroidered handkerchief: 'I don't know what more I can do, Cassy. I'm very fond of him and I think he likes me as well. But what's the use – he's so set in his ways. I thought this time I would be able to coax him or bully him – or trick him' – Jenny laughs through her tears – 'but I'm going back the way I came. He'll never change.'

'I would like to put a bomb under him,' Mama says.

'Conor and Betty, wait till you hear: no more Rathar after this week.'

'What!'

'You won't be going to Rathar school any more.'

'And where will we be going?'

'Wait till I tell you. Come in and close the door; take off your schoolbags. You remember the sweet cake I sent up to the sale of work – for the new roof on the school? Well, Miss Rose came down today to thank me. She couldn't be nicer. "I didn't expect you would give anything, Cassy, in the circumstances," she said. She shook hands with me and the two of us were nearly crying. I told her how happy yourself and Betty were when yous were going to Glengreeny school and how yous hate going to Rathar. Everything is settled. All yous have to do is get two transfer forms from Master Brick. From Monday next you'll be back in Glengreeny school.'

Thirteen candles on Ferdia's birthday cake and thirteen of us around the sitting-room table: Ferdia, Aisling, Betty, Nora Mary, Scunsey, Footsie, Sonny Moylan, Wee Peadar Ó Heascaigh, Boxty, Paddy Anne and Ferdia's two cousins from Glenties, Sean and Seamus.

Ferdia is at the head of the table, propped up in his wheel-bed, his presents scattered about him on the tartan rug that covers his legs: mostly sweets and chocolate and comics and a well-scuffed Rupert annual that Sonny got from Alice for Christmas. Aisling sits next to Ferdia and helps him with his special drinking cup, which has a spout on it. Even though I have been placed two seats down from Aisling, on the opposite

side of the table, nothing that she does escapes me: cutting
Ferdia's cake into tiny pieces, stooping to pick up something
from the floor, turning to Nora Mary, laughing, her necklace
of painted seashells clinking over her high-necked, yellow
blouse. From across the table, her beauty strikes me like a wave
of the sea, tugging me off balance with every move she makes.
This summer there is a grown-up fullness about Aisling, a sort
of aloofness in her manner, as if she is so much older than any
of us. Now and again I can't help glancing directly at her, looking away almost immediately, so that I barely catch the gleam
of her face, bright then vague like a distant star.

On each of our plates are biscuits, currant cake, sweets and
a lollipop. Wee Peadar finds a dead fly under his cup and pokes
at it with his lollipop stick. Peadar's father will allow only Irish
to be spoken in the home and Peadar's grip on English is shaky.
'Who did deaded that fly?' he asks.

Scunsey plays his melodion, then each of us has to sing. How
I wish I had brought my fiddle, but the thought never occurred
to me.

'You should have brought your fiddle,' Aisling smiles across
at me when my turn comes.

'Will I go home for it?'

'Whatever you like.'

When I come back the boys are all around Ferdia in the front
garden; Aisling has stayed inside to help her mother tidy up. I
leave my fiddle case on the sitting-room sofa beside Scunsey's
melodion. Nobody asks either of us to play after that.

The biggest change I notice in Glengreeny school is that
Stonehead has got deafer. Most of the time he teaches from the
front desk, sitting on the lid, with his feet tapping against the
seat, as near to the class as possible. A lot of attention is given
to religion. Even if he starts off teaching some other subject –

history or geography especially – he often gets sidetracked into stories about the Holy Land or the three children of Fatima or Saint Peter crucified upside down in Rome.

At the back of the class sits Sharkey, small button eyes darting and a mouth that shuttles sideways when he talks. Sharkey keeps up a running commentary on nearly everything Stonehead says.

'Charlie Mullins, who won the battle of Clontarf?'

'Humpty Dumpty,' Sharkey answers out of the corner of his mouth.

'When did Our Lord rise from the dead?'

'April Fools' Day,' Sharkey volunteers.

Two seats in front of Sharkey sits Dimmer Floyd from up the mountain. Dimmer is dumber than Big Andy and McGinley put together, but harmless. Every Monday Dimmer is in big trouble.

'Why weren't you at mass yesterday?' Stonehead asks him.

The answer is always the same: 'My father was tired, Master.'

'Don't you know it's a mortal sin to miss mass on a Sunday? . . . Don't you know that?'

'Yes, Master.'

'So now you have a mortal sin on your soul . . . Haven't you?'

'Yes, Master.'

'And if you died this minute, where would you go? . . . To hell, isn't it?'

'Yes, Master.'

'For all eternity: isn't that so?'

'Yes, Master.'

'But you don't give a hoot, do you?'

'No, Master.'

'What! You don't give a hoot if you go to hell!'

Whatever Stonehead says, Dimmer will always agree with him.

Miss Rose takes us for singing: *Bheir mé ó oró bhean ó, bheir mé ó oró bhean í,* with the boys humming a drone and the girls drawling the words. The crows sit at the back, their English readers open, pretending to be learning a poem. Paddy Anne also sits at the back, but for a different reason.

'Paddy Anne is a nightingale, not a crow,' Miss Rose tells us. 'You have to rest your voice, Paddy, until your vocal cords have developed.'

All during singing class Paddy Anne sits at the back resting his vocal cords. It is easy to forget that he is a nightingale because, to look at, he seems no different to any of the other croakers – until once in a blue moon Miss Rose calls him up and tests him against the tuning fork. She tells Paddy Anne that he is coming on nicely, then sends him back again to the crows.

Miss Rose talks to us about Cardinal Mindszenty, who is suffering under the Communists, and about the new Dark Age that is sweeping the world. Every morning we pray for Cardinal Mindszenty and the conversion of Russia.

For the first few days I notice Stonehead studying me out of the corner of his eye, but he never bothers me with a question. Then, in catechism class, where I feel I am exempt, he suddenly asks me to name the seven deadly sins. I can't.

'Can you tell me what is viaticum? . . . Or simony?'

Trying to dredge up something from my Trá Gheal days, I discover that almost every word of catechism I learned has gone clean out of my head. Stonehead says nothing and passes the question along the line.

Next morning when I hand in my sums and get most of them wrong, he turns on me: 'Conor O'Donnell, I'm afraid that you're an idle boy.'

'Look at the fat one! Isn't she a holy show? She's bursting out of her flannens.' Sharkey gives a sideways twist to the words and nods towards the Princess going through her song and dance routine with Ramsbottom.

> Give us a smile;
> Just for a while,
> Light up the lamp of your eyes;
> Tomorrow who knows
> Whether ivy or rose
> Will carelessly fall from the skies.
> Learn how it feels
> To kick up your heels,
> Don't let your season go by;
> Give us a smile,
> Broad as a mile,
> Smile, smile, smi-i-ile.

Scunsey and Footsie snigger at Sharkey's gibe. Secretly I think the Princess is gorgeous, but I smile in agreement. The three have a notion of Ramsbottom. Why, I can't imagine. She is still as bony and skinny as ever – not a bit attractive. True, the Princess has a round, uncouth face, but even this I find alluring. And the rest of her! Wow!

In the funny sketch the Princess usually plays the part of a nagging wife. From the time she comes storming on, I pay no further attention to what anyone else does or says. I relish every toss of her head, her finger wagging, her swaggering walk. Even when she has no part in the action my eyes never wander far from where she bides her time in the background, steaming with temper. I feel like hugging her to calm her down. If I was married to the Princess, she would have no cause for swiping at her husband with the dishcloth or throwing pots and pans at him. We would be happy together.

★ ★ ★

On the top shelf of the wardrobe Betty finds a white shoebox and, inside, a pair of lady's pink high-heel satin shoes. They were put there by Mama for safekeeping years before – and forgotten about; her dancing shoes.

'I wore them only twice. Just imagine. Sadie bought them in Sligo but they were too tight for her so she gave them to me. That was before I met Dada. I was doing a line with Bernard McGrath. Bernard was lovely. We used to meet at the dances in Duhaigh school. He was a great dancer. Bernard went to America – out to his aunt in Brooklyn. It all seems like a lifetime ago now. He was no length beyond until he wrote telling me he wanted me to come out to him. We were to be married in the States. I wrote back saying I would go over as soon as I had my passage money saved – but I never heard from him again. I couldn't understand it – after us being so close.' Mama's bottom lip trembles; she wraps the faded white tissue paper around the shoes and replaces them in their box with a quivering sigh.

'That's the highest so far.'
'It is not so. Footsie went higher.'
'Shut up your mouth, Scunsey!'
'*You* shut up *your* mouth! There's the mark.'
Lunch time and we are having a High Pee Competition against the lavatory wall at the end of the school yard. Boxty is away ahead: he has squirted over halfway up the wall.
'But you stood on your tiptoes.'
'I stood on my feet.'
'You did not so, Boxty – you gave a jump up at the beginning.'
'And *you* gave a jump at the beginning and at the end and in the middle. You were like a jumping Jack-in-the-box.'
Clang-a-lang-a-lang-a-lang! Stonehead's arm sticking out the

window waving the cracked handbell summons us back to class.

The following day the champions are lined up again, ready to let fly.

'You go first,' Footsie tells Boxty. Footsie has pulled back the scutch grass in the corner of the yard and takes out a can of spring water, from which he slurps a long drink.

Boxty steadies himself, aims at the wall, and shoots higher than the scratch line that marks the highest so far.

Footsie then lets fly but falls about an inch short of high-water mark.

'Champ,' Boxty declares, cocking out his belly.

'No, you're not.' Footsie puts the can to his head and glugs down more water. 'Go to the far side of the wall. Everyone.'

'Why have we to go to the far side?'

'Because I'm going to piss right over the shaggin' wall.'

'You are in your shite!'

'Wait till you see.'

As we cross over where the wall is broken Footsie is taking another big gulp of water from the can.

'Ready . . . Steady . . . Goooo!'

A wavering squiggle of piddle appears, straining in spurts to clear the highest part of the wall. It stretches upwards, climbing, slipping, folding back on itself, until it peaks well above the wall, then dips in a sudden arc, sending us scurrying backwards. We are so amazed that an instant cheer goes up.

Puzzled, we climb down into the school yard again; Footsie greets us with a big grin, at the same time brazenly shaking some surplus drops from his wallabaloo.

'How did you do it?'

'Sheer shaggin' talent.'

'You must have cheated.'

'You must have climbed halfway up the wall.'

'Even if he did, no one could pee that high.'

'Do it again.'

'Will you shag off! I did it once. Now it's Boxty's turn.'

Boxty looks down at his fly buttons and raises his eyes towards the top of the wall. It is the same as if he is being asked to pee over the moon.

'Come on, Boxty.'

'Your living best.'

'I have none left.'

'Drink some water.'

'Water is no good.'

'Water is the only thing.'

'Come on, Boxty.'

Boxty takes a long drink and gropes in his trousers.

'Let him out, Boxty.'

'Steady yourself.'

'Give the water time to work.'

'Good on you, Boxty.'

'Drink some more. Go on.'

'Take another slug.'

Footsie reaches the can to Boxty. 'Show us the man you are,' he jeers.

Boxty, holding his pecker in one hand, takes the can shakily in the other and drinks till the water dribbles down his chin. He hands the can to Sonny Moylan, advances a few steps and throws back his head.

'Come on, Boxty, let it rip!'

'Your living best.'

Boxty has taken both hands to his championship pecker, which is pointed skywards, his face screwed up, while we wait . . . and wait . . . and wait . . .

'Put him away,' Footsie says. 'You're only making a mockery.'

★   ★   ★

'Imagine, if anyone came in and saw what he has his wife doing: hammering corks into bottles – while *he's* three thousand miles away himself enjoying a gentleman's life. Not a word any more about bringing us out and not a word about when he'll be home. No wonder I hate to see anyone coming in, when I know they're going to be asking about him. My God above, I'm the laughing stock of the whole parish.'

While Mama continues to pity herself, the stout has been sinking lower in the tub and the pigeon-holed cases steadily filling up with corked bottles. Several times she has skirted around the threat that has always struck terror into Dada, Betty and myself. Though I am fearful, I don't really believe that she would ever speak to me in that cruel way. When she does, the effect is different from any other time. What I feel is a sort of chilling numbness. Her terrible words plunge towards me like a dagger, cutting through the cord which from birth had stretched between us. I look at my mother, but without attachment and – for the first time – without love. The Sunday before, Father McBrearty had preached a sermon about giving scandal.

'Better that a millstone be tied around your neck and that you be cast in the depths of the sea than that you give scandal.' The words have haunted me all week.

'Drown yourself if you want to,' I hear myself saying, 'but don't give scandal.'

Mama's eyes search my face with a frightened look. 'Conor, you know Mama is only joking. I would never drown myself – not in a million years.'

When I ask which way to the circus, the fisherman at the pier in Killybegs lobs a stringy tobacco spit over the side before answering. 'Through the town. You can't miss it. But the matinée doesn't begin for another two hours.'

Only broad-backed work horses grazing from their tethers in the low-lying field, where the wagons are drawn in a half-circle around the back of the tent; the blue and white caravan that sells the tickets still has its shutters closed.

Followed by Betty, I wander in and out between the caravans to the sizzle and smell of sausages frying.

'We never had our dinner, Conor.'

'It doesn't matter.'

'I'm hungry.'

'Eat your chocolate.'

'I'm keeping it for when the circus starts . . . Where are you going?'

'Just for a look in the tent.'

'You're not supposed to go in without paying.'

'No one will notice. Come on.'

'No. You're not supposed to, Conor.'

In the dim and silence under the canvas my eyes search the uppermost rigging. No trapeze. Disappointed, I look around at the high, leaning tiers of empty seats, the bandstand painted in bright, brashy colours, and the sawdust ring, where a single rope dangles from near the top of the central pole. But no trapeze.

To my left a canvas curtain flaps open and a young woman hurries through the performers' entrance. Ponytail bobbing. A red dirndl skirt. Without noticing me, she kicks off her sandals and, taking the rope, quickly begins to scale upwards, her bare feet braced against the central pole. As she climbs, her loose-fitting skirt slides up along her legs, slides and ripples, then as she straightens her limbs, falls back again over her knees. Higher and higher she reaches, her skirt crumpling, gathering and falling, showing for an instant the backs of her legs, her thighs and the plump curves of her bottom.

I know I shouldn't be watching any of this; I should turn and leave immediately, but the devil (which Stonehead says is always on the lookout for an idle boy) tells me to relax, sit down quietly and enjoy what he has sent me.

Near the top of the pole the woman unties a rope and a steel bar swings out over the ring. Trapeze. My eyes have got used to the orange pale light, so that, from where I am now leaning against the edge of a side seat, I can see without straining as the woman secures the ropes and fittings. She is swinging this way and that on the central rope, her legs dangling, parting, and coming together for support against the pole. As she angles one leg around the pole I hold my breath. No knickers! Am I imagining? The woman continues to work on the tackle with both hands, her legs locking and unlocking around the pole. And there it is again! Dark. Fuzzy. Disappearing as she straightens her legs and the folds of her skirt fall down. I watch in a sort of trance, my whole body completely absorbed in the act of staring. There is an upward-reaching movement she makes which I wait for. When it comes, bolts of lightning streak towards me and the devil dances in my pocket...

'Conor. Conor. Where are you?... I'm going back to the town for ice cream.'

'Go ahead.'

'Come with me. I have my chocolate eaten.'

'No.'

'What's wrong with you, Conor? Did you fall?'

'No.'

'Are you hurted?'

'I'm all right.'

The woman has shimmied down the pole and turns towards us, at the same time stepping into her sandals. 'You're away too early. The show doesn't start until three. Come back then.'

★   ★   ★

Betty has dozed off and Mama sits on the edge of my bed, having looked in to kiss us goodnight.

'... One letter was all I ever got from Bernard. After he asked me to marry him, he never wrote again. Wasn't it awful? I wrote to him three times. I waited and waited. Then I thought that maybe he met somebody else. And then Dada came along. I was thirty-four years of age; Sadie was married, Harry was engaged. Three years after I married Dada, Bernard arrived back from the States for a holiday, but he never called. I never saw him again.

'When my stepmother died I went home to help at the wake; Sadie and myself were sorting out her belongings afterwards. In her bureau we found a bundle of letters – all addressed to me. All from Bernard. He even sent me the passage money.'

Stonehead, on his usual perch, has been telling us about Saint Joseph, the carpenter. 'What would you like to be when you grow up?'

Footsie: 'Work in the factory.'

Boxty: 'Go to America.'

Scunsey: 'Go to Australia.'

When my turn comes I say I would like to be a publican, though my secret ambition is to be a magician like Sulliman the Great.

After he has heard us all, Stonehead shakes his head sadly: 'And not one priest among you.'

In the door comes Dimmer; he is dead late but strolls over to his desk without a word of explanation.

'Wait a minute. Where were you all last week?'

'At home, Master.'

'At home. You're supposed to be at school, aren't you?'

'Yes, Master.'

'Then why did you stay at home?... Well?... What's your excuse?'

It is obvious that Dimmer's parents have forgotten to tell him what to say and he is completely flummoxed.

'Well? I'm waiting for your excuse... Where were you every day last week?'

'High mass,' Sharkey prompts.

'You're after being absent for a whole week, aren't you?'

'Yes, Master.'

'Can you tell me why?... Come on... Why didn't you come to school last week?'

'I forgot, Master.'

A big disappointment. Footsie cheated in the High Pee Competition. He squirted from a water pistol.

'Conor. Mrs O'Regan wants you.'

'For what?'

'It's Ferdia. Put on your good clothes.'

'Why have I to put on my good clothes?'

'Ferdia asked to see yourself and Scunsey and Footsie. You're going to be saying goodbye.'

Alone in the Master's sitting room, with a cup of tea which Mrs O'Regan has brought me... Scunsey and Footsie come in together. They are wearing shoes and their Sunday best. Mrs O'Regan pours out more tea and tells us to help ourselves to the cake and biscuits, then goes back to the kitchen.

'My mother gave me a relic of Saint Jude' – Footsie produces a holy leaflet with a small circle of cloth attached.

'Give it to Mrs O'Regan,' Scunsey says.

'Maybe she mightn't be pleased.'

'The three of you can come in now.' Mrs O'Regan leads us through the kitchen to the small boxroom at the back which has been Ferdia's bedroom since he got sick. 'Ferdia, your friends are here to see you' – Mrs O'Regan pounds into shape the bolster and pillow behind Ferdia before leaving us.

Ferdia's breathing has a hoarse gurgling sound and all the life-colour has paled from his cheeks. His arms hang down limply resting on the turned-up sheet, the sleeves of his pyjamas seem empty, his hands faded white and stiff as the starched sheet itself. He seems sleepy, almost in a trance, but the faint movement of his mouth, straining to smile, brings to his face for an instant the flicker of a familiar look.

The three of us crowd together on the one side of the bed not able to say a word. Ferdia's right hand is open, turned up-wards on the sheet. Scunsey lifts Ferdia's hand and squeezes it. Footsie takes his hand next; then I shake hands with him. His hand feels like damp stone, without any trace of life in it, but his look meets mine, flickers wearily over my face, over Scunsey's face and Footsie's – his eyes speaking for him – our eyes answering.

As we leave, Footsie slips the relic underneath his pillow.

'It was a slow death: a day and a night dying.'

'Mary Byrne cried laying him out. Just skin and bone.'

'Strange the ways of the almighty.'

'Ferdia had his purgatory done. He's in heaven the cratur.'

At the *feis* on the strand Mickey Mhór told a rigmarole of a story about a fiddler who bargained his soul away in exchange for all the best tunes in the world. 'But the divil pulled a fast one on him. The fiddler started to play in great glee and he played tunes that he never heard before in his life. On and on he played, tunes from Donegal and Sligo and Sliabh Luachra and the far side of the great ocean, from Mexico and Jericho and China and Siam, one tune sweeter than another, so that he had to pinch himself in the backside to make sure that he wasn't dreaming and that it was really himself was playing, and the powerful fiddler he was after turning into; but lo and behold, when he tried to stop wasn't it a different story altogether: he couldn't even slow down – jigs led into reels and reels led into hornpipes and strathspeys and barndances and mazurkas and polkas and the divil knows what and his elbow was going like a shuttlecock and his poor fingers rushing here, there and everywhere like fleas hopping off a drownded rat. The people watching were dizzy in the head calling to him, "That's enough, Johnny. That'll do you now, and thanks very much", and all he could do was wink at them. He played till the bow was worn down to the stick and the strings were all out o' tune and in flitters and his foot was coming through the sole of his shoe from keeping time, and the men, women and children gathered around began running from the house in terror at the wild appearance of him. Then he started to sink lower and lower in the chair, until his socks began to singe and the turn-ups of his trousers went on fire. Still he didn't take a dang bit notice even though the flames were leaping up his legs. A few friends who stuck by him tried to smother the blaze; they threw water on him, buckets and buckets o' water, and it was the very same as if they were dousing him with paraffin oil. In the end they had to leave him where he was and run for their lives, and the last they saw of him was the fiddle and the bow all in flames and his fingers still sparking away and a fierce blaze where his elbow should be and the rest of him a heap of ashes on the chair.'

For all he put into it, Mickey Mhór's story didn't come first; instead the prize went to Rogan who told a story of his own.

'If she was coming out, she'd be out by now. God save us the day and the night, isn't it a terror! She's like a prisoner at them. Kitty Doogue was telling me all the doors are locked; if anyone comes to visit, the iron key has to be produced. Kitty called in to the ward to see her before she came out for the summer.

Suzanne didn't even know her. And she didn't know from Adam where she was. One minute she was searching for her schoolbag, the next she let a string o' complaints out o' her about everyone around her: all living off her, she said, and she can't get rid o' them. It's doubtful if we'll ever see her in Trá Beag again. And there's no question of any wee sniffle, as the fella says. The pipe was taken off her as well, Kitty told me. They tried to get her on to the cigarettes but she couldn't manage them. She let a cigarette fall down her gansey and burned her vest and her chest. If I could get a lift, I would go up to see her, but maybe I'm as well not to bother; when she doesn't recognise the people, sure what would be the point? God save us the day and the night, does anyone ever know what's in front of them!'

'Conor and Betty, I have great news for you. Conor, you're accepted by the Salesians. The letter came today – an answer to prayer if ever there was one. I finished the Thirty Days' Prayer last night and today we get a lovely letter from the director of vocations. I'm writing to Dada. You write to him, too, Conor. You'll be going away on the seventh of September. He'll have to come home now. I told Molly Dan when she came in for her groceries and she was delighted. Everyone is delighted. "He's the first vocation in Glengreeny since Father Timony," Molly said. "Conor'll be the next ordination." Imagine, the man she compared you to – Father Timony O'Boyle! I hope you'll make a better turnout than poor Father Timony, God bless him. Sit down now and write to Dada. Tell him the whole story.'

Jellybob and Jane were at the *céilí mór*, sitting beside Crusoe for most of the night.

'Crusoe didn't enjoy it one bit. He was waiting for an old

time waltz to be called – but of course Seán Ó Faoistin, who was the *fear a' tí*, would have nothing to do with waltzes. Everything had to be pure *céilí*. Ó Faoistin was planked up on the stage, keeping time with his good leg, calling out the sets. All Crusoe wanted was to get his arms around a woman. He was well on and every time Ó Faoistin called out "The Walls of Limerick" or "The Siege of Ennis", or what not, Crusoe let a string o' curses out of him. "All oul' mechanical stuff," Crusoe said, "in and out and in and out and that's all there is to it." Ó Faoistin was in his element riming off the calls, his wooden leg stretched out in front of him:

> Advance two three, advance two three,
> And back two three, and back two three,
> Gents cross,
> Ladies cross,
> Swing your partner –

and so on. Crusoe never got on the floor all night; he was fumin'. At the end of the dance Ó Faoistin was going around asking people how they enjoyed it and looking for praise for himself. Crusoe was ready for him. "I won't say sheep could do it," says Crusoe, "but with a well-trained sheepdog, they'd make a damn good attempt." '

Luckily the sitting-room window is open when I glimpse Aisling across the street filling the white enamel bucket at the pump. Her brown chequered dress has got too short for her and also too tight where her upper body curves outwards at her armpits. A single broad haircomb holds her hair tightly in place, giving it a flat burnished look and showing the lighter freckles high up on her forehead.

Three winks it takes me to rush downstairs and back up again with my fiddle. 'Souvenir'. The first part. Singing. Soaring.

Away up high on the E string. Hidden by the curtains, I watch the effect I am having. Aisling hears. And she knows that Betty can't play like this; she knows it has to be me. 'Souvenir'. Again the first part. If only I could lash into the second part with all the marvellous double stoppings.

Nora Mary has joined Aisling and stands in my line of sight, talking. Gabby guts. Why can't she shut up for once? The first part again, as loud as ever I can. Long heavy bows. Tremolo. Everything has to go into it this time or I'll be like a record stuck in the one groove.

Aisling raises her eyes towards the window and I take a step backwards. At last she is beginning to pay attention. Don't hold back now. 'Souvenir'. A fourth time. Well, I could be practising. Louder. LOUDER. Nora Mary looks up. I fairly lay into the high notes – sliding up to the high E – down again – up again – up-up-up to the highest note – Aisling still has her head raised in concentration – and down to finish on a long, drawn-out trembling D. I am trembling all over myself and breathing in gasps.

Nora Mary crosses the street calling something back to Aisling. Sounded like 'Show-off'.

Aisling has taken up the bucket, splashing out some of the water, leaning slightly to one side, the bucket held out from her body. Aquarius.

I begin 'The Coolin', turning away as Aisling comes level with the window. When I look again she has passed out of view, but I follow her with the slow, sad notes, knowing that she hears.

On the kitchen table when I come down from the bar is a blue copybook.

'Rogan sent this in with Armada Pat,' Mama tells me.

I had asked Rogan for the story he told at the *feis*; he has written it out in ink in a clear, painstaking script; it has no title.

Long long ago in Éireann there was a young man called Fiach; he was one of the warriors of Partholan and a brave warrior he was. But before being admitted to the inner ranks he was required to bring a message through enemy country as a final test of his valour. He had to take this message from Aileach to Tara, where Partholan then was. And once he started on his journey he was forbidden to rest until he reached his destination.

As night was approaching on the first day, Fiach was hailed by an old man at the crossroads. But he passed him by without slowing his pace. He ran on for a while until he sensed that someone was following him and when he looked back he saw that it was the old man and that he was catching up with him. Soon the old man was running by his side and showing no signs of fatigue. Again he commanded Fiach to stop and again Fiach ignored him. Then the old man put his hand on Fiach's shoulder and suddenly Fiach felt as if he was carrying the weight of the world and his legs refused to move another step. He had to sit down on a stone to catch his breath. And the old man sat on the ground beside him. Fiach held his hand on his dagger but the old man reached out and gently took it from his grasp and Fiach could not resist him.

'Are you one of the enemy?' Fiach asked, 'or one of Partholan's men sent to test me?'

The old man answered out of silence. 'Today you must forget about the enemy; forget about Partholan, too, and all the tests you have ever undertaken or planned to undertake – and think instead of something other.'

'What is that?' Fiach asked, and for the first time in his life he felt an unnatural fear.

The old man's voice grew softer. 'Why does the blackbird sing in Gleann na Smól?' he asked, 'and the salmon leap in the Silver River and the sun rise always over Cruach an Óir?'

'I think I know who you are,' Fiach said.

The old man looked sad. 'You are young, Fiach,' he said, 'but young or old, what matter? Once in his lifetime I come to every man. Once in his lifetime every man sees me face to face.' And he reached out his hand to Fiach but Fiach withdrew and turned away.

'There is an ambush prepared for you,' the old man said.

'I will go around it,' said Fiach.

The old man shook his head.

'Now that I know of it I can avoid it,' said Fiach.

The old man rose and pointed in the distance and Fiach looked and he saw on the horizon a man running. And he knew that the man was himself. Then he turned to the old man and he reached out and with a firm grip he took his hand and in that instant his feet again moved swiftly over the ground and as he ran he knew why the blackbird sings in Gleann na Smól and the salmon leaps in the Silver River and the sun rises always over Cruach an Óir and a great stillness settled upon him so that he hardly felt the sharp hurrying spear that pierced his chest or the twisted barb lodging itself deep in his heart.

Drip . . . Drip . . . Drip – the basin in our bedroom catches the downrain.

'Anthony McGill has a new motorbike,' Betty says.

'I know. Have you still a notion of him?'

'A bit.'

'I thought you got over him?'

'I'm getting over him . . . Do you know who was on the pillion?'

'Mary McBrien?'

'Maybe. But who else?'

'You? Were *you* on it?'

'No. Guess again.'

'I don't know.'
'You have to guess.'
'Give me a hint.'
'Her name starts with A.'
'A?...Not – not Aisling?'
'She was.'
'When?'
'Today. Going down the town.'
'It couldn't be Aisling.'
'I saw her.'
'Are you sure?'
'Do you think I wouldn't recognise Aisling?'
Drip...Drip...Drip. Anthony McGill and Aisling on the motorbike. We are both miserable.

'The last person anyone should have working for them is Jellybob. Jellybob's mother was a real rascal; she was a real tramp. There were eleven of them in the family. Imagine. Eleven. The father used to make poteen. That's what they were reared on. Any time there was a wedding or a funeral or a big night Jellybob's mother would be at the bedroom window busy handing out naggin bottles of poteen. Everybody used to be dead drunk. The priests were mad over it. One night they were doing such a brisk trade that the poteen began to run low and they couldn't get to the well to water it with the crowd around the house. What do you think Jellybob's mother did? She took out the chamberpot from under the bed and got every one of the eleven children to sit on it in their turn and then she got her husband to do a big piddle into it and then she sat on it herself. They filled two chamberpots between them and poured the lot into the barrel. The people were so drunk already that they didn't notice the difference. That's the sort of home Jellybob came out of.'

★ ★ ★

Mickey Mhór grunts when Scunsey and myself come up on the stage beside him with our instruments. Mickey Beag doesn't seem to mind and tunes the fiddle for me. The *céilí* is in the parochial hall and it is the first time for Scunsey and myself to play for money.

'Who taught you, O'Donnell?' Mickey Mhór says to me.

So many fiddlers have had a hand leading me in so many different directions that I have to think before answering: 'Mr Hart and Markey Crawford and Jimmy John and Con Moylan and –'

'Too many cooks spoil the broth.' Mickey Mhór gives another grunt. 'Folley us and keep in time. Strict time when you're playing for dancers.' He glares across at Scunsey, who has drawn his chair in between Mickey Beag and myself, the melodion stretching with a snore of bass notes. 'Where do you think *you're* going! Sit at the far end of the line – and play as soft as you can. The melodion is not a suitable instrument at all. It's only for jazzers.'

Mickey Mhór has been tuning his fiddle and talking at the same time and now a string snaps with a loud ping!

'Did you break a string, Mickey?' Scunsey asks, hoping to humour him.

Mickey Mhór reaches behind us and lands Scunsey a clip in the ear. 'I'll break your mouth, you wee pup you, if I hear another word out o' you the night!'

Dada looks worried stepping out of the train at Killybegs, a bulging American suitcase balanced against one knee. He drops the case as soon as he sees Betty and myself and lifts us off our feet, swinging us around until his broad-brimmed, American hat nearly flies off.

'Yous got big, God bless yous. Yea.' He stands at arm's length to have a good look at us. 'Yea, yous grew all right. Where's Mama?'

'She's at home.'

Dada's face clouds over. He is wearing a light grey American suit spangled with silver threads. His skin has got slightly darker from the sun and there is a small red blotch the size of a shirt button on his forehead which he didn't have before.

Hackney Hill gives a smile and a big handshake before he squeezes the case down into the boot.

Getting into the front seat Dada hesitates. 'Before we head for home – we'll go over to Rogers' for a drink. See what's stirring in the town.'

Standing at the hotel bar, waiting for the drinks, Dada looks up and down the counter, jingling the money in his pockets. Two fishermen come over to welcome him. 'How are times beyond, Jamie?'

'The best. Never better.'

'Plenty o' money stirring?'

'No scarcity o' money.'

'You didn't stay long yourself?'

'Just a year and a half. No help at home any more. Conor is going away to college.'

Out on the street, Dada gives the loose change in his pockets another jingle and hesitates again. 'We'll have one drink in Coen's – one for the road.'

Only a few young fellas at the high counter in Coen's and no one that we know. After buying us all another drink, Dada takes out a packet of Camel cigarettes and offers one to Hill.

Hill taps the cigarette on the back of his hand and smells it before putting it between his lips.

'American cigarettes. They taste stronger, I always think.'

'Better tobacca. The Yank for it every time.' Dada lights Hill's cigarette and another for himself, from a small book of matches with Con Edison written across it.

When Hill goes out the back, Dada puts his arms around

us again. 'I missed yous terrible, that's the truth.'

'We missed you too.'

'Everything all right at home?'

'It is.'

'What kind of form is Mama in?'

'She's in good form.'

'Mama is highly strung, yea – but she's sorry the minute after. We'll say nothing about this wee delay. Time we were moving anyway.'

For most of the journey Dada sits with his hat on his lap, looking out at sea and rock and heather, saying little. As we pass Aisling's house, Big Jodie, who is fitting in new windows, turns to stare at the car and waves to us. Dada waves back.

'Town hasn't changed much, has it?' Dada says to Hill.

'Divil a change, Jamie.'

Ahead of us Tom Tim crosses the street, the cow already on the far side, scratching her neck against Ellen Andy's gable. Tom reaches his hand in the car window to Dada. 'You're welcome home, Jamie. You were gone a good while.'

'No. Just a year and a half.'

'It seemed longer.'

Inside the kitchen door Mama stands waiting for us and turns to take Dada's kiss on her cheek.

'Well – home again,' Dada says.

'Home again.'

A lot of talk about America. Almost everyone who comes in wants to know what times are like beyond. If Dada is out they ask Mama.

'How would I know?' Mama rounds on Crusoe. 'If you want to find out what America is like, why don't you go there yourself?'

★   ★   ★

'Cassy, take a look at this: Anastasia's place is up for sale again.'

'Don't tell me you're getting itchy feet already!'

'I'm just showing you. Sale by private treaty. I knew Barney Flanagan wouldn't last in it for any length – a man that doesn't know the first thing about business.'

'Little and all as he knows about it, the same Barney Flanagan pulled a fast one on us the last time.'

'What the hack! Live and let live. I hear Hobnails is after catching him again; he's in danger of losing the licence. You never know, he might sell cheap.'

'Well, *you're* crazy, surely.'

'No crazy about it. A person could do a lot worse than buy Anastasia's.'

'What are people going to think if they see you moving again?'

'People don't give a hang whether we move or stay, not a rap do they care. Drop him a line and see what price he's asking. No harm in that. We might get a bargain if we strike while the fright is on him.'

'Crusoe is dead, did you hear?'

'Crusoe! No.'

'The doctor is just after leaving' – Old Con follows Dada into the grocery and stands at the counter talking under his breath – 'terrible altogether . . . a basin o' blood . . . won't be any wake in the house . . .'

'Is Crusoe dead?' I ask Dada as soon as Old Con goes out.

'He is, the Lord have mercy on him.'

'What happened?'

'You're too young to understand, Conor.'

'I saw him only yesterday – coming out of Lambert's.'

'Well, he's dead now.' Dada's eyes have misted over.

When Betty comes in from Maggie May's I tell her the sad news, but she knows more about it than I do.

'Do you know what happened?' Betty whispers.

'No.'

'He killed himself.'

'What!'

'Margaret went up to the chapel to put flowers on the altar. When she came back Crusoe was in bed – he was lying on the bed with all his clothes on and him bleeding into a basin.'

'He killed himself?'

'True as God. He cut his wrists with a razorblade.' Betty is silent and seems frightened by her own words. I feel frightened myself. We look at each other and Betty shivers. What we are afraid of is too awful for either of us to mention.

Jellybob's face crumples when he opens the parcel Pete Post has just handed him. The parcel has a bright decoration of American stamps and is addressed to his wife Jane – but Jellybob hasn't the patience to wait until he gets home. Tearing the brown paper wrapping, he takes out a bundle of handkerchiefs and scowls at the other item remaining. 'Oh Auntie Nell, was it worth your while floating this across the Atlantic? A few nose rags for me and a pair o' bloomers for Jane!'

'You'll have to say goodbye to the Master,' Dada tells me; 'thank him.'

'What will I be thanking him for! He'll only tell me I need another year.'

'Well, maybe you do.'

'Are *you* crazy!' Mama's voice rises.

'Go on up to him, Conor. When you come home for the Christmas holidays we'll all be in Anastasia's place. A fresh start.'

Aisling turns around from ironing her yellow blouse on the table when I go in.

'I came to say goodbye to your father.'

'Daddy! Conor O'Donnell is here to see you,' she calls and continues with her ironing.

I watch as she sprinkles water from a saucer, the hot iron turning the droplets to steamy spits. Her hair is loose around her neck, the pale evening light striking, melting, scattering among the tresses gleams of dark brown and russet when she tilts her head. When will I lay eyes on her again? At Christmas? Not if we move to Kilmore. My heart is knocking wildly against my chest, such frantic beating that if I don't say something she must surely hear the thumps. I know that she is going to boarding school in three days' time but still I ask: 'When are you going away?'

'Thursday.'

'I'm going tomorrow.'

'The best of luck to you.'

'I'll probably need it.'

Stonehead comes out of the boxroom, with a dab of shaving cream on his cheek. He shakes hands with me and tells me to concentrate on what I am doing. 'One thing at a time and do it well. You're inclined to be a bit of a dreamer, I'm afraid.'

On my way to the door I summon up enough courage to shake hands with Aisling, nervously raising my eyes to her face. What I feel is an overwhelming anguish: her beauty, her intelligence – not to mention her father being the Master – all these extraordinary blessings tell me that, like Aquarius, she moves in a sphere far removed from the common world where I dwell.

As I turn in confusion to leave, Mrs O'Regan comes in and, without speaking, hands me a pencil case, which I don't immediately recognise. It has F.O.R. carved on the lid.

The vague mix of voices from the bar below recalls other sleepless nights, blue-lit from the gleam of passing bicycles.

Up Dev!

Up the Free State!

Where would we be without the Silent Man? We'd have no factory,
no forestry, no nothing. Up Peadar Bawn every time!

There's no beatin' on him.

White are the sails on the emigrant tide,
As white as the veil on the altar-stone wide,
And broad is the ocean from windward to lee
That rolls between Boston, my true love and me.

Keep it low now, boys. Long after closing time.

Jamie, gimme a penny candle and an ounce o' snuff and let me
out o' here.

A nip, I said. A nip.

Sláinte mhór!

Hudie. A wee breeze.

Give us 'The Girl from Donegal'.

Give us a smoke, Jamie.

On top of Old Smoky –

Shhhhh.

I'm bonified, Jamie.

Bonified.

Bonified, sure.

Ah poor Dinny.

That shuck ya.

A droll wee man.

'Danny Boy', Hudie.

Rogan. A piece o' your own composure.

Ní bhíonn in aon rud ach seal.

A wee wan here.

Killybegs, barrels and kegs,
Kilcar for making báinín –

Shhhh. Away after closing time.
Oh my, oh my, ith my thound athound again?
Hudie, come on.
Come on, Rogan. 'Saint Patrick's Day'.
None o' your tarradiddles.
O Danny Boy, the pipes the pipes are ca-aw-ling –
Quiet now, boys. Hobnails.
From glen to glen and down the mountainside –
Shhh . . . Shhhh . . . Shhhhhhh